PENGUIN BOOKS
The Jungle

Clive Cussler is the author or co-author of a great number of international bestsellers, including the famous Dirk Pitt® adventures, such as *Crescent Dawn*; the NUMA® Files adventures, most recently *Devil's Gate*; the *Oregon* Files, such as *The Jungle*; the Isaac Bell adventures, which began with *The Chase*; and the recent Fargo adventures. His non-fiction works include *The Sea Hunters* and *The Sea Hunters II*: these describe the true adventures of the real NUMA, which, led by Cussler, searches for lost ships of historic significance. With his crew of volunteers, Cussler has discovered more than sixty ships, including the long-lost Confederate submarine *Hunley*. He lives in Arizona.

Jack Du Brul is the author of the Philip Mercer series, most recently *Havoc*, and is the co-author with Clive Cussler of the *Oregon* Files novels *Dark Watch*, *Skeleton Coast*, *Plague Ship*, *Corsair*, *The Silent Sea* and *The Jungle*. He lives in Vermont.

The Jungle

CLIVE CUSSLER
with JACK DU BRUL

PENGUIN BOOKS

PENGUIN BOOKS

Published by the Penguin Group
Penguin Books Ltd, 80 Strand, London WC2R ORL, England
Penguin Group (USA) Inc., 375 Hudson Street, New York, New York 10014, USA
Penguin Group (Canada), 90 Eglinton Avenue East, Suite 700, Toronto, Ontario, Canada M4P 2Y3
(a division of Pearson Penguin Canada Inc.)
Penguin Ireland, 25 St Stephen's Green, Dublin 2, Ireland (a division of Penguin Books Ltd)
Penguin Group (Australia), 250 Camberwell Road, Camberwell, Victoria 3124, Australia
(a division of Pearson Australia Group Pty Ltd)
Penguin Books India Pvt Ltd, 11 Community Centre, Panchsheel Park, New Delhi – 110 017, India
Penguin Group (NZ), 67 Apollo Drive, Rosedale, Auckland 0632, New Zealand
(a division of Pearson New Zealand Ltd)
Penguin Books (South Africa) (Pty) Ltd, 24 Sturdee Avenue, Rosebank, Johannesburg 2196, South Africa

Penguin Books Ltd, Registered Offices: 80 Strand, London WC2R ORL, England

www.penguin.com

First published in the USA by G. P. Putnam's Sons 2011
First published in Great Britain by Michael Joseph 2011
Published in Penguin Books 2012

001

Copyright © Sandecker, RLLLP, 2011

The moral right of the authors has been asserted

Printed in Great Britain by Clays Ltd, St Ives plc

A CIP catalogue record for this book is available from the British Library

ISBN: 978–1–405–93271–4

www.greenpenguin.co.uk

MIX
Paper from
responsible sources
FSC
www.fsc.org
FSC® C018179

Penguin Books is committed to a sustainable
future for our business, our readers and our planet.
This book is made from Forest Stewardship
Council™ certified paper.

Prologue

Eastern China
1281 A.D.

A thick fog filled the valley and spilled out over the surrounding mountains. Borne on a slight breeze, the mist made it look as though the peaks were breathing. From the ground, the dense forests were just shapes and silhouettes rather than individual trees. No animals scurried on the carpet of leaves and pine needles, and no birds were heard crying out. All was eerie silence. Even the army's horses were subdued by the impenetrable gloom. An occasional muted hoof stomp was all that betrayed their presence.

Slowly the sun began to burn away the haze, and like something rising from the depths, the topmost section of the castle's roof emerged out of the fog as though suspended above the ground. The fired-clay-tile roof glistened with moisture. Next to be revealed were the towering walls that surrounded the town. The rampart's crenellations were as even as dragon's teeth. From a distance it was easy to see guards patrolling along the tops of the walls, long spears laid casually over their shoulders. They knew the Great Khan's army was nearby, but they appeared confident that the town's fortifications were more than adequate.

It was said that in China a village without a wall was like a house without a roof, thus every hamlet, no matter how small, had protective bulwarks of stone or at least stockades of wood. Siege and countersiege became the preferred method of warfare, and its tactics had been honed over a thousand years of conflict.

Before their conquest of China, the Mongols had fought as light cavalry, sweeping off the Steppes and decimating their enemies in lightning raids. But they adapted to the Chinese method of battle, albeit reluctantly. The weeks and months, and sometimes years, it took to breach the walls of a fortified city, using captured slaves to fill moats and man battering rams under withering barrages of arrows from the parapets, went against their ingrained desire for a quick victory.

If things went as planned, and the sun burning through the fog indicated it would, a new strategy would be employed this day that would make every walled citadel a trap from which there was no escape. The few warlords in the region who had not yet proclaimed their fidelity to the Khan soon would, or face swift annihilation.

For a week the army of five hundred mounted warriors and another thousand foot soldiers waited in the forests just beyond the city's fields. The harvest was in, leaving the fields cut low and yellowed. It would give the archers within the citadel an excellent opportunity to slaughter anyone foolish enough to launch a direct attack. Just as critical for the defenders, it meant that they had enough food to wait out a long siege. If winter came before the walls fell, it was likely the Mongols would return north to their capital and not come back until spring.

General Khenbish had orders from the Khan to take this town before the first snows dusted the roof of his palace. Though the general had never been graced by the Khan's presence, he would no more disappoint his king than if the man were his best friend. He only wished the Great Leader had not sent an emissary to witness the battle. And such an ugly man at that, with his sallow skin and great hooked nose – plus he had the devil's eyes. Khenbish did give him credit for his beard. While he himself could only grow a drooping mustache and a wispy few strands from his chin, the lower half of the observer's face was hidden behind thick dark curls.

General Khenbish, unlike in any other siege, had not constructed dozens of scaling ladders and towers or built trebuchets and catapults. He'd brought only enough slaves to tend to his soldiers' needs and build but two wood-framed towers placed in the field just beyond the reach of the town's archers. Atop the towers were large copper cones opened to the sky. The inside of each was layered with a fine coat of silver that was polished until it shone as dazzlingly as the sun itself. Under each, a barrel like that of a small cannon protruded from the wooden box supporting the eight-foot cone. The whole upper assembly, held fifteen feet off the ground by a timberwork truss, could be pivoted and elevated on a sturdy gimbal. Four of Khenbish's best men stood on top of each structure.

Had the Khan's ambassador any questions about the strange towers, he held them to himself.

For a week the red *ger* had stood outside the town's tall and tightly sealed gates. As was Mongol tradition, a white tent was erected first and the town's leaders given the opportunity to discuss their surrender without fear of death. When the red woolen tent, the *ger*, replaced the white tent, that indicated an attack was imminent. When the red tent was dismantled and a black tent took its place, that indicated all within the walls would die.

In the days since the red *ger* began swaying and billowing as it abutted the road leading to the gate, rains had fallen or the sky had been heavy with clouds. Today promised the first clear weather, and as soon as Khenbish was certain the sun would burn through the last of the haze, he ordered slaves out across the fallow fields to tear down the red tent and set up its more ominous counterpart.

Archers fired at the slaves as soon as they were within range. Flights of arrows so thick they seemed to swarm peppered the ground around the men. And met flesh as well. Four slaves dropped where they were hit; two more struggled on with thin wooden shafts protruding from their bodies. The others ran unimpeded, protected by the bulk of the bundled black tent.

Replacements were sent out immediately. They zigged and zagged, trying to throw off the archers' aim.

Most were successful but a few went down, driving arrows deeper into their bodies as they plowed into the earth. In all, it took twenty men to erect the tent, and of those only five made it back to the Mongol lines.

'Seems a bit wasteful,' the observer remarked in his thick accent.

'It is how it is done,' Khenbish replied without turning his horse. 'White tent, red tent, black tent, death.'

'The Khan never mentioned why this town is being attacked. Do you know?'

Khenbish wanted to answer, curtly, that the Khan's reasons were his own, but he knew he had to treat the man with the respect due his status. He said, 'The local warlord didn't pay the Khan all of his taxes last year. The amount was trivial and might have been overlooked by the Khan's generosity. However, he was overheard by a royal post messenger bragging of his thievery.'

The Empire was famous for its postal service, with strings of rest houses along all major routes so riders could either switch horses and keep going or pass along messages to rested carriers who were already waiting. In this way news from all reaches of the Khan's vast holdings could reach him in weeks, sometimes mere days.

'Such a transgression', Khenbish continued, 'cannot go unpunished.'

'"Render unto Caesar,"' the emissary said.

The general ignored the unknown reference and glanced skyward. The last of the mist was almost gone, leaving a blue dome over the battlefield. He reined his horse around to check on the men waiting behind him. They all wore full bamboo armor and were mounted on sturdy ponies, descendants of the animals that had allowed the Mongol hordes to attack and then hold the breadth of a continent. Each rider had a special oilskin bag hanging off the side of his saddle. The cloth was completely waterproof, and the contents had been carefully mixed and measured by Khenbish's best alchemist. Behind the cavalry were ranks of foot soldiers armed with pikes nearly twice as tall as the men. The keen blades were honed to a razor's edge.

'General,' an aide called to get his attention.

He turned to face the distant village. On each of the two strange siege towers, a soldier waved a red battle flag – the signal that they were ready.

Khenbish nodded to his own flag-bearer. The man stepped forward so he could be clearly seen and waved a silk standard over his head. Out on the towers, the men dropped their banners and concentrated on the odd machines they had brought to the field. They maneuvered the ungainly contraption so that the small bore in the coffin-sized wooden box faced the top of the fortified wall. One of the soldiers pulled a cover off the cannonlike barrel while the others slowly swung the box back and forth. When either of the two devices was aimed directly at an archer or observer on top of the castle wall, it paused for a moment.

Nothing seemed to change. There was no noise, no projectile fired, no indication at all that anything was happening, yet each time one of the barrels focused on a watchman, that man suddenly ducked away and never showed himself again.

The Khan's emissary looked to Khenbish for some sort of explanation. The taciturn general was studying the parapets through a pane of dark-tinted glass the size of a lady's hand mirror. He finally turned and noticed the look of confusion on the man's face. He kneed his horse to edge him closer, and then reached across to hand over the glass viewer.

The diplomat took it by its ornately carved ivory handle and held it up to his eye. He blinked quickly and then peered over the edge to look at the walled city unobstructed. Just as quickly he looked back through the glass.

The shaded glass cast the entire scene in an eerie twilight despite the bright sun, but that wasn't what had startled him. It was the solid rays of light, as thin as rapiers' blades, that emanated from the two towers. The crimson beams shot like lances from the odd structures and raked across the top of the walls. As he watched, a guard popped his head into the gap between two crenellations. Both beams zeroed in on him instantly. The light raked across his face, and though the distance was too far to be certain, the emissary thought the beams centered in the guard's eyes. It took only seconds for the hapless man to duck down again, his head shaking furiously.

He lowered the glass a second time. The sepia tint was gone; the ruby rays of light too. Everything was

7

still and placid except for the movement of the two wooden boxes being turned back and forth, their purpose, without the glass, unknowable.

His expression was even more uncomprehending than just moments before.

'Dragon's Stare,' Khenbish said without turning. 'That is what my men call it.'

'And you,' the envoy asked, 'what do you call it?'

Khenbish tugged at the reins to wheel his horse around. 'Certain victory.'

'I don't understand. How does it work?'

'There is a long octagonal crystal in each device from an ancient mine far to the south. Do not ask me the science, but using a set of mirrors with holes in them, it somehow channels sunlight captured in the cone on top and focuses it in such a manner that it can temporarily blind a man who gazes directly into it.'

'Yet it is somehow invisible?'

'It appears as a small red dot when it strikes an object, but the beam can only be seen in the air through that glass you are holding.' He turned his focus back on his horsemen. 'Now is the time to end this siege.'

The Khan's man once again regarded the towering ramparts and the thick wooden gate. It seemed as impenetrable as the Great Wall to the north of the capital. He couldn't understand how blinding a few lookouts could possibly end a siege. But then he came from a family of merchants and knew nothing of warfare or military tactics.

'Charge,' Khenbish ordered.

8

Though the emissary expected a wild explosion of man and beast racing for the distant walls, the attack was instead a stealthy and slow walk. The horses' hooves were muffled with thick woolen sacks so they barely made a sound as they moved. Harnesses, saddles, and panniers had all been cinched so tightly that the usual creak of leather was absent, and the men urged their mounts with soft whispers. Closing his eyes, the emissary couldn't tell that fifty horsemen were trotting past. Of all his senses, only his nose detected the faint whiff of dust kicked up by the animals' muffled hooves.

Though not a military man, he knew instinctively that this was the critical phase in the general's plan. He glanced up. The sky remained clear directly overhead, but a single puffy cloud was moving toward the battlefield. Its shadow cut like an eclipse across the hills behind the town. If it swept over them, he feared Khenbish's secret weapon would be rendered useless.

No lookout had shown himself for many minutes. He could imagine the anxiety and confusion among the defenders, not knowing what had struck them or how it had rendered them blind. This wasn't a particularly large community, and he knew from his travels that rural people tended to be superstitious. To what manner of witchcraft had they ascribed their sightlessness?

Like an army of ghost soldiers, the column of horsemen was making deceptively good time across the fields. The mounts were so well trained that none whinnied or neighed.

The cloud was still several minutes away. The emissary

did some quick calculating in his head. It would be a near thing, and yet the riders didn't quicken their pace. The general instilled discipline above all else.

A head popped over the wall, and both light cannons swung on him so quickly that he got the barest glimpse of the battlefield before his retinas were seared by the invisible beams. Khenbish stiffened on his horse, waiting for a cry of alarm that would signal unseen archers to release their arrows. A scream from above caused him to suck air through his teeth. It was nothing more than a crow in the branches of a tree behind them.

The lead rider reached the wooden gate and casually tossed the bag he'd been carrying in the dirt at its foot. A moment later another joined it, and another. And another. The pile grew until it was a misshapen hillock pressed up against the stockade.

Finally someone within the walls showed some intelligence. When he raised his head over the battlements just to the right of the gate, he kept one hand shaded over his eyes and his gaze downward. His warning shout carried clearly across the field. The element of surprise had been shattered.

The riders abandoned their pretense at stealth and quickly had their horses at full gallop. The last few hurled their bags at the gate and wheeled around. They scattered as arrows fired blindly from within the walls once again darkened the skies.

But it wasn't so much the arrows blotting out the sun as it was the cloud that had been so silently approaching. And by some twist of fate the winds that had sustained it ceased, and it hovered like an enormous parasol over the village. Without direct sunlight, Khenbish's ray guns were nullified.

Alert sentries realized what was coming and started throwing buckets of water onto the pile of bags that reached almost halfway up the thick wooden gate. The general had anticipated this and made certain each had been coated with a thick layer of resin so the water couldn't permeate it.

Motivated by desperation, archers appeared along the wall and took careful aim before loosing their arrows. The horsemen wore armor on their chests, and helmets covered their heads, but their backs were exposed, and soon arrows found their marks. In moments there were several jockey-less horses milling on the field, their riders lying sprawled on the ground, some writhing in agony, others ominously still.

One of Khenbish's men raced parallel to the wall, standing high in his stirrups, a nocked arrow ready in his short cavalry bow. Rather than a sharp bronze point, the arrow's tip was a pitch-soaked wad of cloth that burned brightly. He fired and immediately pulled hard on the left rein. The horse knew the signal and went down onto its flank in a cloud of dust, its legs kicking awkwardly while its heavy body shielded the rider from what was to come.

The arrow hit the pile of bags near the base of the gate at the same moment a bucket of water was tossed off the parapet. The flame turned to white smoke and steam, and then nothing. Time on a battlefield has an elasticity that defies all logic. It seemed forever elapsed, but it was less than a half second before the last dying ember of the arrowhead burned its way through the bag and touched off the contents inside.

Alchemists searching for the Elixir of Life had stumbled upon the ratio and composition of chemicals, and so it was called *huǒ yào*, or Fire Medicine. The world would later know it as gunpowder.

Because it is a slow-burning explosive, gunpowder needs to be compressed to do much more than flash and sizzle. The first bag burst into smoky flame, igniting others on the outside of the pile, until flames were shooting dozens of feet into the air. The pyre was enough to detonate the bags buried at the base of the mound, and the weight of the sacks above tamped the expanding gases long enough to produce a titanic explosion.

The concussion wave rippled across the field, sending a wall of hot air as far as the general and his remaining foot soldiers. The blast knocked the ambassador off his horse, and to him it felt as though he'd stood before a potter's kiln. Flame and smoke rose high into the air, while on the other side of the wall the gates were blown inward and shredded. The debris scythed down anyone in its way, while archers and lookouts along the parapet were tossed like limp dolls, their cries shrieking over the roar of the blast.

The Khan's man slowly regained his feet. The ambassador's ears were ringing, and when he closed his eyes, the afterimage of the explosion was burned on the inside of his lids. This was the second miracle weapon he had seen today. First the light gun and now some means of containing fire in bags and unleashing it all at once. Truly this was an amazing land.

On the battlefield, the scattered horsemen turned as though a shoal of fish and began charging for the destroyed gates, where wood smoldered and the dazed defenders ambled in shock. Swords were unsheathed and reflected the sunlight brightly now that the cloud had moved on. The men in the towers searched for victims, but the explosion had taken the fight out of the garrison.

General Khenbish released his reserves of foot soldiers to follow after the cavalry. With a roar almost as loud as the blast of gunpowder, the men tore off across the field, eager to do the Khan's work and restore his honor from being robbed and, worse, made to look weak because of it. They would spare the comeliest women, and boys who could be used as slaves, but everyone else in the town would be put to the sword and the entire village razed. The local warlord's head would be placed on a pike in the nearest settlement as a reminder for those who thought their Khan's wrath was not swift and all-consuming.

'I wish to know more of your amazing arsenal,' the ambassador said as he and Khenbish dismounted. It wasn't common practice for the general himself to take part in the slaughter, and the ambassador had no desire to see what was happening on the other side of the wall.

'I will introduce you to my alchemist. He can explain both in greater detail than I. For me it is enough that they work.' An aide handed him a bone-porcelain cup of strong tea.

As they started off toward the copse of trees where camp servants and staff waited to treat any wounded from the battle, the ambassador mused that there were so many remarkable things that he'd witnessed during his years roaming this strange nation. Some things he would never reveal, like the intimacies he'd enjoyed with some of the Khan's concubines. And some things he would never discuss because they were just too bizarre to be believed. Like the Great Wall – it had the height and breadth of a five-story stone building and yet it stretched from horizon to horizon and beyond. It alone dwarfed every bit of Roman engineering that lay across Europe. There were the rocklike bones of dragons he'd been shown in the central desert, skulls as big as wine barrels, with teeth like daggers and femurs as tall as a man. And then there was what he saw today: a device capable of throwing light intense enough to blind a man.

For his own sake he wanted to know how this weapon operated – Khenbish had mentioned a crystal of some sort – but he knew that this was one more mystery he would take to his grave.

Marco Polo strode alongside the general, unsure that his fellow Venetians would believe even the more banal stories he could tell about his travels in China.

I

Birmingham, England
Four months ago

William Cantor had sneezed into the microphone before he knew he was about to. The need hit him that hard, and he didn't have the chance to turn his head away. The phlegm the sneeze had discharged into his nasal passages had to be snorted back, and that amplified sniff echoed through the nearly deserted meeting room.

'Sorry,' he said miserably and coughed, covering his mouth and turning away so as to show the ten-odd people here for his lecture that he wasn't a complete philistine. 'As an American I knew at Christ Church College said' – that's right, you rubes, I went to Oxford – 'I can shake a hand, I can shake a leg, but I sure can't shake this cold.'

The response from the crowd might have been polite laughter or, most likely, a muted cough.

God, how he hated these lectures, the ones in annex buildings or village libraries, where the only attendees were pensioners with no interest in the subject but nothing better to do with their afternoons. Worse than those, actually, were the ones in cities such as Birmingham, so blighted that the sun never seemed to shine, and the people in the room were just here to get warmed up before heading out to panhandle or line up at soup kitchens. He had counted ten attendees before taking the lectern and no fewer than fourteen overcoats. He imagined a string of rusted shopping carts, overladened with detritus, in the library car park.

'"I have not told half of what I saw."' A much better opening line than spraying the microphone with bogies, Cantor thought ruefully. Still, he had goals, and one never knew, maybe the bundled-up woman toward the back of the fluorescent-lit room was secretly J. K. Rowling in mufti. 'These were the last words uttered by the great Venetian explorer Marco Polo upon his death-bed.

'We know from his legendary book, *The Travels of Marco Polo*, dictated to Rustichello da Pisa while both languished in a Genoese prison, that Polo, along with his father, Niccolò, and uncle, Maffeo' – the names tripped off Cantor's tongue despite his head cold, this being far from the first time he had given this particular talk – 'that he made many incredible discoveries and beheld many amazing sights.'

There was a disturbance at the back of the room as a newcomer entered from the library's brutalist-style reading room. Metal folding chairs creaked as a few people turned to see who had come to hear the speech, probably assuming it was a homeless buddy coming in from Chamberlain Square.

The man wore a cashmere overcoat that nearly swept

the floor over a dark suit, dark shirt, and a matching dark tie. Tall and big, he gave an apologetic wave and took a seat in back before Cantor could see his features. This looked promising, the cash-strapped scholar thought. At least this bloke was wearing clothes that hadn't already been discarded a few times.

Cantor paused long enough for the gentleman to settle. If this was a potential financial backer, he might as well start licking the guy's boots now.

'Even in his day, Polo's *Travel*s sparked debate. People simply didn't believe he had seen and done all that he claimed. They couldn't look past their own prejudices to believe that there was another separate civilization that could rival or even surpass the European states. Later, a glaring omission arose. Simply stated, for all his years in China, and all that he wrote of that distant land, he never once mentioned its greatest achievement, its most iconic image.

'You see, at no point in his dictations to Rustichello da Pisa did he ever mention China's Great Wall. That would be like a modern tourist saying they've been to London but not seen the Eye. Wait. That hideous Ferris wheel may be something a savvy traveler would want to forget.' Cantor paused for laughter. Got more coughing. 'Ah yes, then, his failure to mention the Great Wall, which is just a short distance from Beijing, where Polo spent so much time, led his detractors to discount his entire tale.

'But what if fault lies not with the dic-ta-tor but the dic-ta-*tee*.' Here he had planned to make a play on words and mention the despotic Genoese doge who had imprisoned Polo and the scribe, Rustichello, but decided against it. 'Little is known about the man Polo dictated his story to while they served time in a Genoese prison cell following Polo's capture at the Battle of Curzola. Rustichello himself had been captured some fourteen years earlier after the pivotal Battle of Meloria, which marked the beginning of the decline of the Pisan city-state.

'Rustichello was, to put it in today's vernacular, a romance writer who'd gained some measure of success prior to his being taken prisoner. Think of him as the Jackie Collins of his day. That would give him a strong insight into what would capture the imagination of his reading audience and what would be seen as too fantastic to believe.

'With that in mind, I see him not only as the man wielding the pen that put Polo's story to paper but as his editor as well, a man who could perhaps blunt some of Polo's more controversial discoveries in order to give the manuscript more mass appeal. Medieval noblemen – and that's almost exclusively who writers wrote for at the time – wouldn't appreciate that China rivaled them and in many cases surpassed their achievements in the fields of medicine, engineering, social administration, and especially warfare.'

Cantor paused a moment. Expressions on the faces of his audience ranged from asleep to slack-jawed indifference. So long as they were out of the freezing rain pounding the central English city, they didn't much care what he said. He wished he could see the man in the dark suit, but he was hidden behind a tall homeless fellow who slept in an almost perfectly erect posture.

'It was with this thought in mind – that perhaps Rustichello took notes during their long confinement that were edited out of the final draft of *Travels* and that those notes would account for some of the lapses in Polo's story that have vexed future scholars and made them question the validity of the entire book – that I come to you today.' The line sounded clunky to Cantor's ear too, but he was trying to come off as learned, and all his dons at Oxford spoke in run-on sentences that could fill a page or more.

'I believe,' he continued, 'that somewhere in the world exist those notes, those bits of Polo's story that couldn't get past the medieval censor – that was the Vatican – and would have raised too much doubt among the contemporary readership. Since leaving Christ Church' – no sense admitting that he hadn't graduated – 'I have searched across Italy and into France for a hint of such a book. And finally, six months ago, I believe I found it.'

Did Black Suit stir at this news? It seemed to Cantor that the shadow at the back of the room shifted position slightly. He felt like a fisherman who senses that first nibble on the end of his line. Now he had to set the hook before reeling in his prize.

'I was given access to the sales records of a small antiquarian bookshop in an even smaller town in Italy that has been in business since 1884. They have a record of selling a copy of Rustichello's seminal work, *Roman de Roi Artus*, in 1908. Included with the book of Arthurian legend was a folio of loose pages.

'At this time, Edwardian English families were exploring Italy in order to broaden themselves. Think of E. M. Forster's *A Room with a View*.' To most of this lot it should be *Cardboard Box with a Cellophane Window*, but Cantor knew he was really playing to an audience of one. 'Like any tourist, these travelers brought back souvenirs. Furniture, statuary, just about anything they could get their hands on that would remind them of Lombardy or Tuscany. One particular family fancied books and returned with veritable trunkloads of them, enough to fill a library about the size of this room floor to ceiling. Some of the volumes dated back to a century before Polo was even born. It is this family who acquired the Rustichello works.

'For a fee, I was granted limited access to their library.' Five hundred pounds for an afternoon, Cantor recalled bitterly. He recalled most things bitterly these days. The current library's owner was a right miserable git who, knowing Cantor's desperation to see the library, wasn't above capitalizing on the scholarly interest of a thirty-year-old researcher.

Cantor had scraped together only enough for a single visit, but it had been enough. And that was what he was really doing here today, and for the past few months. He had no interest in enlightening dowagers and the homeless. He was hoping to find a patron who would help him fund his research. The folio's owner had expressed in no uncertain terms that he would not sell it, but he would be willing to allow Cantor access, at five hundred pounds per day.

The young academic was sure that once he published his research, pressure from historical societies would force the owner to, if not donate, at least let a major university authenticate Rustichello's work and thus cement Cantor's reputation and hopefully his fortune as well.

'The text is written in typical medieval French, my specialty along with Italian from the same era. I managed to translate only a small portion since I only discovered it toward the end of my sojourn in the library, but what I read is mind-boggling. It is the description of a battle Polo witnessed in 1281 where a general named Khenbish obliterated his enemies using gunpowder, which Polo had never seen used in such a way, and a most remarkable device that utilized a special crystal to channel sunlight into a focused beam, much like a modern laser.'

Cantor paused once again. Dark Suit had gotten to his feet and skulked from the library annex room, his long overcoat dancing around his ankles like an obsidian cape. Cantor cursed under his breath. He'd failed to set the hook, had in fact scared the fish out of the water entirely. He looked dejectedly at the unshaven and sullen faces arrayed against him. What was the point of continuing? They no more wanted to hear his nasal monotone than he wanted to deliver it.

'Ah, thank you very much. Were there any questions?' He was taken aback when a spidery hand went up. The woman had the scrunched face of one of those dolls made of nylon stockings. 'Yes?'

'Can you spare some change?'

Cantor grabbed up his briefcase, tossed his worn mackintosh over his arm, and strode out to a chorus of hoarse cackles.

Darkness had fallen completely when he stepped through the library's doors. The impersonal expanse of Chamberlain Square was hemmed in by the concrete monstrosity of the library on one side, the three-story classical Council House on another, and by the Greek temple-like Town Hall on a third. In the middle was the monument to Joseph Chamberlain, who'd been someone or another in this dreary city. To Cantor, the structure looked like thieves had made off with an entire Gothic cathedral and left behind the top sixty or so feet of one of its spires.

If the city fathers had intended to design a less harmonious space architecturally, he couldn't see how.

Maybe throw in the odd zeppelin shed, he thought uncharitably, or an Eastern Orthodox onion-domed church.

The rain had slowed to a cold drizzle, and though Cantor raised his collar, icy water found its way down the back of his neck. He longed for a warm shower and a hot toddy, and for his sore nose to stop leaking.

His battered Volkswagen was parked over on Newhall Street, and he had just turned onto Colmore Row when the driver's-side window of a sleek Jaguar sedan whispered down.

'Dr Cantor, might I have a word?' The voice was cultured, with a continental accent – French, German, maybe Swiss, which to Cantor sounded like a combination of the two.

'Ah, I don't have my doctorate yet,' he stammered when he recognized the black shirt and tie of Dark Suit sitting behind the wheel of the luxury sedan.

'No matter, you gave a compelling speech. I would have stayed for the rest, but I received a call I couldn't ignore. Please, just a few moments, is all I ask.'

'It's raining.' Bending to peer into the car sent a spike of pain through Cantor's strained sinuses.

'Not in here.' The man smiled, or at least his lips parted and his teeth were revealed. 'I can drive you to your car.'

Cantor looked up the street. There was no one about and his car *was* five blocks away. 'Okay.'

He stepped around the long sloping bonnet and heard the electronic lock disengage for the passenger seat. He slid into the supple leather. In the glow of the dash lights, the sedan's considerable woodwork shimmered.

The stranger slipped the car into gear and eased it from its parking space. The Jag was so smooth that Cantor hadn't realized the engine had been running.

'An associate of mine heard the lecture you gave last week in Coventry and was intrigued enough to tell me about it. I had to hear for myself.'

'I'm sorry, you are?'

'Oh. My apologies. Tony Forsythe.' They shook

hands awkwardly since Forsythe had to reach under his left arm so as to not release the steering wheel.

'And what's your interest in Marco Polo, Mr Forsythe?' Cantor asked.

He got an odd vibe from the man. He was around forty and had plain, unexceptional features, yet thick dark hair that was so dense it could have been a toupee. Still, there was something else. Cantor realized what it was. His hands had been large and callused. His grip hadn't been overly forceful, but Forsythe's hand had practically swallowed Cantor's. In his experience, men in £1,000 overcoats and £60,000 cars didn't have calluses.

'I'm a dabbler in history, you might say, and I'm interested in this folio and its contents.'

William Cantor had looked for a fish, but he had the sudden feeling he'd nabbed a shark. 'Um, I'm down Newhall.'

'Yes, I know,' Forsythe said, which rather bothered Cantor, but the stranger added, 'Have you there in a jiff. You mentioned the folio's owner had no interest in selling, correct?'

'Yes, the man's loaded. I think he asked me to pay to see his library just to get under my skin.'

'But no price was discussed?'

'Ah, no. It was all I could do to come up with the five hundred quid to see the damned thing for a day.'

'Pity,' Forsythe said almost to himself. 'A simple cash transaction would have been preferable.'

To Cantor's relief, the Jag made the left-hand turn onto Newhall.

Forsythe glanced at him for a second. 'I don't suppose you'd be willing to tell me the gentleman's name?'

'I, ah, I don't think that would be in my best interest, now would it?'

'Oh, but it would, friend William. It is most certainly in your best interest.'

The Jaguar suddenly leapt forward under hard acceleration. Cantor got a fleeting glimpse of his blue VW Polo as they raced past. 'What the bloody hell do you—'

The arm of a person who'd been lying flat and unseen in the spacious rear seat snaked around Cantor's neck with the strength of an anaconda, choking the words in his throat. A sharp jab to the neck, a strange metallic taste in his mouth, and three seconds later William Cantor slumped over in drug-induced unconsciousness.

With his parents long dead from an accident on the M1 and no siblings or girlfriend, it wasn't until his landlord knocked on the door to his tiny one-room flat a month later that anyone knew Cantor had gone missing. The handful of presentations he'd planned had been courteously postponed by a person claiming his identity. It would be another several days before a missing persons report was matched with the headless and handless corpse found floating in the North Sea off the fishing town of Grimsby about that same time.

There were two things on which all the police involved agreed. The DNA found in Cantor's apartment matched that of the body fished from the water. The second was that before the man died he'd been tortured so severely that death would have been a blessed relief.

Because Cantor kept all his notes on the Rustichello Folio in his briefcase, which was never recovered, there was one more crime the authorities never realized was related to his disappearance. There had been a botched break-in of a Hampshire estate down in the southern part of the country near a town called Beaulieu. It happened two days after the last confirmed Cantor appearance. Forensic reconstruction showed that the burglars had been surprised by the widower owner during the robbery, bashed him over the head with a jimmy bar left on the scene – no prints – and fled in panic, not even bothering to take the pillowcases stuffed with sterling silverware they'd already gathered.

None of the police gave a second look at the slim gap in the rank upon rank of books that lined the estate's paneled library.

2

Tribal Region
Northern Waziristan
Today

The mountain village hadn't changed in two hundred years. Except for the guns, of course. They had long been around, that wasn't the issue. Rather, it was the *type* of weapon that had changed. Centuries ago, the bearded men toted bugle-throated blunderbusses. Then came the Tower muskets, followed by the Lee-Enfield rifles, and finally the ubiquitous AK-47s, which flooded into the region thanks to the Soviet invasion of Afghanistan, to the north. And so good were these guns that most were older than the men who carried them. Didn't matter if he was defending the region from a rival faction or heading off to the outhouse, a man without an AK at the ready was no man.

All this ran through Cabrillo's mind as he watched two Pashtun youths from the north, kids barely out of their teens, their beards just shadowy stubble on chin and cheek, try to wrestle a pair of goats onto an open-bed truck. All the while the assault rifles slung around their shoulders would slip and go across their chests, hitting the animals hard enough to make them fight the manhandling.

Each time a gun slipped, the boy would have to pause and redirect it back over his shoulder and then try to calm the satyr-eyed goat. The distance was too great to hear, but Cabrillo could imagine the goats' frightened bleats and the young men's earnest pleas to Allah for easier ways to handle livestock. It never occurred to them to rest their rifles against the rickety stockade fence for the sixty seconds it would take to load the animals unencumbered.

Take away the forty or so other armed men in the village encampment and he would have found it comical.

He had to admire the kids for one thing. Though he was ensconced in the latest arctic gear, he was still freezing his butt off while they cavorted in a couple of layers of homespun woolen clothing.

Of course Cabrillo hadn't moved more than his eyelids in the past fifteen hours. And neither had the rest of his team.

In Northern Waziristan, it was traditional that villages were built like citadels on the tops of hills. What grazing and farming was available was accomplished on the slopes leading to the town. In order for him and his people to find a suitable observation post that let them look down on the Taliban encampment, they had to find cover on an adjacent mountain. The distance across the steep valley was only a mile, but it forced them up a snow-and-glacial-ice peak and left them struggling to draw breath at almost ten thousand feet. Through his stabilized binoculars, he could see a couple of old men smoking a never-ending chain of cigarettes.

Cabrillo rued the last cigar he'd smoked, while his lungs felt as if they were drawing on the metallic dregs of an exhausted scuba tank.

A deep baritone came through his earpiece, 'They wrangling them goats or getting ready to have their way with them?'

Another voice chimed in, 'Since the goats aren't wearing burkas, at least these boys know what they're getting.'

'Radio silence,' Cabrillo said. He wasn't worried about his people losing operational awareness. What concerned him was that the next comment would come from his second-in-command here, Linda Ross. Knowing her sense of humor as he did, whatever she joked about was sure to make him laugh out loud.

One of the young shepherds finally set his wire-stock AK aside, and they got the animals into the truck. By the time the rear gate was closed, the kid had his weapon back over his shoulder. The engine fired with a burst of blue exhaust, and soon the vehicle was chugging anemically away from the mountaintop village. This was an al-Qaeda stronghold, and yet life in the rugged mountains went on. Crops had to be raised, animals grazed, and goods bought and sold. The dirty secret of both al-Qaeda and the Taliban was that while their followers were fanatics, they still needed to be paid. With the money long spent from last fall's lucrative poppy harvest, traditional means of support were necessary to keep the fighters operational.

There were roughly two dozen buildings in the town. Six or so fronted the dirt road that led down to the valley below, while the others rose behind them on the hill, connected by little more than footpaths. All were made of stone that blended in with the bleak surroundings, with low flat roofs and few windows. The largest was a mosque with a minaret that looked ready to topple.

The few women Cabrillo and his team had seen all wore dark burkas while the men sported baggy pants under jackets called *chapans* and either turbans or flattened wool caps known as *pakols*.

'Juan.' Linda Ross's voice had an elfin lilt that went with her pixielike appearance. 'Check out the mosque.'

Careful so as not to draw attention, Cabrillo swung his binoculars a few arc degrees and zoomed in on the mosque's door. Like the other three members of his team, he was dug into the side of the mountain, with a dirt-covered tarp over the foxhole. They were all invisible from just a few yards away.

He adjusted the focus. Three people were coming out of the mosque. The one with the long gray beard had to be the imam, while the other two were much younger. They walked flanking the man, their expressions solemn as they listened to whatever the holy man imparted to them.

Juan tightened the focus. Both of them had Asiatic features and no facial hair of any kind. Their clothing was out of place for this impoverished region. Their parkas, though of muted colors, were top quality, and they both wore new hiking boots. He looked closer at the smaller of the two. He'd studied that face for hours before beginning the operation, committing it to memory for this precise moment.

'Bingo,' he said softly over their secure communications equipment. 'That's Setiawan Bahar. Everyone keep an eye on him. We need to know where they're putting him up.'

The odd trio wandered up behind the main road, walking slowly because the imam had a pronounced limp. Intel said he got that limp when Kandahar fell back in 2001. They eventually reached one of the indistinguishable houses. A bearded man greeted them. They spoke at the doorstep for a few minutes and then the homeowner invited the two boys, both Indonesian, into his home. The imam turned to head back to his mosque.

'Okay, we got it,' Juan said. 'From now on all eyes on that house so we know he hasn't left.'

Cabrillo received a quiet chorus of 'Roger that.'

Then, against his own orders, Juan swept his binoculars back to the main road as a white Toyota sedan that probably had a couple hundred thousand miles on the odometer swung into town. No sooner had it stopped than the four doors were thrown open and armed men leapt out. Their faces were buried behind the tails of their turbans. They brought their weapons to their shoulders as they circled around to the car's trunk. One leaned forward and keyed open the lock. The door raised slowly on its hydraulics, and three of the gunmen leaned in with the barrels of their AKs.

Juan couldn't see what was in the trunk, or most likely who, and waited expectantly as one of the fighters lowered his gun so it hung under his arm and reached into the trunk. He hauled a fifth man from where he'd been lying in a fetal position. Their prisoner wore what looked like standard American-issue BDUs. The boots looked military too. His mouth was gagged, and a blindfold had been cinched over his eyes. His hair was a little longer than Army regulation and blond. He was too weak to stand and collapsed into the dirt as soon as he was free from the car.

'We've got a problem,' Cabrillo muttered. He turned his binoculars back to the house where Setiawan Bahar was sequestered and told his people to turn their attention to what passed for the town's square.

Eddie Seng said nothing, while Linda Ross gasped and Franklin Lincoln cursed.

'Have we heard anything about a captured soldier?' Seng then asked.

'No. Nothing,' Linda replied, her voice tightening as one of the Taliban kicked the captured soldier in the ribs.

In his basso voice, Linc said, 'Could have happened in the thirty hours it took us to hump our butts into position. No reason Max would have passed on news like that to us.'

Without taking his eyes off the house, Cabrillo

switched radio frequencies. '*Oregon, Oregon*, do you copy?'

From the port city of Karachi more than five hundred miles to the south came the immediate reply, 'This is the *Oregon*. Hali here, Chairman.'

'Hali, has anything come over the transom since we started this op about an American or NATO soldier kidnapped in Afghanistan?'

'Nothing over the news wires and nothing from official channels, but as you know we're a bit out of the Pentagon's loop right now.'

Cabrillo knew that last fact all too well. A few months back, after spending nearly a decade enjoying high-level access to military intelligence through his old mentor at the CIA, Langston Overholt, Cabrillo's private security company, known as the Corporation and based on a tramp freighter called the *Oregon*, had become a pariah. They had pulled off an operation in Antarctica to thwart a joint Argentine/Chinese bid to annex and exploit a massive new oil field off the pristine coast of the southern continent. Fearing the geopolitical risks involved, the U.S. government had told them in no uncertain terms not to attempt the mission.

It didn't matter that they had succeeded spectacularly. They were seen as rogue by the new president, and Overholt was ordered not to use the unique services the Corporation provided. Ever again. It had taken all of Langston's considerable influence in the corridors of Washington to keep his job following that episode. He'd confessed privately to Juan that the president had chewed off so much of his butt he hadn't been able to sit for a week.

And that is what brought Cabrillo and this small team here, to one of the few places on earth never to be occupied by a foreign army. Even Alexander the Great had the sense to avoid Waziristan and the rest of the Northern Tribal Regions. They were here because a wealthy Indonesian businessman, Gunawan Bahar, had a son who ran away to join the Taliban, in much the same way youths of a few generations ago back in the United States ran off to join the circus. Only difference was that young Setiawan hadn't developed mentally past the age of seven, and the cousin who'd brought him here had told the recruiter in Jakarta that Seti wanted to be a martyr.

American runaways became carnies. Setiawan's fate was that of a suicide bomber.

Hali continued, 'Stoney and Murph have been trolling every database they can lay their hands on since you left.' Eric Stone and Mark Murphy were the Corporation's IT experts, along with their other duties. 'Nothing much by way of news out of any of the 'stans.'

'Tell them to keep an eye out. I'm looking at a blond guy in NATO gear who looks like he's in a world of hurt.'

'I'll pass it on,' Hali Kasim, the ship's chief communications officer, said.

Cabrillo switched back to the tactical net. 'Recommendations?'

Linda Ross spoke up immediately. 'We can't leave

him here. We all know that in a day or two he's going to be the star of a jihadist beheading video.'

'Eddie?' Juan asked, knowing the answer.

'Save him.'

'Don't even ask,' Linc rumbled.

'I didn't need to.' Juan still had the target house under observation and wouldn't shift his focus. 'What are they doing now?'

'They have him up on his feet,' Linda replied. 'His hands are tied behind his back. A couple of the village kids have come out to see him. One of them just spit on him. The other kicked him in the shin. Hold on. The captors are shooing the kids away. Okay, they're leading him up behind the square, heading in the same direction as our target house. And they're walking, and walking, and . . . Here we go. Three houses left of where Seti's staying.'

'Linc, take the target,' Juan ordered. He paused a beat for the big former SEAL to get his binocs fixated and then switched his own to where the four terrorists were pushing their blond captive into a mud and stone house that was indistinguishable from all the others.

Two of the Afghans took up guard duty outside the simple wooden door. Juan tried to peer through the open window next to it, but the inside of the humble house was too dark to discern more than vague movement.

The Corporation had been hired to get Gunawan Bahar's son away from al-Qaeda, not rescue a foreign soldier, but as was the case in the operation in Antarctica,

Cabrillo's moral compass was the primary force behind their actions. Saving that stranger, while not getting paid the million dollars Bahar had already forked over with the promise of another four when his son was on a plane back to Jakarta, was just as imperative in his mind.

Juan recalled the tears in Bahar's eyes when he had explained during their only meeting about how his son idolized an elder cousin and how this boy had been secretly radicalized in a Jakarta mosque. Because of the mental challenges Seti faced, Gunawan had told him, the boy couldn't rationally join a terrorist organization, so in effect he'd been kidnapped and brought here to this al-Qaeda mountain retreat.

Cabrillo had seen the undying love in the man's tormented expression and heard it in his voice. He had no children of his own, but he was president of the Corporation and captain of its ship, *Oregon*. He loved his crewmates the way a father must, so he could well imagine the anguish Bahar was suffering. If one of his own had been kidnapped, he would move much more than heaven and earth to see them returned.

'You must understand what a blessed child he is,' the father had said, 'a true gift from Allah. Outsiders may look upon him as a burden, but they can't possibly know the love my wife and I have for the boy. It is perhaps wrong for me to say this, but of our three sons little Seti is our favorite.'

'I've heard that from other parents of special-needs kids,' Juan had replied, handing over the white cotton handkerchief from the breast pocket of his suit coat so the man could dab his eyes. Like a lot of Muslims, Gunawan Bahar wore his emotions on his sleeve. 'He is untouched by the ugliness of the real world.'

'That's it exactly. Seti is truly an innocent and will remain that way all his life. Mr Cabrillo, we will do anything to get our boy back. Of his cousin, we do not care. His parents have disavowed him because they know what he has done. But you must return my precious Seti.'

Like many of the private contracts the Corporation handled over the years, this meeting had been set up by a mysterious facilitator named *L'Enfant*. Juan himself had never met the man who called himself The Baby, but the contracts he sent the Corporation's way were always legit, more or less, and in order for potential clients to get on the man's radar, their bank accounts had to be well vetted.

Juan had ordered Eric Stone and Mark Murphy to tear their newest client's life apart and had additionally run the operation by Overholt at the CIA as a courtesy. Just because Langley was upset at Cabrillo and his team didn't mean Juan wouldn't check to make sure Bahar wasn't under investigation.

The last thing they needed now was to unknowingly work for some terrorist mastermind.

Gunawan Bahar had turned out to be just as he had presented himself, a wealthy Indonesian businessman grieving for his kidnapped child who was willing to do anything to have the boy returned to his family.

Upon their handshake, Bahar's most fervid desire

37

had become Juan's, and not only because of the money. He felt a groundswell of anger toward anyone who would exploit a child like Seti, and it was made worse by what they intended the boy to do.

Now Cabrillo had taken responsibility for another life, that of the captured soldier. His desire to rescue him was as strong as his desire to save Setiawan.

Juan flicked his eyes to where the sun was setting over the mountains to the west, judging they had another thirty minutes till dusk and an hour until full dark. 'Eddie, Linc, keep watch on the primary target. Linda, you've got where they're keeping the soldier.'

Juan's binoculars kept scanning the rest of the village and its access road.

The three acknowledged, and their careful observation continued. No detail was overlooked. Linc made sure to point out that there was a gap in the stone wall behind which they were keeping Seti that was big enough for Linda but not his muscled bulk. Linda reported that she'd seen in the flare of a match that there were two Taliban in the house with the prisoner and that he was most likely on the floor, judging by the angle of the Afghanis' heads.

Just as the last of the sun slipped behind an icy peak and turned the underbelly of clouds blanketing the sky a dazzling shade of orange, Juan saw headlights approaching up the road below him. Three vehicles – the goat truck, the sedan with the prisoner, and now this new one – all in one day. Had to be what passed for gridlock in these parts, he thought.

It took several long minutes for the vehicle to make its grinding ascent to the mountain village, and the daylight was almost gone by the time it trundled into the square. A school bus, though half the normal length, it was painted in fantastical colors, with a string of beads hanging across the inside of the windshield and a rack on top that was currently empty. Garish trucks like this were the workhorses of central Asia, transporting people, animals, and goods of all kinds. When the team had passed through Peshawar on their way here, they had seen hundreds of them, no two exactly alike.

Cabrillo switched to night vision goggles. The NVG didn't have the optical resolution of his regular binoculars, but with the light fading he could still make out more detail.

Several men stepped down from the bus. The first one was unarmed and greeted the village headman with a warm embrace. He looked vaguely familiar to Cabrillo, and he wondered if he'd seen that face on a terrorist watch list. The three that followed carried metal suitcases as well as the ever-present AKs.

Juan quickly assumed that this was a senior Taliban official and that the boxes contained video gear for the captured soldier's execution. This was confirmed when one of the guards laid an elongated box on the ground and lifted the lid. The Taliban leader stooped to withdraw a three-foot-long scimitar straight out of *One Thousand and One Nights*, much to the delighted roars of the others.

Subtlety was not a virtue among these men.

Cabrillo described to the rest what he observed, and asked, 'Is anyone thinking what I'm thinking?'

Linc replied, 'That I broke the promise I made to myself after getting out of Tora Bora never to come to this part of the world again?'

'There's that, yes,' Juan said with a chuckle, 'but I was thinking that taking the bus would be a hell of a lot easier than hoofing it the twenty miles back to our SUV. We planned on carrying the kid out. He can't weigh more than a hundred pounds. The variable is if the soldier can walk that far. Stealing that bus negates the unknowns.'

'Sounds good to me,' Eddie Seng agreed.

'Linda?'

'What about its fuel load? Does it have the range to get us out of here?'

'There are no Exxon stations around here, so they must be able to get at least as far as Landi Kotal, the town on the Paki side of the Khyber Pass, maybe all the way to Peshawar.'

'Makes sense to me,' Linc said.

Linda nodded, then remembered no one could see her. 'Okay. We go for the bus.'

The Muslim call to sundown prayers echoed across the deep valley, and the men in the town square and others from the village made their way toward the tumbledown mosque. The guards remained outside the building where they were keeping the soldier, and no one left the house where Seti was sequestered.

There was no generator in town, so as the twilight

deepened some lamps were lit, emitting feeble light through dirty windows in a few of the houses. Both target houses had such lamps. Fuel was expensive, so the lamps were snuffed out one by one within an hour. Like the lives of so much of the world's population, these people's lives were dictated by the earth's stately rotation.

Cabrillo and his team continued to watch the sleeping town through their night vision gear. The two guards maintained their vigilance for another hour before they too succumbed to oblivion. Nothing moved, no smoke from a chimney, no roving dogs, nothing.

They gave it another hour for good measure before emerging from their foxholes.

Juan felt a few joints pop as he unlimbered himself. So many hours of immobility in the chilly air had stiffened him like a board. Like the others, he took a minute to flex feeling back into his muscles, moving slowly so as not to attract attention. His moves mimicked tai chi.

The team was traveling light, carrying just enough weapons and gear for the one night on the mountainside. They all carried the Barrett REC7 assault rifle with tactical lights slung under the barrels, but all armed themselves with their preference of pistols. Cabrillo favored the FN Five-seveN on a shoulder rig so he could clear the attached silencer quickly.

The terrain was rugged, with ankle-twisting boulders and fields of loose stones that could be dislodged into a hissing avalanche with an ill-placed boot, so the team moved cautiously, each covering the next, and always one person watching the village for any sign of movement. Like wraiths, they walked under the thin silver glow of a millimetric slice of moon, their NVGs giving them the advantage over both the landscape and the darkness.

Cabrillo led them into the village, hugging the walls, but not so close that their black uniforms would scrape against the rough-hewn stone. At a preplanned spot, Cabrillo stopped and dropped into a crouch. He pointed to Linda and Eddie before indicating they would rescue Seti. He and Linc would save the better-defended captive.

With the big ex-SEAL covering his back, Juan approached the back of the house where the soldier had been taken. He peered in through a window. Despite the grime caking the single pane of glass he could see three cots in the room. Two of them were occupied by the prone forms of sleeping men. The third cot didn't have bedding, which meant it wasn't likely there was another guy out roaming around.

The prisoner had to be in the house's front room, which if tradition held would be a combination living/dining/kitchen area. Its only window was next to the door, so they would be going in somewhat blind.

Juan made a motion with his hands like he was parting water.

Linc nodded and started down along the left side of the house while Cabrillo padded along the right. At the corner both men paused. A minute turned into three, and Juan was starting to get worried. They had to co-ordinate their assault with the other team. He was waiting for Linda to give him a single click over the tactical radio, telling him she and Eddie were in position.

It was because he was straining his ears so hard that he heard it – a distant whine, like a mosquito at the far end of a long room. He knew that sound and realized they had to move now.

This could be a blessing or a curse, he thought just as Linda signaled they were ready. Linc had heard the click too, and he and Juan moved in such perfect accord that they were around the corner of the house at the same instant, striding forward at the same pace and moving their hands into the exact same position.

Momentum, along with Juan's hundred and eighty pounds and Linc's two-forty, came together as both men slammed into the seated and snoozing guards, cracking their heads together with just a fraction less force than needed to crush bone. The two men never knew what hit them and went from comfortable REM sleep to a near-coma state in a fraction of a second. They eased the guards onto the ground, making sure to hide their AKs under a wooden cart stacked with hay.

They waited a moment to see if the disturbance had been detected. Juan could still hear the faint buzz. He pointed to his ear and pointed up toward the night sky. Linc shot him a quizzical look, not understanding.

Juan stretched his arms wide and waggled them like an aircraft in flight.

Linc's eyes went wide. He knew as well as Juan that

43

there was usually only one kind of aircraft flying in Northern Waziristan – Predator drones.

There was no reason to think that this village was the unmanned aircraft's target, but there was no reason to think it wasn't. Intel on the Taliban leader who'd arrived in the bus might have filtered up the chain of command, and now CENTCOM had an armed drone overhead looking for a target of opportunity.

He wasn't worried about them firing a Hellfire missile just yet. The rules of engagement were pretty clear that confirmation of the target's location had to be verified before the trigger could be pulled. They'd wait until dawn to use the drone's advanced cameras to pick their man. What bothered him was the chance that a local insomniac would hear the aircraft and raise the alarm.

More than anything, Juan wanted to call Lang Overholt and ask the old spook to find out if there was an operation in the works for this village, but two things prevented him. One was that he couldn't risk talking while this close to the target, and the second was that Overholt would freeze him out, or worse, be frozen out himself.

If the Corporation was going to continue enjoying the successes they had, they needed to mend fences in Washington, and soon.

He peered through the window, and when he saw nothing but his ghostly reflection, he realized the glass had been blacked out. He pulled his rifle up behind his back and drew his silenced automatic from its holster. Linc did likewise.

The door had no lock or latch. It was just seven poorly sawn boards held together by a lattice backing.

Cabrillo pressed a gloved hand against it, testing how easily it would open. It moved slightly, the hinges fortunately greased with animal fat so they did not squeak. For the first time on the mission, he started to feel the icy fingers of apprehension. They were putting their primary duty in jeopardy for this, and if something went wrong, Setiawan Bahar would pay the ultimate price.

He pressed on the door a little harder and glanced through the crack with his NVGs. There wasn't enough light for the sophisticated electronics to amplify, so he opened the door wider. He felt it tap gently against something on the floor. He pulled off a glove, squatted, and reached a hand around the bottom of the door. His fingers touched something cold and cylindrical. He explored the shape and found two more. They were metal cans stacked in a little pyramid. Had the door opened farther the cans would have fallen. There would be ball bearings or empty shell casings in the cans so they would rattle when they tumbled. A simple, home-grown burglar alarm.

Juan gently lifted the topmost can, set it outside, and then retrieved the other two. He was able to open the door enough for his goggles to pick up details. A large picture of Osama bin Laden graced the far wall next to the door leading to the bedroom. He saw a stone hearth that was long since cold, a low table without chairs sitting on a threadbare carpet, a few pots and pans, and murky bundles of what he assumed were clothes. Another bed was pushed up to the right-hand side, and reclining with his back to the stone and an AK-47 across his lap was another sleeping guard.

Opposite him was a second indistinct shape. It took a few seconds for Juan to figure out it was a man lying on the floor. He was facing away from Cabrillo and balled up tightly as if protecting his abdomen from being kicked. Prisoner stomping was *de rigueur* for the Taliban.

Unlike in the movies, where a silenced pistol makes no more sound than a blowgun, the reality was that a shot fired here would wake the man in the back room and probably the neighbors as well.

Moving slowly but deliberately, Cabrillo eased into the hovel. The sleeping guard made a snuffling sound and smacked his lips. Juan froze in midstep. He could hear deep snoring from the other room. The guard shifted into a more comfortable position and fell deeper asleep. Covering those last few feet, Juan came up to the man and swung his hand like an ax against his carotid artery. The shock of the blow temporarily short-circuited the guard's brain, giving Juan the time to cut off his air long enough to render him unconscious.

Linc was already in motion. His knife cut through the plastic zip ties securing the prisoner's ankles and wrists while a big meaty hand went over the man's mouth to prevent him from calling out.

The captive went rigid for a moment, then rolled

onto his back with Lincoln keeping his hand in place. It was too dark for him to see what was happening so Linc leaned close to his ear and whispered. 'Friend.'

He felt the man nod under his hand, so he took it away and helped the prisoner to his feet. Linc put one shoulder under the man's arm, and with Juan backing out behind them, his pistol trained on the bedroom door, they made their escape out of the house.

Even with Linc supporting a lot of his weight, the prisoner was limping heavily. They moved away from the building, keeping to the deepest shadows. Cabrillo switched back to his assault rifle. They emerged in the town square near the mosque and found cover behind a stone wall. Out in the street they could see the brightly painted bus. The moonlight gave its paint scheme an ominous cast.

'Thank you,' the captive whispered in a deep Southern drawl. 'Ah don't care who you are, but thank you.'

'Don't thank us until we're well and gone from here,' Cabrillo warned.

Movement farther down the road caught Juan's attention. He sighted down his weapon, his finger just outside the trigger guard. A single click in his radio headset told him that Linda and Eddie had rescued the boy. He looked closer. That was them at the end of the street. He gave her a double click in response, and the two parties met next to the bus.

They had used drugs to render Seti unconscious, figuring it would be easier to deal with him as dead-weight than to risk the possibility of his crying out in

47

panic. Linc immediately took the boy from the much smaller though deceptively strong Eddie Seng and tossed him over his shoulder in a fireman's carry. Eddie popped a small penlight into his mouth, slid through the bus's accordion door, and set about hot-wiring the engine.

Cabrillo scanned the skies, his head cocked as he listened for the Predator he felt certain was still up there. Were they being watched right now? If so, what did the operators at Nevada's Creech Air Force Base think? Were they a choice target, and at this minute was the drone's operator moving his finger to the button that would unleash the deadly Hellfire antitank missile?

To distract himself from something he had no control over he asked Linda, 'Any problems?'

'Piece of cake,' she replied with a cocky grin. 'We released the knockout gas, waited for it to take effect, and just waltzed in and grabbed the kid. I left a window open a crack so the gas will dissipate. They'll wake up with monster headaches and no idea what happened to their young would-be martyr.'

'How many in the house?'

'Parents, two of their own children, plus Seti and his cousin.' A troubled look crossed Cabrillo's face. Linda added, 'I thought that was strange too. No guards, right? But the two Indonesians are here because they volunteered. No need to guard them at all.'

'Yeah,' Juan said slowly, 'you're probably right.'

'I'm ready,' Eddie announced from under the driver's seat, an exposed nest of wires in his hand. All he needed to do was twist two leads together and the big diesel would rumble to life.

The engine noise was certain to attract attention, so once the bus was hot-wired, they had to get out of Dodge as fast as they could.

Setiawan was strapped into a seat using one of their combat harnesses. The prisoner, whose name they hadn't bothered to ask, was in a row behind him. Linc and Linda had the first two seats, so Cabrillo took up a position in the back so he could cover their rear.

It was just then that all hell broke loose.

A shouted cry rose over the sleeping town from the direction of where they'd kept the captured soldier. One of the guards they'd knocked out had come to.

'Eddie, go!' Juan yelled. They had a minute, or less, before the tribesmen got organized.

Seng touched the two wires, creating a tiny arc of electricity, and then twisted them to keep the starter engaged. The engine shuddered but wouldn't fire. It sounded like a washing machine with an unbalanced load. He feathered the gas pedal, trying to finesse the engine, but it still wouldn't start. Before he flooded it, Eddie separated the wires, gave it a couple of heartbeats, and tried again.

The motor snarled and sputtered but refused to catch.

'Come on,' Eddie cajoled.

Cabrillo wasn't paying the drama at the front of the bus any heed. His eyes were glued out the rear window, searching for signs of pursuit. A figure burst from a narrow alley between two houses. Juan had the REC7 to his shoulder and triggered a three-round burst. Glass cascaded to the floor of the bus in a shower of fine chips while the bullets chewed up the ground at the man's feet. Three eruptions of dust stopped the man in his tracks, and he lost his balance and fell to the ground.

Juan noticed in passing that the man hadn't taken the time to arm himself before rushing to investigate the engine noise. He could have shot him dead but instead let him scramble back undercover.

'Eddie?' Cabrillo shouted over his shoulder, certain that the echo of gunfire had awoken every jihadist in a half-mile radius.

'Just a sec,' Seng called back, though there was no sense of tension in his voice. That was Eddie – cool under any circumstances.

Cabrillo scanned the streets as best he could. He saw lamps being lit behind a few windows. The entire village was going to be coming after them in moments. Though the bus would make a pretty good defensive position, the team didn't have the ammo for a protracted gun battle. If they didn't get out in the next few seconds, they never would.

The engine fired, and Eddie didn't give it time to warm up before wrestling it into gear and hitting the gas. The old bus lurched like a startled rhinoceros, kicking gravel from under its bald tires.

A pair of guards emerged from the same alley as the first man and cut loose with their assault rifles, firing wildly from the hip in continuous bursts of unaimed fury. Not a single round hit the bus, but the fusillade kept Juan pinned to the floor, and the men had vanished around the corner by the time he was up and had a sight picture. He put three rounds downrange to keep them back.

The bus had the acceleration of an anemic snail, so as they slowly pulled from the square they were open to more gunfire from hidden alleys and behind stone walls. One burst raked across the row of windows, blowing out the glass and raining shards on the people inside. That particular assault inexplicably cut off, but more bullets pinged against the roof and sparked off the engine cover.

And then they were free, pulling past the mosque where the gray-bearded imam regarded them stoically as they roared by. Juan continued to watch out the rear window to see if anyone was chasing them. Several fighters were out on the main street, their rifles raised over their heads as if they'd won a great victory.

Let 'em think what they want, Juan thought as he slumped onto one of the hard bench seats. The padding had long since vanished, and he could feel a metal support beam digging into his flesh. That little bit of discomfort reminded him of the greater problem they might still be facing. The bus belonged to a senior Taliban officer, someone Cabrillo was now certain he recognized but couldn't name. The odds were good that he was under observation by the U.S. military. While the powers that be might not understand what had just happened back in the village, if they wanted this guy dead, now was the time to unleash the drone's missile.

He scooted back to the shattered rear window and watched the sky. Eddie saw him in the cracked mirror over the driver's seat and called out, 'Anything back there?'

'Not on the ground, but I thought I heard a Predator when we were waiting to go in, and, if my hunch is right, this bus has a big old target on its roof.'

For the first couple miles out of the town, the road followed the valley floor, with wide, open crop fields on either side. But from studying topographical maps before the mission, Juan knew it would enter a steeper grade and snake through about a dozen hairpin turns. To the left of the road was the canyon wall while to the right the landscape fell away in a frighteningly steep grade. Once on that section of dirt tract, they would have no maneuverability whatsoever.

If he was calling the shots back at Creech, he'd wait until they were halfway down and then put the Hellfire up their tailpipe. With that in mind, he shouted over the beat of the knocking engine, 'Hey, soldier?'

'Me?' the blond man asked.

'I know everyone else's name on the bus, so yeah. Are you in any condition to hoof it for about fifteen miles?'

Cabrillo appreciated that the guy took a moment to think through his answer. 'No, sir. Ah'm sorry, but Ah've been through the meat grinder since they grabbed me. Nothing's broken, but a whole lot's sprained.' He lifted his shirt to show a sea of dark bruises across his chest and stomach to go with the shiner around his left eye. 'Ah can do maybe five miles over flat ground, but in these mountains Ah won't make it one.'

'Why are you asking?' Linda wanted to know.

'The canyon up ahead could be a death trap if I'm right about the Predator. I'm thinking about ditching the bus and going back to our original plan.'

It would be asking too much of Linc to carry the guy out, though Juan knew the big man would give it one hell of a try. He considered making the trek in stages, but the longer they remained in the region, the greater the risk of being discovered by the countless roving Taliban patrols.

'Chairman, we've got a problem,' Eddie said suddenly. 'I see headlights approaching.'

Cabrillo cursed under his breath. Thinking it made it happen. The only people out on the roads at night were the Talibs or their al-Qaeda allies.

'What do you want me to do?'

'Play it cool. Maybe they'll leave us alone.'

The twin beams of light lancing out from the darkness bounced along about a half mile farther down the road. Then they swung broadside to the lumbering bus and went still. The approaching driver had angled their vehicle into a roadblock.

The good luck they'd had escaping the village had run out.

'Now what?'

'Give me a sec,' Juan replied in that same cool tone

Eddie had used earlier. 'What kind of vehicle do they have?'

'By the time I'll be able to tell it'll be too late,' Seng replied.

'Good point,' Juan said grimly. Though Juan spoke Arabic like a Riyadh native, he doubted he would be able to bluff their way past a checkpoint, not with an ethnic Chinese, a black guy, a blond one, an Indonesian kid, and the all-American girl next door.

'Go around them, and pray there isn't a minefield next to the road. Guns at the ready.'

'Mr Chairman,' the stranger said. 'My shooting finger's just fine.'

Juan paced forward and handed him his FN Five-seveN. 'What's your name?'

'Lawless,' he said. 'MacD Lawless. Ah was a Ranger before turning to the private sector.'

'MacD?'

'Short for MacDougal. My middle name, which is only marginally better than my first.'

'Which is?'

The guy was handsome, and when he smiled he looked like a recruiting poster or a Calvin Klein model. 'Ah'll tell you when I know you better.'

'Deal,' Juan said, peering out through the windshield.

In the feeble glow cast by the bus's headlamps he could see it was a dark pickup truck that had pulled across to block the single lane. Three men stood in front of it, their heads sheathed in turbans, their weapons trained on the bus. Two more fighters were in the open bed, one hunched over a heavy machine gun, the other ready to feed it a belt of ammunition that he cradled like an infant.

'They get us with that chatter gun,' Linc warned, 'and it's all over but the crying.'

'Looks like these guys didn't get the memo about this being Tommy Taliban's Magical Mystery Tour bus,' MacD quipped. Cabrillo's measure of the man went up a notch. Anyone who could make bad jokes before combat was okay by him.

'I'm going to break left,' Eddie said, 'to put the pick-up's cab between us and that old Russian PKB.'

Juan had already known which way Eddie was going to turn because it made the most tactical sense, so he was already hunkered under a window on the right side of the bus, his rifle barrel just showing above the pitted chrome sill. His mouth had gone metallic as a fresh burst of adrenaline shot into his system.

3

Twenty yards to go. Eddie had slowed a little, to show he was about to comply with the men manning the roadblock, but he kept coming. None of the men arrayed before him looked overly concerned yet, but when they did, one of the soldiers put his hand in the air in a universal gesture to indicate they should pull over.

That was Seng's cue. He mashed the accelerator and gently heeled the bus over onto the narrow gravel verge. Loose dirt hissed under the heavy vehicle, and a tall plume of dust rose in its wake.

The Taliban paused for less than a second at this affront to its authority. Gunfire erupted from the checkpoint. The heavy engine block absorbed round after round while the windshield starred and spiderwebbed in a dozen places before collapsing entirely. Eddie's face was soon streaming blood from glass that had nicked his skin.

The Corporation team gave as good as they got, hosing the pickup from bumper to bumper. Had the ride over the uneven terrain been smoother, they might have had better luck picking individual targets, but from a moving vehicle at this tight range it was all spray and pray.

The interior of the bus became a fine haze of gunpowder residue and pulverized glass. At near-point-blank range the two sides exchanged murderous gunfire. The man behind the pintle-mounted machine gun went down when Linc fired off nearly a full clip at him, though miraculously the ammo loader went unscathed. The three men on the ground had dropped flat, and their view was cut off by the underside of their own truck as the bus rattled past them.

They had just gotten clear when the loader replaced his comrade behind the butterfly grips of the machine gun and opened up. With nearly twice the powder charge of a standard AK-47's, the bullets from the PKB came at them like armor-piercing rounds. The rear of the old school bus was riddled with two dozen sizzling holes, and the bullets had the power to blow through a couple rows of seat before finally losing momentum. A few passed all the way through the bus. Had Eddie not been driving like some old geezer in Florida, with only his hands remaining in view, he would have taken two to the back of the skull.

'Is everyone okay?' Juan shouted, his hearing compromised by the deafening roar of gunfire.

Even as his people acknowledged they were unhurt, Cabrillo was checking on young Setiawan Bahar. The teen remained oblivious in his drug-induced dreamworld. A few chips of glass had fallen on him, but other than that he looked like he could be asleep in his own bed back in Jakarta.

'Are they chasing us?' Eddie asked. 'All my mirrors are shot to hell.'

Cabrillo looked back. The checkpoint was just a short distance behind them, but he could see figures cutting in and out of the pickup's headlights. The men were doubtlessly organizing themselves to track down the fleeing bus and finish what they'd started. Their truck had more speed, maneuverability, and firepower than the bus.

They'd been lucky to get past the checkpoint. Juan knew too well that luck was fickle at best and downright capricious most of the time.

'Oh, they're coming, all right.'

'Hold on,' Eddie suddenly said.

It felt like the bus had driven onto an express elevator heading straight down. They had reached the spot where the road fell away in a series of punishing switchbacks. Any thought of abandoning the bus before reaching the potential target area was moot in Juan's mind. They were too late, with a Taliban technical racing up behind them like the guy was gunning for the checkered flag at the Indianapolis 500.

Tracer fire arced out from the trailing pickup, pulsing trails of burning phosphorescence that reached for the hurtling bus. They had the range but not the accuracy. The gunner had to be struggling just to stay in the truck, never mind manhandling a heavy machine gun.

At the front of the bus Eddie was fighting the wheel like a madman, not daring to look at what lay beyond the right-side tires. The road clung to the side of the canyon, weaving along its face like something out of an old Road Runner cartoon. What he wouldn't give for an Acme rocket right about now.

Inches from the left-hand windows the rock wall rushed by in a blur. Out the right was a vista under the sliver of moon that seemed to drop away forever. Juan couldn't imagine the view from the top of Mount Everest being much broader than this. If he craned his neck, he could see the road below where it had doubled back on itself. MacD Lawless joined him at the mangled rear door. He had Eddie's REC7, and the thigh pockets of his camo pants bulged with spare magazines.

'Figured your man up there can't drive and shoot at the same time.' He handed Juan his pistol. 'That's a fine piece, but Ah think the Barrett here is more apropos to this particular situation.'

He had an accent Juan couldn't place.

When asked, Lawless said, 'New Orleans,' pronouncing it N'Orlens.

'The Big Easy.'

'Coincidentally, that also describes my sister.' Lawless flashed that handsome grin of his. 'Actually, I don't have a sister, but I love that joke.'

The respite lasted another second until the pickup rounded a corner behind them, and the gunner once again had a target. Bullets ricocheted off the canyon wall and arced out over the valley, and some even found their mark, punching additional holes into the bus's rear quarter.

Undaunted, Lawless shot back. His rate of fire was

slow and deliberate, and when Linc and Linda joined them, all four were pouring a lot of lead down the dusty road – enough, it seemed, to deter the driver, because he slowed until the bus pulled one gentle bend away.

Without warning, Eddie slammed on the brakes and kicked the steering wheel hard over. The bus seemed to corkscrew into the earth as it rounded the first dipping hairpin turn. The outside tire of the dual rear axle dangled in space momentarily before Eddie could center all the tires on the road again. The four warriors in back were tossed like rag dolls. Linc slammed his head against a metal pole and lay inert. Linda had blood gushing from her nose from where she'd banged it, and Juan had inadvertently head-butted MacD Lawless so that his breath exploded in a whoosh.

Their gunfire hadn't slowed the other driver. He'd known there was a hairpin coming and that's why he'd applied the brakes.

Bullets rained through the bus's paper-thin roof. The technical had stopped on the precipice above so that the gunner could rain shells down on them. There was no place to hide, no cover. The powerful rounds punched all the way through the floor with barely a check in their speed. It was random chance, and Eddie's hard acceleration, that got them cleanly away.

Juan immediately checked on Setiawan, who continued to sleep peacefully.

A moment later the pickup's headlights swept around the switchback, and the race was on once again.

'Are you a betting man, Mr Chairman?' Lawless asked while gasping to refill his lungs. 'Ah know Ah am, and Ah think these odds are starting to suck.'

Juan had to agree. Something was going to have to give soon. At the next hairpin, they weren't going to be so lucky.

'Look around,' he called out. 'See if there's anything on this heap we can use.'

They scoured under the seats. Juan wrestled an old trunk from under one of the benches. It was sealed with an iron lock that looked as if it had been forged when his ancestor and namesake was discovering California. He drew his pistol, angled it away, and fired. The bullet shattered the wrought-iron lock and ricocheted harmlessly away.

Inside were several women's burkas, but judging by the size they were made for men who would them as disguises. To Cabrillo it was a coward's trick but an effective one. Under the drab clothing was a suicide belt made up of bricks of plastic explosives, sacks full of metal scrap for shrapnel, and a timer that went high up on the back of the vest so the would-be martyr couldn't deactivate it. The belt was worn in such a way that the bomber couldn't take it off.

Juan wondered if this was being delivered to the village for Seti and concluded it probably was. Rage boiled up in him with an acid burn that tightened his throat and tensed up his shoulders so they were as rigid as steel trusses.

'Whatever you're going to do,' Eddie shouted over

the winds that whipped through the bullet-riddled bus, 'make it fast. There's another turn coming.'

Cabrillo and Lawless locked eyes for just a moment, the same thought running through their minds.

'How long, you reckon?' MacD asked.

'Forty-five seconds ought to do it.' Juan manipulated the timer to set it but didn't activate it until they were almost at the hairpin turn.

Cabrillo hit the button to set the clock in motion and tossed the bomb out a window. Eddie braked hard, fighting the wheel with all his strength since the bus lacked power steering. As before, the road fell away in a sharp S-turn and twisted back on itself.

Gravel spit from under the tires when the bus slewed around the corner, becoming light on its inside wheels from the centripetal force of Seng's reckless driving. It settled back on its suspension, and he gunned it again.

Just like at the first switchback, the Taliban pickup had slid to a halt so its machine gun could open fire on the bus's exposed roof. The gunner had just depressed the weapon on its pintle mount so that the barrel was pointed at the bus, and his fingers began exerting the necessary pressure on the trigger, when the bomb, which had landed on the side of the road, unseen in the darkness not four feet away, went up in a mushroom ball of smoke, fire, and steel scrap.

The old Toyota was blown off the road entirely and started sliding down the rocky embankment toward the road below. The gunner had vanished in the blast, while the driver and one of the passengers in the cab were thrown through an open window as the vehicle tumbled onto its roof.

That's when MacD Lawless either saved all their lives or killed them.

Unlike the others, who were watching the truck to see if it was going to miss the bus as it rolled down the hill, he'd glanced out over the valley and saw an odd ring-shaped flash of light in the sky. The Nintendo Commando back at Creech, behind his computer screen and joysticks, had received authorization to fire his Predator's Hellfire missile.

Lawless didn't waste the breath to shout. He raced forward, hurtling past a dazed Franklin Lincoln, and reached the driver's seat in just over a second. He grabbed the steering wheel before Eddie knew he was even there and cranked it hard over.

The front tire sank into the soft shoulder as the bus left the road, followed quickly by the rear wheels, and then the vehicle rolled onto its side, throwing the occupants onto the right wall. Glass shattered, but before anyone could fall against the hard ground, the bus rolled again onto its roof.

An instant later, the Hellfire, with its eighteen-pound shaped charge, slammed into the mountainside at the exact place the bus would have been. The explosion resembled a miniature volcano, with dust and rubble erupting from the hole it had gouged into the stone.

Like a runaway train, the bus slid down the steep embankment, rattling and jarring its hapless passengers.

It crashed into a thicket of bushes just before it was about to fly off the edge of the road where it had been cut into the mountain. Its speed greatly reduced, the bus ponderously rolled onto its side and then crashed to its wheels on the roadbed. After the tumultuous din of the mad slide, the silence was overwhelming.

'Is everyone okay?' Juan called out after getting his wits back. His body ached from head to toe.

'I think I'm dead,' Linc said shakily. 'At least that's the way I feel.'

Cabrillo found a REC7 on the floor and snapped on its powerful tactical light. Linc had a little blood trickling from where his hairline would be if he didn't keep his head shaved. He spotted Linda emerging from between two of the bench seats. She was massaging her chest.

'I think my B's are now A's.'

Juan next turned the light on Seti. The boy had a knot on his head from where he'd banged it against the wall when the bus first overturned, but the harness they had rigged for him had kept him firmly in his seat and the drugs had shielded him from the horror of what had just happened. He envied the teenager.

'Eddie, are you all right?' Cabrillo asked when he reached the front of the bus. Seng was wedged under the seat near the vehicle's pedals.

'I have a newfound respect for anything that goes into a clothes dryer,' he said as he pulled himself free.

MacD Lawless lay crumpled in the stairwell. Juan

bent to check on him, pressing two fingers against his neck to look for a pulse. He found it, strong and steady, and no sooner had Cabrillo moved his hand away than Lawless began to stir.

'So,' Juan said, 'we went from us saving your butt to you saving ours in a little over an hour. I think that might be a record.'

'No offense,' Lawless slurred, 'but Ah'd take it all back if Ah didn't hurt so much.'

'You're fine,' Cabrillo grinned, and grasped the man's outstretched hand. 'And if you're not, well, it's your own damned fault.' He turned serious. 'How in the hell did you see that? And how did you move so fast?'

'Um, luck.' MacD allowed Juan to pull him to his feet. He smiled back. 'And fear.'

'You okay?'

'Ah'm good,' Lawless replied. 'Sorry, but grabbing the wheel was all Ah could think of.'

'It was the right call,' Juan assured him. 'Insane but right.'

Lawless said, 'Marion.'

'What?'

'My first name. You saved my life, Ah saved yours. In my book that makes us tight enough to tell you that my first name is Marion. Marion MacDougal Lawless III.'

Cabrillo considered this for a moment. 'You're right. MacD is better.' They shook hands formally. Juan turned back to Eddie. 'Is there anything left in this poor girl?'

Seng replied by reconnecting the wires and revving the engine. 'They don't make 'em like they used to.'

A rear axle was bent, giving the bus a wobbling sway like a lame horse, but Eddie assured them it would get them to Islamabad by sunup.

4

Brunei

They rose from the sea like modern-day castles, protected by the largest moat in the world. Slab-sided and immense, oil rigs mounted atop massive pilings dotted the ocean, with tall flare stacks belching tongues of greasy flame. One sweep of the horizon revealed two dozen of the monstrosities, while hundreds more were just over the earth's curve.

The huge oil fields made this tiny sultanate on the north coast of the island of Borneo one of the richest countries in the world and its ruler one of the wealthiest individuals.

Above the rigs, choppers ferried men and material to production and drilling platforms while sturdy workboats plied the seas between them. One such chopper, a little Robinson R22, belonged to the Oil Ministry and was carrying an inspector out to one of the larger rigs for its annual going-over. His name was Abdullah. As was common in this part of the world, he had no last name.

Slight, and just twenty-six years old, he was new to the job, this being only his third such inspection. In truth, he wouldn't be performing the main search.

Another team would be following in a couple of hours. His job was to gather and collate the mountains of paperwork required by the Ministry for each of the rigs in their territorial waters. It was scut work that befitted his rookie status. But he knew he'd be amply rewarded once he'd put in his years – senior inspectors made six-figure salaries and lived in mansions with servants and a driver.

He wore heavy-duty coveralls, despite the fact that he wouldn't see anything much beyond the rig's administrative office, and he held a plastic hard hat on his lap. As required, his boots had steel-reinforced toes. Wouldn't want them crushed in a paper avalanche.

The pilot hadn't said more than ten words to Abdullah since taking off, so when he heard a sound coming through his radio earmuffs he turned to see if the man was speaking to him.

To his horror he saw the pilot clutching at the side of his head. With no one holding the controls, the two-seat chopper started moving violently downward. For a fleeting instant Abdullah thought the pilot, a veteran by the look of him, was having fun at the expense of a newbie inspector, but then the man simply slumped over against his door, his body held somewhat erect by his safety belts.

The Robinson started to rotate on its axis.

Abdullah surprised himself by remembering the rudimentary training he'd received. He grabbed the stick and the collective control down by his side and placed his feet on the pedals. He gently applied opposite pressure on the foot bar to correct the spin and gave the aircraft more power to gain altitude. After about fifteen seconds he had the helicopter somewhat steadier, but by no means was it flying as well as it had under a real pilot's control.

He glanced at the pilot. The man remained slumped over, and while he had yet to start losing color Abdullah knew that he was dead. The way he'd grabbed at his head made Abdullah think the older man had suffered a massive stroke.

Sweat trickled down Abdullah's forehead as a lump swelled in his stomach. The rig they were heading for was still thirty miles away, while their base was twenty-five miles behind him. He had no illusions that he could keep the aircraft flying for that long. His only option was to attempt to land on one of the nearby platforms.

'Um, Mayday, Mayday, Mayday,' he called out, not knowing if the radios were set on the right frequency, not even knowing if his headset could access the radio. There was no reply.

When he scanned the instrument panel to see what he could do, he lost concentration momentarily, and the helicopter began to rotate again. Panicked, he over-compensated, losing altitude the whole time. The altimeter showed he was at five hundred feet, but the ocean seemed to surge just below the landing skids. He eased his grip on the controls, remembering that flying helicopters was all about finesse. The light touch, the instructor had said over and over during his two-day tutorial. Though he wasn't allowed to solo, Abdullah had landed an identical helo exactly twice, and both times the instructor's hands had never been more than a millimeter from the controls.

Once he had stabilized the chopper, he looked out across the sea for the nearest oil rig. Uniformly, they all had landing pads either on top of the accommodations block or, more commonly, cantilevered over the ocean. To his dismay, he was in one of the few regions of the oil and gas field that wasn't currently being worked. He saw only one rig, about three miles away. He recognized it as an older semisubmersible. Below its four stout legs, and under the water, were two enormous pontoons that could be filled or emptied via computer control. Such a rig could be towed to any location in the world. Once there, the ballast tanks could be filled to stabilize it, and anchors set on the seafloor to keep it in place. The platform was quite possibly abandoned. He saw no telltale plume of fire spewing from the vent stack, and as he got closer he noted the rust and peeling paint.

It wouldn't matter, he realized. Once he was down he could devote his full attention to the radio and call for help.

Amid the monochromatic gray paint scheme was a faded yellow circle enclosing a yellow letter *H*. This was the rig's landing pad, a steel platform hanging a hundred feet over the water. The pad wasn't solid but rather was a grille that allowed the chopper's downdraft to pass through, thus making it easier to land.

Abdullah coaxed the little Robinson closer and

closer. There was no movement on the deck, no rough-necks working on the drilling floor, no one coming out of the accommodations block to see who was approaching. It was a ghost rig.

He brought the helo to an unsteady hover, slowly easing off the power so it sank down toward the platform. He praised Allah that there was no wind to contend with. Keeping a helicopter in a hover required the same skill and coordination as balancing a Ping-Pong ball on a paddle. A cross breeze would have been deadly. The chopper waggled and wiggled as he brought it lower. He wished he could wipe the sweat from his palms. They were slick on the controls, and a bead of perspiration dangled from the end of his nose.

When he thought he was about four feet from the landing platform, he chopped the power dramatically. But in his unfamiliarity with judging vertical distances through the Plexiglas bubble at his feet, he was closer to ten.

The Robinson slammed onto the deck hard enough to bounce it into the air again, and, when it did, it tilted over onto its side. The rotor blades smashed into the steel grille and splintered, bits of them peppering the sea far below.

The chopper's hull crashed to the deck on its side and fortunately remained still. Had it rolled, it would have plunged off the platform. Abdullah didn't know how to shut off the engines. His only concern was getting out of the aircraft. Everyone who watched as many action movies as he had knew that cars, airplanes, and helicopters always exploded following a crash.

He clicked off his safety belts and climbed over the inert form of the pilot, fear overcoming his revulsion at actually touching a corpse. The four-cylinder Lycoming engine continued to squeal behind the cockpit. He managed to unlatch the pilot's door and thrust it up and over so that it lay flush with the fuselage. He had to physically stand on the pilot's hip to get enough leverage to haul himself from the chopper.

Did he smell gas?

A new burst of fear shot through his body, and he jumped free. No sooner had his feet hit the grating than he was running off the landing pad in the direction of the accommodations block, a huge steel building that took up a third of the deck space on the massive rig. Above it all soared the drilling derrick, a spindly network of steel struts that looked like a miniature Eiffel Tower.

Abdullah reached the corner of the block and turned back. He saw no fire, but smoke billowed from the Robinson's engine compartment, and it thickened by the second.

And then he had the terrible thought that maybe the pilot wasn't dead. He didn't know what to do. The smoke grew more dense. He could see into the cockpit though the nose canopy. Was the pilot moving, or was the image being blurred by heat?

He took a tentative step as if to return to the chopper when flames emerged at the base of the column of

74

smoke. It wasn't the dramatic explosion of Hollywood or Hong Kong moviemakers but a steady fire that quickly engulfed the aircraft. Its roar drowned out the whir of the helo's engine. Smoke poured into the sky.

Abdullah stood frozen. Already he was thinking that he'd be stuck out here forever. If this was an abandoned rig, there was no reason for anyone to come out to it. He was trapped.

No, he told himself. He didn't just survive a plane crash to die on a deserted oil platform. The smoke, he thought. Surely someone will see the smoke and come to investigate. Then he remembered that smoke poured off every rig within a hundred miles, and the fire wouldn't last for very long. The odds that a passing workboat or helicopter would see it before it burned itself out were too long.

But if he saw one coming, he could start another fire to signal them.

Yes, that's what he would do. He took several deep breaths. His hands weren't trembling so badly anymore, and the knot in his gut was easing. He grinned at his good fortune and was soon roaring with laughter. He'd be a hero, once he got back to the office. They would probably give him a promotion, or at least some paid time off. Abdullah had always been able to find the good in any situation. He was an optimist, always had been.

He spotted a large fire extinguisher and, still concerned about an explosion, went for it anyway. The heat was brutal, but as he laid down the chemical suppressant the flames diminished rapidly. It appeared the fire was fed off of gasoline that had leaked out of the helicopter, but most of it had fallen harmlessly through the metal grille. In just a minute the flames were out. He was grateful to see the pilot's body hadn't been too ravaged by the fire.

With that taken care of, he felt he could leave the rig's open deck and explore the accommodations block. There could be a working radio left inside. He retraced his steps and quickly found a hatchway that led into the interior of the four-story block. It was padlocked shut.

Undeterred, Abdullah scoured the deck until he found a length of steel pipe that would suit his purpose. He threaded it through the shiny chain and heaved. The links didn't even rattle, but the pad eye welded to the side of the building twisted and then tore free. He set aside the pipe and hauled on the door. It creaked on its hinges, setting his teeth on edge. It hadn't been opened for months. The hallway beyond was draped in murky shadow. From inside a small pocket sewn to the sleeve of his coveralls he pulled out a penlight and twisted it on. It had been issued by the Ministry and cast a harsh white light that belied its small size.

The walls and deck were steel, utilitarian, and free of dust. It wasn't that they'd been cleaned, it was just that with no human presence there was nothing to create dust in the sealed structure. He peered into several offices. The furniture had been left behind, and a three-years-out-of-date calendar, but there were no files or paperwork of any kind. Even the mundane items like staplers and spare pens were gone.

Although the rig was old, it was still much too valuable to be left abandoned like this. If nothing more, she represented several million dollars' worth of scrap metal. He knew it wasn't unusual for platforms to go unused for months at a time, but years? It didn't make sense.

At the end of the hallway was a staircase leading up to the next level. He climbed it quickly. It was hot inside the steel box, which had been baking all day in the tropical sun. There were two doors leading off the landing. One led to another hallway and probably the crew's rooms. When he opened the second, he was hit by a wall of chilled air. The change in temperature was so acute he staggered back a step before moving into the vast room beyond.

'What the hell?' he said aloud, not sure whether or not to believe what his eyes were telling him.

And then it finally dawned on him. He was on the J-61. Of all the rotten luck, this was the one rig that was off-limits to all Ministry personnel. He didn't know the reason behind the order, only that it came from on high, and he'd been told in no uncertain terms that he was never, ever to set foot on this platform for any reason.

But he didn't understand. What was the big deal? All he saw were a bunch of—

'Hey, you!'

The voice had come from behind him. Someone had

approached down the hallway. Abdullah turned, raising his hands in a placating gesture. 'I'm sorry. You see, my helicopter cra—'

The man slammed a fist into Abdullah's stomach with enough force to knock him off his feet. Before he could even think about defending himself, he was struck again, a punch to the temple that stunned him into paralysis. And then a heavy boot crashed into his face, and Abdullah's world went black.

He came to slowly, like that morning after he and some friends had flouted Islamic tenets and gotten blind drunk. His head ached, his stomach was on fire, and he could barely open his eyes. He saw nothing but blurred edges and blobs of light. Nothing made sense. He heard men's voices and tried to turn his head. His vertebrae felt fused. He had never been in so much pain in his life. What happened? he wondered.

The voices. The man. A guard perhaps. The beating. It came back in a rush. He tried to move but realized he was tied to a chair. Panic seized him, sharpened his senses a little, and to his horror he realized he was back in the helicopter, strapped in next to the singed corpse of the pilot.

Someone had flipped the bird back onto its landing struts and secured him into his seat. He tried to unclasp the harness, but the buckle had been wound with duct tape so many times it was a big silver lump in his lap. He felt movement.

They were pushing the chopper!

He looked out just as the horizon soared over his

head. The windshield was filled with a view of the ocean, and then the acceleration hit him. He was falling, strapped helplessly as the chopper plummeted off the rig.

The Robinson hit the water at near-terminal velocity, snapping Abdullah's neck and mercifully ending his life before he could drown.

Twenty minutes later, when the administrator of the rig he was supposed to start inspecting contacted the Ministry, an alert was sounded. Rescue helicopters and patrol boats were launched immediately. Of the Robinson, its pilot, and its lone passenger, no trace was ever found. One canny chopper jock even circled rig J-61 'just in case,' but it looked as deserted as ever because any trace of the fire had been studiously wiped clean. The secret it harbored was safe once again.

5

Cabrillo had spent the first half hour of the flight in the back of the Gulfstream V's luxurious cabin in contact with Max Hanley. Hanley was the Corporation's vice president, the *Oregon*'s chief engineer, and Juan's best friend. He'd been with Juan since he'd first conceived the idea of a private security company based on a ship. All the crew knew this, but one story few had heard was how the two men had hooked up in the first place.

Cabrillo had spent his professional career as a NOC, a non-official cover, for the Central Intelligence Agency. This was bureaucratic-speak for a spook. Fluent in Arabic, Russian, as well as Spanish and English, he'd been posted to some of the hottest spots in the world and had gotten himself into and out of more jams than he could count.

When he'd come to the realization soon after the Berlin Wall fell that the end of the Cold War would mean an increase in regional conflicts, and that none of America's intelligence agencies were going to be adroit enough to respond, he'd decided to go out on his own as a private contractor. The Corporation would tackle those jobs that were so black no one else could handle them with any kind of deniability. Juan had enough contacts in the government to ensure they would be busy for years.

He'd talked it over with Langston Overholt, his mentor. Lang had regretfully agreed with Cabrillo's assessment. He hated to lose his star agent but also recognized the possibilities the Corporation would give him.

He'd suggested that Juan track down one Maxwell Hanley. When asked who Hanley was, Lang had explained that he'd been the chief engineer aboard the *Glomar Explorer*, the famed Howard Hughes-built ship that had partially raised the Soviet Golf-class submarine, K-129.

Juan had protested that the *Glomar* had done its thing in 1974, which would make Hanley simply too old to work as a mercenary.

Lang had told him, in turn, that Hanley wasn't on that first expedition but a later one that was still classified top secret. Hanley had overseen the ship's operations while she was supposedly mothballed at Suisun Bay in California. In fact, they had mocked up an old freighter to look like the *Glomar Explorer* while they had taken her to a spot off the Azores Islands to raise a Typhoon-class ballistic missile submarine with its full complement of twenty ICBMs and two hundred nuclear warheads. That had been in 1984, and while Hanley had gotten his start as a riverine warrior in Vietnam, he was too ornery to be considered old.

Cabrillo found Max running a scrapyard outside of Barstow, California, and in the course of ten minutes had him tossing the keys to the place to his assistant and heading out the door. By the time the *Oregon* had been selected as their base of operations and her conversion work completed in Vladivostok by a corrupt Russian admiral who loved Yankee dollars and Korean girls in equal measure, the two men were like an old married couple. Sure they argued, but they never lost respect for each other.

Hanley later admitted he would have followed Juan out of the junkyard after the first sixty seconds of his pitch.

'So that's him on paper,' Max said over the secure phone link. He was aboard their ship still anchored just off Karachi.

'Pretty damned impressive,' Juan opined. He'd called Max as they were driving along the six-lane superhighway connecting the Khyber Pass to Islamabad and asked him to run a full background check on Marion MacDougal Lawless. 'Two years at Tulane, but he left and joined the Army as a Nine-Twelve-er.' Meaning the day after the September 11th terrorist attacks he'd walked into an Army recruiting station and signed on as a common soldier, like thousands of other brave men and women.

'Got into the Rangers, excelled by all accounts. He racked up a couple of combat citations, and after eight years opted out to join up with Fortran Security as a private contractor.

'Same skill set as a Ranger,' Max said, 'only ten times the pay.'

'I know Fortran,' Juan countered. 'They're a top-notch outfit, so they pay more like twenty times.'

'Whatever,' Max said in his normally irritated manner. 'He's got an ex-wife and a daughter. Nearly all his pay goes to an address in New Orleans that I can only assume is the ex.'

'Only one, huh,' Juan teased. Max had three, and alimony payments to all of them.

'We're in the middle of a recession. There are thousands of out-of-work comedians out there, and you think *you* are funny? Talk about delusions of grandeur. Anyway. Like I said, that's him on paper, what's the real version like?'

'Max, I'll tell you. He's been beat six ways to Sunday, and while I'm rubbernecking a technical getting blown up he sees the Predator I know is out there fire its missile and moves like nothing I've ever seen before. He saved our lives. No two ways about it.'

'So?' Hanley prompted.

'Since we lost Jerry Pulaski in Argentina, we've been down one gundog. I want to talk it over with Eddie, as head of shore operations, and Linc, as our lead war fighter, but I think we might have our replacement. He was an Army Ranger for eight years and has spent a lot of time deep in the ugliness. Not to mention he managed to impress me in just over an hour of knowing him.'

'What about his contract with Fortran?' Max asked. 'Also, I would like to verify the story of how he got captured. Just playing devil's advocate, but maybe this guy's lost his edge.'

'I'll talk to him and follow up with you before I make any decision,' Cabrillo promised. 'Any word from Setiawan's dad?'

'There's an air-ambulance jet at Karachi Airport. The old man didn't come, but he sent his wife and the kid's grandparents. I let them know as soon as you hit the Islamabad road that you would be here soon. What's your ETA?'

'Another forty minutes.'

'Okay. George is already on the tarmac in the chopper to ferry you guys out to the ship, and we've maybe got another job lined up.'

'Really? That was fast.'

'Came through from *L'Enfant*. Some Swiss financier's daughter crossed the border from Bangladesh into Myanmar, and he now can't raise her on her sat phone. He's afraid something's happened to her and wants us to get her out.'

'Two questions,' Juan said. 'What's she doing in that godforsaken area in the first place and, second, has he been in contact with the government?' The first was really rhetorical. It didn't matter. But the second was critical.

'No. He's a smart guy. He knew that if he reached out to the ruling junta, his daughter would be hunted down and either ransomed or imprisoned for life.'

'That's good. Listen, we'll talk about it when we get back to the ship. Meanwhile, start a background check on the financier and his daughter and anyone she was traveling with.'

'Eric and Mark are already on it.'

'Oh too, if MacD comes back with us, it'll be on a limited access basis for now. Tell Hux to bring her medical bag to meet us. I want her to make sure the guy's not worse off than he's letting on.'

'Ranger tough, huh?'

'Macho 101 is the first class they teach at Benning.' Juan killed the connection.

In the main cabin of the executive jet, Linda was bent over Seti, checking on his condition. He asked how the boy was doing.

'The sedative's starting to wear off. I don't want to risk giving him any more, but I also don't want him regaining consciousness before we transfer him.'

'They have an air ambulance waiting. If you juice him a little, they'll be able to handle it.'

'Okay.'

Linc and MacD Lawless were swapping Afghanistan war stories. Linc's had been one of the first pairs of boots on the ground while MacD hadn't gotten into the country until a few years later. They didn't know any of the same people, but the situations they'd faced were usually similar, especially when dealing with the locals.

'Pardon the interruption,' Juan said. 'MacD, can I have a word with you?'

'Sure.' He set aside the bottled water he'd been sipping and limped after the Chairman to the rear of the aircraft. 'What's up?'

'How'd it happen?'

Lawless immediately grasped what he was being asked. 'There were three of us guarding a Pakistani TV crew – myself and two locals we'd worked with before. We were about an hour out of Kabul when the cameraman asks to pull over. Ah tell him it's a real bad idea, but he said it was an emergency. The terrain was clear, so Ah figure, what the hell. We pull over, and no sooner had the wheels stopped turning than about a dozen Taliban materialize out of the ground. They'd been hiding under blankets that they covered with sand. It was a perfect ambush. Ah didn't even get a shot off.

'The camera crew was a plant. They killed the two Afghan guards on the spot and trussed me up like a Thanksgiving turkey. They stole our truck, and, well, you pretty much know the rest. At some point Ah was transferred to the trunk of a car, Ah think before we crossed into Pakistan, but there's no way to be sure. Whenever they got the chance, they'd smack me around some, and brag about how Ah was going to be a hit on the al-Qaeda version of YouTube.'

He spoke as if he were reporting the events of someone else's life. Cabrillo suspected that it was still too fresh in his mind. The one thing he could tell was that Lawless regretted what had happened to the two Afghans more than his own capture.

'By now,' Juan said, 'you've figured out what we do, yes?'

'Private security, like Fortran.'

'It goes well beyond that. We're also an intelligence gathering operation. We do some consultancy, and we

87

take on some ops for Uncle Sam when he needs complete deniability, though for reasons that aren't important right now that line of work has dried up for the time being. We thoroughly vet all our clients. We work only for the good guys, if you follow my meaning. And we work so far under the grid that only a handful of people in the world know who we are. Your bosses at Fortran, for example, have no idea. You won't see us mentioned in the media because I run a tight outfit that leaves no room for error.'

'Sounds like a pretty good crew,' Lawless said neutrally.

'It's the best at what it does. Each member has been handpicked, and when someone new comes aboard everyone gets a vote.'

'Are you offering me a job?'

'Provisionally. A couple months ago we lost a man. Jerry Pulaski was his name. He was what we called a gundog, a hardened combat veteran used mostly for when the fur starts flying. You'd fill his position.'

'Do you guys mostly operate in this area?'

'No. Actually, this is our first time here. This whole region's lousy with outfits like yours and Blackwater, or whatever they call themselves these days. We'd just as soon leave it to them. This rescue was a one-time type of deal.'

'My contract with Fortran runs for another few months,' Lawless told him.

'Don't you think after what happened to you that they would let you out of it?'

'Yeah, probably,' he drawled. 'Um, listen, though, Ah've got a little girl to support.' He paused, swallowed, and went on. 'My folks are raisin' her, and they need the extra money Ah make.'

'What were you being paid?' Juan asked bluntly. MacD gave him the number, which sounded reasonable.

'Okay, you'll keep making that during your probationary period. After that, if things work out, you'll become a full member of the Corporation and share in the profits.'

'Um, are y'all profitable?'

Cabrillo responded by asking, 'What do you think this plane's worth?'

Lawless looked around for just a second. 'G-Five like this? About fifty million bucks.'

'Fifty-four, to be exact,' Juan told him. 'We paid cash.'

They handed over a still-sleeping Setiawan to his tearful mother on the tarmac between the Corporation's aircraft and a chartered Citation fitted out as a flying hospital. The grandmother too was weeping, while the grandfather watched the exchange stoically. Arrangements had already been made to have Customs and Immigration look the other way. They whisked the boy onto the idling jet, and as soon as the door was closed and sealed it began to roll.

Juan had planned to send their plane out of the country, but with the possibility of a new job soon he told the pilot to park it and find himself a hotel room in the city. They hefted their guns and equipment in nondescript nylon bags and made their way to where a row of helicopters was backed up to a Cyclone fence about fifty yards from the General Aviation terminal building. These were all civilian choppers. For the most part they were painted white with a stripe of color across their noses and along their flanks.

One, however, was a glossy black and looked as menacing as a gunship, though she carried no visible weapons. This was the Corporation's MD 520N, a state-of-the-art helo that vented exhaust through its tail rather than relying on a secondary rotor. This NOTAR system made it the quietest jet-powered helicopter in the world.

The pilot saw the four men and one woman approaching and began hitting switches in the cockpit to fire the turbine.

It would be a tight squeeze, but the 520 had more than enough power to take them all out to the *Oregon*.

'Looks like it went well,' the pilot remarked when Juan opened the passenger door and shoved his equipment bag under his seat.

'Nothing to it,' Cabrillo said in typical fashion.

George 'Gomez' Adams knew better. The veteran pilot could tell by their swagger when they were approaching that things had gotten dicey and that they'd handled it well. 'Who's the new guy?'

'MacD Lawless. He's a Fortran operative who got

nabbed outside of Kabul. Seemed a waste to let them behead him.'

'We keeping him?'

'Maybe.'

'I don't like guys who are better-looking than me,' Gomez said. With his gunslinger mustache and matinee idol looks, there weren't many men in the world who qualified.

'Can't handle a little competition,' Juan grinned.

'Exactly.' Adams looked over his shoulder and thrust out his hand to MacD. 'So long as you never beat me out with the ladies, we'll be fine.'

It was clear Lawless had no idea what to make of that statement, but he shook Adams's hand anyway. 'No problem. So long as you never crash with me aboard, we'll be better than fine.'

'Deal.' Gomez turned his attention back to the chopper, radioing the control tower to get flight authorization.

Juan said to Lawless, 'When we get to the ship, the first thing we'll do is get you a secure link to your people. They must be going nuts, about now. Same thing with your folks, if they've been told.'

'I doubt Fortran would have contacted them yet. I was grabbed less than forty-eight hours ago.'

'Okay. One less thing to worry about.'

A minute later, the turbine shrieked as Adams fed in more power. The airframe shuddered, and then everything became smooth when the skids lifted from the concrete pad.

Gomez fought his instincts to hotdog it, so they rose

at a sedate pace and started flying out over the mangroves and mudflats to the north of the sprawling city of fifteen million. A dense pall of smog cut visibility dramatically so that Karachi's office towers and highrise apartment buildings appeared indistinct in the distance. Everything looked like the color of rust, the buildings, the air, even the water in the enclosed inner harbor. It was only when one looked west, out toward the ocean, that there was any true color. The water was a deep sapphire blue. They flashed over the China Creek, where the main port was located, and Baba Channel, which led to the open sea. It was crowded with all manner of shipping awaiting its turn at the docks.

They flew beyond the barrier islands, and soon the smog gave way to clear air. The sun cast a dazzling silver strip across the waves as it rose higher into the sky behind them.

More ships were streaming toward the port or were outbound laden with goods. Their wakes were like white scars. One ship directly ahead of them showed no wake.

By modern standards, she was just midsized at over five hundred and sixty feet. The containership passing off her port side was over twice as long. Their target was also of an outdated design. Built prior to the industry switchover to standardized containers, she was designed to carry her cargo in five deep holds, each secured with a hatch and serviced by a quintet of spindly derricks. Her superstructure was placed just aft of amidships and was topped by a single funnel. Bridge wings and catwalks hung off it like wrought-iron fire escapes. She carried two lifeboats in davits above the main deck. Her bow was like an axhead while her fantail had a little of that champagne-glass elegance.

All this could be seen from a distance. It wasn't until the chopper was much closer that details emerged. The ship was a rust bucket, a scow that should have been chopped into scrap years ago. Paint peeled in patches all over her hull and decking as if she were infected with some sort of maritime eczema. The paint scheme itself was a patchwork of mismatched colors daubed over one another with no eye at all for aesthetics. Rust formed in pools on the deck, oozed from scuppers and the hawsehole, and streaked the sides of the superstructure like reddish brown guano.

The deck was a tangled jumble of broken machinery, oil drums, and various other junk, including, inexplicably, a washing machine and a massive tire from a tractor.

'You've got to be kidding me,' MacD muttered when the true nature of the ship was revealed. 'Is this some sort of con?'

'She may not be pretty,' Gomez Adams said, 'but she sure is ugly.'

'Trust me when I tell you that it's not what it seems,' Juan assured him. 'For the time being we're not going to let you in on any of her secrets, but secrets she has.'

'What, that she was Teddy Roosevelt's troopship when he went to Cuba?'

Juan laughed.

Linc added, 'No. The *Oregon* was Noah's first attempt at the Ark.'

'I'd believe that one too.'

Gomez swooped around to the aft of the ship, where there was a helipad marked out on the rearmost cargo hatch. A crewman stood by in case the pilot needed help landing, but Adams didn't need any directions. He flared the chopper directly over the big faded letter *H* and settled it in the exact center. He killed the engine, and its persistent whine died down to silence and the rotor blades emerged from their shimmering mirage of motion as they slowed.

'Ladies and gentlemen, welcome to the MV *Oregon*,' Adams said. 'The current temperature is sixty-eight degrees. The local time is eleven eighteen. Please be aware that items in the overhead may have shifted during our flight. Thank you for flying with us today, and we hope you will use us in the future.'

'Forget it,' Linda told him as she opened the rear door. 'Your rewards program sucks, and my peanuts were stale.'

Juan once again marveled at the team he had assembled. Less than twelve hours earlier they had been rolling down the side of a mountain with a Hellfire missile boring in on them and now they were joking as if they didn't have a care in the world. He reminded himself that he shouldn't be too surprised. This was the kind of life they had chosen for themselves. If they couldn't joke about it afterward, they wouldn't last five minutes.

Max Hanley approached from the safety of the superstructure. In deference to the sun, he had a battered Dodgers cap covering what little remained of his ginger hair. Hanley was a little above average in height and was starting to show his age around his middle and in the wrinkles spiderwebbing from the corners of his eyes, but he moved well, and with his anvil-sized hands he could take care of himself with no problem. He wore a pair of tan coveralls that showed a spot of grease on one elbow, meaning he had just come up from the *Oregon*'s revolutionary engine room. With him was Dr Julia Huxley. A Navy-trained physician, Hux wore a customary white coat over her lush 1950s pinup curves, with her hair tied back in a ponytail. Brisk, almost brusque, when she was working on a patient, she was easygoing the rest of the time. She'd been Juan's doctor when he had part of his leg blown off by a Chinese gunboat years earlier when the Corporation was on a mission for NUMA, the National Underwater and Marine Agency.

She'd overseen his rehab, staying by him as he went from a man who couldn't walk to one who could run for miles without a trace of a limp. She and Max were also the only two people in the world who knew that Cabrillo's missing foot and ankle ached every minute of every day.

It was called phantom pain, a common experience for amputees. To Juan there was nothing phantom about it. Just because he couldn't see his foot, or touch it, didn't mean the damned thing didn't hurt all the time.

'I confirmed the wire transfer from Bahar's account to ours,' Max said by way of greeting.

'We're all fine,' Juan countered. 'Thanks for asking.'

'Don't be such a wuss,' Max said flatly. 'I talked to you an hour ago. I know you're fine. Besides, money is more important to me than your health.'

'You're all heart, buddy.' Juan waved MacD forward. 'Max Hanley, Julia Huxley, this is MacD Lawless. MacD, this is my second-in-command and the ship's sawbones. And I mean that literally.' They all shook hands. 'Let's get MacD up to my office so Hux can give him the once-over.'

The interior of the ship was just as bad as her scabrous hide. Chipped linoleum floors, weak lighting, and dust bunnies the size of tumbleweeds. Lead paint and asbestos appeared to be the decorator's preferred mediums.

'Jesus,' MacD cried. 'This ship is like a toxic waste dump. Should I even breathe in here?'

'Sure,' Linc replied, his barrel chest expanding as he filled his lungs. 'Real shallow-like.' He then slapped the back of his hand against Lawless's taut belly. 'Relax, man. It ain't what you think. The Chairman will show you. Go off with the Doc and then you'll see.'

Huxley invited MacD into one of the cabins behind the bridge and set her bag down on the dresser in preparation for her exam. Linc, Juan, and Max continued on to the bridge itself. Linda begged out of the meeting, saying she needed a two-hour soak in the spa tub in her cabin.

There were no officers of the deck or watch standers on the bridge. They would only bother with such a formality if there were shipping close by or a harbor pilot or customs official were aboard. Otherwise the wheelhouse remained empty.

The room was broad, with wood-and-glass doors on either end to access the flying bridges. The wheel was a big old-fashioned spoked affair with handholds made smooth by countless years of wear. The windows were frosted with salt rime and barely translucent. The equipment was generations out of date. The radio looked like something Marconi himself had assembled. The brightwork, like the stand-alone engine controls, hadn't seen polish since it was installed. The wooden chart cabinets were chipped and their tops stained by greasy food and spilled coffee. To all outward appearances, it was perhaps the sorriest excuse for a pilothouse afloat.

Just seconds after they entered the bridge, an elderly gentleman dressed in black slacks and a crisp white shirt with an unblemished apron around his waist materialized as though from thin air. His hair was as white as his starched shirt, his face both gaunt and wrinkled. He carried a sterling silver tray with a dewy pitcher of some tropical-looking concoction and crystal glasses.

'The sun's over the yardarm someplace,' he said in a crisp British accent.

'What's this, Maurice?' Juan asked as the ship's steward handed out glasses and began to pour. Linc looked at his drink sourly and then brightened when the steward produced a bottle of Heineken from his apron.

Linc popped the top by ramming it against the chart table.

'A little juice, a little grog. This and that. I figured you could use something after the mission.'

Cabrillo took a sip, and announced, 'Nectar of the gods, my friend. Absolute nectar of the gods.'

Maurice didn't acknowledge the compliment. He already knew how good the drink was and didn't need to be told. He set the platter aside. Under it was a rosewood cigar box that usually sat on Cabrillo's desk in his cabin. Max demurred, pulling a pipe and a leather pouch from the back pocket of his coveralls. In moments, the air was as thick as an Amazonian forest fire. The steward left the bridge as silently as he'd arrived, his polished shoes somehow not making a noise on the filthy linoleum deck covering.

'Okay, so tell me about this new op,' Cabrillo invited, blowing a plume of smoke toward the ceiling while Max opened one of the wing doors for a little ventilation.

'The financier's name is Roland Croissard, from Basel. His daughter is Soleil, aged thirty. She's got a reputation for being something of a daredevil. She's already got her spot bought and paid when Virgin Galactic starts up their suborbital flights. She's climbed the highest mountains on six of the seven continents. She's been beaten back by Everest twice. She raced as a pay-for-play GP2 driver for a season. For those that don't know, that's one tier below Formula One racing. She's also a scratch golfer, was a world-ranked tennis player in her teens, and just missed the cut for the Swiss Olympic fencing team.'

'Accomplished woman,' Juan remarked.

'Quite,' Max agreed. 'I'd show you a picture, but you'd start drooling on the spot. Anyway, she and a friend went backpacking in Bangladesh. Judging by the GPS logs her father sent, she made a beeline for the border with Myanmar and kept on hiking.'

'Sounds deliberate to me,' Linc said, finishing his beer. The twelve-ouncer looked like a Tabasco bottle in his hand. 'Does he know what she was up to?'

'No idea. He said that she rarely kept him informed of what she was doing. I get the impression there's a little bad blood between them. When I ran the background check on him, it showed there was a divorce when Soleil was seventeen, and he subsequently remarried a few months later.'

'Where's the mother?' Juan asked, nonchalantly tapping ash onto the already-grimy floor.

'Died of pancreatic cancer five years ago. Before that she lived in Zurich, which is now Soleil's home.'

'And what's the father's story?'

'Works for one of those Swiss banks shady people like us keep our money in. Murph and Stone didn't turn up anything through regular and not-so-regular financial channels. Croissard is legit, as far as we can tell.'

'Did you ask Langston? For all we know he's Bin Laden's personal banker.'

'Actually, he's helped the Agency track funds heading to the Jemaah Islamiyah terrorist group.'

'Could this be payback?' Cabrillo wondered aloud. 'Maybe they snatched her.'

'Anything's possible at this point,' Max replied. 'It could be that, or local drug lords, or it could be her phone's on the fritz and she's hiking out as we speak.'

'How long ago did she go dark?' Linc asked.

'She'd been checking in once a week. Missed her regular call four days ago. Croissard let it go a day before he got edgy. He made some calls, first to his contact at Langley over the money-laundering thing, and eventually he tracked down *L'Enfant*.'

'Was the phone transmitting her GPS coordinates the whole time?'

'No,' Max said. 'She only turned it on when she was calling in.'

Juan tapped ash from his cigar. 'So, at the outside, she could have been snatched twelve days ago.'

'Yes,' Max agreed glumly.

'And all we have to go on is her last-known location, which again is eleven days old.'

This time Hanley merely nodded.

'This won't be easy. We're talking minor needle, major haystack.'

'Five million bucks to make the attempt,' Max added. 'Another two if we bring her out.'

They were interrupted by Julia Huxley. She entered the bridge from the corridor that linked the six cabins on that deck – all of which were as shabby as the wheelhouse itself.

'What's the word?' Juan asked.

'Physically, he's fine. He's got some pretty deep contusions across his abdomen and lower chest, his upper arms, thighs, and his cute-as-a-button buttocks. Nothing is sprained, as far as I can tell, but he says his knees and ankles hurt like heck. Give him a week and he'll be good as new. I've still got to run some samples back in my lab, but from what he told me he's as healthy as a horse. I have no reason to doubt that.'

'Send him out to us, and thanks.'

'No. Thank you.'

A moment later, Lawless stepped onto the bridge, tucking a clean T-shirt into his combat pants. He looked around a moment, and said, 'Y'all don't pay your maid enough.'

'It's been her week off since 2002,' Cabrillo deadpanned. 'Well, the doc says you check out, and her word's good enough for me. What do you say?'

'I've got to be honest with you, Chairman Cabrillo,' MacD replied. 'Since coming aboard your ship I'm having second thoughts. You say you make money hand over fist, but living on this scow isn't exactly my cup of joe.'

'What if I were to tell you that under all this rust and grime is a ship that has more luxury appointments than the finest yacht you've ever seen.'

'I'd say you'd have to show me.'

'Juan?' Max said in a questioning voice.

'It's okay,' Cabrillo said. 'Just a taste. Nothing more.'

Cabrillo indicated that Lawless should follow him. They made their way down a flight of internal stairs and through a few dingy hallways until they reached a windowless mess hall. Tacky travel posters were taped to the matte-gray walls. Beyond the pass-through was a kitchen that would turn a health inspector's stomach. Stalactites of congealed grease clung to the hood above the six-burner stove while the flies buzzing around a sink full of dirty dishes rivaled the air traffic pattern over O'Hare.

Juan walked up to one of the posters on the wall opposite the entrance. It depicted a beautiful Tahitian girl in a bikini standing on a beach in front of a grove of palm trees. He bent close and looked to be peering into her navel.

A section of wall clicked open. The door had been so cleverly concealed that Lawless hadn't seen a thing.

Cabrillo straightened. 'Retinal scanner,' he explained, and pulled the door all the way open.

He motioned for MacD to take a look.

He stared, gape-jawed. The carpet on the floor was a rich burgundy and so thick it looked like it could conceal a crouching lion. Polished mahogany wainscoting adorned the walls. Above it was some material that resembled regular residential Sheetrock but couldn't possibly be because a ship at sea vibrated too much. It was painted a subtle gray, with hints of mauve – very relaxing, very soothing. The lighting was either tasteful sconces hanging on the walls or cut-crystal chandeliers.

Lawless was no art expert, but he was pretty sure the canvases in gilt frames were the real deal, and he recognized one even if he couldn't name Winslow Homer as its painter.

This wasn't a passageway on some broken-down old freighter. This belonged to a five-star resort hotel – heck, eight stars, for all he knew.

He looked at the Chairman, confusion written all over his face.

Juan began to answer his unasked question, 'What you see topside is all deception. The rust, the dirt, the sorry state of the equipment. It's all designed to make the *Oregon* as innocuous as possible. Anonymity is the name of the game. With this ship we can pull into any port in the world and not arouse suspicion. It's like when you're on the freeway. You notice the Ferraris and Porsches, but do you give a second's thought to some mid-nineties Buick Regal?

'The best part,' he went on, 'is that we have the ways and means to disguise her silhouette and change her name in about twelve hours. She's never the same ship from mission to mission. We call her the *Oregon*, but that is rarely the name painted on her transom.'

'So the rest of the ship . . . ?'

'Is like this,' Juan said, pointing down the hallway. 'Each crew member has a private cabin – and a decorating allowance, I might add. We have a gym, pool, dojo, sauna. Our head chef and sous-chef both trained at *Le Cordon Bleu*. You've met our onboard doctor, and as you can imagine she demanded, and got, the latest medical equipment available.'

'What about weapons?'

'There's a full armory, with everything from pistols to shoulder-fired antitank missiles.' It wasn't yet time to tell him that the *Oregon* herself was a floating arsenal that would rival most navies' capital ships. That and some of the vessel's other hidden tricks would remain secret until Lawless completed his probationary period. 'Now, what do you say?'

Lawless smiled and thrust out his hand. 'Ah'll call Fortran and give 'em my notice.'

From down the hallway came a whoop from an unseen female crew member. It didn't sound like Hux or Linda, so word had traveled fast about the Adonis-like newbie.

'It might take some time,' MacD continued, 'and Ah'll probably have to go back to Kabul. Ah'm sure they're investigating my kidnapping. Plus, Ah'll need to pick up my passport and personal kit.'

'No problem,' Juan assured him. 'We need a few days to get into position for our next job. We'll issue you one of our encrypted satellite phones and contact numbers. We'll have to fly you out to meet us.' Juan had a sudden thought. 'By the way, how are your tracking skills?'

'Ah'm a redneck at heart. Spent my summers hunting in the bayous. My dad used to boast that he had the dogs carrying the guns and me following the scent.'

6

In the end, the decision of whether to send an advance team to Chittagong, Bangladesh's principal port city, or wait and drive the *Oregon* hard around the Indian sub-continent was made easy by the simple fact that the ship had never been there and none of their contacts had a trustworthy man in the area. If they couldn't guarantee getting the supplies and equipment they needed, there was no sense sending a group ahead to even try.

They would lose five days getting the ship into position, five days in which the trail would grow colder. While this rankled Cabrillo and the rest of the crew, the demand for a face-to-face meeting with Roland Croissard annoyed even more.

When Juan had sent his acceptance email to *L'Enfant*, the reply had been swift, as it always was. The financial terms had already been agreed upon, but Croissard had added the stipulation that he get to meet with Cabrillo. Juan had only agreed to meet Gunawan Bahar because the man had flown to Mumbai, where the *Oregon* had just off-loaded two containers of South African millet that had been lashed to the forward deck. Croissard was currently in Singapore and wanted Cabrillo to come to him.

It meant Juan had to chopper back to Karachi, get on the G-V, fly to Singapore, hold the man's hand for an hour or two, then head off to either Chennai, formerly Madras, or Vishakhapatnam, on India's east coast. Which city would depend on the length of the meeting and the speed the *Oregon* could maintain. Once there, they would need to slow the ship so Gomez Adams could chopper in to pick him up.

Any number of bureaucratic snafus could hold him up. He'd replied to *L'Enfant*, expressing his concerns, but was told the client was adamant.

What bothered Cabrillo was the fact that until he could somehow get the Corporation back in the good graces of the United States government, he had no choice but to accept assignments like this. Like any business, they had overhead and expenses that translated to about two hundred thousand dollars a day.

Taking out entire terrorist cells, thwarting some major attack before it happened – these were the things he'd created the Corporation for. That was why he'd joined the CIA in the first place.

And knowing that, for the time being, he had been marginalized to a degree ate at the back of his mind.

He decided to take Max with him for no other reason than to have his company during the long flights. That left Linda Ross in charge of the ship. After she'd gotten out of the Navy, Linda had captained a rig tender in the Gulf of Mexico. She could handle a ship as well as she could handle a gun.

They landed at Changi Airport, to the north of the

futuristic city-state of Singapore. Its skyline was punctuated by some of the most beautiful architecture in the world, including the new Marina Bay Sands Hotel, their destination. Hanley was nearly inconsolable when Juan told him they wouldn't have the time to hit the hotel's casino.

As was usual when arriving on a private jet, customs was a mere formality. The uniformed agent met them at the stairs when they stepped from the plane, glanced at, then stamped, their passports, and didn't ask to see the contents of Cabrillo's sleek briefcase, not that they were hiding anything in it.

Though they had flown casual, both had put on suits and ties just prior to landing. Juan wore an elegantly cut charcoal, with a faint pinstripe that was picked up in the colors of his two-hundred-dollar tie. His brogues were buffed to a glossy black. Keeping shoes spit-polished was a fetish he shared with the *Oregon*'s steward. Max wasn't wearing off-the-rack exactly, but he looked uncomfortable. His collar dug into the spare flesh around his neck, and there was the tiniest trace of an old stain on his left sleeve.

The air was decidedly warmer here than in Karachi, and while they couldn't detect it over the smell of hot asphalt and jet fuel, it carried the tropical humidity associated with the sea. The Equator was only eighty-five miles to their south.

Juan checked his watch, an all-black Movado that was barely thicker than a piece of paper. 'We've got an hour. Perfect.'

Though offered a super-stretch limousine, they took a less ostentatious town car into the city. Traffic was absolute murder and yet remarkably polite. There were no blaring horns, no aggressive driving techniques. It made Juan recall that for all its wealth and sophistication, Singapore was virtually a police state. Free speech was severely limited, and spitting on a sidewalk could get you caned. This tended to create a homogenous population with a keen respect for the law, and thus no one cut you off or flipped you the bird.

Their destination rose along the water in three gracefully sloped white towers, each more than fifty stories tall. Atop them was a platform that stretched for nearly a fifth of a mile, one part of it cantilevering off the third tower a good two hundred feet. This was known as the SkyPark, and even from a distance they could see the profusion of trees and shrubbery that adorned it. The SkyPark side facing the marina was composed of three infinity edge swimming pools holding almost four hundred thousand gallons of water.

At the base of the hotel towers were three enormous domed buildings housing the casino, exclusive shops, and convention spaces. Rumor had it, the casino resort was the second most expensive on the planet.

The car pulled up to the hotel entrance, and a liveried doorman was there even before the tires had stopped turning.

'Welcome to the Marina Bay Sands,' he said in cultured

English. Cabrillo suspected that had he looked Scandinavian he would have been greeted in flawless Swedish. 'Do you have any baggage?'

Juan jerked a finger at where Max was heaving himself out of the car. 'Just him.'

They stepped through into the hotel's soaring lobby. It was crowded with vacationers. A group of them were assembled for some sort of tour and were receiving instructions in singsong Chinese from a female guide who couldn't have been four and a half feet tall. The line waiting to check in snaked through a velvet-rope maze. With twenty-five hundred rooms, this was more like a small city than a single enterprise.

Juan found the concierge desk and told the attractive Malay girl that she had an envelope for him. He gave his name, and she asked for identification. Inside the envelope was a credit-card-style room key and one of Roland Croissard's business cards. Scrawled on the back was the financier's room number.

They needed to show the armed guard near the elevators that they had a proper room key. Juan flashed it, and they gained entry. They took the car up to the fortieth floor with a Korean couple who were arguing the entire way. Cabrillo imagined that the man had gambled away the family kimchi money.

The hallways were muted and somewhat dimly lit. Unlike the layout of some of the megacasinos they had been in, the three-tower design meant they weren't left walking forever to find the right room. Cabrillo knocked on Croissard's door.

'Moment,' a voice said, dropping the *t* like a French speaker.

The door opened. The man standing there nearly blocking the door from jamb to jamb was not Roland Croissard. They'd seen photographs of him while researching his background.

In that first half second Juan noted that the man's jacket was off, his hands empty, and his expression wasn't overtly aggressive. This wasn't an ambush, and so he relaxed his right arm, which was about to deliver a karate strike to the man's nose that more than likely would have killed him. The man grunted. He'd seen how quickly the Chairman had perceived and then discounted a potential threat.

'Monsieur Cabrillo?' the voice called from farther in the suite.

The gorilla who'd opened the door stepped aside. He was nearly as big as Franklin Lincoln, but where Linc's face was normally open and easygoing, this one maintained a permanent scowl. His hair was dark, cut unfashionably, and looked like something from a 1970s adult movie. He had hooded, watchful eyes that tracked Juan as he stepped into the opulent two-room suite. He had shaved that morning but already needed another.

Hired muscle, was Cabrillo's assumption, and too obvious about it. The good bodyguards were the ones you never suspected. They looked like accountants or entry-level CSRs at a bank, not hulking wrestler types who thought their size alone was intimidating enough.

Juan resisted the impulse to put the guy down for the fun of it. The guard indicated that Juan and Max should fan open their coats so he could see if they were carrying concealed weapons. To get things moving along, the two men from the Corporation indulged him. He didn't bother to check their ankles.

Cabrillo wondered if this guy was really that bad or if he'd been told these were expected guests and should be treated accordingly. He decided the latter, which meant the man had overstepped his authority by asking them to open their coats. His abilities went up a notch in Juan's mind. He took protecting his boss more seriously than his orders to let them enter unmolested.

'Could you button your shirtsleeves, please?' Juan asked him.

'What?'

'Your sleeves are down but unbuttoned, which means you have a knife strapped to your forearm. I've already noticed you aren't wearing an ankle holster, and yet somehow I don't think you're unarmed. Hence the unbuttoned sleeves.'

Roland Croissard rose from a sofa on the far end of the room. A briefcase and papers were strewn across the coffee table. A glass with ice and a clear liquid sat in a puddle of condensation. He wore suit pants and a tie. His jacket was draped across an overstuffed chair that was part of the same furniture cluster.

'It's okay, John,' he said. 'These men are here to help find Soleil.'

The guard, John, scowled a little deeper as he buttoned

his cuffs. When he bent his elbow, the cotton of his shirt bulged against a low-profile knife sheath.

'Monsieur Cabrillo,' Croissard said. 'Thank you so much for coming.'

The Swiss man was of medium height and starting to show a paunch, but he had a handsome face and penetrating blue eyes. His hair, an indeterminate shade, was thinning and combed straight back. Cabrillo's estimation was that he looked younger than sixty-two but not remarkably so. Croissard plucked a pair of wire-rimmed reading glasses off his straight nose as he came across the room with his hand extended. His grasp was cool and professional, the shake of a hand that did it for a living.

'This is Max Hanley,' Juan introduced. 'My second-in-command.'

'And this is my personal security adviser, John Smith.'

Cabrillo held out his hand, which Smith begrudgingly shook. 'You must get around a lot,' Juan said. 'I've seen your name on a lot of hotel registrations.'

The man gave no indication he got the joke.

'Why don't we sit down. May I get you gentlemen a drink?'

'Bottled water,' Juan said. He set his briefcase down on an end table and popped the lid. Smith had positioned himself close enough so that he could see inside.

Cabrillo pulled two electronic devices from the case and shut the lid again. He flicked one on and studied the small screen. Gone were the days when he had to sweep a room with a bug detector. This handheld could check a hundred-foot radius instantly. Croissard's suite was clean. In case there was a voice-activated listening device someplace within earshot, he would leave it on. He then went to the window. In the distance were the silver spires of the skyline, made somewhat indistinct by the heat haze that was forming as morning burned into afternoon.

He peeled an adhesive backing off the cigarette pack–sized device and stuck it to the thick glass. He hit a button to turn it on. Inside the black plastic casing were two weights powered by a battery and controlled by a micro random generator. It set the weights in motion, which in turn vibrated the glass. The electronic generator would guarantee that no pattern would emerge that could be decoded and nullified by a computer.

'Qu'est-ce que c'est?'

French wasn't one of the languages Cabrillo spoke, but the question was easy enough to understand. 'This shakes the windowpane and prevents anyone from using a laser voice detector.' He took one last look at the beautiful view, then closed the sheers so that no one could see into the suite. 'Okay. Now we can talk.'

'I have heard from my daughter,' Croissard announced.

Cabrillo felt a ripple of anger. 'You could have told me that before we flew halfway around the world.'

'No, no. You do not understand. I think she is in more grave danger than I first thought.'

'Go on.'

'The call came through about three hours ago. Here.' He pulled a sleek PDA from his pants pocket and fumbled through a couple of applications until a woman's voice, sounding very tired and very scared, came through the speaker. She said no more than a few words in French before the call abruptly ended.

'She says that she is close. To what, I do not know, but then says that they are closer. She then says that she will never make it. And I do not know who the "they" she references might be.'

'May I see that?' Juan asked and held out his hand.

He fiddled with the PDA for a moment and hit play to repeat the recording. Croissard talked him through it, and once again they heard Soleil's breathless voice. There was a noise in the background, maybe wind through leaves, maybe anything at all. Juan played it a third time. Then a fourth. The background became no clearer.

'Can you send this to my phone? I want to have the recording analyzed.'

'Of course.' Juan gave him the number on the phone he was currently carrying, one that would have its SIM card pulled when the mission was over. 'Were you able to get her GPS coordinates?'

'Yes.' Croissard unfolded a map that had been lying in his briefcase. It was a topographical map of Myanmar done before the country changed its name from Burma. Faint X's had been marked with a fine-tipped mechanical pencil, and the longitude and latitude numbers added next to them. Cabrillo was familiar with them, having seen a copy of Croissard's map already. But there was a new notation about twenty miles northeast of Soleil's last-known location.

'You've tried to call her back?' Juan asked, knowing the answer.

'Yes, every fifteen minutes. There is no reply.'

'Well, this is good news,' Cabrillo said. 'It's proof of life, even if it sounds like she's in trouble. As you must understand, we need some more time to get everything into position. An operation of this nature must be carefully thought out so it can be precisely executed.'

'That has already been explained to me,' Croissard replied, obviously not liking that simple truth.

'We'll be ready in three days' time. Your daughter has already passed effective helicopter range, which will make our jobs a little tougher, but, mark my words, we will find her.'

'*Merci, monsieur.* You have a reputation for success. There is one final piece to this affair,' he added.

Juan cocked an eyebrow, not liking the tone in the financier's voice. 'Yes?'

'I want John to accompany you.'

'Out of the question.'

'Monsieur, this is not a negotiable request. I believe the expression is "my charter, my rules," yes?'

'Mr Croissard, this isn't a fishing trip. We could be facing armed guerrillas, and I simply can't allow an unknown man to come with us.' Cabrillo planned on bringing MacD Lawless, who was a bit of an unknown himself, but the financier didn't need to know that.

Wordlessly, John Smith unbuttoned the cuff where he didn't carry the knife. He pulled up his sleeve to reveal a faded blue tattoo. It showed a flaming circle above the words *Marche ou Crève*. Cabrillo recognized it as the emblem for the French Foreign Legion and its unofficial motto, 'March or Die.'

Juan looked at him levelly. 'Sorry, Mr Smith, all that tells me is that you've visited a tattoo parlor.' It would explain Smith's generic name, though – Legionnaires often adopted *noms de guerre*.

'About fifteen years ago, by the looks of it,' Max added.

Smith didn't say anything, but Cabrillo could see the anger building behind the man's dark eyes. Juan also recognized that he was between a rock and a hard place because ultimately he would have to cave if he wanted the contract.

'Tell you what,' Cabrillo said, and lifted up his trouser leg. Croissard and Smith were startled at the sight of his prosthetic leg. Cabrillo had several that had been tricked out by the wizards in the *Oregon*'s Magic Shop. This particular one was called the Combat Leg Version 2.0. He opened a concealed area behind the flesh-colored calf and pulled out a small automatic pistol. He popped the seven-shot magazine and cleared a round from the chamber.

He showed it to Smith for just a second, and said, 'Eyes on me.'

Then he handed it over.

Smith knew what the test entailed, and, without

moving his gaze from Juan's eyes, he quickly disassembled the small pistol down to its basic parts and then just as quickly put it back together again. He gave it back butt first. It took him about forty seconds.

'Kel-Tec P-3AT,' he said. 'Based on their P22 but chambered for .380. Nice gun to fit in a lady's purse.'

Juan laughed, breaking the tension. 'I tried fitting a Desert Eagle .50 cal in this leg, but it was just a tad obvious.' He slipped the gun and magazine plus the loose bullet into his coat pocket. 'Where have you served?'

'Chad, Haiti, Iraq of course, Somalia, a few other Third World hot spots.'

Cabrillo shifted his attention back to Croissard. 'You've got your deal. He passes.'

'Good, then it is settled. John will accompany you now back to your aircraft and then you will find my Soleil.'

'No. He's going to meet up with us in Chittagong. In case you aren't aware, that's a port city in Bangladesh.' Smith wasn't going to be aboard the *Oregon* a second longer than necessary. 'And that, I'm sorry, is nonnegotiable.'

'*D'accord.* But if you do not pick him up as promised, do not think you will get my money.'

'Mr Croissard,' Juan said solemnly, 'I am many things, but a man who backs out on his word isn't one of them.'

The two men studied each other for a moment. Croissard nodded. 'No. I don't suppose that you are.' They shook hands.

As they exchanged phone numbers with Smith, Max pulled their laser defeater from the window and packed up the bug detector. He snapped the briefcase closed and handed it to Cabrillo.

'If you hear anything from her, no matter the time, call me immediately,' Juan told Croissard at the suite's door.

'I will. I promise. Please bring her back to me. She is headstrong and stubborn, but she is my daughter, and I love her very much.'

'We'll do our best,' Juan said, because he would never promise something he couldn't deliver.

'Well?' Max asked as they were striding down the hallway heading for the elevators.

'I don't like it, but what choice did we have?'

'That's why the face-to-face. To spring Smith on us at the last minute.'

'Yeah. Pretty cagey of him.'

'So, are we going to trust him?'

'Smith? Not on your life. There's something they're not telling us, and he's the key.'

'We should back out of this whole thing,' Max opined.

'No way, my friend. If anything, I'm more interested than ever in what the lovely Miss Croissard was doing so deep into Burma.'

'Myanmar,' Hanley corrected.

'Whatever.'

They exited the elevator and started crossing the busy lobby when Cabrillo suddenly hit himself on the head as if he'd forgotten something and grabbed Max's elbow to turn them around.

'What is it, did you forget something?' Hanley asked. Juan had picked up his pace ever so slightly.

'I noticed two guys hanging around the lobby when we first entered. Both look local, but they're wearing long coats. One of them noticed us when we got into view and quickly turned away. Too quickly.'

'Who are they?'

'Don't know, but they're not with Croissard. If he wanted us dead, he would have had Smith shoot us as soon as we entered his room. And he knows we're going back to the airport, so what's the point of following us?'

Max saw no flaw in Cabrillo's logic, so he just grunted.

They approached the express elevator for the Sky-Park. By feel, Juan was able to insert the magazine back into his Kel-Tec automatic. He even managed to cock the weapon against his hip bone without taking it from his jacket pocket. The two men were making their move, coming across the lobby without taking their eyes off the Corporation duo.

The elevator door pinged open. Juan and Max didn't wait for it to empty before shouldering their way in, all but ignoring the looks of indignation thrown their way. It wasn't even going to be close. The men had waited too long, and now the elevator doors were closing. It was too public out in the lobby to pull any sort of weapon, so Juan threw them a taunting smile as the doors met with a hiss.

'Now what?' Max asked as they were carried skyward.

Juan took the opportunity to load the ejected bullet into the pistol. 'We get to the top, wait about five minutes, and then head back down again.'

'And what will they be doing, pray tell?'

'Splitting up to cover the lobbies of the other two towers. They'll never think we'd stay in this one.'

'And if they decide to follow us up?'

'Never happen,' Juan dismissed with a shake of his head.

'I still wonder who they are,' Max said as they neared the fifty-fifth floor and the SkyPark.

'My money's on the local secret police. Something about our plane's registration or our passports sent up a red flag, and these gentlemen want to ask us a few questions.'

'So how'd they know we'd be here at the—' Max stopped asking his question and then answered it: 'They talked to the car service that brought us to the hotel.'

'Elementary, my dear Hanley.'

The doors opened, and they stepped out onto one of the greatest engineering marvels in the world. The hundred-thousand-square-foot platform sitting atop the three towers was like Babylon's famous hanging gardens, only these weren't the exclusive environs of Nebuchadnezzar and his wife, Amytis. Trees provided excellent shade, while the flowering shrubs perfumed the air nearly a thousand feet above the streets. The long swimming pools, with their dizzying infinity edges, were sparkling blue and surrounded by sun-bathers.

To their left was an eating area cantilevered off the third tower so that it hung suspended in space. Diners were lounging under bright umbrellas while waitstaff danced between the tables, bearing trays of food and drinks. The view over Singapore Harbor was absolutely breathtaking.

'Man, I could get used to this,' Max said as a woman in a bikini passed close enough for him to smell the coconut in her tanning lotion.

'You ogle any harder, your eyes are going to pop out.'

Juan led them away from the elevator and took up a position so they could see it on the off chance that the two secret policemen had followed them up. He was pretty sure they wouldn't, but he hadn't stayed alive in such a dangerous profession for so long by not being cautious.

A moment later the elevator doors parted again. Cabrillo tensed, his hand in his pocket, his finger resting along the trigger guard. He knew he wouldn't shoot it out with these guys – Singapore had the death penalty – but, if need be, he could toss the pistol into a bush to his right and avoid a major weapons violation. Provided they didn't find the second, one-shot gun embedded in his artificial leg.

A family dressed for a little time under the sun emerged, the father holding the hand of a little pig-tailed girl. An older boy immediately rushed to look over the railing at the miniature cityscape so far below.

The doors started to close. Juan blew out his breath and was about to make a snarky comment to Max when a hand appeared between the gleaming elevator doors and stopped them from closing entirely.

Cabrillo cursed. It was them. They looked out of place with their long dark coats and their darting eyes. He backed a little deeper into the trees. They would have to sneak along the back side of the restaurant to get to the elevator housing for the third tower. To do that they would need to scale a concrete retaining wall and that might attract the attention of one of the servers or pool attendants. It couldn't be helped.

He put his foot on the first tier of the wall and was about to boost himself up when an eagle-eyed lifeguard a dozen yards away shouted for him to stop. He must have been watching them the whole time and suspected they were up to something.

The two agents immediately were on guard and started moving toward them, even though Juan and Max were still out of their direct line of vision.

The time for subtlety was over. Juan heaved himself up onto the wall, climbing the three tiers with the agility of a monkey. When he reached the top, he lowered a hand to help Max. The lifeguard began climbing off his little mahogany tower and blowing his whistle to attract additional security. He either hadn't noticed or had dismissed the two men in trench coats.

The agents burst into view. One threw open his coat and brought up a vicious-looking machine pistol. Max was halfway up the wall, as exposed as a bug on an entomologist's lab table. Juan had a split second to make a decision, and he did so without hesitation.

He dropped Max.

Just as the agent pulled the trigger. Cement dust and chips exploded off the wall where Max had been dangling. People started screaming and stampeding away from the chain saw–like whine of the machine pistol as the entire thirty-round clip was emptied against the concrete wall inches above Max's prone form.

Not knowing what was going on but acting on instinct and adrenaline, Cabrillo drew the Kel-Tec and returned fire. His first rounds were snap shots, just trying to break the gunman's fixation on perforating Max. The gunman jerked slightly as a more carefully aimed yet still a little wild bullet struck the crown of his head.

The second agent started opening his coat, where he doubtlessly had his own weapon. Juan shifted his sights and, to his horror, saw that the 'agent' was wearing a heavy suicide vest. He could see the packs of explosives and other bags that would contain metal scrap for shrapnel.

'*Allahu Akbar,*' the man shrieked.

Juan put a bullet down his open throat, and the man fell back like a marionette with its strings cut.

The first gunman had blood sheeting down his face and was staggering backward, dazed by the .380 caliber bullet that had gauged a trench through the top of his skull. He'd dropped his machine pistol down onto its sling and was fumbling in his coat pocket.

Juan couldn't get a clear shot at him as people continued to streak past, not realizing they were blundering into the middle of the gunfight. He knew this first guy was probably also packing a vest and made the decision that hitting one of the civilians with a stray bullet was preferable to dozens of them getting mowed down in an explosion.

A hotel guard finally arrived. He'd been on the far side of the platform and hadn't seen a thing. He noticed the one man down on the ground in a pool of his own blood, paid no attention to the guy with blood on his face, and instead trained his attention on Cabrillo, an obviously armed target.

He started to raise his pistol and nearly had it centered on Cabrillo when Max threw himself across the intervening ten yards and hit him like a linebacker. They crashed to the ground in a tangle of limbs, bowling over another man in the process.

Juan took a chance and fired again. He hit the bomber in the chest, but the man merely staggered back from the impact. The bullet had hit one of the bags of nails, which stopped it like body armor. The Kel-Tec's slide was locked back over an empty chamber.

Cabrillo flipped himself around so that his foot was pointing toward the gunman. The barrel of the .44 caliber pistol hidden inside his prosthetic leg made up its central support strut to give it as much length, and thus accuracy, as possible. There was only one round, so essentially the weapon was just a tube with a dual-trigger firing mechanism that ensured it couldn't accidentally discharge.

When he hit the second trigger, it felt like someone had slammed the bottom of his stump with a sledge-hammer. The round punched through the sole of his shoe, and the recoil almost knocked him off his perch. The heavy 300-grain bullet entered the bomber's body in the abdomen, its kinetic energy lifting him off his feet like he'd been jerked from behind.

He hit the pool, his body parting the water, and sank from sight when the vest detonated. Water geysered in a solid white column that rose forty feet over the deck before crashing back like a torrential rain. The blast had been big enough and close enough to blow out part of the pool's steel side. Water gushed through the open-ing, dancing and twisting as it fell over the side of the building on its long journey to the ground. The once-bucolic swimming pool had become one of the tallest waterfalls in the world.

There was nothing left of the bomber, and with the pool absorbing so much of the explosive force and the shrapnel, it didn't appear that anyone had been injured, at least seriously.

Cabrillo's hearing was just returning after the sonic assault of the blast. More people were screaming now, running, panicked and unsure of where to go or what to do. Over all this, he detected a high keening wail, a sound of true mortal danger that cut above the fearful bleating of hotel guests.

There was a little boy still in the pool, his arms supported by plastic water wings. He'd been in the shallow end, playing by himself, when all the adults had scrambled from the water at the opening salvos of the attacks, and apparently his parents hadn't had the time to rescue him.

As the water drained through the twisted opening, sucked through it like it was a high-speed pump, the floating child was being drawn inexorably toward the shattered metal.

Juan leapt off the eight-foot retaining wall and sprinted across the deck. He threw himself into a perfect dive that would have gotten applause from Olympic judges and struck out for the boy. He could feel the current pulling on his body. It was like trying to fight a riptide. He had been a strong swimmer his entire life and had been able to stroke his way out of some pretty dangerous situations, but nothing had prepared him for the raw power of the pool draining through its blown-out side. The hole was at least four feet in diameter.

He reached the child when they still had about ten feet to go before he would be sucked through. The kid flailed his arms, crying beyond all reason. Juan grabbed him by the hair to get out of the reach of his thrashing arms and tried to tow him clear, but the surge was simply too much to fight one-handed. He looked around in desperation. No one had seen what he was doing.

The hole was a bright spot near the bottom of the pool where sunlight illuminated the eddies and whirl-pools that formed and dissolved as the water poured into infinity.

Cabrillo put on a burst of speed, his legs pistoning and his free arm hauling back with everything he had.

For every foot he gained, the pool took back two. The vortex was just too strong. He had seconds before he was pulled through the rent in the side of the pool. He did the only thing open to him.

He stopped swimming.

And then twisted around so that he was facing the gaping tear. As they were drawn closer he held the child up in his arms. He would have one shot, one instant, when he could make this happen and save them both. If not, he and the boy would be sucked out of the pool and sent plummeting a thousand feet to their deaths.

They were less than two feet away. The water was still too deep to stand in, so Cabrillo kicked hard, raising his upper body out of the water. He threw the boy at the ledge surrounding the swimming pool, sank down to the bottom, and sprang up again. He launched himself partially out of the water and hit the side of the pool directly over the tear in its side. The relentless pull sucked at his dangling legs and nearly drew him back in again before he managed to get a better grip on the cement and haul himself completely free. He looked to his side. The boy was just pulling himself upright, tears cutting through the water on his face, his right elbow bent as he examined the scrape he'd gotten when he hit the deck. Only when he saw that it was beginning to bleed a little did he began to wail like a fire engine.

Juan got to his feet and snatched up the kid so he wouldn't fall in again. He hooked up with Max, dumped the sniveling boy next to a potted palm, and joined the frenzied exodus off the SkyPark.

127

Ten minutes later, just as police were starting to arrive at the resort en masse, they hit the lobby. Any attempt at a security cordon at this point was never going to happen, and the cops seemed to realize it. People streamed out of the building like a herd of frightened animals. Cabrillo and Hanley allowed themselves to be borne along with the tide of humanity. Once out of the building, they made their way down to the far end of a line of taxis and hopped into the last cab in the string.

The driver was about to protest that he couldn't take fares until it was his turn but stopped himself when he saw the three hundred Singapore dollar bills in Cabrillo's hand.

He didn't even care that they were wet.

7

Max broke the minutes-long silence. It had taken him that long to get his breathing under control and for his normally florid complexion to return from the far end of the crimson color palette. 'Mind telling me what just happened back there?'

Juan didn't respond right away. Instead, he reached into his pocket for his phone, saw that it had been ruined by his time in the pool, and shoved it back in his pocket. Hanley handed over his undamaged cell. Cabrillo punched in a memorized number. On these disposable phones they never preprogrammed the extensions of other team members in case they were ever confiscated.

The line rang once and was picked up. 'How you doing, Tiny?' Juan asked. Chuck Gunderson, aka Tiny, was the Corporation's chief pilot. Though he spent little time aboard the *Oregon*, he was an integral part of the team.

'As one of my flight instructors told me, if you don't have patience, you'll never make it as a pilot.' Chuck had that peculiar Minnesota drawl made famous in the movie *Fargo*.

Had the pilot inserted the word 'fine' into his answer, it would have indicated that he wasn't alone and was most likely under duress.

'We're on our way back right now. Contact ATC and get us a slot out of here.'

Gunderson must have heard something in the Chairman's voice. 'Trouble?'

'All kinds and then some. We should be there in twenty minutes.' Juan cut the connection and handed back Max's phone. A pair of ambulances screamed past in the opposite lane, their lights flashing and their sirens going full bore.

'Are you going to answer my question?' Hanley asked.

Cabrillo closed his eyes, picturing the scene when they'd first spotted the suicide bombers. He concentrated on the people around them, not on the gunmen. The picture firmed up in his mind, and he studied the faces of the hotel guests and staff who had been in the lobby at that instant. It wasn't an innate skill but rather something drilled into him during his CIA training so that when all hell broke loose he could distinguish additional threats or identify accomplices. Oftentimes in assassinations or bombings there was an observer nearby to report back on the operation.

'I think,' he finally said, 'that we happened to be in the wrong place at the wrong time.'

Hanley was incredulous. 'You honestly think that was a coincidence?' he demanded.

'Yes,' Cabrillo replied, hastily raising a hand to stave off Max's next remark. 'Hear me out. As I mentioned earlier, if Croissard wanted to set us up, he could have had his goon, Smith – nice name, that, by the way –

130

shoot us as soon as we were in the suite. Stuff our bodies into some big trunks, and no one would ever be the wiser. With me so far?'

Max nodded.

'That puts him in the clear, which means it's unlikely he told anyone about the meeting since he really does want us to find his daughter. Right?'

'Okay,' Hanley said, drawing out the word.

'Now, who was around us when the bombers made their move?'

'Hell, I don't even recall what they were wearing,' the Corporation's number two admitted.

'Overcoats, which in this heat should have tipped me off that they weren't Singapore security forces. Anyway, you and I were the only two Caucasians in the lobby when they started after us. Everyone else was Asian. I think this attack has been in the works for a while, but it was seeing our white faces that triggered them into executing their plan.'

'Seriously?' Max asked, his voice dripping with doubt.

'Just because there has never been a terrorist attack in Singapore doesn't mean it isn't a target. The casino's brand-new, a shining example of Western decadence. Any jihadi worth his salt would be drooling to blow up the place. We just happened to be there when it happened.'

Hanley still didn't look convinced.

'How about this,' Juan offered. 'If by tonight some group hasn't laid claim to the attack, we'll assume we were the targets and we'll back out of our deal with Croissard, since he was the only person who knew we were going to be at the hotel. Would that satisfy you?'

More emergency vehicles went barreling by, followed by a pair of SUVs painted in jungle camouflage colors.

When Max didn't say anything, Juan caved. 'Fine, I'll call Croissard and tell him we're out and that he needs to find someone else to save his daughter.'

Hanley shot him a look. 'That is the feeblest attempt at manipulation I've ever heard.'

'Is it going to work?'

'Yes, damnit,' Max spat, angry at himself for being so predictable. 'If some group claims responsibility, our mission's still on.' He crossed his arms and stared out the window like a petulant child.

Cabrillo felt no qualms about using his friend's emotions like this. Hanley had done it to him a million times before. And it wasn't that either needed to be nudged to do the right thing. It was that they needed to be in total agreement. Their relationship was the foundation on which the Corporation was built, and if they didn't see eye to eye on nearly everything, the entire team would lose its edge.

Juan had the driver drop them about a quarter mile short of the General Aviation area. Just because Tiny had said everything aboard the plane was all right didn't mean that the area was secure. The pair approached cautiously, using cars parked along the access road as cover. The cement building, with its row of green-tinted glass windows, looked normal. There was an armed guard out front with a valet, but he'd been there when they had first arrived.

Planes were taking off and landing normally, meaning the airport was still operational. That, coupled with the fact that the uniformed rent-a-cop didn't look particularly wary, told Cabrillo that the authorities had yet to issue any sort of alert.

They were eyed as they entered the building. Juan's suit had stopped dripping but was still soaked, and Max's was scuffed-up from the attack.

'Our taxi hit a fire hydrant,' Juan explained as they passed.

Moments later they were escorted by a pretty Malaysian hostess to their Gulfstream and were entreated to return to Singapore soon.

'What happened to you two?' Tiny asked as they mounted the stairs. Despite the cabin's ample headroom, Gunderson had to stoop over to keep his flight cap atop his blond head. His shoulders seemed to brush both sides of the fuselage.

'Later,' Cabrillo said. 'Get us the hell out of here.'

Tiny ducked back into the cockpit and set about following the Chairman's order with his copilot. Juan got on the aircraft's satellite phone and dialed Roland Croissard's cell. It rang eight times, and he was sure it would go to voice mail when the Swiss financier picked up.

'Mr Croissard, it's Juan Cabrillo.' The background din was a symphony of sirens. 'What's happening there?'

'A bombing on the roof of the hotel.' Croissard's voice was edgy, near panic. 'They have evacuated all the guests. It is a good thing, because ten minutes after the first explosion another ripped through part of the casino.'

Juan covered the handset's microphone and relayed that last bit of information to Max, adding, 'See, we were nowhere near the gaming floor. It was a coincidence.'

Max's perpetual scowl deepened, but he knew the Chairman was right.

'Are you and Smith okay?'

'*Oui, oui*, we are unharmed. Just a little shaken up, perhaps. Well, at least I am. Nothing seems to bother John.'

'That's good. I think we are all victims of being at the wrong place at the wrong time.' Juan had to raise his voice when the Gulfstream's twin engines began spooling up. 'I want to assure you that this will not affect our transaction. Do you understand?'

'Yes, I do. And I am most relieved.'

'Let Mr Smith know that I will be in touch with instructions for how we will pick him up. As I said earlier it will most likely take place in Chittagong, Bangladesh.'

'*D'accord*. I will tell him.'

Juan cut the connection. He rummaged through a storage locker and found a pair of mechanic's overalls. They were sized for Tiny Gunderson, but a dry tent was preferable to a well-tailored but wet suit.

They took off a few minutes later, and no sooner had the undercarriage clicked into the fuselage than Tiny's voice came over the intercom. 'Singapore control just shut down all departing aircraft. They're requesting we return to the airport, but I figure we'll be beyond their twelve-mile limit before they can do anything about it. Whatever you and Max got into back there, Chairman, it sure has their dander up.'

Hanley and Cabrillo exchanged a look. Max leaned forward to a small refrigerator and pulled out two beers, a Peroni for Juan and a Bud Light for himself. The 'Light' was an admission that his personal battle with the bulge was ongoing. 'I'd say,' he said, 'that we just barely kept our butts out of a Singapore Sling.'

Cabrillo groaned.

Eight hours later, and half an ocean away, Gomez Adams held the Corporation's MD 520N over the rearmost of the *Oregon*'s five cargo hatches. The ship was pitching mildly, but there was a freshening breeze off the port quarter. He massaged the controls, matching pitch, yaw, and speed, and set the big chopper onto the deck. As soon as the skids kissed steel, he cut the turbine and announced, 'We're home. And, believe it or not, there might just be a little vapor left in the gas tanks.'

A technician immediately rushed forward to secure the chopper.

The eleven-thousand-ton tramp freighter was at the helicopter's maximum range off the eastern coast of the Indian subcontinent as she drove through the gentle rollers for her rendezvous in Bangladesh. Far to the west the setting sun painted the undersides of the clouds in hues of orange, red, and purple and cast a wavering gilded beam atop the waves.

Nowhere on earth was a sunset as beautiful as those found at sea, Cabrillo thought as he ducked under the chopper's still-spinning blades. The downdraft made his oversized jumpsuit snap and whip like it was attacking him.

Max grinned at him when the collar slapped Juan across the face.

'Welcome back, boys,' Linda Ross said as she stepped forward to greet them. She wore a pair of cutoff shorts and a tank top. 'You have a knack for finding trouble, don't you?'

Hanley pointed a thumb at Juan. 'Blame him. The guy attracts nothing but suicide bombers, terrorists, and madmen.'

'Don't forget loose women. What's the latest on the bombings?'

'Some new group called al-Qaeda of the East has claimed responsibility for the attack. No dead and only five slight injuries. The two blasts on the roof were standard vests packed with Semtex and scrap metal. You know, couture for killers. The explosion in the casino was much smaller. No word yet on what it was, or at least it's not being reported. Mark and Eric think they can hack into the Singapore police mainframe, but they didn't sound too certain.'

'Tell them not to bother,' Cabrillo said. 'My guess is the primary bombers' handler tossed a grenade in a trash can to cause more chaos. I'd hate to think of the death toll had Max and I not been there.'

'Amen,' Hanley said, and ambled off to give Adams and his mechanics their orders.

Off along the starboard rail, a crewman had opened the lid of what had started out as a regular fifty-five-gallon steel barrel. It was as dented and neglected as everything else aboard the *Oregon*. Rather than just some bit of nautical junk left to litter the deck, the barrel was a carefully positioned redoubt for a remotely operated M60 machine gun. The technician from the armory had the lid open, and the gun raised and pivoted to the horizontal position while he cleaned it and checked for any signs of salt-air corrosion. This was one of several identical weapons placed around the main deck's perimeter that were used primarily to repel boarders.

'Why there?' Linda wondered aloud as she and the Chairman walked to the towering amidships super-structure. Its white paint was faded to the color of curdled cream and was flaking off the ship like she was some prehistoric reptile shedding her skin.

Because there were no other vessels within visual range, they hadn't bothered pumping ersatz smoke though the ship's single funnel. Unlike any other water-craft plying the oceans today, the *Oregon* relied on magnetohydrodynamics. The high-tech system used supercooled magnets to strip free electrons from the briny water. This free electricity was then used to force water through two pump jets. Eventually such propulsion would become standard on all shipping since it was environmentally sound, but the staggering cost and still-experimental state of development made the *Oregon* the only vessel afloat to use it.

'The casino's owned by an American company, and, according to the tenets of Islam, gambling, or *maisir*, is forbidden,' Cabrillo replied. 'That place is the church of all things unholy. Anything on the bombers themselves?'

'Just what was captured on the hotel's surveillance cameras when they were in the lobby and elevator. They were either Malay or Indonesian. No IDs were found. And it'll take days to do a DNA search, and most likely these guys aren't on any databases. Their pictures might match with something, but nada for now.'

'It's early,' Juan remarked.

They stepped over the coaming of a watertight door and into the superstructure. The lighting was fluorescents bolted to the ceiling, and the hallways were painted steel. When there was no prospect of outsiders entering the ship, the air was kept comfortable, but it could be changed at a moment's notice. In cold climes, if an inspector or customs agent was aboard, they cranked up the big Trane air conditioners, or in the tropics they would pump in additional heat just to make the interlopers want off the ship as fast as possible. Also, the lighting could be set to flickering at microburst frequencies designed to interfere with neural activity. For some it brought a mild headache and a little nausea. It could send an epileptic into a seizure.

That had happened only once, fortunately, and Doc Huxley was there in moments.

Since an incident involving Somali pirates a few months back hadn't gone as planned, Max had installed injectors that could flood the entire superstructure, or individual rooms, with carbon monoxide, again under the watchful eye of Julia Huxley. The odorless and colorless gas induced drowsiness and lethargy at first, but prolonged exposure would bring brain damage and death. Because individuals react differently depending on their size and physical condition, Cabrillo considered this to be a last-ditch option.

They stepped into a little-used janitor's closet, and Linda twisted the taps of a slop sink like she was working the dials of a safe. The water that splashed from the faucet was rusty brown and somehow lumpy.

No detail was too minor.

A secret door clicked open to reveal the opulent core of the *Oregon*, the spaces where the men and women who manned her spent most of their time.

They went one deck lower to where most of the crew's cabins were located, and Juan paused outside the door of his own suite. Linda made to follow him in and continue the briefing.

'Sorry,' he said, 'but I need a shower and to get out of these clothes. I look like a *Star Wars* action figure dressed in an old G.I. Joe doll's outfit.'

'I wasn't going to mention your need for a new tailor,'

she grinned saucily. 'You look like I did wearing one of my dad's shirts as an art-class smock when I was a little girl.'

'We hired Tiny for his flying ability, not his uniformity of size.' He turned away, then stopped. 'One more thing. Go down to the boat garage and tell them we need to strip one of the RHIBs of every ounce of weight they can think of. That includes pulling one of her outboards and centering the other. Max has Gomez Adams and his team doing the same thing to the whirlybird.'

An RHIB was one of the two Rigid Hulled Inflatable Boats the *Oregon* carried, one in a starboard-mounted chamber where it could be launched into the sea and another in storage in a forward hold as a backup.

Linda didn't point out the obviousness of Cabrillo's plan. Once they choppered into Myanmar, the only real way around the interior was by boat. 'Aye, Chairman. Enjoy your shower.' Linda sauntered off.

The Chairman's cabin was decorated like it had been the stage for the film *Casablanca*, with all sorts of archways, finely carved wooden screens, and enough potted palms to seed an oasis. The tile floor was laid over a rubber membrane so the ship's vibration wouldn't crack it.

Before he saw to his own needs, and inspired by the gun crew up on deck, he retrieved the Kel-Tec pistol from his overalls' pocket and set it on the blotter on his desk next to what looked like an old Bakelite phone but was actually part of the *Oregon*'s sophisticated communications array. Behind his desk was a gun safe. He opened the heavy door, ignoring the assortment of arms and the bundles of currency and gold coins stored within. Instead, he retrieved a gun-cleaning kit. He knew the little automatic's chamber was clear, but he jacked the slide several times, once he'd pulled out the empty magazine. After carefully scouring the barrel and chamber, he wiped all the parts with gun oil. He loaded fresh .380 ammunition into the magazine. He would have chambered a final round, but he wanted the armorers and Kevin Nixon down in the Magic Shop to give his artificial leg a going-over after its dunking, so he just put the pistol into his desk drawer.

An unchambered bullet wasn't a danger until someone touched the gun.

He fought his way out of the XXL-sized jumpsuit, pulled off the prosthetic leg, and hopped easily into his luxurious bathroom. It had a copper tub big enough for elephants to laze away an afternoon in, but it was rarely used. Instead, he got into the shower, adjusting the heat and the multiple heads until his body was being pummeled by tsunamis of water just a few degrees cooler than scalding.

He dressed casually in lightweight khakis and a rich purple polo shirt, his feet shod in soft leather moccasins without socks. Unlike his combat leg, the prosthesis he had on now was a virtual twin of his flesh-and-bone limb.

His cabin was the closest to the Op Center, the electronic nerve center of the freighter. It was from this room, as high-tech as the bridge of a science-fiction starship, that all the *Oregon*'s weapons, defensive systems, damage control, helm, and propulsion were controlled. The semicircular room, dominated by a massive flat-panel display and kept dimly lit, had a helmsman and fire-control officer sitting toward the front, with duty stations for communications, radar and sonar, and a dozen others ringing it. The watchkeeper sat at the middle of the space in a single chair with its own monitor and controls that could supersede all others. Mark and Eric had dubbed it the 'Kirk Chair' the first time they had seen it, which secretly pleased Cabrillo since that had been his inspiration when he'd designed the space.

Eddie Seng had the conn but leapt to his feet when Juan entered the Op Center.

'As you were, Mr Seng.' On the split screen were feeds from multiple cameras mounted at strategic locations around the ship. 'Anything to report?'

'We're all alone out here, so I've got her humming along at forty knots.'

'Any word from young Mr Lawless?'

'He's still in Kabul but will make our pickup in Bangladesh.'

'Get word to him that he'll be choppering out to the ship with another passenger, and that discretion is the better part of valor. A loose lip could sink this ship, and all that.'

'Who's the other passenger?' Eddie asked.

'A corporate minder named John Smith,' Juan said.

'Ex-Legionnaire. He's Croissard's muscle, and Croissard's insisting that he come with us.'

'And I take it by your tone you're none too happy about it.'

'Truer words have never been spoken, but we don't have much choice in the matter.' Cabrillo didn't like variables he couldn't control, and Smith was definitely one of them.

MacD Lawless was another. He wasn't sure if this would be the right first mission for him, not with Smith along and Lawless's abilities still unevaluated. He'd have to think it over further. By now his research team of Mark Murphy and Eric Stone should have all the details of the man's military career and the circumstances of his capture in Afghanistan. He'd read through it after dinner and then decide if Lawless would be on the mission with the Corporation rescuing Soleil Croissard.

The *Oregon*'s dining room had the hushed sophistication of an English gentlemen's club from a bygone era. It was all polished brass and dark woods. The furniture was heavy with subtly patterned fabrics, and the carpet was muted and plush. All that was missing were some stuffed animal heads on the wall and a couple old men smoking cigars and regaling each other with tales of safaris and imperial wars.

Juan caught a break from having to read Lawless's dossier because Murph and Stony were sitting at one of the tables.

Eric Stone was a Navy vet but hadn't been a fighting

143

sailor. Like Mark, who'd been with a Defense contractor before joining the Corporation, Stone was a technology guy. It was only after he'd come aboard that his innate sense of ship handling came to light. After Juan himself, Eric Stone was the best helmsman on the *Oregon*. Stone, a shy man by nature, retained a little of the deportment he'd learned in the Navy. He still tucked in his shirts, and his hair was always in place.

Mark, on the other hand, cultivated a nerd-chic vibe, though it seemed pretty heavy on the nerd and light on the chic. His dark hair looked like he dried it in a wind tunnel. He had tried, unsuccessfully, to grow a beard and had since given up, but his shaving schedule was erratic at best. Both men were of average height, though Eric was the slenderer of the two. Because he lived mostly on junk food and energy drinks, Mark had to spend time in the gym to keep from packing on the pounds.

Tonight he wore a T-shirt with a picture of a dachshund puppy lying asleep on a dinner plate with some potatoes and a serving of traditional German spätzle. Next to the plate was a half-full beer mug and eating utensils. Under the picture were the words 'Wienerdog schnitzel.'

'That's just wrong,' Juan said as he approached the table.

'I Photoshopped it myself,' Murph said proudly. 'I made another for chimi-chihuahuas.'

Cabrillo took a chair opposite. 'Are you eating canned ravioli?'

'You can't beat Chef Boyardee,' Mark replied, taking a spoonful.

'I sometimes wonder if you're twenty-eight or just eight.' Cabrillo plucked the crisp linen napkin from the table and draped it over his lap. A moment later a wedge salad with strawberry balsamic dressing was placed in front of him.

'I was actually thinking about a Caesar,' he said to the server without looking up.

'You'll eat the wedge,' said Maurice, the ship's impeccably dressed but irascible steward. He added as he walked away, 'You'll have the beef bourguignon too.'

He returned a moment later with a bottle of Dom Romane Conti, a rich French burgundy that would be the perfect accompaniment to the Chairman's meal. He poured with a flourished twist so as not to spill a drop. 'I had to drink two full glasses to be sure it hadn't turned to vinegar.'

Juan chuckled. Maurice's little tasting stunt cost the Corporation around eight hundred dollars. Times might be a little leaner than normal, but the retired Royal Navy valet wouldn't be denied 'a touch of the grape,' as he would put it.

Cabrillo turned to his dinner companions. 'You guys could save me from staring at my computer for the night by giving me the condensed version of what you've found out about MacD Lawless.'

'I see absolutely nothing wrong with staring at a computer all night,' Murph said, setting down a can of Red Bull.

'So, Lawless?'

'Linda used a contact left over from her days on the Joint Chiefs' staff and was able to pull his service record.' Eric's tone was now serious. 'Marion MacDougal Lawless was an excellent soldier. He's racked up a Good Conduct Medal, a Purple Heart, and a Bronze Star. These last two for the same engagement outside of Tikrit. After Iraq he qualified for the Rangers and aced the school at Fort Benning. He was then shipped to Afghanistan and saw some pretty heavy fighting up near the Pakistan border.

'He put in eight years and left the Army as an E7. He was immediately approached by Fortran Security Worldwide, offered a slot as a bodyguard back in Kabul, and, as far as we could tell from their records without triggering any computer alarms, he's been a model employee for the past year.'

'What about his capture. Anything on that?'

'Reports are still sketchy, but it appears to be the way he told you. The Pakistani camera crew he was hired to protect had come in from Islamabad, but there's no record of them ever working in Pakistan. The two Afghan security guys with him were legit. They were former Northern Alliance fighters who'd gotten additional training by our Army and then went freelance. The truck was never found, but an Army patrol reported seeing several large holes dug next to the road where Lawless says he was nabbed.'

'Big enough to hide a bunch of ambushers?' Juan asked, and Stone nodded.

Murph added, 'The whole thing sounds like an al-Qaeda setup to get an American on tape being hacked to pieces. They haven't produced one in a while.'

'The Tikrit incident,' Eric said, 'where he was wounded.'

'Yes?'

'I read parts of the after-action report that weren't redacted. Lawless went alone into a building and took out eleven insurgents who'd pinned his team and were turning them into mincemeat. He had a bullet in his thigh when he killed the last three. You want my opinion, he's the real deal.'

'Thanks, guys. Good job as usual. How are you coming along with getting maps of the Burmese jungle?'

'Hah,' Murph barked. 'There are none. Where that girl got herself lost is one of the remotest places on the planet. Other than the major rivers, no one knows what the hell's in there. For all the good they've done, the maps we've found should all be labeled "Beyond this point, there be dragons."'

Those turned out to be prophetic words.

8

'Sorry about the accommodations,' Cabrillo said, swinging open the door to one of the cabins in the *Oregon*'s superstructure. 'But with Smith aboard we have to keep up the appearance that this is all the old girl has to offer.'

MacD Lawless sniffed, made a face, then shrugged. 'Y'all said my bein' here was probational. I guess this is the price I pay.'

'When things quiet down, I'll personally give you a tour of the parts of the ship we can't let Smith know about. Oh, and he has the cabin next to yours. Keep your ears open. I'm sure he'll be in touch with Croissard, and these walls are paper-thin.' There were microphones in every room and cabin in this part of the ship, but Juan wanted MacD to feel like he was already doing something to earn his pay.

Lawless threw his duffel bag onto the cabin's single cot, where it sagged a good six inches into the near-springless mattress. The porthole was grimy, so the room was cast in shades of shadow and murk. The deck was covered in a mouse-brown carpet with such a thin nap that it could be mopped, and the walls were bare metal painted battleship gray. There was an adjoined private head with stainless steel fixtures like those seen in prisons and a medicine cabinet without a door.

'This place has the charm of an old Route 66 trailer court a decade after they closed the road,' Lawless said, 'but I've slept in worse.'

He and John Smith had just been heloed to the ship from Chittagong Airport, and the *Oregon* was already steaming east at sixteen knots, heading for the northern coastline of Myanmar.

'I noticed you're not limping,' Cabrillo said.

MacD slapped his leg and intentionally thickened the Big Easy lilt in his voice. 'Feelin' fine. A couple days' R and R, and Ah heal good. My chest still looks like a Rorschach test, but it doesn't hurt. You let Doc Hux check me out, and Ah'm sure – Can Ah ask you somethin'?'

'Fire away,' Juan invited.

'Why me? Ah mean, well, you know what Ah mean. You just know me one day and offer me a job.'

Cabrillo didn't need to think of a response. 'Two reasons. One was the way you handled yourself when we were in Pakistan. I know how you think and fight when the bullets start flying. That's something I can't get from just reading a résumé. The second is just a gut feeling. I was a NOC for the CIA. Do you know what that is?'

'Non-official cover. You went into foreign countries and spied on 'em without any embassy help.'

'Exactly. I recruited locals. It's one of those jobs where you learn to get a feel for people quickly or you end up dead. As you can plainly see I'm not dead, so I must have a pretty good sense about who I can and can't trust.'

Lawless held out his hand. 'Thank you,' he said simply, but the words were loaded with meaning.

'Thank you. We're holding a briefing after chow in the mess hall, one deck down on the starboard side. Follow your nose. Dinner's at six.'

'Black tie,' MacD quipped.

'Optional,' Cabrillo called over his shoulder.

The kitchen off the mess hall was still filthy, but it didn't matter since the food was being prepared in the main galley and delivered via a dumbwaiter. Juan had reminded the chefs not to display too much of their culinary skill so that John Smith wouldn't suspect any of his surroundings. It wouldn't do for a five-star meal to come out of a two-roach kitchen.

Crew members, dressed like engineers, deckhands, and a couple of officers filled the spartan room but gave Cabrillo a table for himself, Lawless, Smith, Max Hanley, and Linda Ross. Linda was going to be the fourth on this mission. She was more than capable of handling herself, and she spoke some Thai, which might come in handy.

Smith was dressed in jeans and a T-shirt with matte-black combat boots on his feet. His disposition was little improved from the first meeting in Singapore. His dark eyes remained hooded and were in constant motion, scanning each face at the table and occasionally sweeping the room. When they'd entered prior to a meal of baked lasagna and richly buttered garlic toast, Cabrillo had allowed Smith to choose his own seat at the round table. Not surprisingly, he took one so his back was to a wall.

When he was told that Linda Ross would be joining the team searching for Soleil Croissard, a small, contemptuous sneer played at the corners of his mouth before his expression returned to a blank mask.

'As you wish, Mr Cabrillo.'

'Juan will be fine.'

'Tell me, Mr Smith,' Linda said, 'your name is English, but your accent is something else.'

'It is the name I chose when I joined the Legion. As I recall, there were about eight of us in my basic training class.'

'And where are you from?' she persisted.

'That is a question you never ask a Legionnaire. In fact, you never ask about his past at all.' He sipped from his glass of ice water.

Max asked, 'You're sure that Soleil hasn't tried to contact her father since that last communication just before we met?'

'Correct. He's tried her phone numerous times, but there is no answer.'

'So our starting point,' Juan said, 'will be the GPS coordinates we got off that last call.'

'I noticed there is something next to the helicopter, covered with a tarp. A boat, I assume?'

'Yes,' Cabrillo replied to Smith's question. 'Even stripped as she is, our chopper doesn't have the range to reach Soleil's last known location. We'll use it to airlift a boat into the country and track her from the water.'

'A good plan, I think,' Smith admitted. 'By boat is about the only way one can travel in the jungle. I recall my training days in French Guiana. The Legion guards the European Space Agency's launching facility there. They would drop us into the jungle with a canteen and a machete and then time how long it took us to get back to base. It was so thick, the best of us averaged a mile a day.'

'We've all been there,' MacD Lawless said. 'I'd match the Georgia swamps to any jungle in South America.'

'Ranger?' Smith asked, recognizing that the Ranger training school was at Fort Benning, Georgia.

'Yup.'

'And you, Miss Ross, what is your background?'

Linda threw him a cocky grin that told him she could give as well as take. 'You never ask a lady about her past.'

Smith actually smiled. '*Touché.*'

Juan unrolled a map he'd brought to the mess and anchored the corners with a coffee cup and a plate laden with what remained of a blueberry cobbler that he was relieved Smith hadn't tried because it was about the best he'd ever tasted.

'Okay, we're going to bring the *Tyson Hondo* in here.' He pointed to a spot just off Bangladesh's southern coast. *Tyson Hondo* was the name currently painted across the *Oregon*'s fantail, and it was what they'd been calling her since Smith came aboard. 'There's nothing much out there. Just a few fishing villages and nomadic clans who live aboard their boats. I wish we could fly at night, but lowering the boat onto this river here' – he pointed to a spot about a hundred miles inland, well across the border with Myanmar – 'is just too dangerous in the dark. There are no military bases that far north, so we don't really need to worry about being spotted, but we'll fly nap-of-the-earth the whole way in.'

'Is your pilot qualified?'

'We grabbed him away from the 160th SOAR,' Juan replied, referring to the U.S. Army's elite Special Operations Aviation Regiment.

'So he's qualified.'

'More than. From there, we'll motor upstream. These maps are terrible, but as near as we can tell the river will take us to within a couple of miles from where Soleil and her companion were last heard from. Now, as you can see from these two plotted positions, she hadn't wandered too far from when she'd made her last scheduled check-in with her father.'

'Is that significant?' Smith asked.

'Don't know,' Cabrillo replied. 'Maybe. It all depends on what's in that particular patch of jungle. In her last call, she said she was close to something but that someone else was even closer.'

'If I may venture a guess,' Linda said, and continued when the men were looking at her. 'From what I've read about her, Soleil Croissard is a daredevil, but she really doesn't publicize her adventures. She's not into seeing her name splashed across the tabloids. She just sets herself insane goals and then checks them off her list when she's done. Car racing, check. World's tallest mountains, check. Scuba dive with great whites, check. My guess is that whatever she's looking for isn't something she's going to tell the world about. She's after something for herself.'

'It would be a hell of a feat to cross Burma on foot,' Max said. 'It's not just the terrain, but you've got opium smugglers, and one of the most repressive governments in the world that would like nothing more than to capture her for a show trial.'

'Could it be that simple?' Juan asked Smith.

'I do not know. She never told Monsieur Croissard why she was doing this.'

'If that were the case,' MacD said, 'why hasn't she moved more than ten miles in almost two weeks?' To that, there was no answer. 'What if she sees herself as a real-life Lara Croft? Are there any ancient temples or anything in that jungle?'

'Possibly,' Juan said. 'The Khmer empire stretched pretty far. There might have been other significant civilizations before or since. I really don't know this history as well as I should.'

'I do not see what it matters why she is there,' Smith interjected. 'Getting her out should be our only interest.'

Cabrillo could see that Smith had a follower's mindset. He took orders, executed them, and moved on without giving them the slightest thought. It showed that he lacked imagination, unlike MacD Lawless, who could see the benefits of understanding Soleil

Croissard's motivations. Why she was there was an important factor in how they would get her out.

What if she'd gone in to make a major opium buy? Cabrillo doubted that was the case, but if it were true, it would alter how he would want to approach the situation. Dope peddlers don't like being interrupted in the middle of a deal. What if she'd gone to meet some escaped human rights activist who had an entire army chasing after him? Speculating about her presence there now might save lives later.

He didn't expect someone like Smith to understand that. He recalled his first impression at the Sands resort in Singapore. The guy was just hired muscle, a thug who Croissard had polished up a little so he fit into decent society and could do the financier's dirty work.

'Since time is of the essence,' Juan said with a nod in Smith's direction, 'we'll let that rest for now. Since none of us could pass as a native, there's no sense trying to blend in in terms of the weapons we bring. John, what's your preference?'

'MP5 and a Glock 19.'

'Okay. Tomorrow morning at oh-eight-hundred, I'll meet you at the fantail with one of each. You can test them as much as you'd like. MacD, do you want the Barrett REC7 like we had in Afghanistan?' Cabrillo asked it in such a way as to make Smith think Lawless had been with the Corporation for a while.

'Saved our butts quite well, as I recall. And a Beretta 92, just like the one Uncle Sam gave me.'

'Linda?' Juan asked to make this sound like normal operating procedure. 'So I can tell the armorer.'

'REC7, and I'll take a Beretta too. Uncle Sam showed me how to use one, but he never gave it to me.'

'Truth be told,' MacD said mischievously, 'Ah kinda stol'd mine.'

Smith must have sensed the meeting was winding down. He cleared his throat. 'I myself am not a parent,' he said, 'so I do not know the anguish Monsieur Croissard must be suffering right now. Young Lawless here told me on the chopper ride out to the ship that he has a daughter back in the States. Perhaps he can imagine what my boss is suffering.'

He looked pointedly at MacD. Lawless nodded. 'If anything were to happen to my little girl, Ah would hunt down and butcher the person who did it.' The mere thought of his daughter being hurt brought a flush to his face and real anger into his voice.

'I can see that. And that is exactly what Monsieur Croissard expects of us. If, God forbid, something has befallen Soleil, we must be prepared to exact his revenge.'

'That isn't exactly what we signed up for,' Cabrillo said, not liking the direction the conversation was going.

Smith reached into his back pocket for his wallet and withdrew a piece of paper. He unfolded it and laid it on the table. It was a bank draft for five million dollars. 'He has given me sole discretion to give this to you if I feel it warranted. Fair enough?'

Cabrillo met his steady gaze. For a moment electricity seemed to arc between the two. All the others at the table could feel it. Ten seconds went by, fifteen. If this had been the Old West, the room would have cleared in anticipation of a gunfight. Twenty seconds.

The ex-Legionnaire glanced down and picked up the bank check. He'd blinked.

'Let us hope it doesn't come down to that, eh?'

'Let's,' Juan replied, and leaned back to throw an arm over the back of his chair in a studied relaxed pose.

The following morning Smith met Cabrillo at the fantail as they had arranged. This morning both men wore camouflage fatigue pants and plain khaki T-shirts. A folding card table had been set up next to the rust-caked railing and on it were the weapons Smith had requested and extra magazines as well as several boxes of 9mm ammunition, since both pistol and submachine gun used the same. There were also two sets of earphones and several blocks of yellow-dyed ice in a cooler under the table.

The big MD 520N helicopter sat squarely on the rearmost hatch cover, its blades folded flat and covers installed over its jet intake and exhaust. Usually the chopper was lowered into the hull on a hydraulic lift, but, as with everything else Juan had done since Smith came aboard, he didn't want to tip his hand about his ship and her true capabilities.

The gray tarp had been removed from over the RHIB that was resting on the second aft-deck cargo hatch. Two crew members were giving the lightened craft a final inspection.

'Sleep well?' Juan greeted. He thrust out a hand to show there were no hard feelings over last night's little staring contest.

'Yes, fine. Thank you. I must say, your galley produces delicious coffee.'

'That's the one thing this outfit doesn't skimp on. I'd have a mutiny on my hands if we served anything other than Kona.' There was no sense in being petty and feeding Smith swill.

'Yes, I've noticed other places where you are not so, ah, generous.' He wiped a finger along the rail, and the tip came back stained red.

'She may not be much to look at, but the old *Tyson Hondo* gets us where we need to go.'

'Odd name. Is there a story behind it?'

'That's what she was called when we bought her, and no one felt any great urge to change it.'

Smith nodded to the pristine weapons. 'I see another area where you do not pinch pennies.'

Cabrillo played up the mercenary bit a little. 'A carpenter's judged by how he treats his tools. These are what we use to ply our trade, so I insist on nothing but the best.'

Smith picked up the Glock, hefted it for a moment, and then checked that the chamber was empty. He stripped it down, eyeing each component critically before putting it all back together. He did the same with the Heckler & Koch MP5. 'These seem adequate.'

Juan handed Smith a pair of ear protectors while he slipped on his own set. He then reached under the table for one of the yellow ice chunks and heaved it as far over the rail as he could. It hit with a splash and vanished for a second before bobbing back to the surface.

Smith jammed home a magazine in the H&K and cocked the stubby little weapon. He flicked off the safety, selected single-shot, and brought it to his shoulder. He fired, paused, and fired three more times in rapid succession. All four shots hit the ice, which at the speed the ship was carving though the water was nearly a hundred yards off the port quarter by the time the last bullet struck. Smith waited for the ice to drift a little farther astern, letting it get right to the machine pistol's maximum effective range, and fired twice more. The first bullet missed and kicked up a tiny fountain of water. The second hit the chewed-up ice dead center and split it into two pieces.

'Nice shooting,' Juan called. 'Another?'

'Please.'

Cabrillo threw a second chunk of ice overboard. This time, Smith fired three-round bursts that sent ice particles flying. The block literally disintegrated. They repeated the drill with the pistol. Smith fired off the entire clip with the precision pacing of a metronome. Every shot was a hit.

'Satisfied, or do you want to keep going?' Cabrillo had to acknowledge that Smith knew his business.

'I have to confess I haven't had much practice lately on automatic weapons. The Swiss authorities frown on their ownership. So I would like to continue firing the MP5.'

'No problem.'

They kept at it for another twenty minutes. Juan would load magazines while Smith destroyed chunks of ice. By the end he was hitting with every pull of the trigger no matter how far his target had floated away.

Max's voice suddenly blared over the loudspeaker mounted under the second-level catwalk that ringed the superstructure. 'Cease fire, cease fire. Radar has a contact five miles out.'

'Wouldn't do for them to hear us,' Juan said, and took the machine pistol from Smith's hands. He pulled out the magazine and ejected the cartridge that was already in the chamber. 'The ammo stays with me, the guns go with you. Security precaution. No offense intended. I'll have someone drop off a cleaning kit at your cabin. We eat lunch at noon and take off at one. Is there anything else you need?'

'I have my satellite phone, but what about tactical communications?'

'You'll be issued a radio.'

'Then I'm good.'

'Yeah,' Juan said, 'I think you are.'

Smith took the compliment with a little nod of the head.

9

With the doors pulled off and all the soundproofing bats removed, the interior of the chopper was as loud as an iron foundry during a pour. And that was just with the turbine at idle. Only Gomez Adams had a proper chair. All the others had been removed to save weight. This left Linda, MacD, and Smith strapped directly to the rear bulkhead with tie-downs intended for cargo. Juan sat next to the pilot on a jerry-rigged folding lawn chair that had been screwed to the deck.

Between the passengers was a mound of personal gear, including food, weapons, ammunition, a GPS tracker, and tactical headsets for the combat radios. Along with Smith's sat phone, Cabrillo and Linda had phones of their own.

Juan had never considered stowing their gear in the boat on the off chance something happened to it on the flight in. The only provisions he would allow to go with the RHIB were twenty gallons of drinking water. With the tropical heat and soaring humidity, he figured each of them would drink nearly a gallon per day.

Gomez finished the preflight warm-up and asked, 'Everybody ready?' His voice was muted through the headphones everyone was wearing.

He didn't wait for a response before putting on more

throttle. Rotor wash whipped through the chopper like a gale-force wind. The headphones kept Linda's baseball cap in place, but her bunched and rubber-banded hair danced like the tail of an agitated cat.

The noise and wind built to a crescendo that rattled the helicopter within what seemed like an inch of its life. And then the ride smoothed as it lifted gingerly off the deck. The *Oregon* was at a dead stop, and there was no crosswind, so Gomez easily kept the craft centered over the large *H* painted on the cargo hatch. Ahead of them a loadmaster was watching the steel cable trailing up to the aircraft's winch. As the chopper rose higher into the air, more and more cable was taken up until it went taut. The whole time, Gomez had inched the chopper forward so that at the exact instant the line started taking the load he was directly over the rigid-hulled inflatable.

As delicately as a surgeon, he lifted the boat off its cradle. They were at the very limit of what the helo could take, and for a moment Adams paused, as if to let the chopper get used to the great weight hanging from its belly. And just as quickly he heaved it farther off the deck and sent the helicopter crabbing sideways, plucking the boat from between the stern derricks. As soon as they had cleared the rail, Adams applied even more power, and they started eastward to where the jungle crouched just over the horizon.

'How's it feel?' Juan asked the pilot.

'Like we've got a two-thousand-pound pendulum swinging free under us. That boat might be pretty sleek in the water, but it's got the in-flight aerodynamics of a barn door. I hope you aren't expecting to chopper it back to the ship when you're done.'

'I'd like to, if we can,' Juan told him. 'I recall, though, that our contract does mention being reimbursed for expenses.'

'Good. Write the damned thing off. The strain we're putting on the airframe and rotors ain't worth bringing it home.'

Cabrillo laughed. Complaining was Adams's way of dissipating stress. Max Hanley was the same way. Juan felt humor helped him a little, but the truth was that before a mission he liked to keep that stress bottled up inside. It was like the coiling of a watch spring; it was energy he would release later as he needed it. The more dangerous the situation, the tighter, and thus more explosive, he became. Right now, and until they crossed the border into Myanmar, he was truly relaxed. After that, he knew the tension would mount. Like always, he hoped he wouldn't need to let it out, at least not until he was back aboard the ship soaking in a hot shower after a hundred or so laps in the *Oregon*'s indoor swimming pool.

Because the chopper was so grossly overloaded, Adams kept the speed down to around sixty knots, but it seemed only a couple of minutes passed before they thundered over a white sand beach at just enough elevation for the bottom of the RHIB to clear the mangrove swamp beyond. That was it, a thin pale strip of sand delineating a world of blue water from an equally monochromatic world of green jungle.

It seemed to stretch forever, rolling and undulating with the vagaries of the topography, but always covering every square inch of the ground below them. They were still in Bangladesh, but Juan knew the jungle stretched uninterrupted all the way to the coast of Vietnam and that it really was *terra incognita* – land unknown. Neil Armstrong once described the surface of the moon as 'magnificent desolation.' This was the same, only this landscape was verdant yet nearly as hostile to human life.

They were so overloaded the chopper was barely able to keep the dangling boat from smashing into the taller trees. Gomez Adams wasn't so much flying the aircraft as he was fighting to keep it airborne and on course. His snarky comments had long since dried up. The sweat that shone on his face was only partially due to the high humidity.

Cabrillo plucked a handheld GPS from a pouch hanging from his combat harness. In a moment it told him that they were about to cross into Myanmar's airspace. He didn't bother announcing it to the others. But he kept a sharp eye on the jungle below for any sign the frontier was protected.

They had planned their route in to avoid rivers or major streams because any settlements in this remote part of the country would be built along their banks. There were no roads, and for as far as Cabrillo could see there were no signs that loggers had been attacking the jungle. Judging from the view alone, it was as if the human race had never existed.

The ground below started rising, and Adams matched the earth's contours. Below them their shadow leapt and jumped across the canopy. It was not as crisp as it had been earlier because clouds were moving in from the north. Behind the grayness loomed ominous black thunderheads that towered into the sky. They flickered with lightning.

'I'd say you're in for a spot of weather,' Gomez said, his first words since making landfall.

'Of course we are,' Cabrillo replied. 'If it wasn't for bad luck, I'd have no luck at all.'

They continued on for another hour and were now deep into Myanmar. Adams had flown masterfully, and, just as they had planned, they crossed over a hillock and there was the target, the river, a narrow slash through the jungle with trees almost meeting overtop. The pilot checked his fuel gauge and did some quick calculations.

'Sorry, but this is as far as I go. As it stands, I need the ship to come east to meet me if I'm going to make it back.'

'Roger that.' Cabrillo twisted in his makeshift seat so he could look at the trio in the cargo area. 'Did you hear that? We need to do this quick. Linda, you've got point, then MacD and you, John. I'll be right behind. Linda, make sure you wait to unhook the boat.'

'You got it,' she replied, and kicked a rappelling rope out the hole where a door had once been.

Adams maneuvered the big chopper into a hover directly over the fifty-foot-wide river. The tops of the trees danced and swayed in the rotor wash as he threaded the RHIB through them on its way to the water below. Such was his skill that the boat barely made a splash as it hit. And no sooner was it in place than Linda Ross threw herself down the rope. She dangled precariously for a moment, then arced her body over the RHIB's inflatable skirt and landed on her feet on the deck. MacD Lawless was halfway down and dropping fast. Linda positioned herself to release the winch hook and waved up at Adams, who was watching the procedure through the Plexiglas windows at his feet.

'See you later,' Juan said to the pilot as he unstrapped himself for his turn down the line.

Before following the others, Juan clipped a D ring from the bundled packs to the line and looked down at the three people in the boat. All were looking up at him. Linda made a gesture to indicate they were ready, so Juan pushed the packs out. They hit the deck hard, but there was nothing in them that could break. Juan slung his carbine over his shoulder and threw himself down the rope, his hands protected by special gloves with leather palms and fingers. He arrested his fall an inch from the boat before letting go. No sooner had his boots hit than Linda released the winch, and Gomez Adams torqued the chopper up and away, heading back to the ship, and flying even closer to the ground now that he didn't have to worry about the RHIB.

After so much time in the helicopter, it took several minutes for the ringing in their ears to subside.

They were on a deserted stretch of the river, which

at this point flowed at a snail's pace. The banks were about a foot above the water, composed of reddish soil that crumbled in places. Immediately behind the banks exploded a riot of vegetation that was so dense it appeared impenetrable. Cabrillo stared at a spot as hard as he could and estimated he could only penetrate maybe five feet before his view was completely blocked. For all he knew, a division of Myanmar's Special Forces was lurking six feet in.

The temperature hovered around ninety degrees, but the lack of wind and the thickness of the moisture in the air made it feel like they were breathing in a sauna. In moments, perspiration stains bloomed under Cabrillo's arms, and sweat trickled down his face. The coming rainstorm would be a welcome relief that couldn't get there fast enough.

'Okay, we've got about sixty miles to cover. I want MacD and John on the bows as lookouts. Linda, you're with me, but keep an eye on our six. The guys back on the ship beefed up the outboard's exhaust, but anyone upstream will still hear us coming, so stay sharp.'

With that, Juan took his place at the control console slightly aft of amidships. Other than the ring of rubber fenders that encircled the boat, it was the only thing that stuck up above the deck of the spartan assault boat.

'Gear all secured?' he asked.

'Yup,' Linda said, straightening from where she'd bungeed the packs to a flip-up pad eye.

Cabrillo pressed the starter, and the engine immediately rumbled to life, as he knew it would. He let the single outboard warm for a moment and then bumped the throttle. The boat fought the river's current until they were holding still relative to the banks. He pressed the accelerator harder. Water boiled behind the transom as the prop bit into the black tannin-laced river. In seconds he had them up to about fifteen miles per hour, far below the boat's capability even with one of its engines removed, but a speed he judged would allow them plenty of reaction time if someone was coming downstream.

The wind created by their forward progress was a blessed relief.

When they neared a sharp bend in the river, Cabrillo would throttle the boat down so it was barely making headway and peek it around the corner to make sure there was nothing lurking in their blind spot.

After a half hour, two things happened almost simultaneously. The nature of the river changed. The banks drew in closer, which sped up the current, and boulders appeared, creating eddies and pools that Cabrillo had to steer around. These weren't exactly rapids, but they quickly could become so. The second thing was that, after a brutal spike in humidity that seemed to soak their lungs with each breath, the rain clouds, which had arrived overhead and washed all color from the jungle, opened. It was a constant drumming rain that hit like fists. It came down in sheets, it came down in buckets, it came down as if they were being blasted by fire hoses.

Juan fumbled a pair of clear goggles from the tiny compartment under the wheel and slipped them over his eyes. Without them, he couldn't see the bow of the boat. With them, his vision wasn't extended too much farther, but enough for them to keep going.

He gave thanks that tropical downpours, while brutal onslaughts to the senses, were blessedly brief. Or so he kept telling himself as ten minutes turned into twenty, and their speed barely made headway against the still-strengthening current.

The three others hunched miserably at their stations, looking like drowned rats. When he glanced down at Linda, who had her back against the rubber fender, she was hugging herself, and her lips were quivering. MacD was making a halfhearted attempt to bail out the RHIB using his boonie hat. A solid inch of water sloshed back and forth whenever Cabrillo steered them around an obstacle.

The riverbanks rose higher still, hemming them in, oftentimes looming over the boat. Loose soil had given way to gravel and rock. The once-tranquil river was becoming a torrent, and as much as Cabrillo thought it might be a good idea to pull over and wait out the storm, there were no sheltered coves, no places to tie off a line. They had no choice but to forge ahead.

Visibility was measured in inches, while overhead thunder cracked an instant after the lightning snaked across the heavens.

But he kept them driving onward. Every time the boat hit an obstruction, or the stern sank deep as they powered over a cataract, he was grateful that the single propeller had a shroud to protect the blades.

Otherwise the prop would have chewed itself apart on the rocks.

It took a keen eye to notice when the water suddenly turned muddy brown, and an even sharper mind to understand what it meant.

Cabrillo reacted instantly. He turned the boat sharp right to get out of the center of the raging river just as the rubble of a collapsed bank farther upstream choked the waterway with debris. Whole trees arrowed down the river, their branches reaching out for the RHIB, each easily capable of capsizing the craft or at the least tearing away the rubber fenders that acted as the boat's gunwales. Had Juan not twisted the wheel, they would have been sunk for sure.

Trunks as big around as telephone poles hurtled past, their root-balls exposed. Erosion was eating away at the soil that had been ripped from the ground when the trees tumbled into the river. At one point Juan had to slew the boat around the drowned body of a water buffalo, its horns coming close enough to brush the boat's flank before the current carried the pitiable creature away.

Some objects were too low in the water for Cabrillo to see, so he maneuvered the boat by listening to MacD's shouted warnings. They were forced to cut left and right as the river continued to throw flotsam at them. Juan had reduced power as much as he dared, but still trees and shrubs flew past at dizzying speeds, while the sky continued to rage overhead.

If anything, the storm was intensifying. Along the

banks of the river, trees were bent nearly horizontal by the wind, and leaves the size of movie posters were stripped off and tossed through the air. One whipped across Cabrillo's face and would have gouged out an eye if he hadn't been wearing the goggles.

If there was a bright side to this, he thought fatalistically, the chances were nil that anyone else would be crazy enough to be on the river with them.

The last of the trees schussed down the river, and the water regained its black-tea color, and all at once the rain stopped. It was as if a tap had been turned off. One second, they were enduring the worst torrent any of them had ever experienced, and, the next, the water that had been pummeling them for so long was gone. Moments later the dark storm clouds cleared away from the sun, and it beat down on them with a mocking cheeriness. The humidity spiked. Steam rose from the forest, creating a fog that was at first eerie and spectral but quickly grew to an impenetrable haze.

'Is everyone all right?' Cabrillo asked. He received nods from three dripping heads. From the storage cabinet under the steering console he grabbed a hand pump and tossed it to Smith. 'Sorry, but the mechanical pump was removed to lighten the boat.'

The craft wallowed under the hundreds of pounds of water that sloshed across the deck and filled its bilge. MacD continued to bail with his hat, and Linda made do with her hands, dumping palmful after palmful over the gunwales. The pump was by far the most efficient means of clearing the craft, but its stream seemed insignificant when compared to the volume of rain the boat had taken on.

Twenty laborious minutes later the craft still wasn't empty, but they had come upon an obstacle that looked like it had doomed the trip before they had really gotten started.

A three-foot-high waterfall spanned the width of the river, its flow a glossy black over the rock. The banks here were high sloping hills of loose gravel and till.

'How far have we come?' Linda asked, her clothes not yet dry.

'We have at least another sixty miles to go,' Juan said without looking at her. He was studying the riverbank behind the RHIB.

'I guess we have to start hoofing it,' MacD said with the eagerness of a prisoner heading for the gallows.

'Not so fast. Linda, did you bring explosives?'

'About two pounds of plastique and some timer pencils. A girl has to be prepared.'

'Excellent. MacD, I want you to reconnoiter at least two miles upstream. Make sure there aren't any villages within earshot. John, sorry, but you get to keep bailing. We need to get the draft as shallow as possible.'

'*Oui,*' the taciturn man said, and just kept pumping the handle back and forth, shooting a thin jet of water over the side with each stroke.

MacD grabbed up his REC7, shook water from the receiver, and leapt over the side of the boat. He waded to the right bank, climbed up, using his free hand for purchase on the shifting mound of gravel, and disappeared over the crest at a jog.

'You're not thinking—' Linda began.

'Oh, but I am,' Cabrillo said.

He had her rummage through her gear for the explosives while he fashioned a shovel out of a carbon fiber oar. They jumped from the boat, Cabrillo with a line in his hand to tie off around a piece of beached driftwood. The bank was steepest about thirty yards behind the RHIB, so they slogged their way there, loose rock sliding and hissing wherever they stepped.

Cabrillo eyed the hill, which rose a good fifty feet above the river even as flooded as it was. He had one shot to get this right or they were looking at a days-long march through the jungle. They were already so far behind Soleil Croissard that her trail was ice cold, and getting colder by the minute.

Satisfied with his decision, he dropped to his knees and started digging. For every awkward shovelful of pebbles he pulled from the hole, half as much tumbled back in. It was frustrating work, and soon his breathing was labored because of the soggy and molten air. He finally reached a depth of about three feet, then moved down the hillside about eight feet and repeated the process, while Linda separated her explosives into five equal measures.

It took nearly thirty minutes to complete the holes. Cabrillo's pores were like faucets, and he'd drunk nearly a quarter of the camelback water harness he'd had Linda fetch from the boat. He was just getting back to his feet when he sensed movement behind him. He whirled, drawing a pistol in the same motion so that when he completed his turn he had a bead on the man who emerged from the scrub.

He lowered the weapon the instant he recognized MacD Lawless. If anything, the native Louisianan was breathing even heavier than the Chairman.

Juan looked at his watch as Lawless stepped gingerly down the bank.

'Two miles?' he queried.

'I can keep a seven-minute-mile pace for five miles,' Lawless said, blowing like a stallion after the Kentucky Derby. 'That slows to ten minutes with a full pack.'

Juan was impressed with both Lawless's stamina and the fact that he knew his body's capabilities and limitations. Information like that could one day save an operator's life.

'Anything up ahead?'

'Just jungle. The good news is, it looks like the worst of the rapids are behind us.' He sucked at the water tube from Cabrillo's camelback and used a dingy tan bandanna to wipe his face. 'Man, it's thicker out there than the swamps of Lafourche Parish.'

'Get back aboard. We'll be ready in a minute.'

The Corporation used digital devices rather than chemical timers to set off the explosives. These had an accuracy unmatched by their older brethren and would allow Cabrillo split-second timing. He set the timers and quickly laid the explosive in each hole, frantically shoveling dirt back in to cover the plastique.

He was back aboard the idling RHIB, painter line in hand, with about two minutes to spare. He edged the boat closer to the waterfall to put as much distance as possible between them and the blast. Everyone lay flat on the deck, not even peering over the gunwale because of the debris that would be blown from the beach.

The blasts went off in a sequence that was so tightly controlled, it sounded like one long, continuous explosion. Rock and debris erupted from the earth in fountains of flaming gas that echoed across the river and sent hundreds of birds into startled flight. Seconds later, pebbles peppered the RHIB, bouncing off the inflatable fenders or pinging against the plastic deck. One fist-sized rock gave Smith a charley horse when it hit his thigh. He grunted once but said nothing more.

Before the dust had fully settled, Juan was on his feet, looking aft. The underpinnings of the riverbank had been excavated by the explosion, and, as he watched, the entire mass – nearly forty feet of it – slid ponderously into the river, bulling aside the water, before the leading edge smashed into the far shore with enough force to block the waterway entirely.

'*Voilà*,' Cabrillo said, obviously pleased with himself. 'Instant cofferdam.'

With its outlet cut off by the landslide, the water trapped between it and the falls began to rise. It was now a race to see if the river would erode the temporary dam before the level got high enough to force the boat up and over the falls.

'I've got another idea. Linda, take the helm. John, MacD, with me.'

Cabrillo grabbed up the boat's painter once again and used hand signals to get Linda to tuck the boat directly below the waterfall. It was barely higher than the RHIB's bow. The three men leapt atop the falls and found footing on a rock poking up from the water like a tiny island.

The area between the falls and the dam continued to fill. But, at the same time, the downstream current was eating at the cofferdam, exploiting any crack or flaw to tear it away. The RHIB's bow rose higher still until the front of the keel rested on the rock face of the falls. The men coiled the nylon line around their wrists in the most important game of tug-of-war they'd ever fought. Linda kept the engine revs up, forcing the craft higher and higher. Behind them, a trickle of water worked its way through the cofferdam, rejoining the river's normal flow. The breach was tiny, no more than a few seeping drops, but would expand exponentially.

To make matters worse, the lowest section of the dam, near the bank opposite to where Cabrillo had set off the explosions, was close to being overtopped by the rising water.

'We're going to have one shot at this,' Juan said, bunching the muscles in his arms and shoulders as they prepared to pull the boat over the falls. 'Linda, watch behind you and tell us when.'

Linda peered at the cofferdam and the riverbanks to make sure the water was still filling their man-made lagoon faster than the earthen dam was letting water pour through. She judged it finely. The water level reached its crest, with the falls being no more than a six-inch riffle, when the dam let go in a gush of mud and debris.

'Now!' she shouted, and firewalled the outboard.

The three men heaved back on the line, their bodies as taut as marble statues, the effort playing across each of their faces. The ten minutes it took to fill the basin was washed away in seconds. As the level dropped, more and more weight pressed the RHIB's keel into the rock and made the load on the men that much heavier.

The river sluiced out from under the outboard's prop so that it screamed as the blades met air. And still the men pulled, gaining fractions of inches with every strained heave.

Linda idled the engine and jumped out of the RHIB so that she was standing on the very lip of the falls, inky water rushing past her shins. But that last one hundred and eleven pounds of extra weight was all the men needed removed to do the trick. The boat slid over the rocky bottom and then hit deeper water and began to float. The current turned it sideways against the escarpment and gave it a bad list, but it was now too low in the water to be forced back over the falls.

MacD and John Smith both fell back into the river when the boat lurched forward. They came up sputtering, and laughing that they'd done it. Cabrillo had somehow kept his balance, and when Linda cut the boat across the current and brought it up to his little rock island, he stepped over the gunwale as casually as a commuter gets aboard a train.

In turn, Lawless and Smith hauled themselves out of the river and lay panting on the deck, big grins plastered on their faces.

'That wasn't so bad,' Juan remarked as he took his place behind the console.

'Like hell,' MacD said when he noticed he had leeches stuck to his arms. 'Oh God, there's nothin' Ah hate more than leeches.' He fished in his pocket for a disposable lighter.

'I wouldn't do that,' Linda warned as Lawless worked the little flint wheel to dry it out.

'That's how my daddy taught me.'

'Oh, the leech will drop off, but it will also regurgitate everything it ate. Which, a, is disgusting, and, b, might carry disease. Use your fingernail and scrape its mouth off of you.'

Following her advice, and making faces that a little girl might make, MacD got four of the bloodsuckers off his arms, and one off the back of his neck with Linda's help. Smith hadn't been attacked by the loathsome parasites.

'You must have sour blood, John,' Lawless teased, putting his shirt back on. With a tightened belt and drawstrings closed around his ankles, he wasn't worried about anything getting into his pants.

Smith didn't reply. He took up his station at the bows and prepared to act as lookout once again. MacD exchanged a look and a shrug with Linda and Cabrillo, and went to join Smith at the bow.

Because of the waterfall covering their rear, there was no need for Linda to keep watch for anyone overtaking them. And with riverine transportation the only way to negotiate the jungle, Cabrillo drove with the confidence that there wouldn't be any villages up ahead either. The people wouldn't have been able to get back upstream once they floated past the falls, and he had seen no indication of portage paths on either side of the cataract.

He kept up a good twenty-five-mile-an-hour pace and slowed only at the truly blind corners as the river meandered deeper into the jungle. Their speed finally dried everyone's clothes.

As the sun arced its way across the sky, the river remained as tranquil and easy to negotiate as a meandering canal. The rain forest was the other constant. It lined the waterway as densely as a garden hedgerow. Only occasionally would there be a gap, usually when a small stream fed into the main channel, or where the banks were especially gentle and animals coming down to drink had worn away game trails. One of the trails was particularly large. Juan suspected it might have been cleared by some of the country's estimated ten thousand wild elephants.

Lurking in that impenetrable wall of broad-leaved plants were Asian rhinos, tigers, leopards, and all manner of snakes including the biggest pythons in the world and the most deadly species of cobra, the king cobra. All in all, he thought, not exactly a good place to be lost.

It was nearing early evening when Juan cut the power so that the boat was barely making headway against the gentle current. The dramatic reduction in engine noise left their ears ringing for a moment.

'We're about ten miles from Soleil's last-known GPS coordinates. We'll stay with the motor for maybe another five and then we break out the oars. Everyone, keep sharp. We have no idea what we're going to find, but Soleil was convinced there was someone else in the jungle with her.'

Cabrillo's eyes never lingered on any one spot for more than a moment. He scanned the forest ahead and off to the sides, knowing that someone could be watching them with total impunity. If there were rebels, or drug dealers, or an army patrol out here, they wouldn't know until they had walked into the ambush. He had to resist the urge to glance over his shoulder. He knew Linda was watching their back, but he couldn't shake the sense that someone was watching him.

A bird screech high in a nearby tree squirted a healthy dose of adrenaline into his bloodstream. Linda gave a little gasp, and he saw MacD jump. Only Smith hadn't been startled. Juan was beginning to suspect the man had ice water running through his veins.

When they'd covered the allotted five miles, Juan cut the engine and lifted the outboard from the water so it wouldn't act as drag. With two rowers on each side of the RHIB, they started paddling. Smith had pumped most of the water out of the bilge, but it was still a big boat, and, no matter how mild the current, it was tough going.

In times like these they usually deployed a small electric motor that could power them along silently, but like so much other equipment it had been left back on the *Oregon* in order to save on weight.

People who have never rowed a boat together before usually go through several awkward minutes as they adjust to one another's timing. Not so here. Despite the fact that Smith and MacD were virtual strangers, all four set a tempo instinctively and worked the carbon fiber oars with the symmetry of the Harvard crew.

Every few minutes Juan would check his handheld GPS, and when he spotted a rare clearing ahead on the right bank, he knew they had reached the end of their time on the river. It was a natural trail into the jungle, and he suspected this was where Soleil and her companion – Cabrillo couldn't recall his name – had exited the water.

He steered them toward the small open glade, noting that a thin trickle of water was running through it. Beyond towered a riotous wall of vegetation. Soleil had last been heard from three miles from this spot.

They edged the boat into some reeds lining the tributary, pushing it as far into cover as possible. No sooner had they stopped than Smith had his machine pistol up high on his shoulder, scanning the area through its scope. There was nothing but the background din of insects and birds and the sound of the water burbling past the RHIB's transom.

It took just a few minutes to gather up their gear. All of them wore camelbacks for water and lightweight nylon rucks, weighing from twenty-five pounds for Linda to nearly forty for Cabrillo and the other two men.

With luck, they wouldn't need anything other than the water.

Cabrillo looked back at the RHIB to make sure it was well concealed. He walked a few paces from the others to check from a different angle and that's when he saw the face. It was watching him through hooded, unblinking eyes. It took him a breathless moment for his brain to comprehend what he was seeing. It was the head of a statue of Buddha that had toppled to the jungle floor just up from the river. Behind it, cloaked in creepers and vines, was a stone building much like the step pyramids at Angkor Wat in neighboring Cambodia, though nowhere near that massive scale.

The structure was maybe thirty feet tall, with the Buddha head once resting on the roof of the tallest tier. It all looked ageless, as if the complex had been here since time immemorial and the jungle grew up around it.

'I think we're at the right place,' he muttered.

'No kidding,' Linda said. 'Look.'

Juan tore his eyes away from the pyramid and glanced over to see that Linda had pulled aside a leafy branch to reveal two one-person plastic kayaks. The sleek craft were commercially available at outfitters all over the world. The pair were dark green in color, and were a logical choice for getting upstream because they could be carried around obstacles by the paddler.

'They must have carried them overland from Bangladesh,' Smith said.

Cabrillo shook his head. 'It's more likely they entered the river where it meets the sea. They must have chartered a boat in Chittagong to carry them on the first part of the trip. Soleil definitely had a destination in mind. She knew right where she was heading. Check that out.'

They all followed his pointed finger to where the last rays of the sun shone on the head so that for a brief few seconds the gray stone visage appeared gilded.

Linda's hand went to her mouth to stifle a cry of surprise. 'It's beautiful,' she said breathlessly.

'Ah guess we ain't in Lafourche Parish after all,' Lawless remarked.

Smith made no comment. He looked at the temple for just a second before tucking his machine pistol under his arm and glancing at Cabrillo with an expression that said gawking at antiquities wasn't on their agenda.

Juan didn't doubt Smith's loyalty to Roland Croissard, nor his desire to rescue his employer's daughter, but he thought the former Legionnaire needed to lighten up a bit and enjoy the surprises life sometimes throws at you. There were probably less than a handful of outsiders who'd ever seen the temple complex. Knowing that sent a charge through his system, and he wanted nothing more than to explore its mysteries.

But he also knew Smith was correct. They were on a mission, and studying archaeological treasures wasn't part of the deal. They could cover the remaining miles to their GPS target before the jungle became too dark to see. He did let Linda snap a few pictures and slide her cell phone camera back into its waterproof sleeve before giving the order to move out.

10

Juan had thought the easiest way to travel would be to keep to the little stream, but it was a muddy morass that sucked at their boots with each step. When he lifted his foot from the muck, thick clots of it clung all the way to his ankle, and every step seemed to accumulate more. After just a dozen paces he could barely lift his legs free of the ooze.

This forced them out of the streambed and into the bush.

Juan knew immediately what soldiers fighting in the barbwire-entangled trenches of World War I had gone through. The sharp leaves pulled and ripped at his clothing and opened shallow yet painful cuts on his arms and face. There was no trail to speak of. He had to battle his way through snarls of vines and shrubs with the finesse of a bull in a china shop.

MacD, who marched directly behind Cabrillo, tapped him on the shoulder and made a gesture to say that he should take point. Cabrillo silently bowed to him. Lawless stepped ahead of the Chairman, studied the wall of bushes facing them, and moved a few feet to the left, closer to where tree trunks were just barely visible. He started forward, moving his body like a contortionist. It looked awkward, but he more than tripled their pace, with each team member mimicking the moves of the person ahead. And where Cabrillo had sounded like a rhinoceros crashing through the bush, Lawless moved as silently as a snake.

Still, the going was slow, and thirty minutes later so little sunlight was filtering through the canopy, it was as if they were fifty feet underwater.

'We should stop for the night,' MacD said in a whisper. 'Ah can't see nothin'.'

'All right,' Juan had to agree. Looking upward, it was next to impossible to see any daylight at all. 'We'll start out again at first light.'

Everyone's first order of business was to get the flameless heating units from their MREs to start chemically warming their entrées. Next came laying out nylon sleeping pouches with built-in mosquito netting. Finding areas big enough to lie comfortably in the dense jungle was a chore unto itself, so the single machete MacD had been carrying was put to good use.

By the time their food was ready everyone had their pouches rolled out but still tightly sealed to keep the armada of insects, which had plagued them from the moment the RHIB had come to a stop, from joining them for the night. No one said a word the entire time. When the meal was over, Juan pointed at Smith, then at himself, then at MacD, and finally at Linda. This was the order for guard duty. He checked his watch, calculating in how many hours the sun would rise again, and held up two fingers. They nodded their understanding.

Cabrillo deliberately gave Smith the first watch

because he knew he himself could stay awake to make sure the Legionnaire did his job.

The night passed smoothly, if not exactly comfortably. A jungle at night contains an earsplitting symphony of bird and monkey cries, with a backup chorus of insects' incessant chirping. Juan's concerns about Smith were unfounded.

A clammy mist clung to the ground when they awoke, deadening the sounds of the forest and giving everything an eerie, otherworldly quality. They broke camp as silently as they made it, and within ten minutes of there being light enough to see they struck out again, MacD at point and Cabrillo in the drag position.

Mercifully, the jungle began to thin, and when MacD found a game path, they could move on at an almost-normal pace. Lawless paused every so often, to listen, for one, but also to check the trail for any signs that a human had used it recently. Given the amount of rain that fell on a daily basis, Cabrillo doubted he would find anything and was amazed when after a quick detour into the adjoining bush he came back holding a balled-up piece of silvered paper. A gum wrapper. He opened it and held it under Cabrillo's nose. He could still smell the mint.

'Our Miss Croissard,' he whispered, 'is no environmentalist, littering like this.'

Lawless pocketed the scrap while Juan checked the GPS. They had about a quarter mile to go.

Their pauses became longer and more frequent the closer they got, and everyone held their weapon at the ready, not knowing what to expect but prepared none-theless. It was a good sign that birds and tree-dwelling animals cavorted in the canopy. It was usually a sure sign that there was no one else around.

The forest suddenly opened up into a small glade of knee-high grass. They paused at the edge, like swimmers contemplating jumping into a pond, and surveyed the area. A gentle breeze made the stalks of grass sway and ripple, but otherwise nothing moved. Cabrillo judged that Soleil had made her final transmission from the right side of the open field near where the jungle started again.

Rather than cross the glade, they backtracked into the bush and approached the site from the side. When they were fifteen feet away from the GPS coordinates, Cabrillo spotted stuff on the ground at the very edge of the field. He realized immediately it was what remained of a camp. He spotted a dark green tent that had been slashed apart, its lightweight frame mangled beyond recognition. Stuffing from shredded sleeping bags looked like cotton balls. There were other items too – a small camping stove, plastic plates, articles of clothing, a hiker's walking stick.

'Looks like we are much too late,' Smith said in a low voice. 'Whoever attacked here is long gone.'

Cabrillo nodded.

He hadn't known what to expect they would find, but this confirmed his worst fears. All that remained was to find what the animals had left of the bodies. It was a grisly but necessary step to prove to Croissard that his daughter was truly dead.

'You and MacD watch the perimeter,' Juan said. 'Linda, you're with me.'

With the two men keeping guard, Linda and Cabrillo moved closer to the little encampment. As they did, they saw that the tent had been riddled with small-arms fire. The nylon was peppered with tiny holes whose edges were singed black by the heat of the bullets.

Linda hunkered down to pull open the collapsed tent fly, her arm reaching out to the zipper like it was on automatic pilot. Her expression was one that said she wanted to be anywhere but here and doing anything but this. Juan stood bent behind her

The viper had been resting in the cool shadow of the tent, just out of view. The vibrations of two large animals' hearts beating and their lungs breathing had woken it seconds earlier, so when it struck, it did so with the fury of the disturbed.

It moved so fast that high-speed cameras would be necessary to capture its strike. As its hood opened, and its needlelike teeth hyperextended from its mouth, drops of clear venom had already formed on their tips. It was one of the most powerful neurotoxins on the planet and worked by paralyzing the diaphragm and stopping the lungs. Without antivenom, death occurs about thirty minutes after the bite.

The lightning-quick snake aimed straight for Linda's forearm and was about three inches from clamping its jaws around her skin and sinking its teeth an inch into her flesh when Juan's hand snapped around its neck and used the awesome power of its uncoiling body to redirect the strike and hurl the serpent into the jungle.

The entire episode took a single second.

'What just happened?' Linda said. She hadn't seen a thing.

'Trust me,' Cabrillo said, a little breathlessly. 'You don't want to know.'

Linda shrugged and bent back over her task. There were more items inside the tent – food wrappers, a mess kit, more clothes – but there was no body, or even blood. Juan reached over Linda's shoulder, moving stuff around with his hands, concentrating on what he wasn't seeing more than on what he was. He cast around in the grass, eventually finding Soleil's satellite phone, or what was left of it. A bullet had passed clean through the sleek high-tech device. He also found a bunch of spent shell casings. 7.62mm. They were doubtlessly fired from AK-47s, the old Soviet Union's legacy to the world of violence.

He called softly for Lawless and Smith.

'They're not here,' he informed them. 'I think they were ambushed but managed to slip into the jungle. The attackers swept through the camp, took what they wanted – food, apparently, since we didn't find any – and then went off in pursuit.'

Smith's expression didn't change except for a little tightening at the corners of his eyes.

The guy really was made of stone, Juan thought.

'MacD, think you can track them?'

'Give me a sec.' He ambled over to the edge of the

192

jungle closest to the ruined camp. He dropped to a knee, studying the ground, and then examined the branches of the nearest shrubs. He took almost five full minutes before waving the others to him. Cabrillo had used that time to call the *Oregon* and give Max Hanley an update. In return, Max had told him that everything was quiet on their end.

'See here?' MacD pointed to a broken branch. The pulpy wound had turned ashen. 'This here looks like sumac to me. This level of discoloration means the branch was snapped a week ago, maybe ten days.'

'So, you can track them?' Smith prodded.

'Ah sure will try, but no guarantees.' He looked at Juan. 'Did y'all find any shoes or boots?'

'No.'

Lawless put himself into the minds of two terrified people running for their lives. They would go in as straight a path as possible. They hadn't found shoes, which meant they weren't asleep when the attackers struck, meaning it had probably still been daylight, or dusk. Yes, they would run in a straight line since the pursuers would be able to see if they veered left or right.

He entered the jungle, confident that the rest of his team would keep him covered so he could concentrate on the hunt. Twenty yards in he found a red fiber that had been snagged by a thornbush and knew he was on the right path.

And so it went. At times, there were plenty of signs that a group of people had passed through the forest.

At others, they'd go a quarter mile before spotting some vague clue, usually a broken twig or a smeared and barely discernible footprint. The morning wore into a steamy afternoon. They didn't pause to eat but rather wolfed down protein bars and drank from their camelbacks.

Cabrillo thought they'd come at least ten miles when the jungle ended in a gorge that cut through the landscape like an ax stroke. At the bottom, nearly a hundred feet down by his estimation, raged a churning river that twisted and curled around rocks and fought against the stony banks.

'Left or right?' he asked MacD.

He scanned the ground in both directions, casting ahead nearly a hundred yards. 'Oh my,' he called.

The others jogged to where Lawless stood, and they all saw what had given him pause. It was another temple complex like the one they'd seen when they left the main river only this one was built on the opposite cliff, clinging to the rock almost organically. It reminded Cabrillo of the Anasazi cave city at Mesa Verde, Colorado, only this had typical Oriental architectural flairs, with gracefully arching roofs and round, tiered pagodas. Some of the structure must have collapsed over time because under the buildings, down in the river channel, were mounds of dressed stonework, some with decorative carvings still visible. Amid the rubble was the remains of a waterwheel that must have powered a mill inside the temple. Most of it had rotted away, but there were enough of its metal struts and supports left to show it had been enormous.

Very little of the complex rose above the far rim of the chasm, and what little bit did was covered in vegetation, like the vines and creepers that snaked their way down the façade. The original builders had constructed the temple so that it was next to impossible to find.

'I'm definitely getting that Lara Croft vibe,' Linda said as she gazed awestruck at the remarkable feat of engineering.

They moved farther along the edge of the canyon and came across two additional surprises. One was that a village had once stood on this side of the river. Though the jungle was reclaiming it bit by bit, the land had been cleared and diked to form rice paddies, and there were remains of several dozen stilted huts. Most were piles of rotted wood, but some still stood on shaky legs, like tottering old women too proud to rest. The people who'd lived here must have tended to the monks who resided in the temple.

The other surprise was the rope bridge that spanned the eighty-foot-wide chasm. It sagged in the middle and looked ready to collapse with the next puff of wind. The main cable was at least a foot around, with two guide ropes that were at shoulder height secured to it with strands of line like the cables of a suspension bridge. Because they were thinner and more susceptible to rot, many of these supports had parted and hung dejectedly from the main hawser.

'You don't think?'

'It's possible,' Juan answered Linda's almost-asked question.

'There is no way I'm crossing that,' she said.

'Do you fancy climbing down, crossing what look to be class five rapids, and then free-climbing up the other side?' He didn't wait for her response. 'MacD, see if you can tell if Soleil or her partner came this way.'

Lawless was standing next to the stone pillars that anchored the bridge. They'd been set into holes carved into the rock and then reburied so that about four feet of each of them rose above ground level. Bronze caps with dragon heads had been placed over both pillars. One of them had snagged a small patch of red cloth in a dragon's open mouth, the same shade as the fiber he'd found earlier.

'They came this way, all right,' he said, and showed off his discovery.

'Juan,' Smith called. He held a dull brass shell casing like the ones they'd found at the campsite.

Cabrillo eyed the rickety bridge with little enthusiasm, but he figured that if others had crossed it in recent days, it should support them. He slung his assault rifle over his shoulder as he approached the span. 'Keep an eye out,' he said, and grasped the shoulder-high guide ropes.

The main cable was made of woven fiber and felt as hard as iron, though the guidelines had the slimy feel of rotting vegetation. He made the mistake of looking down. Below him the river looked like it was boiling, stones as sharp as knives littering the roaring waterway. Everything seemed jagged and deadly. If he hit the river, he'd be drowned for sure, and an impact with the rocks would split him open like a ripe melon.

Carefully placing one boot in front of the other, and testing each spot before putting his weight on it, Cabrillo inched his way out over the gorge, the sound of water cascading below him like a screaming jet engine. When he hit the halfway point, he glanced back and saw his companions watching him. The cable had sagged enough that he could only see their faces. Linda looked anxious, MacD intrigued, and Smith bored.

Climbing up the catenary-arced rope was trickier than going down, and once Juan's foot slipped off completely. He clutched at the guideline, which shivered with tension. He slowly rebalanced himself and glanced back with a rueful shrug. He made it the rest of the way without incident and exhaled a long relieved sigh when his feet hit solid ground.

Linda came next, moving with the agility of a monkey, her pixie face set with determination. MacD followed, grinning like this was all a game to him. When he got to their side, Cabrillo looked up to see that Smith had disappeared.

'He said he needed to take a leak,' Lawless said, and went immediately to the vine-shrouded temple entrance. It looked like a perfectly square cave, and the air that whispered from it carried the cold chill of the earth.

Smith emerged from the jungle on the far side and quickly crossed the gorge, with Juan covering him with his REC7 should anyone step out of the forest behind him.

'All set?' Cabrillo asked him.

'*Oui.*'

'Here!' Lawless's hushed voice came from inside the temple.

The three quickly stepped inside the stone building, which was just one story and unadorned. Lawless was halfway to a set of stairs carved into the rock that descended down to the lower reaches of the complex. He was hunkered down, holding a flashlight steady on the body of a young man.

He was blond, with a few weeks' worth of beard, and dressed in sturdy cargo pants, a red long-sleeved T-shirt, and boots. There didn't appear to be a mark on him. If not for his deathly pallor, it would be easy to imagine he was simply resting. MacD gently pulled him forward. There were four bullet holes stitched across his back. They hadn't been immediately fatal or he wouldn't have been able to prop himself against the wall. Or perhaps Soleil had done it as a final act of kindness.

'That is Paul Bissonette,' Smith said. 'He was a frequent climbing partner of Soleil's.'

'*Vaya con Dios,*' MacD muttered.

'What about Soleil?' Linda asked.

'She either kept running or she's somewhere down there.' Cabrillo pointed to the stairs.

Flashlight beam preceding them, and pistols drawn because the confines were too tight for their assault rifles, three of them made their way cautiously down the stairs. Cabrillo ordered MacD to remain at the entrance and keep watch.

Unlike the plain walls of the uppermost chamber, the staircase was ornately carved with mythical figures and geometric designs. When they reached the bottom, they found themselves in another windowless room, but this one had a stone bench ringing three walls and a fireplace on the fourth. It was covered in mosaic tiles of deep red and bright yellow that had lost none of their luster over the years. A doorway led to another staircase. This one had windowlike openings that overlooked the cataracts below.

On the next level they discovered small rooms like jail cells that must have been where the priests slept. There was also a kitchen, with a built-in oven, and a fire pit set in the middle that would have been used to boil rice.

Below that was what had to have been the main temple. It had been stripped bare but at some point in the past would have been heavily gilded, with beautiful rugs on the floor and an ornate statue of Buddha high up on a dais overlooking the monks. The windows here all had Juliet balconies of intricate stone.

'Wow!' Linda's eyes opened wider when she looked out over the gorge.

On the opposite cliff, where they had been when they first spotted the temple, the priests had carved an image of Buddha into the living rock. It was inexactly rendered, as if it were a work in progress. Some parts were beautifully sculpted while other sections were merely crude outlines.

'They must have hung from bosun's chairs to work on that,' Cabrillo said.

'This place should be a World Heritage Site,' Linda remarked.

'Maybe that's what Soleil and . . .' Why did he keep blanking the poor guy's name?

'Paul,' Linda offered.

'Maybe that's what they were doing here.'

Smith was over studying the platform where a statue had once sat. It was constructed of closely fitted wooden planks that had been sanded until they were glass smooth. Wind and rain lashing though the open windows had pitted and stained the side closest, but the one protected by its own bulk still showed the loving craftsmanship that went into making it.

On a closer look, Cabrillo saw that the rougher side had been broken into. The wood had been pried apart, and a few pieces littered the floor amid the leaves that had blown into the room. Because of the age of the wooden dais, it was impossible to tell how long ago the vandalism had occurred. He joined Smith and peered into the hole. It had been a hiding place for whatever the monks considered their holy of holies – a relic of some sort, no doubt.

Had this been what Soleil had come after, a religious treasure that had long since been plundered? It seemed like such a waste. He turned away, shaking his head sadly.

There was one more level to the complex below the main temple. This was the section that had partially collapsed into the river. When they stepped out the doorway from the staircase, they found themselves on a platform maybe ten feet above the raging waters. The stone was wet from the splashing current and slick with moss. Below them was the skeletal framework of the waterwheel, and around them were the remains of a machine made of iron that was so badly rusted it crumbled to the touch.

Cabrillo studied what remained of the contraption, following along where gears and axles connected, and determined that it had been a large pump. He could tell that there had once been a bellows, most likely leather, which would have formed the vacuum chamber. It was sophisticated for its day and, judging by the size, very powerful.

This begged the question of its intended use. Even though it was large, it couldn't have made a dent in the level of the river, even during the dry months. It had to be something else.

He walked to the right side of the platform, moving carefully in case the stonework was unstable, and peered over the edge. All he saw was white water shooting by like it had burst from a dam. Then he saw that directly below him was the entrance to a cave that bored back into the side of the cliff below the temple complex. It would have been accessible through the waterwheel building before it gave way.

'I bet they built here because of the cave,' he muttered to himself. It had to have some religious significance. His knowledge of the Buddhist faith was limited, but he knew that some caves and caverns were considered sacred.

The cave opening was out of reach without sophisticated climbing gear and more rope than the team had brought with them, but he wondered if Soleil had made the attempt. Is that why they hadn't found her? She had slipped trying to reach the cave entrance, and her body was swept downstream?

'Hey, Juan. Come here for a sec.' Linda waved as she called him over. She and Smith were staring down into the river just above where the waterwheel sat in the current. 'Do you see something down there, tangled with the wheel?'

Juan looked over the edge of the platform. It was difficult to make out any details – the rapids turned the river white from bank to bank – but it did look like something was ensnared in the upstream side of the wheel. He first thought it was branches that had been swept along with the flow. The metal framework would be a trap for such flotsam. And then he put two and two together. When he did, the picture came into focus. It was a body wedged into the wheel's spokes.

'Jesus! It's her!'

He quickly shed his pack and dug through it for the twenty-foot coil of rope he had packed. As he tied it to the back of his combat harness Linda secured the other end around the stone foundation of the ancient pump. The metal was just too brittle to trust.

'Should you have MacD here instead of me?' she asked.

Lawless had more physical strength than she, but Cabrillo didn't want to be belayed by two people he barely knew. He shook his head. 'You and John can handle it.'

He scooted to the edge of the platform directly above where Soleil's body was trapped. He wished he could remove the boot on his real foot to keep it dry, but the metal and rocks were as sharp as knives. 'Ready?'

'Yes,' the pair said in unison.

Cabrillo flipped onto his stomach and eased himself over the precipice. Linda and Smith took his weight and slowly lowered him down. The droplets of water that bubbled up from the river were icy cold. Juan twisted a bit as the rope unkinked, then stabilized. They let out more line, and he reached with the tip of his foot for the waterwheel. As they lowered him farther still, his weight shifted to the old contraption, and soon the line went slack.

Now that he was closer, he could see that the body was slender, but it was facedown so he couldn't make a formal identification. He got down on his knees and reached an arm into the frigid water. The current almost plucked him off his perch. He steadied himself and reached again. He grabbed onto the shirt collar and pulled back with everything he had.

At first the body didn't move. It was too tangled and the river too powerful. He shifted to get more comfortable and tried again. This time he felt her shift. Soleil's corpse twisted around the stanchion that had pegged her in place since she fell into the water and for a fleeting second almost took Cabrillo with her. He managed to hang on, but the current was brutal. He fought to drag the body up onto the wheel. His grip was slipping on the wet clothing, and his hand was going numb. He realized that she had a bag over her shoulder, and his fingers soon slipped so he was only gripping its strap. When that happened, her body slipped free of the carry-all and vanished down the river. It happened so fast there was nothing Cabrillo could do. One second he had her and the next she was gone.

Juan cursed at his own stupidity. He should have tied her off before trying to move her. He looked up at his companions.

'Was it her?' Smith asked over the river's roar.

'Yeah,' Cabrillo said. 'The hair color and build were right. Though I never saw her face. I am sorry.'

He slipped the strap for the leather satchel over his shoulder and let Linda and Smith haul him up. As soon as he could reach for the stone platform he used the strength in his arms and shoulders to scramble over the lip. He lay panting on the stone platform for a moment, more in disappointment than exhaustion.

Linda finally extended a hand to help hoist him to his feet.

That's when they heard the unmistakable whooping beat of a fast-approaching helicopter.

11

The three reacted as one. Cabrillo tossed Soleil's bag to Smith, since he was as close to the rightful owner as he could get, and together they raced for the stairwell up and out of the temple complex.

His supposition that Soleil and what's-his-name had been attacked by rebels or drug smugglers was obviously false. The chopper had to belong to the military, which meant these were reinforcements for a patrol that had to be someplace close by. Soleil must have either stumbled onto it or run into a group that had betrayed them to the military. Either way, it was rotten luck for the two hikers, and was now just as bad for Cabrillo and his team. They raced through the main temple, flew past the dorm level, and ran up to the ground-level entrance.

'We've got company,' MacD said unnecessarily.

The helicopter came in low enough for Cabrillo to recognize it through the canopy as an old Russian Mil Mi-8. They could pack more than two dozen combat soldiers in one.

'Okay, we've got one shot at this,' he said. 'We've got to get across the river and into the forest before the pilot can find a place to set down.'

'Why not try to hide on this side and cross later?' Smith asked.

Cabrillo didn't waste the breath explaining that guards would doubtlessly be posted on the rope bridge, and he didn't fancy hiking days or even weeks to find another way across. 'Linda, you go first, then Smith, MacD, and me. Got it?'

With the helicopter drumming the air, the four of them sprinted from the temple entrance, keeping as much cover as possible between them and the aircraft overhead. Given how dense the jungle was, it wasn't too difficult. They only had a hundred yards to cover, but the problem would be once they reached the bridge. It was totally exposed.

The beat of the rotors changed as the pilot transited into a hover. Juan knew that meant the men were coming down fast ropes and would be on the ground in seconds. This was going to be close.

Linda reached the bridge and kept on going, not breaking stride. Her feet danced along the main cable, one hand bracing along the guideline, the other clutching her REC7. Smith let her get a few paces out before he committed himself to the rickety structure. His added weight gave the bridge a burgeoning sway. It creaked ominously, and several of the support ropes snapped free.

Cabrillo and MacD ran side by side, knowing that less than a hundred yards back the Mi-8 had disgorged its passengers and begun lifting clear, its huge rotor beating at the hot, fetid air.

A stream of tracer rounds ripped across their path, forcing both men to dive flat. Juan flipped around and opened fire, laying down a suppressive wall of lead to allow MacD to start across the bridge. Cabrillo wriggled behind a rock, and whenever he saw movement in the jungle behind them, he triggered off a three-round burst.

A grenade came lobbing out of the bush. Juan made himself as small as possible behind his rock as the poorly thrown explosive went off with a concussive whoosh. Shrapnel chewed the dirt around him, but nothing struck home. Lawless was halfway across. On the far side, Linda made it to solid ground and immediately twisted around one of the support pylons and added her own cover fire. From Cabrillo's position, the muzzle flash looked like twinkling stars.

He changed out his half-depleted magazine for a fresh one, loosed a long burst of autofire, and exploded from his hidden position. He felt like he had a giant target pinned to his back and that his legs were encased in lead. It seemed harder to run than when they'd hit that ooze just off the boat. Cabrillo slung his rifle across his back when his boot hit the bridge. It jolted and jumped like it was carrying a live electrical current. Ahead of him, MacD was moving as fast as he could, while Smith made it to the other side. Like Linda, he found cover behind the support pillar and opened fire.

Bullets cut the air all around Juan as he tried to both keep his balance and run. He didn't recall the thick-braided rope being so narrow. A hundred feet below him the water was a white frothing nightmare. Expecting a bullet in his back at any second, he kept running, the cable swaying all the while like an old hammock.

With his eyes on his feet, it was a miracle he looked up at the instant he did. A little ways ahead of MacD, bullets slammed into the cable, fired no doubt by the Burmese soldiers. It disintegrated in a furball of hemp fibers, and, as soon as the two ends parted, the guide ropes took the added strain.

'Down!' Cabrillo shouted over the din of battle, and threw himself onto the quivering main cable. MacD dropped flat, clutching at the foot-thick rope with his arms and leg.

Even when the structure was first built, the guide-lines were never designed to carry the load of the main cable. They lasted the seconds it took Cabrillo to spin himself around so he was facing the temple. He had one instant to see that a pair of soldiers in jungle fatigues had also started across the bridge, their AKs slung low across their bellies.

First one guideline split apart, rotating the entire bridge in a gut-wrenching jolt. The second let go an instant later, and Cabrillo was suddenly in free fall, clinging to the rope as it arced back toward the Buddhist sanctuary, accelerating with every second. Wind whistled past his ears while the world tilted and spun. The two Burmese soldiers hadn't seen what was coming. Screaming, one hurtled off the span, his arms and legs pinwheeling until he smashed into the rocks below. The river washed away the crimson smear he'd left on the stone and carried the body away. The second soldier managed to grab at the guidelines as they sagged like deflated balloons.

Juan redoubled his grip and braced for impact, knowing that if he lost his tenuous hold he also lost his life. He hit unyielding stone like he'd been struck by a bus. He felt his collarbone snap like a green twig and his entire left side go numb for an instant. And then his brain rebooted, and the agony struck his nervous system from his ankle to his head. Blood dripped from a gash on his temple, and it took everything he had not to just let go and be done with it all.

The soldier who'd clutched at the rope at the last second gave a warning shriek as he lost his hold and came tumbling down the cliff face. There was nothing Juan could do. The guy struck him a glancing blow that caused him to slip a little farther down the cable, and then he was gone.

Cabrillo looked down to see him sail past MacD, who had somehow stayed on even though he'd fallen farther and hit even harder. The soldier plummeted into the water headfirst and vanished. Juan never did see him surface.

He was stuck. With his broken collarbone there was no way he could climb up the cable, and he knew there was no way he'd survive a plunge into the river. He thought that maybe he and MacD could swing the rope across the cliff and somehow land on the waterwheel platform, but that wouldn't work either. It was just too far away.

Cabrillo looked up, expecting to see the triumphant

faces of soldiers aiming down at him. He could no longer hear any firing from Linda's side of the chasm and assumed that when the rope parted, she and Smith had beaten a fast retreat. The soldiers could be choppered over in just a few minutes, so it made no sense for them to linger over a situation over which they had no control.

The cable began to shake with a slow rhythm, and it took him just a moment to realize that the Burmese soldiers, rather than shooting the two of them off the rope like flies, were hauling him and MacD up to the canyon rim, to a fate that would probably make dropping into the river seem like the lesser of two evils. But as long as he was alive and had Max Hanley and the rest of the Corporation as backup, Juan Cabrillo would never give up.

Twenty-four hours later, he wished he had.

It took the soldiers nearly ten minutes to haul first Cabrillo and then MacD out of the gorge. By then Juan's shoulder felt like it had been lanced with a hot poker, and his arms and legs burned with an unholy fire from clutching the cable. He was disarmed by a soldier wielding a combat knife who cut the REC7's sling before he had been brought fully to the ground. Another soldier plucked his FN Five-seveN from its holster and yanked a throwing knife from its scabbard, hanging inverted from his harness strap.

The same was done to MacD when they brought him up from the depths. He'd been so much farther out on the rope than Cabrillo that when it collapsed, he had actually been dragged into the river. His pants were wet from the knees down. That little bit of a cushion was what saved him from being crushed against the cliff.

They were forced to stay on their knees, with two men covering them and a third removing the rest of their gear. It was during the pat down that they discovered Cabrillo's broken collarbone, which the soldier made sure to knead with both hands until the bones ground together.

The pain was intense, but only when the soldier let go did Juan let out a little whimper. He couldn't help it. They also discovered the artificial leg. The soldier turned to an officer wearing aviator-style sunglasses for instructions. A few words were exchanged, and the soldier pulled Juan's combat leg free of its stump and handed it to his superior. The man looked at it for a moment, gave Juan a rotten-toothed smile, and hurled the limb over the edge.

He hadn't known what a small arsenal the leg represented or how Juan had planned to hijack the chopper using the pistol secreted within it. He just wanted to show Cabrillo that he was totally powerless and that from this moment on the army of one of the most ruthless dictatorships in the world controlled his fate.

Cabrillo had to fight to keep the disappointment from showing on his face. Instead of giving the bastard the satisfaction of knowing how much this really meant, he shrugged as best he could and just looked around at the scenery as if he didn't have a care in the world. If his mouth hadn't been so dry, he would have tried to whistle.

The officer didn't like that his demonstration of power hadn't elicited the proper amount of fear, so he barked an order at one of the soldiers covering them. An instant later the butt of a Kalashnikov smashed into the back of Juan's head, and his world went black.

Cabrillo came to in fits and starts. He remembered the awful racket of a chopper flight and being manhandled a couple of times, but each of these memories felt as if it had happened to someone else, like a scene from a movie he'd watched long ago. He never came close enough to consciousness to feel any pain or have any idea where he was.

The first sensation when he finally returned from the abyss was an intense ache at the back of his head. More than anything, he wanted to explore the area with his hand and make sure his skull hadn't been crushed in, like he was sure it had been. But he resisted the urge. An instructor at Camp Peary, the CIA training facility known as The Farm, had once told him that if he were ever captured and was uncertain of his surroundings, he should lie as quietly as possible for as long as possible. This allowed him to rest, but, more important, he could gather intelligence on where he had been taken.

So with the back of his head screaming for attention and other parts of his body sore, he lay dormant, straining to glean anything from his surroundings. He could tell he was still clothed, and knew, by the ease with which he could breathe, that his head wasn't in a bag. As best he could tell, he was lying on a table. He strained his ears but could hear nothing. It was difficult to concentrate. His head pounded in time with his beating heart.

Ten minutes grew into fifteen. He was pretty sure he was alone, so he risked opening an eye a fraction of a millimeter. He could make out no shapes, but he saw light. Not the brightness of a noonday sun but the murky glow of an incandescent bulb. He opened his eye a bit more. He could see a bare cement-block wall where it joined a concrete ceiling. Both were stained with Jackson Pollock–esque swirls and splashes of a rusty red substance Cabrillo knew to be blood.

He remembered that MacD Lawless had also been taken prisoner, so he could only pray that Linda and Smith had gotten out. If they escaped the ambush, he was confident that they would rendezvous with the *Oregon*. Once they were far enough downriver in the RHIB, Gomez Adams could extract them with the helicopter.

The steady beat of pain lancing though his head continued unabated. It was making him a little nauseated, which meant he probably had a concussion. Though he was almost positive he was alone in a cell of some kind, he dared not move his head. There could be hidden cameras or a two-way observation mirror behind him. He did shift a little, like an unconscious person thrashing out. His feet and wrists were bound to the table with steel cuffs. He lay still once again.

He was in no shape to stand up to an interrogation, and if they'd brought him to the capital, Yangon, he was most likely in Insein Prison. Pronounced 'Insane,' it was perhaps the most brutal penitentiary on the planet, the deepest of black holes, where escape was impossible and survival had even longer odds.

It housed around ten thousand prisoners, though its capacity was less than half that. Many were political activists and monks who'd spoken out against the regime. The rest were criminals of every kind. Diseases like malaria and dysentery were endemic. Rats outnumbered both the prisoners and the guards. And the tales of torture were the stuff of nightmares. Cabrillo knew they loved to employ rubber hoses filled with sand to beat people and used attack dogs to force prisoners to race each other across a gravel path on their elbows and knees.

His only hope lay in the fact that there was an electronic tracking chip embedded in his thigh and at this very moment Max and the rest of the crew were working on getting them out.

Out of nowhere, a fist slammed into his jaw, nearly dislocating it.

He could have sworn there was nobody else in the room with him. The guy had the patience of a cat. There was no use pretending any longer. He opened his eyes. The man who'd struck him wore a green military uniform. Juan couldn't identify his rank but managed to take a little satisfaction in the fact that he was massaging his right fist. His head felt like a struck bell.

'Name?' the soldier barked.

Juan saw two additional guards had come through a metal door. One stayed close to it while the other took up a position next to a table with a sheet draped over it. He couldn't tell from its outline what lay underneath.

When he didn't give his name fast enough, the lead interrogator pulled a length of ordinary garden hose from his belt. By the way it sagged Juan knew it was a weighted sap. It cracked across his stomach, and no matter how tightly Cabrillo had flexed his abs the blow felt like it had sunk all the way through to his spine.

'Name!'

'John Smith,' Cabrillo said, sucking air through his teeth.

'Who you work for?' Again the cudgel whipped across Juan's stomach when he didn't answer instantly. 'Who you work for? CIA? UN?'

'No one. I work for myself.'

The hose came down again, this time across Juan's groin. It was too much. He turned his head and retched from the pain.

A cultured voice with a tinge of a British accent said, 'I can tell from your accent that you're American.'

The unseen speaker was up near the head of the table, where Cabrillo was strapped. Juan heard him light a cigarette, and a moment later a plume of smoke wafted over his face. The man moved so Cabrillo could see him. He was Burmese, like the others. Juan put his age as in his mid-forties. His face was nut brown, with lines around the eyes and mouth. He wore a visored cap, but Juan could see his hair was still jet-black. There wasn't anything necessarily malevolent about the officer, but Cabrillo got a cold chill down his spine.

'How is it that you came to be in my country, armed no less? We get so few visitors from the United States that we know exactly how many are within our borders at any given time. You, my friend, should not be here. So tell me, what brings you to Myanmar?'

A line from *Casablanca* popped into Cabrillo's head. 'My health. I came here for the waters.'

The officer chuckled. 'Very good. One of my favorite movies. Claude Rains then says, "The waters? What waters? We're in the desert," to which Bogey replies, "I was misinformed." Truly a classic.' His voice then cracked, 'Muang!'

The hose struck twice in rapid succession, both blows hitting the exact same spot on Juan's broken collarbone. The pain traveled up from his shoulder and slammed into the top of his brain, where it felt like his head would come apart along the cranial sutures.

'Mr Smith,' the lead interrogator went on smoothly, 'I mentioned that I believe you are American. I would like to know your feelings on torture. It is a sore subject in your country, I believe. Some feel that even sleep deprivation and exposure to loud music are cruel and inhumane. Where do you stand on this subject?'

'I agree wholeheartedly,' Juan said quickly.

'I would imagine a man in your position would,' the officer said, a smile plucking at the corners of his mouth. 'I wonder if you felt that way yesterday, or last week. It doesn't matter. This is your fervent belief now, of that I am certain.'

He did something to a mechanism under the table so that it tipped back slightly, leaving Cabrillo's feet about twelve inches higher than his head. While this was going on, the guard near the table ripped off the sheet to reveal several folded towels and a one-gallon plastic jug.

'What I really want to know,' the officer continued, 'is if you believe waterboarding constitutes torture, hmm?'

Juan knew he had a high threshold for pain. He had hoped to hold out for the couple of days he figured it would take Max to bust them out, but he'd never faced the waterboard before and had no idea how he'd react. As a kid he'd spent countless days swimming off the Southern California coast, and though he'd had water forced up his nose on more than one occasion, he'd never really been as close to drowning as he was about to come.

A towel was laid across his face while two powerful hands grabbed his head to keep it from moving. Cabrillo's heart went into overdrive. His hands tensed. He heard water splashing. Felt a couple of drops hit his neck. And then he felt moisture on his lips, a dampness at first, but soon his skin was wet. A drop slid down his nose and burned its way into his sinuses.

More water was dumped onto the towel, soaking it through. Juan tried to exhale through his nose to stop the water from invading the delicate membranes. It worked for seconds, almost a minute, but his lungs could hold only so much air, and the towel was sodden, a great clammy weight pressing down on him. At last there was no more air to fight the inevitable, and water poured into his sinus cavities. Because of the angle of the table, it pooled there and went no farther along his respiratory tract.

That was what waterboarding was all about. Make the victim feel he is drowning without actually drowning him.

It wasn't a matter of will. Over this there was no control. When the sinuses fill with water, the brain, having evolved since the first primitive fish walked out of the sea and breathed in its first lungful of air, knew the body was drowning. It was hardwired. Juan could no more control his body's reaction than he could force his liver to produce more bile.

His head felt like it was burning from the inside out while his lungs went into convulsions, sucking small amounts of water into them. The sensation was worse than anything he could imagine. It felt like he was being crushed, like an ocean's worth of water had invaded his head, scalding and searing the fragile air sacs behind his nose and above his eyes.

The pain now more intense than any he'd experienced. And this had only gone on for thirty seconds.

The weight of it all grew worse still. His head was ready to explode. He wanted it to. His throat pumped in a gagging reflex, and he choked on more water pouring down his windpipe.

He heard agitated voices speaking in a language he didn't know and wondered if he was hearing angels calling to him.

And then the towel was taken away and the table tilted so that his head was much higher than his feet. Water jetted from his nose and mouth, and he retched painfully, but he could breathe. And while his lungs still burned and the air tasted of death, it was the sweetest breath he'd ever taken.

They gave him less than a minute before the table slammed back down and the soaking-wet towel was once again pressed over his face. The water came, gallons of it, tons of it, tsunami waves of it. This time, he could only exhale a few seconds before it again pooled inside his head. His sinuses filled up to the rim of his nostrils, and they could hold no more. With that came the agony, and the panic, and his brain screaming at him to do something – to fight, to struggle, to break free.

Cabrillo ignored the pitiable cries of his own mind and took the abuse without moving a muscle, because the truth was that he knew he wasn't drowning, that the men would let him breathe again, and that *he* had control over what his body did, not instinct, not his hindbrain. It was his intellect that ruled his actions. He lay as calm and still as a man taking a nap.

At some point one of the guards was sent to fetch another gallon jug of water, and for a total of fifteen times Juan was drowned and then allowed to breathe, drowned and then allowed to breathe. Every time, the soldiers expected Juan to break and beg for mercy. And, every time, he lay back down after catching his breath and goaded them by nodding to them to do it again. The last session, they let it go so long that he passed out and they had to unshackle him quickly and force the water from his body and revive him with a couple of slaps to the cheek.

'Apparently,' the interrogator said while Juan panted and snorted water out of his sinuses, 'you do not want to tell me what I want to know.'

Cabrillo shot him a look. 'Like I told you earlier. I came here for the waters.'

He was heaved off the table and dragged to a cell down a short, stark corridor. The room was unbelievably hot, with absolutely no air movement. Juan was dumped on the bare concrete floor, the metal door was slammed, and the lock shot home. There was a single caged light high up on a wall, a slop bucket, and a few handfuls of dirty straw on the cement floor. His cell mate was about the most emaciated cockroach he'd ever seen.

'So, what are you in for, buddy?' he asked the insect. It waved its antennae at him in response.

He finally was able to examine the back of his head and was amazed that the bone wasn't broken. The gash had doubtlessly bled, but the waterboarding had cleaned out the wound. His concussion was still with him, yet he could think clearly, and his memory was unaffected. It was a medical myth, that unless showing symptoms of brain injury, a concussed person should stay awake following the injury, but with his lungs afire and his body aching all over, he knew that sleep would not come. He found that the only comfortable position was flat on his back with his injured arm bent across his chest.

He thought back to the firefight in the jungle, examining every instant like he had with the terrorist attack in Singapore. He saw Linda on one knee behind the stone pillar, her petite body shaking every time her rifle discharged. He saw MacD's back as he ran ahead of him, recalling that Lawless's foot almost slipped from the rope once. There was Smith, reaching the far cliff and whirling around the second anchor pillar. Juan recalled looking at his own feet again and trying not to stare into the maddened river almost a hundred feet below him.

He then looked up and saw Smith open fire, and then the rope disintegrated ahead of MacD. Cabrillo ran the scene through his mind again and again, like a cop reviewing surveillance footage. He concentrated on Smith's rifle as it roared on full auto. He was aiming across the river at the soldiers chasing them. He was sure of it.

So who had fired the rounds that hit the rope bridge? It couldn't have been anyone on the cliff behind him. They were all under cover far enough from the edge that they couldn't get an angle to shoot at the dropping rope. The two soldiers who'd fallen down the gorge when the rope came apart wouldn't have done it.

He clearly saw Linda blasting away, but Smith's out-line was blurred in his memory.

Juan blamed his headache. Usually he could recall every detail and nuance, but not now. Besides which, cold was leaching up through the concrete and settling into his bones. He stood, feeling dizzy enough to need to place a hand on the wall. Without his artificial leg, there really wasn't anything he could do. He waited until the dizziness passed, but didn't trust his balance enough to hop around the cell. On a lark, he measured it out using his exact six-foot height. It was twelve by twelve. He did the math in his head. The diagonal would be a touch under seventeen feet. He tested his calculation, knowing that his boot was thirteen inches long. His arithmetic was spot-on.

'The brain's still working,' he said to the cockroach, which was moving about in the scattered stalks of hay. 'Okay, think! What the hell is bothering me?'

There was something about the destroyed camp. He recalled a feeling of confusion, that there was an item out of place. No! Not out of place. Missing. There were certain things a woman out camping for more than a month would have brought with her, and they were things that men had absolutely no reason to steal. Soleil Croissard's pack had been in the tent, and emp-tied. There hadn't been any face cream, or lip balm, or feminine products of any kind.

Had the body he'd almost recovered been a woman's? He hadn't seen her face, but the build and hair color had been Soleil's. It had to be her. And whatever female luxuries she'd packed into Myanmar must be in the ditty bag he'd recovered and handed off to Smith. It had been waterlogged, so there was no way to judge its true weight and thus no way to guess at its contents, but that had to be it. She and her companion, ah, Paul Bissonette – hey, the memory ain't so bad after all – must have heard or seen the army patrol approaching. She grabbed up her most personal items, and together they lit out into the jungle and eventually to the ruined Buddhist temple.

Then why wasn't he satisfied? Had he seen her face, there would be no doubt, but he hadn't. He couldn't make a positive identification, and that left a loose end, something he professionally and personally hated. Of course, he had bigger things to worry about than the past.

Cabrillo hoped against hope that their Burmese captors would leave MacD alone. It was obvious from his and Lawless's ages that Juan was the senior man here, so they should concentrate all of their attention on him. He just didn't think that was going to happen. He had an idea of what Lawless was made of. He was tough and resourceful, but did he have the kind of mettle it took to go through what Juan had just experienced and not break? Cabrillo hadn't known that about himself, so he had no idea if the kid could take it.

In the end, Juan thought, what did it really matter if MacD broke? What did he know, really? The client's name and the mission to go find his daughter wandering the Burmese jungle. The *Oregon*? He knew her name but had no idea of her real capabilities. Juan's identity? Who the hell would care? He'd been out of the CIA long enough that he couldn't be considered an intelligence asset.

No, he thought, MacD could spill his guts out and it wouldn't really change a thing. He now hoped that Lawless was bright enough to see this and spare himself any pain.

Somehow, as exhaustion began to dull his own aches and he felt himself drifting toward sleep, he suspected that MacD would keep quiet if only to prove himself worthy of joining the Corporation.

Cabrillo had no idea how much time had passed – he'd come to on the waterboard without his watch – when he woke with a start. He was bathed in sweat and panting.

'Son of a bitch,' he shouted aloud.

It had come to him during his sleep – a clear vision of John Smith firing at the cable. He had intentionally shot the thing to pieces. Rage boiled in Juan's veins.

Smith had set them up. No. Roland Croissard had set them up. That hadn't been a woman's body in the river; it had been a slender man. And the bag didn't contain feminine toiletries. In it was something they had plundered from the temple, something hidden beneath the dais where the Buddha statue had once sat, and Juan had handed it to Smith pretty as you please.

This had never been about rescuing any daughter. Croissard had sent his own team into the jungle and they'd failed to recover some item, so he'd hired the Corporation to finish their mission.

'God, what an idiot I am.' Then through the fog of anger came the realization that Linda Ross was with Smith and had no idea he had a completely different agenda than she knew.

Would he just kill her now that he had what he wanted? The question burned in Juan's mind. Logic said that he wouldn't. It would be easier for him if she were to explain to Max and the rest what had happened to MacD and Cabrillo. And once he was aboard the *Oregon*, he simply needed to wait until transport back to civilization could be arranged.

He felt a measure of relief. Linda would be okay. But the idea of Smith and Croissard's betrayal sent his blood pressure through the roof. How could he not have seen it? He thought back, looking for signs or clues. That audio message Croissard supposedly had received from his daughter was obviously faked. It had just the right note of mystery and desperation to whet Cabrillo's interest. He had wanted this mission because there was a frightened young woman, a damsel in distress – he thought bitterly of his own stupid sense of chivalry – who needed saving.

Croissard had played him for a chump. Cabrillo looked at the suicide bombing at the hotel under a new light, but he couldn't see an angle that benefited the Swiss financier's master plan. That wasn't staged. Those men were looking to kill as many people as they could. It was just luck that he and Max had survived. There was no way Croissard was behind it. Of that, he was certain.

He couldn't recall the last time he'd been duped. He couldn't remember the last time someone had even bluffed him at poker. He'd always prided himself on knowing all the angles, thinking three steps ahead, and having an edge over everyone he dealt with.

How could he not have seen it?

The question played though his mind on a never-ending loop. There was no answer. Mark and Eric had vetted Croissard. The guy was just a businessman. What the hell was he playing at? Why the subterfuge? And then came another question he couldn't possibly answer: What had been in the bag that made it worth sending the first pair of explorers and then shelling out millions to the Corporation when they fell off the radar?

Cabrillo lay with his back propped up against the cement wall of his cell while a sea of unknowns filled his brain.

12

To Smith's surprise and her credit, the woman didn't argue when he said they should head into the jungle after the rope bridge parted. They stayed just long enough to see that the Burmese soldiers were hauling up their two new prisoners before they ran for cover in the forest.

With the bridge out, the soldiers wouldn't be able to follow until they could find a place to land their chopper. Smith and Linda would have more than enough of a head start to elude capture. But just in case the Burmese had a tracker as accomplished as Lawless, they made certain to sweep the trail behind them.

After an hour of hard going, covering ground they had just crossed that morning, Smith called for a five-minute break. His companion wasn't even breathing hard. Smith plopped himself onto the ground, panting heavily. In the background was the omnipresent sound of birds and insects. Linda squatted next to Smith, her expression grim, her mind doubtlessly on the fate of her captured companions.

She wiped at her eyes and turned away from Smith. It was the opening he'd been waiting for. He silently drew his pistol and placed the barrel at the back of her head.

'Drop your rifle, carefully,' he ordered.

Linda had drawn air through her teeth and gone stiff. She had the REC7 across her knees. She slowly placed it on the ground in front of her. Smith kept up the pressure with his pistol as he reached out and dragged the rifle out of her range.

'Now pull out your pistol. Two fingers only.'

Like an automaton, Linda unsnapped her holster and, using just her thumb and index finger, drew the Glock 19 she favored. The instant her fingers opened, she ducked her head and spun, throwing up a blocking arm to push Smith's pistol into the air. She'd known his attention would be on her weapon and used that as a distraction. She stabbed out with stiffened fingers and caught Smith in the throat just above where the collar-bones met. Then she hit him in the side of the head with a left cross. The punch wasn't her best because they were close together, but with his airways con-stricted from the jab it dazed the former Legionnaire.

Linda sprang to her feet and reared back to kick Smith in the head. Fast as an adder, he grabbed her foot out of the air and twisted it over so that Linda had no choice but to fall to the ground. He leapt onto her back with both knees, blowing the air from her lungs, and his weight made it difficult for her to refill them. He slammed the pistol into the nape of her neck.

'Try something like that again and you're dead. Understand?' When Linda didn't reply, he repeated the question and screwed the barrel deeper into her flesh.

'Yes,' she managed to croak.

Smith had a length of wire ready in his pocket. He grabbed Linda's arms and placed them at the small of her back. One-handed, he looped the wire around her wrists and twisted the two ends closed. The wire was high enough up her forearms that she couldn't reach it with her fingers. A second piece of wire bound her wrists to the reinforced belt loop of her camouflage fatigues. In just seconds Linda Ross was trussed up like a Christmas goose. Only then did he take his weight off of her. Linda coughed violently as her lungs began working again. Her face was bright red, and her eyes burned with rage.

'Why are you doing this?'

Smith ignored her. He retrieved his satellite phone from his pack and powered it up.

'Answer me, damnit!'

He stripped the baseball cap off her head and stuffed it into her mouth. With so much jungle overhead he couldn't get a clear signal. He grabbed Linda and started walking toward a clearing about fifty yards away. He dumped her into the grass and sat opposite her. He noticed he had an e-mail that had come in first thing this morning:

Change of plans, my friend. As you know my intention all along was to use official channels for our search. Going with the Corporation was a risky choice. My negotiations have finally paid off. I have made expensive arrangements with a Myanmar official for a squad of soldiers to be sent out to the monastery. They know who you are. Together, you should be able to wipe out the Corporation team and complete the mission.

Smith scratched at the stubble on his jaw. This changed everything, and explained how the chopper happened to show up at the exact right time. This meant the first team sent into the jungle was probably attacked by smugglers rather than the army. Just bad luck on their part.

Smith wrote out his text:

> Wish I'd read your e-mail sooner. I've spent the last hour running from the patrol. No harm done. BTW I have them. Cabrillo and another taken prisoner. I have their woman with me. Bound and gagged. Instructions?

A minute passed before the reply lit up the screen:

> I knew you could do it! And three Corporation members grabbed in the process. Interesting. It seems the Oracle gave them far more credit than they deserve. It appears they are no longer a threat. What of the other team I sent? Any ideas?

Smith replied:

> Basil was shot, most likely by drug runners. Munire drowned. He had them in a bag. They had been under the dais, just like it said in the Rustichello Folio I stole in England. I am about an hour away from the army unit. How do I make contact?

The response came a moment later:

> I will get word to them that you are coming back to their location. They will stand down. You can fly with them back to Yangon. A jet is waiting.

That beat having to hike out. In the cosmic scheme, it made up for being in a firefight where he was never a target. He thumbed in another message and hit SEND:

What do I do with the woman?
Is she attractive?

Smith looked over at Linda and assessed her the way a butcher looks at a cut of meat.

Yes.
Bring her along. In case the Oracle didn't misjudge as badly as we think, she makes a good bargaining chip. If we don't need her, we can sell her. See you soon, and well done, my friend.

Smith shut off the satellite phone and put it back in his pack. He again looked over at Linda. She glared at him with laser intensity. He smirked. Her anger had absolutely no effect on him.

'On your feet.'

Linda continued to stare defiantly.

'I was just told to keep you alive,' he said, 'but that is an order I needn't worry about obeying. Either get on your feet or I shoot you now and leave your corpse to the vultures.'

Her defiance lasted another heartbeat or two. He could tell when she finally accepted that she no longer had choices. The fire remained behind those eyes, but her shoulders sagged just a little as tension ran out of her body. Linda rose. With her in the lead, and Smith just behind her enough so that she couldn't try anything, they retraced their path and headed back to the monastery.

Juan marked time by the twin ravages of hunger and thirst. The hunger was a dull ache that he could handle. It was the thirst that was driving him mad. He had tried pounding on the door to get someone's attention, but he knew that they hadn't forgotten him. They were breaking him down bit by bit through deliberate deprivation.

His tongue felt like a seared piece of meat that had been rammed into his mouth, and his skin had stopped sweating so that it felt papery and brittle. No matter how he tried not to think about it, images of water flooded his mind – glasses of it, lakes of it, whole oceans of it. It was the worst form of torture. They were letting his mind betray him the way Croissard and Smith had. He realized that the waterboard treatment had only been a lark, a way for them to amuse themselves. If it had worked, fine. If not, they already had the second phase of his interrogation mapped out.

This was their tried-and-true method of breaking prisoners, and he was quite sure it had never failed.

Suddenly the bolt securing his door snapped back with a metallic echo, and the hinges squealed like nails on a chalkboard. Two guards were there. Neither had weapons other than the rubber truncheons slipped under their belts. They stomped into the room and lifted Cabrillo from the floor. The Burmese are not usually big people, and these two were no exception. In his exhausted state, and with only one leg, Cabrillo was deadweight, and the soldiers staggered under him.

Cabrillo was dragged down the corridor toward where he had been waterboarded. The dread he felt was like a load of stones had been packed around his heart.

But they continued past the door and went farther down the hallway to another interrogation room. This one was square, cement, and had a table and two chairs. One was bolted to the floor, the other was occupied by the interrogator with the cultured voice. On the table was a carafe of water, its sides dewy from the humidity, and an empty glass.

'Ah,' the interrogator greeted him with a smile that was part bonhomie, part reptilian. 'Good of you to join me, Mr Smith.'

They were still using that name, Juan thought. They either hadn't tortured MacD or he hadn't broken. Or this guy was smart enough not to reveal what he'd learned from their other prisoner.

Juan was dumped into the chair, and it took everything in him to remain erect and keep his eyes on the interrogator and not ogle the pitcher. His mouth was too dry to speak.

'Allow me to introduce myself,' the interrogator said, pouring water into the glass so that the ice cubes clicked musically. 'I am Colonel Soe Than. In case you were wondering, you have been our guest here at Insein for two and a half days.'

He set the glass in front of Cabrillo. Juan sat as still as a statue.

'Go ahead,' Than encouraged. 'I will not think any less of you.'

With a studied deliberation, Juan reached for the water and took a measured sip.

Then he set the glass back onto the table, less than a quarter of it gone.

'I do admire your strength, Mr Smith. You are one of the most disciplined men I've ever come across. By now, most people would have upended the carafe and sucked it all down. Of course, the abdominal cramps that accompany such a foolish mistake are as brutal as the original thirst.'

Juan said nothing.

'Before our time together comes to an end' – he glanced at his watch; it was the black military-style chronograph that Cabrillo had brought on the mission – 'which should be in a half hour or so, I wonder if you would at least tell me your real name.'

Cabrillo took another slow sip of water. His body craved it, but he forced himself to put the glass back on the table. He cleared his throat. When he spoke, his voice was a hoarse croak. 'No joke. It really is John Smith.'

Than's forced civility vanished in an instant, and he swung a fist into Juan's hand, which was lying palm down on the table. The blow wasn't enough to break bone. He could see a smug look cross Than's otherwise bland face. By reacting like he had, he was telling Juan that he knew the truth. MacD had broken.

'Chairman Juan Cabrillo,' Tran said, civility back in place, 'of the Corporation. Preposterous name, by the way. You're based out of an old freighter called the *Oregon*. Which, as of first light this morning, our navy and air force are searching for. They have orders to sink it on sight. That was what I got out of a bargain that's been made: the satisfaction of punishing your people for transgressing on our soil.'

'Bargain?' Juan asked.

'Oh, I should tell you that when we told our friends to the north your identity – you see, we share everything with them since they are so supportive of our government – they were very interested to hear of your capture.' Cabrillo knew Than was talking about China, Myanmar's largest trade partner and only real ally in the region. 'They very much want to speak with you. Your compatriot, young Mr Lawless, as well, but I get the impression that General Jiang is most anxious to speak with you. It seems you were once in the employ of the CIA and that you might have insight into certain espionage events that have taken place over the years.'

Juan had never worked in China during his time with the Agency and couldn't fathom why a Chinese general would think he would know anything. He couldn't even guess why his name would pique their interest. He'd been out of the game for years.

Than went on. 'Though I've never worked directly with the general, I must tell you his reputation precedes him. You will look back at our time together with fondness in the coming months and wish that you had remained in my gentle and loving care.'

Another thought struck Juan just then. He still had his tracker chip, so the crew would know where he was, but getting him and MacD out of China was going to be damned close to impossible. His hand was a little unsteady when he drank more water. Than refilled his glass.

'Not so glib now, eh, Chairman?' Than taunted. 'Still want to remain defiant?'

There came a knock on the door. Than nodded to the guard stationed next to it to open it. In strode a middle-aged Chinese man in a beribboned uniform with a peaked cap placed firmly on his salt-and-pepper head. His face was deeply wrinkled, the skin of a man who spent a great deal of time out in the field rather than in an office, pushing papers. Behind him was a tall woman, also in uniform. She was about thirty, with long, straight black hair and horn-rimmed glasses, with her bangs obscuring parts of her face.

Than stood quickly and extended a hand. He and the general conversed in Chinese. Jiang didn't introduce his aide, nor did the general even glance in Cabrillo's direction. Juan took the opportunity to keep sipping at the water, hoping that the fluid would give him strength for whatever hell Jiang had planned for him. Cabrillo studied the general a little closer. There was something familiar about him, but he was certain he'd never met the man before. Maybe he'd seen a photograph in a briefing. He wasn't sure.

'On your feet,' Than said in English.

Cabrillo stopped wracking his brain and did as he was ordered, balancing as best he could on his only foot. One of the guards grabbed his arms and pinned them behind his back so he could whip on a pair of Flex-Cuffs. The plastic bit deep, but Juan had kept his wrists slightly apart so when the guard stepped away the binding wasn't so tight. It was an old trick that on rare occasions had allowed him to get out of bindings or, at a minimum, make them a heck of a lot more comfortable. Well, less uncomfortable.

A minute later, MacD appeared with two more guards. They had to prop him on his feet. His uniform was hanging off him in rags, and fresh bruises covered his face, masking the old ones inflicted by the Taliban. His head lolled drunkenly, and if not for the guards, he would have collapsed. Spittle oozed from his lips. Jiang hardly gave Lawless a look, but his aide gasped when she saw him and had to stop herself from reaching out to him in a gesture of compassion.

They made a sad little procession. MacD was barely conscious, and Juan had to be dragged because he didn't have the strength to hop. His guards sort of carried him under the shoulders and let his good leg take long steps.

They were taken into a large loading dock/motor pool. Sunlight blasted through the big overhead doors, forcing Juan to squint. The air reeked of diesel and spoiling food. Prisoners under the watchful eyes of more guards were unloading sacks of rice from the back of a Chinese-made stake truck with the baldest tires Cabrillo had ever seen. Its driver sat in the cab and smoked. Another truck was being loaded with produce grown on the prison grounds.

Parked just outside the big room was a white van without rear windows. The back doors were opened to reveal a cargo bed separated from the cab by a metal grille. The two prisoners were tossed into the back. MacD's head hit with a thump and he lay still. There was nothing Cabrillo could do.

More Flex-Cuffs were used to secure the two men to hooks built into the floor. This wasn't a regular prison vehicle, just a commercial van, but without internal door handles it was just as effective as an armored car. The doors slammed shut with a finality Juan felt in his bones. This was not going to end well.

A few more minutes went by. He could imagine Than and the general comparing torture techniques the way housewives swap recipes. Even with the front windows open the rear of the van grew as hot as a Dutch oven.

Jiang finally broke free from Than and got behind the wheel himself, his demure aide at his side in the passenger seat. They didn't speak to each other as the engine was fired and the vehicle put into gear. A little wind puffed into the cargo area as they threaded through the prison grounds and headed toward the main gate. Juan couldn't see anything but sky from his position on the floor, but he recalled that Insein Prison was a massive complex in northern Yangon built around a central hub like the spokes of a wheel. He also remembered that families were allowed to bring non-political prisoners food at the perimeter wire and that, without it, many would simply starve to death.

Society is said to be measured by the condition of its prisons. Myanmar had to be at the bottom of the barrel.

The van slowed to a stop at the main gate. Guards checked the underside and opened the back doors. One pointed first at Juan, then at MacD, checked a clipboard, counted them a second time, and nodded. The doors were slammed closed.

They were a block from the prison, and Juan was about to try talking to the general when his aide opened the steel grille confining them in the back. She'd removed her glasses.

Juan gaped at her, unable to believe what he was seeing. She started crawling back into the cargo bed, carrying a small black case.

'How?' he rasped.

Her eyes' shape changed with latex appliances and her hair dyed and lengthened with extensions, the *Oregon*'s chief medical officer, Dr Julia Huxley, threw him the warmest smile he'd ever seen.

Then it dawned on him why he recognized the general. It was Eddie Seng, also heavily made up to appear older.

'Eddie and I were in the neighborhood.' She quickly cut Cabrillo's Flex-Cuffs with a scalpel from her medical bag and started examining MacD Lawless.

'Don't get cocky,' Seng warned from the driver's seat. 'We just passed a motorcade heading toward the prison and, if I don't miss my guess, in the backseat of the second car was the real General Jiang. We're not out of the woods yet.'

'What?' Cabrillo cried. 'The Chinese really want me? What the hell for?'

Seng glanced over his shoulder. 'It was before I joined the Corporation, but didn't you sink one of their navy's Luhu-class destroyers?'

'The *Chengo*,' Juan recalled. 'It was the first time we ever worked with NUMA's current director, Dirk Pitt.'

He took Hux's seat in the van's cab. On the center console was a liter bottle of water. He drank a third before rescrewing the cap. He wanted more, but cramping was a real concern. Outside, Yangon was like any other modern megalopolis. The air was thick with smog and the stench of leaded gasoline being burned in untuned engines. This part of town was poorer than most. The road was a strip of crumbling asphalt. The curbs were open sewers. The single-story houses all seemed to lean on one another for support while half-naked children watched traffic with vacant eyes. Mangy dogs lurked in alleyways, looking for whatever scraps the kids hadn't gotten to. Car horns blared at every intersection and usually for no apparent reason. In the far distance, Cabrillo could see some high-rises, but they had the institutional blandness of 1970s Soviet architecture. Occasionally there were signs of the city's Oriental nature, a pagoda or

Buddhist shrine, but other than that Yangon was indistinguishable from every other Third World city on the planet.

'Where's the *Oregon*?' Of the dozens of questions swirling through Cabrillo's mind, that was the most pressing.

'She's about twenty miles southeast of us,' Eddie replied.

'Do you have a phone or a radio? I need to tell Max that the air force and navy are hunting for her.' Seng fished a two-way radio from his uniform pocket. Juan called the ship and told the duty officer – Hali Kasim, as it turned out – about the search under way and to place the *Oregon* on battle stations. The ship's klaxon was wailing by the time the last words were out of the Chairman's mouth.

Next, Cabrillo spun in his seat so he could look into the rear. 'How is he, Hux?'

'Head injury for sure,' she replied in her clinical voice. 'Can't tell how severe until we get him back to the medical bay and I run an MRI.' Like everything else on the *Oregon*, her infirmary was state of the art, and would qualify as a Level One Trauma Center. 'How about you? Any injuries?'

'Dehydration and a broken collarbone. I had a concussion, but it's cleared up.'

'I'll examine you in a little while.'

'Concentrate on MacD. I'm fine.' Cabrillo turned back around. 'Okay, what's been happening? Oh, first, Roland Croissard double-crossed us. I don't know what he's playing at, but his man Smith is why MacD and I were captured.'

'We figured something was up when yours and Linda's tracking chips showed you both heading out of the jungle at over a hundred miles per hour. Figured it was a chopper.'

'An old Mi-8. Wait, Linda came with us? Where is she now?'

'A few hours after you landed in Yangon, she went to the airport and flew out to Brunei. The signal went dark when she was moved to a location just off the coast. I assume she was heloed out to a ship.'

'Brunei?' It made no sense. Unless Croissard had business dealings there, which was entirely possible.

'Murph and Stony are looking into it and digging deeper into Croissard's background.'

Cabrillo asked, 'How'd you set up the rescue from Insein?'

'We took the *Oregon* south as soon as your signals started to move and we couldn't raise you on your phone, and when we were within range we started monitoring all military communications, especially stuff coming out of the prison. When Soe Than – he's the warden, by the way – made his deal with General Jiang, we saw our opening. The trick was to time it so we arrived earlier than him, but not so early that we aroused suspicion.'

'I have to congratulate Kevin and his magicians. The makeup is amazing.'

'Remember, he once barely missed out on an Academy

Award. This was a piece of cake to him. He said a real challenge would have been to make Linc into Jiang.'

'How'd you two come to shore?'

'On the *Liberty*.' That was one of the *Oregon*'s two lifeboats. Like her mothership and her twin, the *Or Death*, the *Liberty* was a lot more than she seemed. 'We came in during the night and docked her at an old boarded-up fish-packing plant across the river.'

Traffic was growing thicker and the sound of car horns louder. Big city buses and little three-wheeled tuk-tuks overloaded with passengers and their possessions vied for the same real estate with equal disdain for the other's presence. It was bedlam. They saw no traffic cops, but plenty of soldiers patrolled the sidewalk, all armed with AK-47s and aviator shades. Pedestrians went around them like water around a boulder, parting and merging again, and making sure to never jostle them.

To Cabrillo, they didn't look particularly alert. They were menacing, but they didn't have the look of soldiers on the hunt for something in particular. That meant Than hadn't sent out an alert. Yet.

'Where'd you get the van?' Juan asked as they sat behind an old truck carrying lengths of teak logs.

'Rented it from a delivery company first thing this morning.'

'No problems?'

'For the thousand euros cash I paid him, the clerk would have offered to kill his own mother,' Eddie replied. Like Juan, Seng had been a deep-cover operative for the

CIA, so he had a way about him that made strangers trust him and had an ease in foreign countries as though he'd lived there his entire life.

As they drove and the neighborhoods improved, they saw stores selling just about everything under the sun and street vendors who sold anything else. There was a more commercial vibe, and a vibrancy, though nowhere near that of other Asian cities. It was the pall of the military dictatorship that sapped people of energy. Traffic was snarled not because there was so much of it but rather because the drivers were in no hurry to get to their destinations.

'On the left?' Eddie said.

Juan knew immediately who he was referring to. Midway down the block of stores selling knockoff clothing and bootleg CDs and DVDs was a soldier holding a walkie-talkie to his ear. He nodded, spoke a few words, and clipped it onto his belt. He had a partner who'd been standing at his side. The first one relayed information to the second, and the two started paying the traffic a lot more attention.

'What do you think?'

'I think,' Cabrillo replied, 'that the jig is up. Do you have a weapon?'

'Glove box.'

Juan opened it and retrieved a Glock 21 chambered for .45 caliber. The big slugs would put down just about anything short of a charging elephant.

The two soldiers saw the big white van amid the sedans, taxis, and bicycles, and their carriage changed in an instant. Hands tightened on weapons, and their posture stiffened. They started walking with purpose.

'I don't want to have to kill these guys,' Juan said.

'Hold on.'

Eddie crushed the gas pedal and turned the wheel so that the front of the van clipped the back of some Chinese-made subcompact neither had ever heard of. Its wheels burned off rubber as the van pushed the tiny little car out of the way.

The soldiers started running. Juan stood with his head out the window and fired across the sloping hood. He aimed for the smoking brazier of a street vendor selling some sort of meat skewers. The metal drum toppled off its stand and crashed to the ground at the same time the two soldiers dove flat for cover. Glowing embers peppered the sidewalk in smoking heaps, and enough landed on the soldiers that their immediate concern was immolation and not the van.

Seng finally bulldozed the car out of the way, which allowed him to steer the van onto the sidewalk on the other side of the street from the soldiers. He laid on the horn and kept going. People leapt aside, and wares displayed outside shops were blown through. He spun the wheel at the next cross street, which thankfully was clear, and got back onto the tarmac.

'We've bought seconds at most,' he said, checking his wing mirrors. 'Any ideas?'

'Ditch the van.'

Hux must have heard him because she said, 'I want to move MacD as little as possible.'

'I'm afraid we don't have much of a choice. This city's crawling with soldiers on the lookout for us. We need another vehicle.'

Eddie pulled off the road into the parking lot of a gilt-topped shrine. The building towered more than seventy feet and managed to shine despite the smog. Several monks in saffron robes were sweeping the entrance steps. Off to the side were a string of tuk-tuks for hire. He stopped the van next to them and jumped out. The motorized tricycles, powered by 50cc engines, could seat three, and were as anonymous as yellow cabs in Manhattan.

Seng pulled the keys from the ignition and approached the nearest driver. His negotiation consisted of dangling the keys, pointing to the van and then to the man's three-wheeled scooter. This must have been the best day of his life because the driver couldn't nod fast enough.

While this was going on, Juan tucked the pistol into his waistband and made sure his T-shirt covered the butt before stepping out of the truck. He could hear police sirens. He jumped to the back doors and opened them. With Hux's help they got MacD out and over Cabrillo's good shoulder. The broken one shot out spears of agony with every move. He walked on his knees, and placed MacD as gently as he could in the tuk-tuk's rear bench seat, Julia cradling his head the whole time.

She got in on one side of Lawless, Juan on the other, and Eddie placed himself behind the handlebars. The engine belched a cloud of noxious blue smoke with the first kick of the starter and fired on the second.

A whistle shrilled behind them. A policeman was rushing up the road on a bicycle, waving a hand and blasting away with his whistle.

Eddie popped the clutch as the cop fumbled for his sidearm. The tuk-tuk had the acceleration of a boulder rolling uphill. Its woefully underpowered engine strained to get them moving. The cop was thirty yards away when the little jitney started going and was coming at a breakneck pace.

The other tuk-tuk drivers sensed trouble and vanished behind a hedge of blooming shrubs while the man who'd made the Faustian bargain yelled at Eddie to get off the bike. He ran alongside and pulled at the handlebars.

Seng reached over, grabbed the guy's face, and shoved. He tumbled to the ground in a heap of flying arms and legs. The cop was still gaining but was having a hard time pulling out his weapon. His whistle blasts were becoming shriller as his breathing became more ragged.

He was almost beside them when they hit the street in front of the glittering temple. His uniform was soaked with sweat, but his face showed nothing but resolution. Juan could have simply shot the man, but he was just doing his job. Instead, Cabrillo found a ratty umbrella on the floor at his feet, a convenience for the tuk-tuk's passengers during the rainy season.

He grabbed it up and thrust its point into the spokes

247

of the bike's front wheels at the same time the cop finally got an ancient Makarov pistol out of his holster. The umbrella whipped around and jammed against the front forks, stopping the two-wheeler instantly and launching the cop over the handlebars. He flew a good eight feet before crashing into the road. He rolled a few times and lay still, dazed but alive. The tuk-tuk roared on.

'I think we're clear,' Eddie said after a few moments.

'Let's hope so,' Juan told him.

'Kind of feel bad for the owner of this thing. He'll never get to keep the van, and now he's lost his scooter.'

'Just goes to show that it's as true here as anywhere.'

'What's that?'

'If it sounds too good to be true, it probably is.' Cabrillo turned serious. 'You know that cop's going to tell the military that we're in a tuk-tuk now. Three Westerners riding around with a Chinese driver can't be an everyday occurrence.'

'I know, but there are a hell of a lot more tuk-tuks than white panel vans. Here.'

There had been a straw coolie hat dangling from a handlebar. Eddie passed it back to Juan, who settled it atop his head.

Despite the detours, Eddie seemed to know his way, and soon they were driving on a road parallel to the river. Eventually they found the on-ramp to the Hlaing River Road and its suspension bridge across.

A third of the way up the arching span, the tuk-tuk had slowed to a crawl. A line of traffic behind them honked as if one voice. Julia jumped over the rear seat, and with her weight gone and her pushing with everything she had they managed to crest the bridge and putter down the far side. As soon as there was room drivers zipped past them, glaring.

'Only about another two miles,' Eddie told him.

They all felt a measure of relief being outside of the city proper. This side of the river had nowhere near the congestion, and there were even some open fields. They headed south, passing swampland on their right and industrial facilities abutting the river on their left. Some of the warehouses appeared abandoned, the metal siding coming off their skeletal frames. Squatter families clustered near them, using them as makeshift homes.

'Oh hell,' Eddie said. Up ahead, in a copse of mangrove, was a short canal dug into the riverbank so that fishing boats could tie up to a pier without being struck by the main current. There was a cluster of large buildings around it that had once been a cannery. Now it was a rust-streaked ruin with a collapsed roof, and the pier built along the three-hundred-foot canal was more rot than wood. The *Liberty* was tucked partially under the quay, her normally safety-orange upper deck sporting matte-black paint.

What had upset Seng was the navy patrol boat hovering about thirty feet from the *Liberty* with a crewman standing in the bow training a .30 caliber at their craft. Also, a police cruiser was parked in the cannery's lot, and two officers were walking toward the lifeboat with their weapons drawn.

Eddie motored past the cannery's entrance gate and pulled into the next driveway, which happened to be for another abandoned warehouse. An old woman in a dingy dress was cooking over an open fire pit and didn't bother looking up from her chore.

'What do you think?' Eddie asked.

Cabrillo considered the situation. The police would soon figure out there was no one aboard and, since the engine was tamperproof, would eventually tow it away behind the fifteen-meter patrol boat. They had to act fast. Juan unlaced his remaining boot and pulled off his sock.

'Whew,' Julia exclaimed at the odor.

'Be grateful you're upwind of this thing,' he quipped. 'Eddie, you're going to have to carry MacD. With my shoulder broken I can't do it and run.' Though Eddie wasn't particularly big, a lifetime of martial arts training had given him phenomenal strength. 'Julia, you're with Eddie. Get the boat fired up as fast as you can and meet me on the point at the end of the canal. Oh, I need a lighter.'

Eddie flipped him a Zippo. 'What are you going to do?'

'Create a diversion.' Juan had gotten out of the tuk-tuk and come around to unscrew the gas cap. It was three-quarters full. He pressed the sock into the tank, and soon gasoline wicked up through the cotton fibers.

This time, with Juan on the driver's seat, they drove slowly past the cannery again, and just when they lost sight of the police cruiser because of the mangroves he stopped to let out the other three. Eddie's expression remained the same as he deadlifted MacD Lawless onto his shoulder.

'I'll give you ten minutes to get as close as you can. By then the cops will have holstered their pistols, and the guy on the machine gun should be relaxed.'

It was bad luck among the Corporation team to wish someone good luck, so they parted without another word. Julia and Eddie stepped into the mangrove forest, sloshing through knee-high water, and soon vanished from sight.

Juan had no watch, but his internal clock worked with quartz-powered precision. He gave them exactly five minutes before kicking down on the starter. It refused to fire. He jumped on it twice more with the same result.

'Come on, you stupid thing.' He kicked again. Each thrust with his leg caused the broken ends of his collarbone to grate together.

He feared he'd flood the motor, so he gave it a few seconds before trying again. He got the same result. In his mind's eye the marine patrol was securing tow ropes to the *Liberty*'s bow and the cops were headed back to their car.

'Okay, you sweet little jewel of a tuk-tuk, cooperate with ole Uncle Juan and I promise I'll treat you nice and gentle.' It was as if the vehicle knew its fate and wanted no part of it.

Then finally on the tenth kick the motor sputtered to life. Juan rubbed the fuel tank fondly. 'Good girl.'

Without a foot to shift the pedal into gear, he had to bend over and move it manually at the same time he let out the clutch. The tuk-tuk came within a hairsbreadth of stalling, but he managed to keep the engine fired. As soon as he could, he popped the transmission into second, and then was in third by the time he cut through the cannery gate. The cops stood on the quay while the patrol boat was backing toward the *Liberty*.

So intent on their prize, none of them paid attention to the buzz-saw whine of the tuk-tuk barreling into the complex. Juan made it to the parked cruiser, its single dome light still pulsing, before one of the officers started back to see what was happening.

Cabrillo slid off, lit the gas-soaked wick sticking out of its tank, and started to commando-crawl as fast as he could.

The sock burned in an instant and detonated the gasoline seconds later. Juan felt the searing heat on his back when the mushroom of flame and smoke erupted like a miniature volcano. Had he been running, the concussion would have blown him off his feet, but he was slithering like a snake and never slowed his pace.

The tuk-tuk blew apart like a grenade, with shrapnel piercing the side of the cruiser on the rear quarter. The car started leaking fuel, and it too went up in a conflagration many times larger than what had just gone off. The rear half of the vehicle lifted five feet into the air before smashing back onto the concrete apron hard enough to snap its frame. The cop who'd left the dock to investigate the three-wheeler's arrival was blown back ten feet.

Through all the carnage Juan continued to crawl, unseen amid the debris littering the open parking lot and the forest of grasses and shrubs that grew up through the cracked pavement. He whimpered each time he moved his bad arm but fought through the pain.

Back in the canal, Julia and Eddie, towing the unconscious MacD, had used the cover of the pier to reach the *Liberty* after making it through the mangrove swamp. The lifeboat was big enough to accommodate forty passengers in its fully enclosed cabin. She had two conns. One was a fully enclosed cockpit at the bow, and the other was an open helm at the very stern, with a door leading down into the hull. A band of narrow windows ringed the cabin, and there was a second hatch to gain entry just behind the cockpit. It was low enough that Julia could tread water and still manage to open it. She popped the lock as soon as the jitney cab detonated.

Kicking her legs and pulling with her arms, she managed to wriggle through. Forty feet away, and in plain view, the four men on the sleek patrol boat were watching the fireworks and paying no heed to the lifeboat. Juan's distraction was working flawlessly.

By the time the police cruiser exploded, Eddie had passed up MacD and was halfway into the *Liberty* himself. The interior was low-ceilinged but bright. The bench seats all had three-point harnesses for the passengers almost like the safety gear on a roller coaster, because in heavy seas the *Liberty* could flip completely over and still manage to right herself.

Julia went straight for the cockpit while Eddie bent over the bilge cover to recover a long plastic tube clipped down in the dank recess of the craft. The twin engines rumbled to life, and Julia gave it no time to warm up before advancing the throttles to their stops.

Eddie staggered back under the brutal acceleration but kept on his feet. As soon as he got a better stance he unscrewed one end of the tube and slid out an FN FAL, a venerable Belgian assault rifle, and two magazines. No one really knew why Max had cached a weapon like this on a lifeboat, but Eddie was grateful for it now because once they had the Chairman, he knew the fight was far from over. He rammed home one of the mags and joined Julia in the cockpit. She intentionally brushed against the slightly smaller patrol boat as they shot past. The hit scraped paint off both vessels but, more important, dumped the guy manning the machine gun into the canal.

They left him bobbing in their wake even as another crewman scrambled to get behind the weapon.

In just a few seconds they were adjacent to the small promontory at the end of the man-made canal, but there was no sign of Cabrillo. And the patrol boat was halfway turned around for a pursuit. Juan suddenly emerged from where he'd been lying behind an overturned barrel. His face was a mask of determination even if his body looked utterly ridiculous as he hopped one-legged for the boat. Each leap carried him almost four feet, and his balance was such that he barely paused before flinging himself forward again.

Eddie ran aft to open the upper hatch, and as soon as he popped out into the sunshine he loosed a short burst from the FN at the patrol boat. Angry fountains of water erupted all around the black-hulled craft, and the men ducked for cover beneath the gunwales.

Julia throttled back but didn't kill power entirely as she came abreast of Cabrillo. He gathered himself for one more leap and hurtled across the open space between the shore and the boat and crashed onto the upper deck in an ungainly belly flop. She buried the throttles as soon as she heard him hit. The speed with which the *Liberty* got on plane was such that, had Eddie not grabbed him, Juan would have tumbled over the stern.

'Thanks,' Cabrillo panted. He pressed himself into the molded jockey seat that was little more than a padded shelf for your butt and rubbed at his thigh. The muscle burned with built-up lactic acid.

They had at least a hundred yards on their pursuers, but now that the patrol boat wasn't under fire it was quickly accelerating. The gap narrowed deceptively fast. The sailor behind the machine gun bent to take aim. Juan and Eddie ducked a second before he opened fire. He raked the seas to their port side and then swept the barrel across the transom, high-powered rounds chewing at the fiberglass.

Julia juked the *Liberty* to throw off his aim, but the

maneuver cost her speed, and the gap tightened further. Eddie rose from behind cover and opened up. This time he was aiming to hit something, but even on a smooth river a boat is not the best firing platform, and his shots went wide.

Traffic on the water was heavy, with barges under tow and all manner of shipping, from small one-man skiffs to five-hundred-foot freighters. The two boats raced each other like competitors. The Burmese skipper knew he had superior speed to the bluntly ugly lifeboat, but he couldn't get too close to the gunfire. It was a standoff that lasted for a mile as both craft tried to get an advantage by using other ships as moving obstacles.

'Enough of this,' Juan said when he felt he was sufficiently rested. He ducked his head into the cabin and shouted over the engine's roar, 'Julia, I'm taking the conn.'

'Okay. Good. I need to check on MacD. This can't be doing him any good.'

The control panel at the rear helm station was simple and straightforward except for one switch hidden under the dash. Cabrillo eyed the speedometer for a second and saw they had more than enough speed. He hit the button. Activated by hydraulics, it extended a series of wings and foils under the hull that knifed through the water with almost no resistance. The hull was lifted until only the foils and her prop were in contact with the river.

The acceleration was twice anything they'd experienced before, and the lifeboat/hydrofoil was soon doing sixty knots. Juan glanced back in time to see a look of awe on the patrol boat skipper's face before the distance grew too much and he became just a dot on a rapidly receding horizon.

They cut across the water with the beauty of a porpoise, swinging around slower ships like a Formula One car chasing the checkered flag. Juan knew there wasn't a boat in the Myanmar navy that could touch them, and he seriously doubted they'd get a chopper into the air in time.

Two minutes later Julia popped up through the hatch. She handed Juan a bottled water and helped him ease his arm into a sling. She also taped a chemical ice pack to his shoulder and shook some painkillers into his hand.

'And that, fearless leader, is the best medical science has come up with for a broken collarbone,' she said, giving him a couple of protein bars from an emergency rations kit. She then grew a little sheepish. 'Sorry, I forgot this tub has turbo boost. I would have kicked it into high gear sooner.'

'No worries. Get on the horn and tell Max we're heading home. Wait. How's Lawless?'

Her expression darkened. 'Don't know. He's still nonresponsive.'

They continued to thunder down the river, flashing under two more bridges. To their left the city scrolled by – container ports, cement works, lading piers – and finally they were past the downtown business district, with its clutch of high-rise office towers and apartment blocks.

A police boat had been launched to intercept them. Juan could see blue lights flashing on its radar arch as it skimmed across the waves on an intercept course. If this was the best the city had to offer, it was sadly short. Cabrillo calculated the vectors as the speedboat came at them and realized that it would pass at least a hundred yards astern of the *Liberty*.

He gave the captain kudos for effort, because even when it became clear they had no chance of catching the hydrofoil, he kept his two outboards pegged until he swung into the lifeboat's wake at the exact distance Juan had figured. He chased them for almost a half mile, the distance lengthening with each second, until he finally admitted defeat and broke off. Juan threw him a wave as if to acknowledge the game attempt.

The river widened the closer they came to the sea until the banks were distant blurs of jungle. It grew muddier too as tidal action and ocean waves stirred up sediment from the bottom. Traffic thinned to just the occasional containership or fishing smack. Juan knew the smart thing to do now was to throttle back and act just like any other vessel out here, but he hadn't forgotten that the navy had assets in the air and along the coast hunting for the *Oregon*, so the quicker they made their rendezvous, the quicker he could get them all safely over the horizon.

Julia came back with a spare radio, since Eddie's had been in the drink. Juan called his ship on a preset frequency. 'Breaker, Breaker, this is the Rubber Duck, come back.'

'Rubber Duck, you've got the Pig Pen, ten-four.'

'Max, it's great to hear your voice. We're almost to the mouth of the Yangon River. What's your twenty?'

Hanley read off some GPS coordinates, which Eddie jotted down and then entered inversely into the *Liberty*'s navigation computer. It was a simple ploy on the off chance someone who understood idiomatic American CB lingo was paying them any interest.

'We'll be there in about twenty minutes,' Juan said when the readout flashed their ETA.

'That's good, because the Burmese navy will have one of their Chinese-built Hainan-class missile destroyers on our doorstep in about twenty-five. She's got a mess of cannons and packs antiship rockets up the wazoo. We've been swatting at helicopters for the past hour. Haven't splashed any of them yet since no one's fired at us, but things are going to get real hairy real soon.'

'Copy that, good buddy. Smokey's a-comin'. Best if we transfer to the boat garage and deep-six the *Liberty*.'

'Sounds like a plan, just so long as we don't have a problem and sink being one lifeboat short.'

'Never a fear,' Juan said with typical bravado. 'Oh, and alert medical that we have a head-trauma case. Have a gurney standing by. The secret police did a number on MacD in prison.'

Cabrillo pressed the throttle levers to see if he could coax another knot or two out of the *Liberty*'s engine, but it was giving everything it had. The air lost a lot of its humidity and freshened as they made the transition from the river to the ocean. The seas remained calm, so Juan could keep the hydrofoil up on her wings and skipping across the water.

The next fifteen minutes passed without incident, but then Juan spotted something in the distance, a speck floating just above the horizon. It soon resolved itself into another Mil helicopter that was thundering toward them at full military power. The big helo was flying at less than five hundred feet when it roared overhead, the whop of its rotors sounded like crashing thunder.

The pilot must have satisfied himself with a positive identification, because when he came around again the side door had been rolled open and a pair of soldiers stood ready with AKs. Points of light winked at the muzzle tips, and lead rained from the sky. Their aim was thrown off by the speed of the chase, but the amount of ammunition they were pouring down on the hydrofoil was staggering. Holes erupted on the *Liberty*'s unarmored roof while bits of chewed-up fiberglass whipped by Eddie and Cabrillo at the helm. Eddie fired a controlled burst back at the chopper and managed to score a hit. A spray of blood pattered the inside of the copilot's window.

Juan weaved the hydrofoil back and forth, trading a little speed to keep them out of another deadly assault.

'My kingdom for a Stinger missile,' Eddie said.

Cabrillo nodded glumly.

'Rubber Duck, we have a chopper on radar at about your position,' Max called over the radio.

'He's right above us. Anything you can do?'

'Wait two minutes.'

'Roger.'

The chopper dove in for another run once the soldiers had reloaded. Juan cut the hydrofoil hard to starboard, skipping it across the waves like a stone and nearly tearing away her underwater wings. His quick maneuver put the boat directly under the Mil and robbed the gunman of their open shots, and Cabrillo matched the pilot's every turn as he attempted to shake them out of his blind spot. Eddie put the FN to his shoulder and fired straight up, peppering the underside of the chopper with a dozen perfectly aimed rounds.

This time it was the helicopter that was forced to retreat. It took up a station at around two hundred feet in altitude and more than a thousand yards off the *Liberty*'s starboard rail. The pilot maintained their speed but showed no interest in coming closer. That last attack had cost him.

Then from over the horizon came a streaking blur that cut the air like lightning. It was a burst from the *Oregon*'s 20mm Gatling gun dialed up to its maximum of four thousand rounds per minute. At that setting it wasn't individual bullets she threw into the sky but a solid wall of tungsten hitting hypersonic speeds. Such was the ship's targeting system that the rounds came within three feet of the chopper's spinning rotor without hitting it. Had they wanted, they could have blown the helicopter into a falling meteor of scrap aluminum, but the demonstration of such awesome firepower was more than enough.

The Mil banked away violently and soon vanished.

A moment later Juan spotted the *Oregon* as she waited patiently for her wayward children. Under her patch-work coats of naval paint and artfully applied rust streaks she was the most beautiful sight in the world to him. The garage-style door of her boat garage was opened at the waterline amidships on her starboard side. While Eddie made ready to open the sea cocks and send the *Liberty* to a watery grave she did not deserve, Juan guided her in to a perfect stop. Max stood on the sloping ramp with two orderlies from medical and a gurney for MacD. Behind them loomed a second RHIB assault craft like the one they had abandoned in the jungle. It sat on a launching cradle that could shoot it out of the ship using hydraulic rams.

Juan tossed Hanley a line, which he tied off to a cleat.

'Good to see you.'

'Good to be back,' Juan said with a weariness he felt all the way to his bones. 'I tell you, my friend, this has been a nightmare from the word go.'

'Amen to that,' Hanley agreed.

The orderlies boarded the lifeboat, carrying a back-board to stabilize Lawless and prevent any more injuries. They moved quickly, knowing that they were minutes away from engaging in a battle with Myanmar's finest gunboat.

Once MacD was lifted clear and was on his way to the infirmary with Julia huddled over the speeding gurney, Eddie opened the seacocks and leapt from the lifeboat.

'Sorry,' Juan said, and patted the *Liberty*'s coaming before making the jump himself.

Max mashed an intercom button that linked to the high-tech Op Center. 'Punch it, Eric. We're out of time.'

Then came an echoing boom from across the sea followed by the high-pitched shriek of an artillery shell in flight and then an explosion of water thirty yards beyond the wallowing *Liberty*. Hanley was right. They were out of time. Almost immediately they were bracketed by a second shell. The *Oregon* was pinned.

13

Deep inside the ship's hull, her revolutionary engines came online with a command from Eric Stone. The supercooled magnets sitting encased in liquid nitrogen began stripping free electrons from the seawater being sucked through her drive tubes, creating an incredible amount of electricity that was transformed into horse-power by the pump jets. Like a thoroughbred that breaks from a standstill to a full gallop, the *Oregon* took off, a bone in her teeth and a creaming wake at her stern. The cryopumps' whine soon went ultrasonic and disappeared above the normal range of hearing.

A third blast concussed the air, and an explosive shell hit the ocean in the exact spot the ship had occupied moments earlier. It blew up a towering fountain of water that stayed suspended for what seemed like an impossible amount of time before collapsing with a guttural splash.

Cabrillo's first order, as he was hobbling to the Op Center with Max supporting one arm, was to send a crewman to his cabin to get him another prosthetic leg.

The high-tech room buzzed with coiled energy that gave the air an electric tang. Eric and Mark Murphy were in their customary seats. Hali Kasim was to the right, monitoring communications, and Linc had taken over the radar station generally manned by Linda Ross when the ship was facing danger. Gomez Adams was at a spare workstation, flying an aerial drone over the area. The drone – really, just a large commercial RC plane – was fitted with a high-def Minicam that relayed incredible real-time pictures.

'Sit rep,' Juan commanded when he threw himself into the Kirk Chair.

'Single Hainan-class missile destroyer about twelve thousand yards off the port beam and coming in at about fourteen knots,' Eric reported.

'Wepps, how are we looking?' That was Cabrillo's nickname for whoever commanded the *Oregon*'s array of weaponry, usually Murph.

'I've got target lock with an Exocet missile, and I've run out the 120mm cannon. I've also got two Gatlings deployed for antimissile defense.'

The Exocets were launched from tubes mounted in the deck with hatches designed to look like typical inspection ports. The Gatling guns were placed in the hull and protected by metal plates that could swing out of the way. The big cannon, which used the same fire-control system as an M1A1 Abrams main battle tank, was housed in the bow. Clamshell doors opened outward, and the gun was run out on a hydraulic carriage that gave it almost one hundred and eighty degrees of traverse. This system's only drawback was that the gun had to be decoupled from its autoloader at the extremes of its swing.

On the main view screen was an aerial image of the

Myanmarian ship cutting through the waves. Every few seconds what appeared to be a cotton ball would burst from one of the twin muzzles of her turret-mounted main guns as they continued to fire at the *Oregon*. The ship was about one hundred and seventy-five feet in length, with a knife-edged prow and boxy superstructure. The resolution was crisp enough to see she was a tired-looking boat.

Cabrillo called up the specifications of the Chinese-built gunboat and grunted aloud when he saw it had a top speed of over thirty knots. The *Oregon* could still outrun her, but they would be in range of her 57mm deck gun for an uncomfortable interval.

'Wait, how fast did you say she was approaching?' he asked.

'Fourteen knots, steady.'

'Gotta love the Third World,' Juan said. 'They don't have the money for proper maintenance. I bet that's all the speed she's got.'

A warning alarm went off at the radar station. 'He's got a lock on us,' Linc warned.

'Jam it!'

'Missile launch detected.'

'Murph?'

'Got it.'

The portside Gatling gun, with its own radar, scanned the sky and spotted the big missile as it came at them at wave-top height. With its three-hundred-pound shaped explosive warhead, the rocket would blow a hole into the *Oregon* big enough to rival the damage done to the

USS *Cole*. The Gatling's computer processor designated the threat, adjusted its aim slightly, and let rip with a four-second burst. It didn't sound like a gun as it fired but rather some sort of mechanical saw. It was the sound of tearing on an industrial scale.

At the same time, chaff launchers threw up a curtain of thin aluminum strips that obscured the *Oregon* from enemy detection on the off chance the missile got past the Gatling. And luminescent flares to confuse its heat-seeking capabilities were launched with the gusto of a Fourth of July fireworks show.

The missile tracked in dead level and ran into the hail of 20mm Gatling rounds when it had traveled less than three miles. Two hundred and seventy-six rounds completely missed the rocket and plummeted harmlessly into the sea. One round did connect, and the missile exploded, smearing the sky with an elongated trail of fire as its charge went off and the remaining solid rocket fuel detonated catastrophically.

But that wasn't the end of the battle. The destroyer's deck guns continued to fire at nearly eight rounds a minute. With both ships on the move, and the *Oregon*'s cross section half of what it should be because of some radar-absorbing material applied to her super-structure, the shots were falling pretty wild.

Juan checked their speed and guesstimated that they would remain in range for the better part of fourteen minutes. That left the potential for more than a hundred rounds coming at them. A few were bound to be magic bullets and hit. His ship was armored against the types of weapons pirates employed – heavy machine guns and RPGs fired at the hull. An explosive round arcing in on a high parabola would slice through the deck plates, and the charge would detonate inside the ship with deadly results. If it managed to hit the liquid nitrogen storage tanks, the resulting explosion would unleash a deadly cloud of superchilled gas that would freeze the entire crew solid and so distort the hull's steel that the ship would crush herself under her own weight.

It was a risk he couldn't take. He noted too that a Hainan-class destroyer carried a crew of seventy. An Exocet launch would sink them. And there was no close-by shipping to rescue survivors.

He made his decision quickly.

'Helm, bring us hard about one hundred and twenty degrees. Wepps, when you have a bearing on that ship, engage with the one-twenty. Let's see if we can convince him that this is a fight he can't win.'

The *Oregon* dug her shoulder into the sea as her directional jets, with the help of an athwartship thruster, threw her into the tightest turn she could make. Loose items flew off shelves, and everyone had to lean into the turn to keep balanced. As the bow came about, Mark Murphy waited until he had a lock and then opened fire. Typically, they could fire twice as fast as the Burmese ship, but the gun was at its most oblique angle so the autoloader had to reengage after every round.

Unlike the smaller gun firing at them, the 120 fired at a flat, lancing trajectory. The *Oregon* shuddered when the gun roared.

All eyes were on the view screen. A second after the cannon discharged the discarding sabot round, the tungsten dart hit the destroyer square in the turret. The kinetic energy blew through its thin armor without a check in speed, and it impacted the breech of one of the two 57mm guns and detonated the round that was in the chamber. The turret came apart like an opening umbrella, its skin flaying up and out in a blistering cloud of fire and smoke. The smoke curled and coiled over the ship's deck as she charged on blindly for a few seconds.

Juan gave them a count of ten, and, when the Mayanmarian ship didn't slow, said, 'Fire two.'

The big cannon had gone through the complicated loading sequence automatically, so when Mark pressed a key on his computer, it discharged another round.

This time he put the shot right through a bridge window. Had he used a high explosive, it would have killed everyone in the room. As it was, the sabot round hit with massive force, blowing out all the windows, wrecking helm control, and turning the radio room just aft of the bridge into a charred ruin.

The Hainan-class destroyer began to slow. She would have sheered away on a different course but could no longer control her rudder, and it would be several minutes before anyone senior enough left alive transferred steering to auxiliary control.

'Nicely done, Wepps,' Juan congratulated. A smile tugged at his lips when he saw Maurice enter the bridge, carrying one of his artificial legs. This limb was all titanium struts and exposed mechanics and looked like something out of a *Terminator* movie. The steward had had the foresight to bring Juan another pair of shoes. 'You don't know how ridiculous I feel without that thing.'

'And look, Captain,' Maurice deadpanned. 'How ridiculous you look too.'

'What's our new heading, Juan?' Eric asked.

'Get us to Brunei at the best possible speed. Maurice, rustle up some food and bring it to the conference room. I want all senior staff except Hux, who has to stay with MacD, in there in thirty minutes. We have a lot of ground to cover.'

Cabrillo gave them a tight deadline because he had no intention of luxuriating in a long, steamy shower. He didn't want to unwind. He wanted to stay as tight and focused as possible until Linda Ross was safely back aboard the *Oregon*.

Juan was the first to arrive in the boardroom. The thick glass table could seat a dozen comfortably on black leather ergonomic chairs. The walls were painted a chocolate/gray with recessed pin spotlighting and flat-panel screens on the two shortest walls. Louvers could be lowered over large square windows to let in natural light, but Maurice had rightly left them closed. The steward was just finishing laying out silver chafing dishes filled with several Indian curry dishes.

An orderly in blue scrubs was also there with an IV bag on a skeletal metal stand.

'Doctor Huxley's orders,' he said when Juan questioned his presence. 'The amount of dehydration you suffered has unbalanced your electrolytes and played havoc with your kidneys. This will help.'

Cabrillo had to admit he wasn't anywhere near a hundred percent. His head ached, and he felt fluey. He sat at the head of the table while Maurice prepared him a plate of food and an iced tea and the orderly threaded the IV into his left forearm, freeing his unhurt right to eat.

'Any word on MacD?' he asked.

'Sorry, no change. He's still in a coma.'

Eddie Seng and Max Hanley came in moments later, followed by Eric Stone and Mark Murphy. The two techno-junkies were carrying laptops that could jack into the ship's dedicated Wi-Fi and were discussing the most useless apps for the iPhone.

Everyone helped themselves to the food and took their customary places around the table. Linda's empty seat was a grim reminder of why they were there, and the absence of her elfin face and quick wit made for a somber mood.

'Okay,' Juan began. He set a napkin aside. 'Let's go over the knowns. Roland Croissard double-crossed us. His hiring us to find his daughter was just a pretense to help his henchman, Smith, get into Myanmar and presumably steal whatever was in a small satchel we found on the body of someone I can only assume was a member of a team he had sent into the country earlier.'

'Their failure was why he brought us in,' Max said in

an acknowledging tone. It made sense, and everyone nodded.

'What was in the satchel?' Eddie asked.

'No idea,' Juan replied. 'Probably it was something looted from a long-lost Buddhist temple. As I look back on it, there was damage to a wooden dais in the main prayer chamber. Whatever it was had probably been hidden there.'

'Just to play devil's advocate,' Max said. 'What if Croissard's clean and it was Smith who pulled off the double cross?'

'Has anyone been able to contact Croissard since this mission turned sour?' Juan looked around the table.

'No,' Hanley admitted.

'Besides,' Juan added, 'we were sent out supposedly to find his daughter. I'm sure now that the body in the river was that of a slender man with longish hair. You have tried calling Croissard's office number and not just his cell?'

'Yeah. We even managed to get to his private secretary. She says that he is traveling and can't be reached.'

'Typical runaround,' Juan summed up. He looked to Mark and Eric. 'I want you two to track him down. He flew into Singapore on a private jet, I'm sure. Find out which and track where it went after our meeting. It's probably owned by his company, so it shouldn't be too tough.'

'What about the attack in Singapore?' Max asked. 'Does our thinking change on that, knowing what we know now?'

'I had time to consider it while I was being held

prisoner. I can't see how Croissard's betrayal changes our perception of that assault. I really believe it was just like we thought originally. Wrong place, wrong time. The big question on my mind is, why? Why did Croissard do this? Why hire us only to betray us?'

'Because whatever he was after was something he knew we wouldn't get for him,' Eric said. 'Croissard came to us through the Cypriot information broker *L'Enfant*, right? He knows the kinds of missions we deal with. So in order to get us to accept, Croissard had to make it something he knew would interest us. And come on, Juan, could you resist saving the beautiful daughter of a billionaire? Could any of us?'

'Damsel in distress,' Max grumbled. 'Oldest ploy in the book.'

'The other thing I'm wondering,' Mark Murphy interjected. 'How did the Myanmar military get mixed up in all this? I mean, if Croissard had contacts in the government, why not use them instead of sneaking around?'

The question hung unanswered because no one had a logical answer.

Eddie finally said, 'Could he have brokered a last-minute deal?'

Everyone agreed quickly since it was the only suggestion put forth. Cabrillo knew that this was dangerous groupthink, but he also had a feeling that in this instance it was the correct answer.

He asked, 'How are we coming on a more in-depth look at Croissard?'

'Ah,' Mark started, but then Eric Stone stepped in.

'Max has had us digging since you and Linda dropped comms and began choppering out of the jungle. Of course we looked into his background as a standard part of taking on a new client. That check showed he was squeaky clean. And as much as it pains us to admit it, the more we've dug, the shinier the guy is.'

Mark Murphy nodded. 'But we know there's something, right? I mean this guy has serious ulterior motives. We've even double-checked on his daughter, Soleil. The upload to her Facebook account that talks about her upcoming trip came from a personal laptop using a Wi-Fi connection at a coffee shop two blocks from her apartment in Zurich. She was booked on a Lufthansa flight from Zurich to Dubai and then on to Dhaka, Bangladesh. She checked into her room at the Hotel Sarina and caught a flight the next day to Chittagong, where she said she and her friend—'

'Paul Bissonette,' Cabrillo offered, knowing now that name would be seared on his brain forever. 'Smith positively ID'd his body, but I guess that was bogus.'

'Anyway, his travel itinerary matches hers, though he had a standard room and she slept in the Imperial Suite. It was from Chittagong that they had planned to start their trek.'

'Any idea how she was getting into the jungle or her exact destination?'

'No. She was cagey about that on Facebook. She did send a Twitter message from Chittagong, saying that the real adventure was about to begin, and then nothing other than what Croissard says she phoned in.'

'So Croissard used his daughter's planned expedition into the jungles of Bangladesh as cover for his own mission. We have to assume that she'll return soon enough with her buddy, yes?'

'More than likely,' Murph agreed.

Cabrillo went silent for a moment, his chin resting on his hand. 'Okay, that's all in the past,' he said. 'Tell me about the present. Where did they take Linda?'

Eric flipped open his laptop and worked the keys for a second. An overhead image of the open ocean appeared on the two flat-panel displays at either end of the room. The picture was tight so the resolution was poor. 'This is a Google Earth shot of the exact coordinates where her tracker chip's signal went dark.'

'And there's nothing there,' Cabrillo snapped. He was looking for answers, not more enigmas. 'She was ferried out to a ship, probably Croissard's private yacht, and it's long gone by now.'

'That was the first thing we checked,' Stone said. He hit another couple of keys, and the picture of a snowy-white luxury cruiser snapped up on the screens. She looked to be well over two hundred feet long and capable of cruising through the roughest seas. 'This is the *Pascal*, Croissard's private yacht, and she's been anchored off Monte Carlo for the past five months. I confirmed with the harbormaster this morning. She hasn't gone anywhere.'

'Okay, so another boat.'

'Maybe not.'

Eric returned to the original picture of the ocean

where Linda vanished and started zooming out so that a greater and greater swath of the sea was revealed. Small square objects appeared at the edge of the picture. Stone moused the cursor over one, clicked to center it, and started zooming back in.

'What the . . .'

In seconds the image resolved itself to reveal a massive offshore oil platform, complete with a flare stack, loading crane, and a chopper pad cantilevered over the side.

'These are some of the most oil-rich parts of the world,' Eric remarked. 'There are literally hundreds of drilling rigs off Brunei's coast. That's how the sultan got so rich. Also, there's more than enough metal on one of those behemoths to block Linda's tracker chip.'

'But there wasn't a platform anywhere near where her signal dropped out,' Max said.

'No,' Mark chimed in, 'but who knows how long ago these pictures were taken? Google update their maps all the time, but they still lag far behind the real world. An oil rig could have been installed just a couple months ago and it might not show up for years.'

'Then we need more updated imagery,' Juan said.

'We're doing one better,' Eric told him. 'We're trying to hire a chopper to fly out there and put some eyeballs on the target.' Stone put up his hands in a defensive posture when he saw a look sweep across Cabrillo's face. 'Don't worry, we'll make sure he stays far enough away so no one gets suspicious.'

'When will you hear back?'

'I'm hoping today. The helicopter-charter company is mostly booked up, taking workers and equipment out to the oil fields, but they told me that they might be able to divert one of their helos this afternoon for a quick look-see.'

'Good idea.' With his belly full and the IV clearing his mind and restoring his body, Cabrillo needed all his focus to stay awake. 'What's our ETA?'

Eric pulled up another screen on his computer that detailed the ship's position and speed and had a running estimate of their journey. 'Forty-five hours.'

'Eddie, I want you and Linc to dust off our contingency plan for storming an offshore oil rig. Go over them with the rest of the gundogs and make sure everyone's up to speed. Eric and Mark, keep digging up anything you can find on Croissard and his pet Neanderthal, John Smith. I bet he really was in the French Foreign Legion. Maybe you can snoop through their electronic archives.'

'You got it.'

'What about me?' Max asked.

Juan got up from the table and winked. 'Just sit there and look pretty.'

He was back in his cabin, the drapes closed, the air-conditioning cranked, and his covers pulled up tight less than sixty seconds later. Despite his exhaustion, his mind was troubled with images of Linda Ross being held captive, and the nagging feeling they had all missed something critical. Sleep came grudgingly.

The jangling of an old-fashioned telephone dragged

him out of the abyss. He threw aside the blankets and grabbed up the handset. The matte-black telephone looked like it had come from the 1930s, but it was a modern cordless.

'Chairman, sorry to bother you.'

'No bother, Eric,' Juan said. 'What's up?'

'Eh, we just heard back from the helicopter-charter company.'

'I take it it's not good news?'

'No, sir. Sorry. There's nothing at the coordinates we gave them. They say the pilot overflew it directly.'

Juan swung his legs out of bed. If it hadn't been a rig, then Linda had been transported to a ship. A ship that had several days' head start, and they had no idea in which direction it was heading. Linda was well and truly lost.

'How are you coming along to get better satellite photographs of that area?' he asked after a short pause.

'Well, we, ah, hadn't really looked. The chopper was our best shot.'

'You're right, I know, but humor me. Find some recent pictures anyway. There might be a clue. Maybe they took her aboard a drill ship of some kind. If that's the case, we at least know which needle in the Pacific haystack we're looking for.'

'Okay.' Stone was about to hang up but remembered his report wasn't complete. Like anyone, he was reluctant to admit failure. 'We're still drawing blanks on Croissard, and, as for Smith, we can forget it. Just a quick hack into Foreign Legion archives shows roughly fourteen thousand John Smiths have served with the unit over the past fifty years. It's a popular *nom de guerre*.'

'I figured as much,' Juan admitted, 'but we have to try everything. Keep me posted.'

After a quick shower and shave, Cabrillo stopped in the medical bay. MacD Lawless lay on a standard hospital bed surrounded by some of the most high-tech lifesaving equipment in existence. A heart monitor beeped a strong measured cadence. He was able to breathe on his own, but a clear plastic cannula carrying pure oxygen had been fitted around his ears and under his nose. Juan noted that Lawless's bruising was fading fast and that most of the swelling had gone down. Along with his good looks, the guy had the constitution of an ox.

Hux came around the curtain separating MacD from the rest of the sleek medical ward. As always, she wore her hair in a ponytail and sported a lab coat. Her face bore a doctor's professional blankness.

'How is he?' Juan asked, trying not to sound grave.

Julia suddenly smiled, a beaming grin that lit up the already bright room. 'He's asleep.'

'I know. He's been in a coma—'

'No,' she cut him off quickly. 'He came out of the coma about three hours ago. He actually just barely fell back asleep.'

For whatever reason, there wasn't a doctor in the world that was bothered by waking a patient no matter how badly his body needed sleep. Julia Huxley was no different. She gently shook MacD's shoulder until his eyelids fluttered open. He stared blankly until his jade-green eyes could focus.

'How you doing?' Juan asked warmly.

'Great,' MacD replied, his voice raspy. 'But, man, you should see the other guy.'

'I did,' Cabrillo said. 'He had some of the worst bruised knuckles I've ever seen.'

Lawless started chuckling, but the pain made him moan. 'Don't do that. Don't make me laugh. It hurts too much.' MacD suddenly grew sober as he remembered who he was talking to and how he had crumpled under Soe Than's torture. 'Ah'm sorry, Juan. Ah really am. Ah had no idea it would be so bad.'

'Don't worry about it. All you gave was my name and the name of the ship – a name, I might add, that rarely graces her fantail. Had you not told them who I was, the Chinese government wouldn't have made a deal to haul us back to Beijing, and Eddie wouldn't have been able to figure out a way to rescue our sorry butts. You unwittingly saved our lives.'

Lawless looked dubious, as if there couldn't possibly be an upside.

'Seriously,' Cabrillo went on. 'We'd both be in a Chinese prison right now, looking at life sentences, if you hadn't told Than what you did. If you want to feel bad about breaking, man, I can understand that, but you also have to own up to the fact that in doing so you made our escape possible. It's the whole gray cloud/silver lining thing. What you have to figure out is, which

281

one you want to concentrate on. Choose wrong, and I have no use for you. Okay?'

MacD sniffed back to clear his throat. 'Ah understand. And thanks. Ah hadn't thought about it that way. It looks like that's the second time Ah saved your life.' He tried to smile but couldn't make it stick.

Juan knew that Lawless would come around, and he knew too that hiring him had been the smartest thing he'd done in a long while. 'You get some rest. We're tracking Linda as we speak, so in a few days it'll all be just a story we tell each other over drinks.'

'What? Wait. You're trackin' Linda?'

'Every Corporation operative has a tracker chip embedded in the thigh. It runs biometrically and can be seen from satellites. We're en route to Brunei right now. The last place her chip transmitted from. We'll get her back. No worries.'

'No worries,' Lawless parroted.

Cabrillo nodded to Hux and left medical.

14

The *Oregon* pounded onward, driven as much by her anxious captain as by her remarkable engines. It was fortunate for them that the seas remained calm because the speeds they reached would have meant a terrifying ride had there been significant chop. Usually the ship would stray from a direct route so that no passing vessels would get an inkling of its capabilities, but not this time. Cabrillo didn't care who saw them cutting through the waves at better than forty knots. They were hailed several times, usually by bored radio operators who wanted to know who or what they were. On the Chairman's orders, the *Oregon* maintained radio silence.

The only attempt to look remotely normal was the fake smoke belching from the ship's single funnel. Most sailors who saw her pass by assumed the old tramp freighter had been retrofitted with gas turbines.

Sitting in the Op Center, his arm still in a sling, Cabrillo watched the sea's passage on the big monitor. A glance to his right showed him a big radar repeater dotted with nearby shipping. The Straits of Malacca were perhaps the busiest shipping route in the world, and the near-traffic-jam conditions had forced the *Oregon* to a fraction of her capabilities.

This wasn't Juan's normal watch. It was eight o'clock

at night, and the third shift had the conn. The sun was sinking rapidly behind them, turning the sea into an undulating sheet of burnished copper. When it vanished completely, he knew the shipping would slow even further. The big containerships and tankers had modern navigational aids and could maintain their speed in nearly any condition. The delay would be caused by the dozens of fishing boats and small coastal freighters that they would need to go around.

His only consolation was that they were approaching the end of the narrow strait. Once they reached open waters again, he could give his beloved ship free rein and crank up the magnetohydrodynamics even higher.

'Good evening, everyone,' Julia Huxley announced herself as she entered the Op Center from a passage at the rear of the room. Seated in a wheelchair in front of her, and wearing a hospital johnnie, was MacD Lawless. 'I'm giving my patient the nickel tour. You may recall, Juan, all he saw before was the hallway on the other side of the mess hall.'

'Wow,' Lawless said, wide-eyed. 'This is like the bridge of the *Enterprise*. That's where Chris Pine sat.'

'Who?' Cabrillo asked.

'Chris Pine. He plays Kirk in the movies.'

Juan let the comment pass rather than reveal how far behind the times he was. 'How you doing?'

'Goin' stir-crazy, to be honest,' he drawled. 'The mind is willing, but the flesh is weak. Ah can't stand lyin' around in bed all day. Say, where are we?'

'Malacca Straits.'

'We're makin' good time,' Lawless commented.

'The old girl has a little something extra under the hood, though right now we're down to fifteen knots because of the damned traffic.'

Lawless studied the view screen and said, 'Looks like the I-10 back home.'

'I grew up in California,' Juan told him. 'You don't know traffic until you've seen the 405. So what else has Julia shown you?'

'Your dining room, which Ah have to say is about the swankiest Ah've ever seen. Um, the pool, which was amazin', the gym, some of the crew's quarters. What else? The boat garage and the hangar.'

'You haven't seen the half of it. Down at the keel are doors that open to the sea where we can launch and recover submarines, and the *Oregon* packs more fire-power than just about any ship afloat.'

'Don't ruin my tow,' Julia interjected.

'Once you're feeling better,' Juan said, 'we'll talk about your cabin. It's empty right now, but you start figuring out how you want it set up, and we'll make it happen.'

'Ah've been bunking with a bunch of other operators in a former auto body shop in Kabul, and, before that, housin' was courtesy of Uncle Sam. Ah don't know the first thing about decoratin'.'

'Talk to Linc, then. He opted for a cot and a metal locker and put the rest of his allowance into a Harley Fat Boy he keeps in the hold.'

'Ah like his style.'

Julia intervened, 'You can start your biker gang later. Right now, I'm taking you back to medical.'

'Yes, ma'am,' Lawless said, making his voice sulky like a recalcitrant child and throwing Cabrillo a wink.

Just then Eric Stone and Mark Murphy burst into the room. 'Chairman, we got it,' they said in unison. Neither looked like he'd slept much in the past thirty hours.

'What did you get?'

'Good night, y'all,' MacD said as Hux wheeled him out of the room.

'There was an oil rig there,' Eric said.

He had an open laptop in his arms, which he set down at a spare workstation. In seconds he had an overhead image of an oil production platform on the main viewer. Details were hazy because the shot was so tight, but Juan could see a chopper pad hanging off the side of the rig and make out the shadow of her tall derrick falling across the deck. If he had to guess, he'd say the platform was easily a square acre.

'It's designated the J-61 and hasn't been in use for two years.'

'Who owns it?'

'Dummy front companies. Mark and I are still working on piercing the corporate veil.'

'Is it self-propelled in any way?'

'No. She's a semisubmersible with no propulsion whatsoever. If they moved her, they had to tow her.'

'We know damned well they moved her,' Juan said, staring at the screen as if a satellite picture could give him answers. 'The only question is, when?'

Mark helped himself to coffee from the urn. 'A rig that size would need at least two tugs. We're checking all the big firms to see where their largest boats are now. So far we haven't turned up any in the area recently.'

'Does Croissard have any connection to oceangoing-tug operators?'

'I don't think so,' Mark replied. 'I know he has no dealings in oil or gas exploration.'

'Double-check,' Juan said. He thought about everything that moving a structure of that size would entail. If Linda was on it just a couple of days ago and now it was gone, Croissard would be moving quickly. Coordinating multiple ships in a tight space and then building up enough speed from a dead stop would take how long? he wondered. Four days? Five? That's if everything ran smoothly, and how often did that happen?

If he was in charge of the operation, he'd want something more efficient. How would he do it? How would he transport twenty thousand tons of steel quickly and quietly out of an anchorage it had occupied for years?'

'Wait,' he said aloud as the answer hit him. 'Not a tugboat. A FLO-FLO.'

'A what?'

'FLO-FLO. Float-on/float-off. A heavy-lift ship.'

'A heavy-lift . . . ? Damn, you're right,' Mark said. He took Eric's laptop and typed into a search engine.

The picture that flashed up on the view screen was of a ship unlike any other in the world. Her superstructure was pressed well forward over her bows, with two boxy stacks and bridge wings that extended over her rails. The rest of the nearly eight-hundred-foot-long vessel was open deck space that barely rose above her waterline. This particular picture was of the MV *Blue Marlin* as she carried the crippled USS *Cole* back to the United States for repairs.

This extraordinary class of vessel had ballast tanks that could sink the ship to a predetermined depth. It would then maneuver itself under its load, be it a bomb-damaged guided missile destroyer or an oil platform. Once in position, the ballast tanks were pumped dry, and the entire vessel rose up once again, its cargo piggy-backed atop one hundred and twenty thousand square feet of deck space. When the load was secured with chains, or even welded to the deck, the FLO-FLO could cruise comfortably at around fifteen knots, far faster than a traditional tow, which rarely exceeded five with a load as cumbersome as an oil rig.

Eric took back the laptop, his fingers blurring across the keys, as he searched databases and company records. After four minutes, in which the only sounds in the Op Center were the background thrum of the ship's engines and the whoosh of air through the vents, he looked up. 'There are only five heavy-lift ships in the world big enough to carry a rig like the J-61. Two are under contract to the U.S. Navy, ferrying combat ships so they don't waste engine time and needless mainten-ance while in transit. Another one is approaching the North Sea, carrying a rig to the gas fields from its build-ers in Korea, and one just delivered another oil platform to Angola. The fifth is ferrying a bunch of luxury yachts from the Mediterranean to the Caribbean. Seems the cruising season's about to change over. Sorry, Juan, but your idea doesn't pan out.'

A look of bitter disappointment clouded Cabrillo's face. He was sure that he'd been onto something.

'Not so fast,' Mark Murphy said. While Stone had been busy with his laptop, Murph had been working with his iPad, which also linked wirelessly to the ship's Cray supercomputer. 'Croissard maintains a series of dummy shell companies all incorporated in the Channel Islands. None of them have been active until about a week ago. Since this is obviously a long-range plan, I merely skimmed the file. The company's called Vantage Partners PLC, and it was funded by an offshore bank in the Caymans. Its sole act as an incorporated entity was to sell itself to a Brazilian company. I stopped looking, figuring this was a legitimate business deal that had nothing to do with Croissard's plans in Myanmar.'

'I take it you just dug a little further,' Juan said.

'Yup. The Brazilian company has a division in Indonesia that operates a ship-breaking yard. No financial figures for the deals have been disclosed, but I think what Croissard did was to sell Vantage Partners for significantly less than he funded it for as a way to buy the breaker yard and all the ships they're under contract to dismantle.'

'Is one of them a heavy-lift ship?'

'Give me a second, my hacking into their computer system's almost complete.' Even as he said it, his eyes glued to the iPad, he started grinning. 'Got it. They're taking apart three ships right now. Two commercial fishermen and a bulk carrier. The next job is the MV *Hercules*, a heavy-lift FLO-FLO that's being dismantled as part of its owner's bankruptcy deal. Says here she arrived under her own steam, so she's still in working order.'

'Bingo,' Cabrillo shouted in triumph. 'That's how they're moving the rig. Croissard bought himself a heavy-lifter.'

'This brings up the next question,' Eric said. 'Why? Why move the rig at all?'

'It's not because Linda's aboard,' Juan replied, 'so there's something else on it Croissard doesn't want found.'

'It has to be something pretty big,' Murph pointed out. 'Otherwise they would just take it off the rig and go.'

Cabrillo stayed silent, thinking. Why? wasn't the question that interested him. He wanted to know where Croissard was taking the rig. He tapped at the integrated keyboard built into the arm of his chair and called up a map of the South China Sea. There were the big Indonesian islands of Java, Sumatra, and Borneo, where Brunei was located, and literally thousands of others, most of which were uninhabited. Any one of those would make a perfect hiding spot. The problem was the volume of shipping passing through the region. A vessel as unusual as the *Hercules*, laden with an oil platform, was sure to be noticed and reported.

Just as in his first meeting with Croissard in Singapore, Juan felt like he was missing something. Maybe Eric's question was more pertinent after all. Why risk moving the rig? Murph had said that there was something aboard it the Swiss financier didn't want found. But you can't really hide an entire platform. Not easily anyway.

And then Cabrillo saw it. He typed at the keyboard again, and the water of the South China Sea seemed to evaporate off the map projected on the big video screen. Less than a hundred miles from Brunei the continental shelf fell away sharply into the Palawan Trough, a fifteen-thousand-foot chasm that split the seafloor like an ax stroke.

'That's where they're heading,' he said. 'They're going to deep-six the rig with Linda aboard her. Navigator, plot us a course to a point on the trough's rim closest to the rig's last-known location.'

Eric Stone, who was the ship's chief helmsman, took over the navigation workstation and made the calculations himself. It took the *Oregon* a few degrees more northward on their northwesterly heading. They would be cutting a corner on the busy sea-lanes, but as the ship's bow came about, Stone was calculating the speeds and relative positions of all the vessels near enough to show on their broad-range radar.

'If we increase to thirty-five knots, we'll thread right through them,' he announced.

'Do it, and once we're clear of all traffic, put the hammer down.'

*

Dawn found Cabrillo up in the wheelhouse, a big mug of black coffee in hand. The seas remained calm, and fortunately free of shipping. The water was a green as deep as the finest emerald, while the rising sun, diffused through distant clouds, smeared the horizon in a red blush. Somewhere along the line, probably during their slower passage through the Straits of Malacca, a large gull had landed on the starboard wing bridge. He was still there, but with the ship traveling so fast he'd hunkered down behind a wall plate to shelter himself from the ungodly wind.

Cabrillo continued to use the sling for his broken collarbone. Because of it, he wouldn't be joining the raid on the J-61. He would have to confine himself to being a spotter in their MD 520N chopper, which was being preflighted down in the hangar under the number 5 cargo hatch. They would be in position to launch in another thirty minutes.

He hated sending his people into danger when he wasn't there to lead them, so his passive role in this operation was especially maddening. Once the *Hercules* had been sighted, Gomez Adams would return to the *Oregon* to pick up the combat team, leaving Juan to sit on the sidelines. Linc, Eddie, and the other gundogs were more than capable of taking down whoever Croissard had guarding Linda.

The central elevator whispered open behind him in an alcove at the rear of the pilothouse. The crew knew that when the Chairman was up here alone, it was best to leave him that way, so he was mildly irritated at the interruption. He turned and the reprimand died on his lips. Instead, he smiled. MacD Lawless wheeled himself off the elevator. It was clear that he was struggling, but also just as clear that he was determined to make it on his own.

'Ah'd forgotten what a pain it is getting into and out of elevators in these damned contraptions.'

'You're preaching to the choir,' Cabrillo said. 'After the Chinese blew off my leg, I was in one for three months before I could walk on a prosthetic.'

'Ah thought some fresh air would do me some good, but Ah was warned to stay clear of the main deck.'

'Unless you like that windblown look, it's good advice. We're making better than forty knots.'

Lawless couldn't hide his astonishment. Because he was in a wheelchair, he could only see the sky through the bridge windows. Cabrillo got up from his seat and crossed to the portside flying bridge door. It was a sliding door, so that it could be opened or closed no matter the conditions. As soon as it was slid back just a couple of inches, hurricane-force winds howled through the gap, rustling the old chart held to the table with equally out-of-date books on navigation. Though it was early morning, the air was hot and heavy with humidity, but at the pounding velocity with which it blew into the bridge it still felt refreshing.

Cabrillo opened the door completely and stood back so MacD could maneuver his chair out onto the flying bridge. His hair whipped around his head, and he had to raise his voice to be heard over the gale. 'This is incredible. Ah had no idea a ship this big could move so fast.'

'There isn't another like her on the high seas,' Juan told him pridefully.

Lawless spent a minute staring out to sea, his face unreadable, and then he backed himself inside once again. Cabrillo closed the door.

'Ah should get goin' on to medical,' Lawless said with some reluctance. 'Doc Huxley doesn't know Ah'm AWOL. Good luck today.' He held out a hand.

Juan kept his arms at his side. 'Sorry, but we kind of have a superstition about that. Never wish someone luck before a mission.'

'Oh, sorry. Ah didn't . . .'

'Don't sweat it. Now you know and you won't spook the others.'

'How's this? *See you later.*'

Cabrillo nodded. 'You got it. See you later.'

On Juan's orders the *Oregon*'s engines were reversed when they were at the absolute limit of their chopper's range. They would have very little time over the target area, but he wanted to find the *Hercules* as quickly as possible. If he had miscalculated and the FLO-FLO heavy-lift ship wasn't transiting toward the Palawan Trough, there was virtually no chance they'd spot it from the helicopter no matter how much time they had on target. The ship, and its cargo, would be long gone.

The impeller blades inside the gleaming drive tubes had their pitch reversed, and the water that had been blasting through the stern was suddenly jetting out the forward intakes. It looked for a moment like two torpedoes had struck the ship, with frothing water exploding up and over the bows. The deceleration was enough to buckle knees. As soon as her speed dropped below ten knots, the rear hatch cover rolled forward, and a hydraulic lift pushed the black chopper into the daylight. Cabrillo was already buckled into the front passenger seat, a large pair of binoculars over his shoulder. Max Hanley sat in back to act as a second spotter.

Technicians locked the five folding rotor blades into place as soon as they cleared the ship's rail, and Gomez fired the souped-up turbine. When he had greens across the boards, he engaged the transmission, and the big overhead rotor began to beat the sultry air. Because of her NOTAR configuration, the 520 was a much quieter and steadier helicopter as the blades reached takeoff velocities. Adams fed her more power and gave the collective a slight twist. The skids lifted off the deck, and then he goosed her hard, pulling up and away from the *Oregon* in a blinding climb that kept them well aft of her forest of derrick cranes.

They had to loop far to the east so that they would approach the search area from behind the *Hercules*. They did this for two reasons. One, they would be coming out of the rising sun, effectively making them invisible to any lookouts. Second, with the big oil platform straddling her cargo deck, the ship's forward-mounted radar would have a huge blind spot back over her fantail. They would never see them coming.

The flight was tedious, as any flight over water tended to be. No one was in the mood for conversation. Usually there would be banter between the men, a way to alleviate the tension gripping them all, but cracking jokes while Linda Ross's life hung in the balance wasn't appealing to any of them. So they flew on in silence. Juan would occasionally scan the sea through his binoculars, even when they were still far outside their target area.

It was only when they were about forty miles out that he and Max started studying the ocean surface in earnest. They worked in tandem, Max looking forward and left, Cabrillo forward and right, both men sweeping the binoculars back and forth, never allowing themselves to be mesmerized by the sun glinting off the shallow waves. They were ten miles from where Cabrillo estimated the ship would be, and just shy of where the continental shelf plunges into the Palawan Trough, when Juan spotted something ahead and off to starboard. He pointed it out to Adams, and the pilot banked around slightly to keep their backs to the sun.

Cabrillo was instantly concerned. They should have found the ship by first spotting her miles-long wake and following it in. There was no wake. The *Hercules* was dead in the water.

It was an otherworldly sight. The ship itself was nearly twice the length of the *Oregon*, but what was so remarkable was the towering drill rig sitting astride her open deck. Her four legs were as big around as above-ground swimming pools. The floats beneath them,

296

covered in red antifouling paint, cantilevered a good seventy feet over the *Hercules*'s rails and were the size of barges. The platform itself was easily several acres in area, far larger than Cabrillo's initial estimate, and the distance from the deck to the top of the drill tower was more than two hundred feet. All told, the combination of ship and rig weighed in at well over a hundred thousand tons.

'What do you think?' Adams asked. Their plan was to find the rig and immediately return to the *Oregon*. But with her lying at idle, he was unsure.

Cabrillo wasn't. 'Get in closer. I want to check something.'

Adams dropped them lower until the skids were dancing over the waves. Unless a lookout was stationed at the fantail, they would still be pretty much invisible. It was when they were within a half mile that Juan realized the *Hercules* had developed a list to port. He wondered briefly if they had miscalculated the load and stopped to adjust it.

But when they came around the back of the ship, he saw heavy steel cables dangling off the superstructure's boat deck, and the metal arches of her davits were extended. The lifeboat had been launched. At the waterline he could see roiling bubbles caused by water filling her ballast tanks and expelling air. They weren't readjusting the load – they had abandoned ship because they were scuttling her.

15

'Swing us around the other side,' Cabrillo called urgently.

As nimbly as a dragonfly, Adams maneuvered the chopper around the heavy-lifter's bow and along her starboard rail. Like on the opposite side of the ship, the davits were swung out and the lifeboat long gone. However, here there was no indication that the pumps had been activated. They were filling the tanks on only one side so that the *Hercules* would capsize under the tremendous weight of the J-61 rig.

'Get us down there as fast as you can! We have to stop those pumps.'

'Juan,' Max said, 'what if they took Linda with them?'

Cabrillo called the *Oregon*. Hali Kasim answered right away. 'Go ahead, Chairman.'

'Hali, have we received a signal from Linda's tracker chip in the past hour or so?'

'No, and I've got one of my screens dedicated to her frequency.'

'Wait one.' Cabrillo flipped back to the internal helicopter comms channel. 'There's your answer, Max. She's still aboard. Gomez, get us down there. Hali, you still with me?'

'Right here.'

'We've found the *Hercules*, but it looks like they're scuttling her. You have our location, yes?'

'I show you eighty-two miles out at a bearing of forty-six degrees.'

'Get here as fast as you can. Bust the guts out of the *Oregon*, if you have to.' Juan killed the connection. 'Change of plans. Gomez, put me on top of the rig, then you and Max try to find a way of disabling the pumps.'

'You're going to look for Linda?' Hanley asked.

'If all else fails, she and I can jump for it,' Juan said, knowing that his idea was born of desperation and would probably end up killing them both.

The look of concern that flashed across Max's face told Cabrillo that Hanley thought it was pretty dumb too. Juan shrugged as if to say, what else can we do? He accepted a walkie-talkie that Max had grabbed from an emergency cache kept under the rear seat. Max would carry its twin.

'You don't want me to get more people from the *Oregon*?' Adams asked as he lifted the chopper up the towering side of the oil platform.

'I don't want her slowing for any reason,' Cabrillo told him.

Gomez centered the helo over the landing pad. Cabrillo didn't waste the time it would take to settle the helicopter properly. He unsnapped his harness, threw open the door, and dropped three feet to the deck, his clothes and hair battered by the rotor's thunderous downdraft. The 520 peeled away toward the stern, where there was enough deck space to safely land.

The landing jarred Juan's injured shoulder and sent a stab of pain through his chest. He winced and then ignored it.

At more than two hundred feet up in the air, the slight list they'd seen from the chopper was much more pronounced, and Cabrillo was forced to lean slightly to maintain his footing. He had no idea if the *Oregon* would arrive in time.

He looked around. It was clear the rig was old. Rust showed through faded and chipped paint. The decks were heavily stained and dented where pieces of equipment had been slammed into it by careless crane operators. There was very little in the way of loose gear sitting around. He spotted a large bin loaded with thirty-foot lengths of pipe called drill string that was threaded together under the derrick and used to bore the hole into the earth. Heavy chain dangled through the drill tower like industrial lace. To Juan, all that was missing to indicate the platform was abandoned was the cry of a coyote and a few tumbleweeds.

Cabrillo made his way to the accommodations block, a three-story cube with the ornamentation of a Soviet apartment building. All the windows on the first level were small portholes no bigger around than dinner plates. He examined the single steel door. He could see that at one time it had been chained closed. The chain was still attached through the handle, but the pad eye had been snapped off the jamb. Now crude beads of solder had been used to weld it shut. He pulled at the handle anyway, heaving until his arm ached, but it didn't budge even a fraction of an inch.

He hadn't taken a sidearm with him because this was supposed to be a scouting mission. He looked around for something he could use to smash a window. It took ten frustrating minutes to locate a discarded cover for an oxyacetylene tank. It was roughly the size of a grapefruit and heavy enough to shatter the glass. With his one arm still in a sling, his aim was off, so it took him three tries before he could even hit the window, and that blow merely starred the shatter-resistant pane. He used the metal cover like a hammer and beat the glass out of the frame.

'Linda?' he shouted into the empty room beyond. He could see it was an antechamber where workers could strip out of their oil-soaked coveralls before making their way to their cabins. 'Linda?'

His voice was swallowed by the metal walls and closed door opposite him. He bellowed. He roared. He thundered. It made no difference. His answer was silence.

'Linda!'

Max jumped from the 520 as soon as its skids kissed the deck and ran crouched under the whirling disc of its rotors. He had two football fields to cover before he even reached the fortresslike superstructure. He knew after the first dozen steps that he was woefully out of shape. Yet he kept moving, his stout legs pumping, his arms sawing back and forth. Behind him, Gomez settled the chopper and cut the turbine.

It was only when he reached the slab-sided pontoon float that Max realized they had made a critical error. The pontoon stretched the entire width of the *Hercules*'s deck and was as sheer as a cliff, a vertical wall of steel nearly thirty feet tall without a ladder or handhold. The ship's crew would need access to the aft of the vessel during transit, so he began retracing his steps, looking for a hatch.

'What's wrong?' Adams asked. He'd ditched his flight helmet and unzipped his one-piece jumpsuit to the navel.

'There's no way over the float. Look for an access hatch.'

The two men scoured the deck to no avail. The only way to get to the superstructure was over the oil rig's two enormous pontoons, an impossible feat for either man.

'Okay,' Hanley said, coming up with an alternative. 'Let's get back to the chopper. There must be someplace on the superstructure where you can hover and I can jump.'

Because the engine was still hot, they were airborne a few moments later. The *Hercules*'s bow was a jumble of equipment and antennae, and the roof of the pilothouse was obscured by the guy wires supporting its radar mast. Gomez Adams had thousands of hours at the controls of nearly every helicopter in the world and could thread a needle with the MD 520N, but there was simply no place large and open enough for Max to safely jump. After five frantic minutes, Adams banked away.

'New plan,' Hanley announced. 'Put me on top of the forwardmost pontoon.'

He climbed between the two front seats and rummaged around in the emergency kit for twenty feet of half-inch nylon rope. It wasn't long enough, but it would have to do.

Adams edged the helo under the soaring platform and just above the rust-red pontoon, the rotordraft buffeting them from above and below. He held the 520 rock steady with its skids just inches above the pontoon so that Max merely had to step out of the craft and onto the rig itself. Gomez pulled away once again and settled the chopper onto the fantail. He throttled down the Rolls-Royce turbine but didn't cut it completely.

As soon as he was down, Max tied off one end of the rope to a support bracket near the rig's stout leg and tossed the other end over the side. It hung a good fifteen feet from the deck of the *Hercules*. He groaned.

'I'm getting too old for this stuff.'

He maneuvered until his legs dangled over the pontoon and slowly lowered himself down the rope, clutching tightly with his thighs because he feared his belly was more of a load than his arms could take. When he reached the rope's end, he simply let go.

The deck slammed into his feet, compressing every vertebra in his spine and sending electric jolts of pain throughout his body. He hadn't rolled properly, and that mistake cost him a thrown back. He strung together a run-on sentence of expletives the likes of which he hadn't uttered since his days in Vietnam.

Slowly getting to his feet, he shuffled toward the rear of the superstructure. But where others would collapse in pain, Max gutted it out, moving like an old man but moving nevertheless.

'How are you coming down there?' The question was tinny and indistinct. Then he remembered the walkie-talkie clipped to his belt.

He raised it to his lips. 'I threw my damned back out, but I'm almost to the superstructure. How about you?'

'The door to the accommodations block is welded shut,' Cabrillo replied. 'I busted out a window and yelled for Linda, but I got nothing back.'

'Can you crawl through?'

'No, it's just a small porthole. I'm looking around now for another way in. This thing's built tighter than a castle.'

'Some rescue team we are, huh?'

'We'll get her back,' Cabrillo said with utter certainty.

Max continued on, a fist pressed to his lower back to ease some of the pain. The superstructure was painted in a dull white that showed the ship's hard years of operation. Corrosion ate at the metal in places, leaving behind rust streaks that drizzled down her plating. There were two hatches giving access to the interior spaces, and when Hanley reached the first one, he found that it had been locked from the inside. He tried pulling on the handle harder.

The second door was also battened down. He looked up. A catwalk ran the width of the building-sized superstructure, but it was twenty feet above him. Farther up on the bridge deck was a second walkway, and above that loomed two squared-off funnels covered in soot. There were no windows, and no way to access anything forward. Max was trapped, and he had noticed since they'd landed that the *Hercules*'s list had noticeably steepened.

Cabrillo walked around the accommodations block, searching for any way inside. Two sides of it abutted the edges of the rig and were nothing more than open grilles over the water, with handrails at waist height. There were two more doors, but each was locked from the inside.

Staring up the blank sides of the structure, he saw that a pulley had been rigged in order to fly a flag off an aerial that rose ten feet above the roof. The metal cord was badly abraded and fraying, but it just might work.

He opened the turnbuckle that converted the wire into a continuous loop and looked around for something to tie off one end. A half-full drum sat a short distance away. Able to use only one hand, he took several minutes to walk it closer to the pulley. He lost more precious time tying off an end of the wire around the middle of the barrel. If the knot failed, he'd probably break his neck, so it had to be perfect.

Then he made a one-foot loop in the other end of the wire. The hardest part was wrestling the metal drum onto its side. He had to get down low and press with his back and legs, straining to tip the barrel until it crashed over with a sloshing clang. He slipped his foot through the loop and pushed the barrel so it was parallel with the rig's deepening incline.

For a few seconds, his weight was enough to keep him anchored to the ground, so he put his other foot against the barrel and gave it a shove. Gravity did the rest. The drum started rolling across the deck, and, as it did, the wire went through the pulley, and Cabrillo made a stately ascent up the side of the building, his foot in the loop, his good hand clutching the line. He made it to the roof in just a couple of seconds and nimbly jumped clear. The loop jammed in the pulley, arresting the barrel's journey across the deck.

The top of the block was a maze of looping vents and commercial-grade air handlers. It took Cabrillo a few minutes to figure out which trunk lines went into the building and which were the returns. When he knew which one he wanted, he flicked open a pocketknife. It was an Emerson CQC (Close Quarters Combat) that Linc had turned him onto.

Rather than mess around with the tarred screws securing the two-foot-square ducts, Juan plunged the blade straight through the metal and hacked open a big enough hole like he was slicing paper. There wasn't a mark on the blade when he was done.

He crawled into the duct, mindful of his aching shoulder, and slithered forward until he came to an elbow that bent down through the roof. The insides of the duct were coated in a thick layer of dust that clouded around his head with every movement and forced him to sneeze hard enough that he banged his head. Just enough light leaked through the opening and around his body for him to see that the duct dropped away four feet and then bent in another ninety-degree corner.

He muscled his way back out of the duct and re-entered it feetfirst. When he got to the elbow, he flipped onto his stomach and eased himself over the edge, his shoulder screaming in protest. He felt with his toes until he touched the bottom of the duct and then shifted his weight entirely. The metal popped and echoed as it adjusted.

A minute later he was lying prone in the lower section of ductwork, grinning to himself when he saw light up ahead. He pushed with his feet until he was over a ceiling vent that was easily large enough to crawl through. He'd assumed he'd have to cut his way out of the air-conditioning system. Instead, he pounded out the grille with his heel, oozed his way into the opening, and allowed himself to drop to the floor of the oil worker's cabin. The room had a single porthole overlooking the ocean and an iron bed frame without a mattress. Whatever else had been in here had been removed long ago.

He stepped out into a hallway beyond, calling Linda's name as he searched thirty identical rooms and a large space in the middle of the building that had been a rec center or conference room. It was nothing now but bare walls, linoleum floors, and fluorescent lights affixed to the ceiling.

The stairwell to the next level down was pitch-black. He pulled a halogen penlight from his pocket and rotated the bezel until it threw a tight shaft of light.

'Linda,' he called when he cleared the stairwell. His voice echoed and crashed back like he had entered a massive space. The air carried the lingering effects of an ozone tang. It smelled of old electronics and burned wire.

He could tell right away that the room had been extensively modified. The dropped ceiling had been removed as well as all the partition walls. The windows had been blacked out, and additional vents in the form of silver collapsible tubes rose up another stairwell and snaked across the floor. What drew Cabrillo's attention, though, was what else had been added. Floor-to-ceiling racks in tight rows filled the entire space, and on them were rank upon rank of powerful-looking computers, all linked into one massive parallel processor. There had to be ten thousand or more machines all working as a single computer. The amount of processing power boggled the mind. It probably rivaled that of a large university or even NASA. The extra ductwork was to dissipate the heat buildup created when the machines were in operation.

He searched the room as quickly as he could on the off chance Linda was here and then descended to the next level, where he found an identical setup. Thousands of computers sat mutely in their racks with thick data cords linking machine to machine.

He puzzled at what Croissard needed all this

number-crunching capability for. Somehow it must tie in with whatever his man Smith had recovered from the Buddhist temple in Myanmar, but he had no idea how.

Again, Cabrillo swept the room and failed to find Linda Ross.

He hated to think that she was on one of the lower levels under the rig's main deck. It would be a rabbit warren of crawl spaces, corridors, and storage rooms that could take hours to search. He didn't want to even consider that she could be stashed down in one of the rig's legs or giant floats. He flicked the light onto the face of his watch and was dismayed to see that he'd already been aboard the J-61 for more than an hour. He also estimated the rig's list had increased a few degrees in that time. She was still solidly planted on the *Hercules*, but for how much longer?

The next level was the accommodations block's ground floor. His first task was to unlock and prop open one of the doors leading to the catwalk that hung off the seaward side of the structure. The fresh air helped dispel the ozone stench. He also took a moment to check in with Max. Hanley had yet to find a way into the ship. He told Juan that Adams was about to move the chopper onto the rig's pontoon and use its undercarriage winch to haul him up.

This level, Cabrillo discovered, was mostly offices as well as changing rooms for the roughnecks. There was no sign of Linda, so he set off once again, descending into the guts of the rig, his tiny light unable to do more than push at the murky gloom.

A screech of steel on steel boomed and roared through the platform like the shriek of a speeding train slamming on its brakes. Juan felt the whole structure shift and then stabilize. The list increased another couple degrees in as many seconds.

They were running out of time.

Eric Stone pushed the *Oregon* mercilessly. Rather than take the command chair in the middle of the Op Center, he remained in his customary seat at the helm, where he had a better sense of how the ship was responding to the waves and therefore could make minute adjustments to eke out the most speed.

The tramp freighter had never let them down before and she was delivering again, cutting across the sea like an offshore powerboat, her bows slicing cleanly through the water while a boiling wake astern marked her passage.

They covered the eighty miles to the *Hercules* in record time, but when they arrived, he knew immediately that they were too late. The heavy-lifter was so far over that she looked ready to capsize at any moment. The towering oil rig astride her deck leaned far out over the water, casting a long shadow that darkened the sea. He imagined only its tremendous weight was keeping it glued in place.

'Well done, lad,' Max's booming voice came over the ceiling-mounted speakers. He was in the MD 520N, heading back to the ship to pick up men and supplies that were already waiting.

'What do you want me to do?' Stone asked, secretly relieved that he wouldn't be responsible for the rescue attempt.

'Lay her right up under the rig and shove with everything she's got,' Hanley said without pause.

'What?' Eric couldn't believe his ears.

'You heard me. Do it.'

Stone snapped on the ship's intercom. 'Deck crew, lay out every fender we've got along the portside rail.' He wasn't worried about ruining either ship's paint scheme but was concerned about staving in hull plates.

Afraid that making waves near the *Hercules* would send her plummeting into the depths, Eric coaxed the *Oregon* alongside the ship like she was a skittish colt, all the while ballasting her down so that her rail would slip under the rig's projecting pontoons. The J-61 loomed over them like a castle on a sinking foundation.

'Chopper is down,' Max announced as Stone made tiny corrections to their position.

The two ships came together as gently as a feather falling to earth, the thick pneumatic fenders compressing and easing the contact even further. When the vessels were pressed against each other as snugly as possible, Eric slowly ramped up the *Oregon*'s athwartship thrusters and cranked the directed-thrust drive-tube nozzles to ninety degrees.

The effect was immediate. Burdened by tens of thousands of gallons of water flooding her starboard tanks, the *Hercules* was over nearly twenty degrees, but as soon as the power came up, the *Oregon* managed to shove her eight degrees closer to vertical. The forces in play were titanic but so carefully balanced that the slightest mistake on Stone's part would send the twenty-thousand-ton oil platform tumbling off the *Hercules* and crashing down, and ultimately through the *Oregon*. The worst part was that unless they could shut the heavy-lifter's sea inlets and pump her dry again, this was a delaying action at best.

Max's dangerous ploy bought them time. Just how much was anyone's guess.

No sooner had the helicopter settled onto the deck than Hanley, with his back aching, practically fell out of his seat in an effort to get out quickly. Julia Huxley was waiting with a wheelchair, her lab coat billowing around her in the rotor wash. Max was grateful for the chair but had no intention of allowing her to wheel him to the infirmary. He locked the wheels with his hands and watched as Mike Trono, Eddie Seng, and Franklin Lincoln – the men who had planned on spearheading the armed takedown of the *Hercules* – load up gear they would need to breach the ship's superstructure and stave off a disaster. They couldn't simply jump aboard the sinking vessel because there was too much of a gap caused by the rubber fenders sandwiched between the two ships.

In order to save even more time, Eddie would fly over to the ship clipped to the chopper's winch so he could be lowered onto the pilothouse directly. Three minutes after he landed, Gomez Adams ramped up the

313

engine and lifted away, mindful of his friend dangling beneath the helo's belly.

He flew up and over the *Oregon* and came down again seconds later, peering though the Plexiglas at his feet in order to put Eddie on target. He deftly lowered Seng onto the pilothouse roof just inboard of one of the jutting bridge wings.

Eddie unclipped himself from the winch, threw a wave, and leapt down to the catwalk.

Adams then set the chopper down on the forward pontoon, where he'd had to rescue Max moments earlier. Mike and Linc tossed out their gear and jumped free so that Gomez could fly up to the oil platform's chopper pad and wait for the Chairman to make his appearance.

Eddie hit the flying bridge in a tuck roll, springing to his feet an instant after landing. He didn't bother with the lock but cross-drew a 9mm, shot out the glass half of the door, and leapt through. He hit the deck in another roll and came up next to the navigation console, a massive piece of electronics that spanned almost the entire width of the pilothouse. The room was nearly two hundred feet wide, spartan, and, he quickly discovered, dead. There was no power. All the flat panels were blank, the controls inoperable, and the readouts unlit. It wasn't only that the crew had killed the engines, but they'd taken the battery backup off-line. The *Hercules* was truly a ghost ship.

'Max, you there?' he radioed.

'Go ahead.' He was halfway to the Op Center.

'We are seriously screwed. Main propulsion is down. Auxiliary is down, and it looks like they pulled the feeds off the backup batteries.'

'Do you have anything?' Hanley asked.

'No,' Seng replied. 'That's what I'm trying to tell you. This thing's dead across the board.'

A moment passed while Max considered their options. 'Okay,' he finally said, 'here's what I want you to do. Down in the engine room there will be manual valves to shut off the inlet pipes. You need to reach them and close them. We can't pump her out, but at least we can stop her from sinking farther.'

'Is that really enough?' Eric Stone had been listening on the open channel. In the few minutes since he'd laid the *Oregon* alongside the heavy-lifter, they'd started pushing the *Hercules* laterally through the water, creating waves that rocked both ships. Already one of the indestructible fenders separating them had exploded under the pressure. 'I don't know how long I can hold her.'

'Do your best, lad.'

Linc and Mike Trono went for the direct approach. Rather than mess around with torches or blasting charges, Mike fitted an RPG to his shoulder as soon as Adams was clear and fired down at the doorway leading into the ship's superstructure. The resulting explosion blew the door completely off its hinges and sent it clattering along an internal hallway. He and

Linc clambered down the rope that Max had left behind. The paintwork around the destroyed door was on fire from the blast, but they were ready, and Linc sprayed it with a small fire extinguisher and cast the little canister aside when the flames were gone. The metal was still blisteringly hot, so they eased their way through carefully.

Both carried powerful three-cell batteries and matching 9mm Sig Sauers in case the *Hercules* wasn't as deserted as they believed.

Entering the ship in the condition she was in was the same as a fireman running into a burning munitions factory, but neither man gave it a second thought.

The interior of the *Hercules* was in rough shape. The walls were peeling, the floor was lifted in places, and the cabins had all been stripped bare. Wire conduits sagged from the ceiling and walls where their brackets had snapped over the years. She didn't look quite as bad as the *Oregon* was meant to, but it was clear she belonged in the breaker yard where her previous owners had sent her. Mike and Linc were making their way up to the bridge when they overheard Eddie and Max on their tactical radios. They turned as if in lockstep and retreated the way they had come.

The ship's motion in the water remained sluggish because her ballast tanks continued to fill. However, when she yawed to starboard, she went deeper and recovered slower than when she pitched the other way. With her belly so full she was struggling to remain upright, and no matter how skillful Eric Stone was at the controls of their ship, it was inevitable that the *Hercules* would capsize.

To make matters worse, the clouds Cabrillo had seen at dawn had moved into the area, and a freshening breeze was affecting the surface waves, making them march in long columns that slammed into the side of the ship.

Moving even faster than them, Eddie Seng soon caught up to the pair. All their expressions were the same mask of grim concentration. Juan's and Linda's lives depended on them staunching the gush of water flooding the ship's cathedral-sized tanks.

While every oceangoing vessel was different, the efficiencies built into the field of maritime architecture meant there were only so many ways to access the engine room, and its placement was always logically thought out. It was because of this that the men quickly descended three decks and came across a metal door stenciled ENGINE ROOM. A chain had been wrapped around the handle and padlocked.

Linc set about blasting the chain apart, since shooting the lock off with a pistol in such a confined space would most likely end with the shooter catching the ricochet. He stuck a wad of plastique the size of chewing gum onto the padlock, jammed a detonator to it, and hustled the other two men down the hallway and around a corner.

The blast wave hit them like a hurricane gust, and the noise was deafening even with their ears covered. A thin wisp of acrid chemical smoke hung in the air. The padlock and half the chain links were gone. Eddie quickly stripped away the rest of the chain and was about to throw the door open when the *Hercules* was caught by a particularly strong wave that seemed to bury its rail in the ocean. For thirty long seconds she hung there, while the massive oil platform shrieked its way closer to oblivion as it slid across her deck.

The *Oregon* fought her with everything she had, but the damage was done. The rig had moved enough to upset the heavy-lifter's center of gravity, and her list was now as bad as ever. The wave had dealt her a fatal blow.

'That's it,' Max called over the radio. 'Get out of there. That goes for you too, Juan.' He waited a beat. 'Chairman, can you hear me? Juan? Juan, if you're receiving this, get off the rig. Damnit, Juan. Answer me. You are out of time.'

But Cabrillo never answered.

16

Juan was so deep into the J-61 rig that its steel blocked his walkie-talkie from sending or receiving. He probably wouldn't have heeded Max's warning anyway. He'd pushed too hard to fail now.

The guts of the platform were as confusing as a Cretan maze, with countless passageways that crisscrossed and doubled back on themselves. It didn't help that his little light stabbed just a few feet into the darkness. He'd cracked his head several times on unseen obstructions and had bruises on his shin and quite possibly dents in his prosthesis.

Cabrillo had a highly developed spatial sense and had known when the *Oregon* had first arrived and shouldered the ship closer to an even keel. He could also tell that she was now losing the fight to keep the *Hercules* on the surface. The ship's list was the worst it had ever been, and when the rig had slid across the deck several feet, he knew he was out of time, and yet he didn't falter and didn't question if he had done enough and should get out.

He tore down a flight of open metal stairs two at a time, cradling his bad arm with his good to lessen the impact. Down this deep the rig was an industrial forest of massive cross braces, bulkheads, and thick columns.

The floor was bare metal coated in a thin layer of spilled crude that had congealed to the consistency of tar. It was slick and sticky at the same time.

'Linda?' he roared, and in the silence that followed his fading echo he thought he heard something. He called her name again, louder.

There!

It was muffled and indistinct, but he heard a response. He raced toward the sound of a woman screaming for help. In the far corner of the space was a closed-off room without windows. A wedge had been rammed under the door as an added precaution, though the handle was locked from the outside.

'Linda?'

'Is that really you?'

'Galahad to the rescue,' he said, and dropped onto his butt to hammer at the wedge with his artificial leg.

'Thank God!' Linda breathed. 'You have to get us out of here!'

'Us?' Juan said between blows.

'Soleil Croissard has been a prisoner here for weeks.'

Even as he worked to free them, Cabrillo's mind went into overdrive. There was no logical reason for Roland Croissard to imprison his daughter and then try to kill her. She was here as a hostage and thus leverage to get him to do someone else's bidding. Smith? He didn't seem the type. He was a henchman, not a mastermind. Someone else entirely. They'd spent untold hours tearing into Croissard's life, only there weren't any clues to his goals because they weren't his goals at all. Some other person was offstage pulling all the strings, and they had no idea who. And if getting the mysterious item out of the jungle temple had been the goal, Croissard was most likely dead, leaving the Corporation with nothing.

The wedge finally popped free and skittered away. Cabrillo got to his feet and ripped open the door. Linda Ross came at him in a rush, ignoring his slinged arm. She wrapped her arms around him in a hug that for Juan was equal parts pain and joy.

Behind Linda was another woman, who in the weak glow of the penlight and after so many days of deprivation still managed to be stunningly beautiful. Her raven hair was raked back into a ponytail, exposing large brown eyes.

'Miss Croissard, I'm Juan Cabrillo.'

'*Oui*, I would have recognized you from Linda's description.' Her accent was charming.

'We need to get out of here, like now.'

With Cabrillo in the lead, they made their way back up through the labyrinthine oil platform. Juan was on automatic pilot, trusting his memory to find the straightest route out to freedom, while another section of his mind worried over the identity of whoever was behind the enigmatic John Smith. He'd pump Soleil for information later. Maybe she had an inkling of what was happening, but, for now, Cabrillo looked at the problem with just the facts he knew.

He tried the walkie-talkie now that they were closer to the main deck. 'Max, can you hear me?'

After a squelch of static he thought he heard, ''Ta 'ere.'

'Max?'

''Et outta 'ere 'ow.'

'We're almost clear.'

As they kept rushing up the final set of stairs, the reception improved. 'Juan, Gomez is standing by on the pad, but you have less than a minute. We can't hold her any longer.'

'Max, listen carefully. Put an armed guard on MacD Lawless. If he tries to get to a phone or radio, shoot him.'

'What? Why?' Hanley's incredulity made his voice crack.

'I'll explain when I see you. Do it.'

The last steps were so slanted, it was like running through a fun house, and when they finally burst out the door to the catwalk suspended over the sea, all three of them crashed into the railing because they couldn't stop their onward rush. Running along the walkway, with the *Oregon*'s deck one hundred feet below them and at a twenty-plus-degree angle, made them all realize that Max's promised minute was overly optimistic. They had seconds before the rig toppled.

Gomez Adams held the 520 over the helipad, one skid touching the deck, the other hovering over a massive gap. He was level. It was the platform that was skewed. The tips of the rotor blades on one side of the chopper thrummed dangerously close to the deck.

'Go! Go! Go!' Juan shouted.

Below them, the rig screeched once again as gravity pulled it closer to the tipping point. The *Hercules*'s rail was buried in the sea, and a gap began to show under the uphill side of the platform as it started going over.

In the Op Center Eric Stone redirected the drive-tube nozzles and put on a burst of speed, redlining the engines in a desperate bid to get the ship clear of the steel avalanche crashing toward them. Aboard the capsizing heavy-lifter, Eddie, Linc, and Mike had no choice but to hold onto any solid surface they could find, so they clung to the topside railing with everything they had.

Cabrillo unceremoniously shoved both women into the chopper as Adams started lifting clear and leapt in after them as the rig slid the rest of the way off the deck. The stress was too much for the platform's spindly drill tower and it broke free, twisting steel wrenched apart as though it were a balsa wood model. The rig moaned like amplified whale song.

The helicopter's tail boom cleared the helipad with inches to spare, its three passengers staring agog at the destruction they had just escaped. The platform crashed into the ocean scant feet from the fleeing *Oregon*'s jack staff and created a titanic wave that lifted the ship like a toy in a bathtub and nearly drove her bow into the swells. Eric deftly steered them across the wave front like a surfer peeling down the face of one of the big ones off Oahu's North Shore.

The top-heavy rig turned turtle as soon as all of it was in the water, upending so that the air-filled pontoons were pointed at the sky. It bobbed almost merrily. Unburdened of so much deadweight, the *Hercules* pendulumed back until she was almost straight, before the inertia of water sloshing in her tanks returned her to a deadly list. The three men holding fast to the rails were thrown violently but managed to maintain their grip.

When they let go, each slid across the deck on his backside, maintaining a safe speed by pressing gloved hands and shoes against the plating. When they came up against the lower rail, all three simply stepped into the ocean and started swimming away. Adams maintained a hover over them to direct the rescue launch racing from the *Oregon*'s amidships boat garage.

The RHIB reached them just moments before the *Hercules* succumbed to the inevitable and rolled ponderously onto her side, her barnacle-scaled bottom exposed to the sun for the first time in her long career. Air trapped in the hull burst out through portholes and vents, spewing and sputtering as though the old ship was fighting her fate.

And then he remembered that this wasn't the end of the affair but the very beginning, and all thoughts of humor vanished.

'Gomez, get us back to the ship ASAP.'

MacD Lawless had betrayed them from that very first night in Pakistan, and Cabrillo wanted answers.

No sooner were they down and the RHIB back up the ramp in the boat garage than he ordered the *Oregon* to stand off the platform and rake its waterline with the ship's 20mm Gatling gun. The depth here wasn't optimal – the *Hercules*'s crew must have been rushed after all – but they were over the continental slope, and, with luck, the J-61 would tumble down the undersea cliff and end up in the crushing depths of the abyssal plane.

Juan wanted no evidence that this act of sabotage hadn't gone off as planned. The heavy-lifter wouldn't last another ten minutes on the surface, and once they'd peppered the rig's floats with a couple thousand holes it would join the ship on the bottom.

Because he was covered in gooey oil from his search for Linda, Cabrillo went to his cabin first, while the two women were escorted to the infirmary for a checkup. As much as he longed for a shower, he simply stripped out of the clothes he'd been wearing, balling them up for the trash rather than tossing them into a hamper, and threw on a navy blue jumpsuit and clean boots.

He was down in medical seven minutes after Adams got them safely home.

Max was there waiting, a look of concern on his bulldog face. 'First off, glad you're okay. Second, what the hell is going on?'

'We're both about to find out,' Juan said, and led him through the door.

'About time I get some answers,' Dr Huxley said with mild irritation. 'Why is my patient under guard?'

'How are Soleil and Linda?'

'They're fine. Soleil is a little wrung out from her ordeal, but up until they moved the oil platform she was cared for. How about it, Juan?'

'Croissard was duped the same way we were and by the same person.'

'MacD?'

'Nope. But let's go have a chat with him.'

Juan could see that the guard had taken the added precaution of securing MacD's wrists to the frame of his hospital bed. Cabrillo dismissed him with a wave and spent several seconds eyeing their newest member turned prisoner.

Cabrillo started, 'I'm going to tell a story and I want you to correct me where I get it wrong. If I'm satisfied when we're finished, I'll untie you myself. Deal?'

MacD nodded.

'At some time during your most recent posting to Afghanistan when you worked for Fortran, you befriended a local, probably someone younger than yourself.'

'His name was Atash.'

'You told him all about your daughter back home in New Orleans, never considering the kid was part of a terrorist cell and that the information you gave him would be used against you.'

Shame washed over Lawless's face.

'When they were ready, the cell sent a team to the United States to kidnap her. Proof of her abduction was somehow provided, and you were told that if you didn't do exactly what they said, she would be killed. You had no choice. They set up a bogus ambush to get you across the border into Pakistan, where you were roughed up a little to make your capture appear legit.

On a night they knew we were watching that village you were paraded around, setting us up to rescue you at the same time we nabbed the little boy, Setiawan.

'I always figured our escape out of that town was too easy,' Cabrillo said. 'Not the ambush on the road later. That was a separate group that had no idea what was going on. But the people in the village were under orders to let us go with minimum fuss.'

'Hold on,' Max said. 'I thought you said they opened fire on the bus.'

'Oh, a couple of Johnny Jihadis shot at us, but they either missed entirely or fired up at the roof so as not to hit anyone. It was a show to convince us that we'd made the greatest escape in history. All hat and no cattle, as the old saying goes. Later, after we escaped the roadblock, we had a Predator launch a missile at us. I never even saw it, but MacD here did, and moved faster than an Olympic sprinter. He saved our lives. It was an impressive feat for someone supposedly beaten half to death by the Taliban and stuffed into the trunk of a car for a few days. No way would you have been able to move like that. Your injuries were mostly faked.'

Lawless didn't deny it.

'I don't get this,' Hanley persisted. 'How did they know when we were going to rescue that kid?'

'You don't see it yet?' Juan asked. 'That kid didn't need rescuing because his father had sent him to Pakistan in order to lure us to that village.'

'I must be dense or something. Why lure us there?'

'The whole thing was set up so that we would take

MacD into the fold. Gunawan Bahar is the mastermind of everything we've been through these past couple of weeks. He wanted to plant a spy on the *Oregon*, so he hired us to "rescue" his son from the Taliban while he also planted a man whose daughter's life he controls in place for us to rescue too.

'It was a brilliant piece of misdirection. As soon as we were double-crossed by Smith in Myanmar, all suspicion automatically went to Croissard. No one ever considered there was another layer to this onion and that Croissard was no more in control of his actions than MacD.'

That last statement wasn't entirely true. Since his time at Insein, Cabrillo had harbored a nagging doubt about something. He did not know what, but he sensed that some piece of information he'd been given was off in some way. It was instinct, but that was a feeling he'd learned to trust over the years, so when he saw Soleil on the rig he knew what had eluded him for so long.

'What gave it away,' he continued, 'was the timing of the rig being sunk. Bahar knew from Lawless that we'd escaped Insein Prison and had Linda's location because of the tracker chip. That pushed up his deadline to deep-six the J-61 platform by a few days or weeks. The clincher was when MacD came up to the bridge this morning. He'd been told we were steaming hard but had no idea of the speeds the *Oregon* is capable of. As soon as he left me he called his handler, Smith, I assume, because of the way he seemed to get under your skin when we were back in the jungle. He told Smith that we were just hours away rather than days. The *Hercules* still wasn't over the Palawan Trough, but they were out of time. They immediately opened the sea cocks and hit the lifeboats. To not only kill Linda and Soleil but also to hide the fact that the platform was home to perhaps one of the largest collections of interlinked computers outside a government lab. How'd I do?' He directed that last question to MacD.

Before Lawless could reply, a searing blast of sound made conversation impossible. It was the buzz-saw clamor of the Gatling raking the sides of the oil rig's ponderous floats. It went on in staccato bursts for a full minute so that by the time the weapon was withdrawn back into the ship and its redoubt cover slid back into position, three thousand fist-sized holes had been blown through the floats, above and below the water. It would slip beneath the waves within the hour.

'How about it?' Juan prompted when it was clear Mark Murphy had finished the job.

'Nailed it. Everything.'

'I get it now,' Max exclaimed. 'Croissard was controlled because Bahar had kidnapped his daughter too. All that crap on her website about going to Burma was bogus. They must have tried to get to that temple themselves, failed, and so he used Croissard to hire us, somehow knowing we'd get the job done.'

Cabrillo nodded. 'And with both Smith and his spy on the team, Bahar had regular updates of our progress.'

'It all seems so elaborate. Why bother forcing MacD

into this? Why the ruse? Bahar could have simply hired us to go into Myanmar.'

'Wouldn't work,' Juan said. 'No motivation. We would never take on some job to go tomb raiding. He needed the type of mission he knew we wouldn't refuse. He'd already proven our soft spot for wayward kids, with the whole deal to save his son, so he just pulled the same trick again, only this time using Roland Croissard's daughter as bait. Then, once he had whatever was in that bag, he called in his friends in the government to take us out.'

'Why not work with the government all along?' Max wondered aloud.

'No idea, but there was some reason. Otherwise he wouldn't have bothered with us at all. My guess is that bringing in the military was a last-minute deal. MacD, any thoughts?'

'No, sir. They never gave me any information. Just took it.'

'So you have no idea what was in that bag we recovered from the body in the river?'

'None at all. And before you ask, Ah never even knew the name of the guy above Smith. I knew Smith wasn't calling all the shots, but Ah didn't know who was behind him.'

'Another mystery solved,' Max said, turning back to Cabrillo, 'is the bombing at the hotel.'

'What? It wasn't random?'

'It's obvious that Bahar considers us such a threat that he felt the need to infiltrate our team, but he also took a shot at blowing us up in Singapore to end that threat early.'

Juan considered this for a moment and shook his head. 'I don't think so. As I said before, why not just have Smith blow our brains out as soon as we entered the room?'

Hanley's face split into a wicked grin. 'Because he would know the rest of the Corporation would search the ends of the earth for the shooter. But if we'd died in a suicide bombing, who would they hunt down?'

Cabrillo thought that his old friend might be onto something, but a lingering doubt remained. For the time being the past was unimportant. 'For now, we need to concentrate on Bahar. We need to find out what he has planned. It's something he sees us threatening, and it's linked to whatever they pulled from the temple.'

'That's specific,' Max said sardonically

'What about my little girl?' MacD asked, mustering as much dignity as he could. 'Now that Smith, or this Bahar guy, knows Ah've been found out, they're goin' to kill her. They've let me talk to her over a webcam. The guys with her are strapped with explosive belts. They're going to blow up my baby.'

'Who said anything about Smith and Bahar knowing we've discovered why you're here?'

'Ah don't understand.'

'It's simple, really. You contact Smith like you're supposed to and report that the rig was gone by the time we got to it.'

'Okaaay,' Lawless said, drawing out the word as if to draw out more information.

'And then we rescue your daughter, figure out what these sons of bitches are really up to, and nail them to the nearest outhouse door.'

After the longest, hottest shower he'd had in a long time, Cabrillo went to find Linda Ross. She'd write up a full report of her ordeal, but he wanted to get the highlights quickly to help establish their next course of action. He went first to her cabin to discover that Soleil was there and just out of the shower herself. She had one towel wrapped around her and tucked under her arms and another wrapped in a turban, covering her hair.

'Again, you catch me when I am not at my best,' she said with a coy smile.

'Story of my life,' Juan replied. 'Good timing with everything but the ladies. Linda didn't show you to one of the guest cabins?'

'She did, but your selection of feminine toiletries is a little lacking. She was kind enough to let me use hers.'

'I'll get onto the steward,' he promised, and then asked with genuine concern, 'How are you?'

A shadow passed behind her Gallic eyes. And, just as quickly, it faded. 'I have endured worse.'

'I read up on some of your accomplishments,' Cabrillo said. 'And I was very impressed. However, there is nothing quite like being held against your will. That lack of freedom and control can get to anyone. Powerlessness is perhaps the worst feeling in the world.'

She opened her mouth as if to reply, then suddenly plopped herself on Linda's bed and buried her face in her hands. She sobbed quietly at first, but soon it grew, until her whole body was shaking. Juan wasn't the type to be put off by a woman crying, at least when she had a reason. Pointless histrionics just irked him, but something like this naked expression of fear was something he understood all too well.

He sat on the bed next to her but kept his hands to himself. If she wanted human contact, it would be up to her to initiate it. His instincts at times like this were spot-on. In seconds, Soleil had pressed her face into his shoulder. He put an arm around her and simply waited for her to get it out of her system. Less than a minute later she straightened and sniffled. Juan plucked a couple of tissues from the box on the nightstand and handed them to her. She dabbed at her eyes and blew her nose.

'*Pardonnez-moi*. That was not very ladylike.'

'You'll be all right now,' he predicted. 'I can tell you are a strong woman, but you've bottled up your emotions for a long time. I suspect you never showed weakness to your jailers.'

'*Non*. Not once.'

'But that doesn't mean you don't have any. So they come out in a rush in the end. Nothing to it.'

'Thank you,' she said softly. Her voice strengthened, and a little smile played at the corners of her mouth. 'And thank you for saving my life. Linda has such faith in you that she never doubted our rescue. I was not so sure. But now?' The smile turned into a grin. 'Now I think you can do anything.'

'Just as soon as I get my red cape back from the cleaners.'

The reference confused her for a moment. 'Oh, your comic-book Superman.'

'That's me, but I don't do tights.' Juan turned serious. 'I need to ask you some questions. If it's too difficult, we can do it another time.'

'*Non*. I will do my best.'

'Or I can come back when you're dressed.'

'I have a towel. It is enough,' she said with European pragmatism.

'Did you overhear anything during your captivity? Anything that would give us a clue what this is all about?'

'No. Nothing. They took me from my home in Zurich. Two men broke into my house and attacked me while I was asleep. While one held me down the other gave me a shot. It knocked me out. When I came awake again, I was in that cell where you found me. I did not even know that it was an oil platform until Linda told me. You see, they had drugged her too. But she says she woke in a helicopter on its way out to sea.'

Juan knew that, like himself, Linda would have remained motionless after coming to in order to get a sense of her surroundings. It was a trick he'd taught her.

'Do you have any idea why you were targeted?'

'I assume it has to do with my father,' Soleil replied. 'He is a wealthy and powerful man.'

'I met him in Singapore when he hired us to go into Burma to look for you.'

'It is true that I was planning on going to Bangladesh with a friend of mine on an extreme backpacking trip.'

'We know. The man behind your abduction went so far as to update your website to make it look like you'd left for that trip. They covered themselves well. Anything specific about your father? Any recent business deals?'

'We are not so close anymore,' she admitted sadly.

Cabrillo knew that pretty soon she'd have to be told that in all likelihood her father was dead. Bahar had what he wanted, so Roland Croissard had become a loose end. They would keep searching, of course, but the odds were long that the Swiss financier had been left alive.

'Okay, then,' Juan said, and stood. 'You get some rest, and we'll talk more later.'

'There are some people I'd like to call. My father and some friends.'

'I might as well tell you now. Your father is missing. We've been trying to reach him for several days but haven't had any luck. Also, I'm afraid that until we have a better handle on the situation we need to keep up the pretense that you died back on that oil rig.'

'My father? Missing?'

'And the last time anyone saw him he was with the man that most likely kidnapped you in Zurich.'

Guilt, fear, and anger played across her face in a kaleidoscope of emotions. She sat as still as a statue, a beautiful mannequin, her soul having just been torn out.

'I am sorry,' Juan said softly. He wished she hadn't asked about making calls. She wasn't ready to hear this kind of news. Not now.

Soleil finally looked up at him, a pleading look in her eyes that he wanted more than anything else to satiate. He'd never seen such naked vulnerability. Now he was in territory where he wasn't all that comfortable because it brought up feelings of his own loss. He hadn't been told about his wife's death until he'd returned from a mission for the CIA and she'd been in the ground for weeks.

With relief he saw her firm up, straighten her shoulders, and harden her eyes. 'I think I would like to get dressed and walk the deck, if that is okay. I have not seen sunshine or felt fresh air in a long time.' She pointed to a suitcase just outside the bathroom that he recognized as coming from the wardrobe section of the Magic Shop. Linda and Kevin Nixon had already kitted her out.

'Of course,' Juan quickly agreed. 'If you need anything, feel free to ask any of the crew. Even though we didn't find you where we expected to, they're all relieved that you're safe.'

'Thank you for everything.'

'Cocktails in the dining room at six. Dinner's casual, but I'll wear my cape for you.'

She smiled wanly at his attempt at humor, and Cabrillo took his leave. He finally tracked down Linda.

She was in the exercise room with Eddie Seng. Both were dressed in the traditional *gi* of martial arts training and were locked in a fight for dominance on the dojo floor.

'Not enough action for one day?' Juan teased.

Linda flared. 'That dirtball Smith got the drop on me back in the jungle, and I want Eddie to show me what I did wrong.'

Seng had degrees in several styles of fighting and was the Corporation's instructor.

'It can wait. We need to talk.'

Linda bowed to Eddie and came across the padded mats in bare feet. 'I'll tell you right off the top that Smith didn't give away much. As soon as he got me to Yangon he hit me with happy juice.'

'And you woke up on the chopper, heading out to the rig.'

'How did you know that?' she asked, one eyebrow arching.

'I'm Superman. Actually, I just had a chat with Soleil.'

'Chat, eh?'

Juan didn't take the bait. 'Was Smith with you in the chopper?'

'Yes. And he had the bag. And he made his only mistake. It was on the floor between him and the pilot, and, just before we landed, he opened it. Inside were ruby crystals, big ones. I'd say a foot long or longer, and they'd already been cut and polished. I'd never seen anything like it in my life.'

Cabrillo had a hard time believing this was all an

337

elaborate smuggling scheme. There had to be something beyond that.

Linda was still talking. 'Once we landed I continued to play rag doll. They took me straight to the cell with Soleil, so I don't know if Smith hung around for the final act or not.'

'I suspect not. Bahar went through a lot of trouble to get that bag. He'd want the stones as soon as possible. Let me ask you something. I discovered that two entire floors of that rig were crammed with computers. I'm talking thousands of interlinked machines. Any ideas?'

'Ask the brain trust. Mark and Eric are the computer nerds.'

'Aren't we supposed to call them ITs?'

'So I'm not politically correct. Sue me. Seriously, you'd have to ask them. I was shoved into the black hole of Calcutta as soon as I was aboard.'

Cabrillo found Mark and Eric in Stoney's cabin. They were playing a video game on a giant flat-screen that was actually four edgeless panels mounted in a square. Juan understood that some games promoted actual skills, but he saw no redeeming features in the two of them racing a cartoon car with what looked like an aardvark behind the wheel through a shopping center.

'I guess you guys haven't heard.'

'Heard what?'

'Croissard's daughter was on that rig too. He was used to get to us. And MacD Lawless was a spy.'

338

'What?' the two crowed in unison.

'The real bad guy turns out to be Gunawan Bahar. He was the mastermind behind everything. So your priority is tearing into every part of his life. I want to know who he really is and what he's after. When we first contacted Overholt about Bahar, he said that he wasn't on the CIA's radarscope, so you're going to have to dig deep.'

'Hold on a sec,' Mark said. 'MacD's a spy? For who?'

Cabrillo laid out the whole convoluted story, summing up by saying that he and Max both agreed that Bahar felt the Corporation represented a direct threat to whatever he had planned. 'Two final pieces,' he added as a further aside. 'Linda saw a bunch of foot-long polished rubies in the bag we recovered in Myanmar, and I discovered that two decks of the oil platform had been converted into a massive server farm. Any thoughts?'

The two young geniuses glanced at each other for a moment as if syncing their minds. Mark finally spoke up. 'Whatever they were, they weren't rubies. Corundum, the base material for both rubies and sapphires – the difference being the presence of trace minerals that give them color, chromium for ruby, iron or titanium for sapphire – has a hexagonal crystal structure, but it's tabular rather than linear.'

Cabrillo kept his face impassive while inside he was screaming, Speak English!

'What he's saying,' Stone translated, 'is that rubies don't grow lengthwise like emerald or quartz, so it is unlikely that Linda saw foot-long rubies. They were some other type of crystals.'

That supported Juan's theory that this wasn't about gem smuggling, but this information got him no closer to the truth. 'What about all the computers?'

Mark said, 'Obviously Bahar needed to crunch some major numbers, but without knowing more about him or his goals it's impossible to say exactly what or why.'

'Then you have your marching orders. I want answers.'

'You got it, boss man,' Stoney replied.

17

John Smith stepped off the boarding stairs of the private jet and into the arms of Gunawan Bahar. The two embraced like brothers.

'You have done well,' Bahar said, holding Smith at arm's length to look him in the eye.

'It was easier than we anticipated, especially after you brokered the deal with the army.' They spoke in English, the only language they had in common.

Smith really had taken the anonymous *nom de guerre* when he'd joined the Foreign Legion. He'd been born Abdul Mohammad in Algeria and, like many in his homeland, had a great deal of French blood in his veins after one hundred and thirty years of colonial occupation. Also, like many in his homeland, more than forty years of independence hadn't eroded the hatred he felt for his nation's former overlords. But rather than fight as an insurgent in his own country against a government he saw as corrupted by Western influences, he had decided to fight the beast from within and joined the Legion as a way of gaining military training and learning how to ingratiate himself with Europeans so that he could easily pass as one.

After his initial five-year contract, he left to join the Mujahadin, fighting the Russians in Afghanistan. The warfare he enjoyed, but the level of ignorance he encountered among the people came as a shock. He found they were all superstitious peasants who spent as much time warring among themselves as they did fighting the Soviets. Even the Great Sheik Bin Laden was a paranoid fanatic who actually believed that once the Russians were expelled they should take the fight directly to the infidels in the West. Though he'd been a playboy in his youth and enjoyed himself in European cities, Osama never understood the true might of a Western army. Battling Russian conscripts on soil that was foreign to them was a far cry from taking on the United States.

Bin Laden came to believe that martyrdom operations, as he liked to call suicide bombers, would bring about the destruction of the Western world. Abdul Mohammad wanted to see America brought to its knees, but he understood that blowing up a few buildings wasn't going to change anything. In fact, it would harden the victims' resolve and bring swift and deadly reprisals.

Though he did not know how, he knew there was a better way. It wasn't until years later, long after Bin Laden took down the Twin Towers and ignited a powder keg that had hurt the Muslim world far more than the West, that Mohammad met Setiawan Bahar, Gunawan's brother and namesake to his son. (The boy used in the Afghan operation had been a street urchin they had carefully coached not to talk to the infidels.) By the time they met, Mohammad was working for a private

342

security company in Saudi Arabia, the flames of jihad having cooled in his belly. The Bahar brothers were in the country at a time when Wahabi fundamentalists were targeting Western interests. The pair were touring oil production facilities that were interested in buying electronic controls from one of their companies back in Jakarta.

Mohammad was their bodyguard for two weeks, and their full-time employee ever since.

They used him for their own corporate security as well as what they dubbed 'special projects.' These ranged from corporate espionage to kidnapping rivals' family members in order to win contracts at lower bids. The Bahar brothers, and then only Gunawan after Setiawan died of lung cancer, were very careful to shield themselves from any consequences of their more aggressive business dealings. The fact that the Corporation couldn't trace their ownership of the J-61 oil platform was a testament to their care and caution.

What had bonded the three men originally was their belief that Bin Laden's tactics were doomed to fail. They agreed that they wanted the West to end its persistent meddling in the Middle East, but terrorism would never bring that about. In fact, it caused more interference. What the Muslim world needed was leverage over the United States. Since both sides needed oil, the one to run its factories and cars, the other for the tremendous revenue, something else had to be found.

It was four years earlier when Gunawan had read an article in a science magazine – in his dentist's office, of all places – that he found a way to get that leverage. He had placed Abdul in charge of the venture and gave him near-limitless resources. The very best and brightest in Bahar's vast empire were put to the task, and outside contractors were brought in as needed. The project was so cutting-edge that secrecy was a given and needn't be explained to the employees, while only a select few knew the ultimate use of the device they worked feverishly to build.

They had been ready for nearly a year except for one critical component and that's what Abdul had finally found, thanks to an obscure British researcher who'd put together the pieces of an eight-hundred-year-old legend and led Mohammad to a remote temple lost in one of the most impenetrable jungles in the world.

Muhammad unslung the bag from his shoulder and carefully opened the top. The bright sunshine beating down on the airport tarmac made the crystals gleam like solid fire.

'Congratulations, my friend,' Bahar said warmly. They started toward a waiting limousine. 'This has become your obsession as well as mine. Tell me, was the temple as Marco Polo described it to Rustichello?'

'No. The monks expanded it greatly over the years. The original cave where the crystals were first mined was still there, but they had constructed buildings going down to it from the cliffs above and had started carving more idolatrous images on the opposite side of the chasm. Judging by the level of decay, I would say it was abandoned at about the time the current junta took control.'

'Interesting that they left the last of the stones behind,' Bahar mused as a chauffeur held open the door for him.

'They took their foolish statue but abandoned the gems. Perhaps over the centuries they lost the knowledge of their existence. Polo said that only the head priest knew about them, and that he was told only because he carried the Khan's seal.'

'Perhaps,' Bahar muttered, already uninterested in the conversation. 'It's enough that you were able to track them down at all.'

Abdul had had teams of researchers and archivists searching the globe for these particular crystals after finding a tiny sample in the shop of a Hong Kong antiquities dealer and learning they possessed the special internal structure needed to make their device work. And his superior was correct in saying this had become an obsession. He had amassed and retained so much information about crystals that he could probably get his gemology certification. He'd personally visited stores and mines from Scotland to Japan, but his break came after one of the hired researchers, a bit of a Marco Polo fanatic himself, had sat in on William Cantor's moneygrubbing lecture in Coventry, England. When Mohammad heard the tale about crystal-powered weapons, he had flown to England that night with an assistant and met with Cantor when he gave his next lecture. He had to give Cantor credit – he'd actually tried to hold off telling Abdul who the actual owner of the Rustichello Folio was and where he lived. Once they'd disposed of Cantor's body, they'd broken into the drafty mansion in the southern part of England, killed the old man, taken the Folio, and staged the scene to look like a robbery gone bad.

They were safely out of the country before either crime was discovered.

A hired translator then spent several weeks on the document, eliciting details of Polo's observations of the battle and his later journey to find the mine where the crystals that had blinded the village's watchkeepers had originated. Abdul knew that the mine held the same stones as the tiny sliver he'd found in Hong Kong.

Of course they would need to be tested, but the optical properties Polo described were the same as they needed for their project. It couldn't be coincidence.

'And the sinking?' Bahar inquired. 'Did it go as planned?'

'We had to hurry but were only a few miles from our target area, and no one spotted us heading back to Brunei in the *Hercules*'s lifeboats. Our American mole had reported that the ship they used is much faster than we were led to believe. He should call me soon to tell me how it went, but I think we destroyed all traces of the Oracle before they reached it.'

'That is good. As it turns out, the Oracle was right about the Corporation posing a potential threat. They did manage to escape Insein Prison, a feat I don't believe has been accomplished by many.'

Abdul recalled his meeting with Cabrillo in Singapore. He'd had a feeling then that the man was dangerous. That reminded him of another loose end that needed seeing to. 'What of Pramana?'

'We're going to see him now. That is the reason for our delay here in Jakarta. I knew after his failure in Singapore that you would wish to speak with him. It was only your quick thinking that prevented it from becoming a fatal mistake. Once your chat is over we'll head to Europe with the crystals. Oh, what about Croissard?'

'Weighted down and tossed into the Malacca Strait.'

Thirty minutes later the sleek Mercedes limousine pulled into the parking lot of a run-down warehouse on the outskirts of the teeming city of ten million. The lot was cracked and weed choked, and the building looked as though it hadn't seen paint since the Dutch granted Indonesia its independence.

'I can't believe that fool Pramana didn't have tighter control of his people,' Mohammad said, his temper beginning to grow.

Some of the enforcers he employed came from the Islamist group Jemaah Islamiyah. In fact, Pramana had accompanied him to England and had carried out the torture of William Cantor. What Abdul hadn't known is that when Pramana sent two of his men to the Singapore meeting as lobby backup in case something went wrong, they brought suicide vests on the private jet with the intention of killing the very men Abdul was there to meet. Abdul didn't know the reason or particularly care. He supposed it was to avenge the fellow Muslims the Corporation had killed in Pakistan. Abdul himself had warned them all about how good these operators were, so perhaps they'd decided to martyr themselves by taking out such a formidable foe.

It mattered little. What mattered was that Pramana had betrayed them either deliberately or by not being able to control his men, and they'd nearly ruined everything. Had Mohammad not realized the situation and quickly improvised another explosive device with gunpowder from his pistol and chemicals he found on a maid's cart, he felt certain that Cabrillo would have realized the meeting had been a trap and not taken the contract. The third blast he'd set off in the casino had been just enough to convince the two Americans that they had been in an unfortunate place at an unfortunate time.

'If you don't mind,' Bahar said when Abdul swung open the car's door, 'I'll remain behind.'

'Of course.' Mohammad stepped out into the humid air and unsheathed the knife he kept strapped to his forearm.

18

Washington, D.C.
Three weeks later

The president's secretary had been with him from the very beginning when he decided to parlay his up-by-the-bootstraps story and gift for oratory into a political career. He put his law practice on hiatus and ran for mayor of Detroit and won in a landslide when his opponent had withdrawn from the race to 'spend more time with his family.' The truth was, his opponent's wife had found out her husband had been cheating and was preparing divorce proceedings. From there he did two terms in the House and another in the Senate before launching his presidential run. Eunice Wosniak had dutifully followed him from his one-man practice to the mayor's office and on to Washington, and now to the most powerful post in the world.

She guarded her boss almost as fiercely as his chief of staff, Lester Jackson. Jackson was a Washington insider who'd latched onto the president's coattails early on and never relinquished his grip.

While she had a support staff of several dozen under her, one of the tasks Eunice insisted upon performing herself was giving the president his coffee when he strode through her office on the way to his. She'd just finished adding milk – the First Lady insisted on two percent, but it was actually whole milk poured into a two percent carton – when her fax line rang.

It wasn't without precedent, but faxes were somewhat archaic in today's world so the machine usually sat mute for weeks on end. When it had spit out a single page into the tray, Eunice scanned the contents, bewilderment turning to genuine concern as she read.

This had to be a hoax, she thought.

But then how did the sender get this line? It wasn't listed in the White House directory because of all the prank faxes sent to the president, along with the prank letters and e-mails. Those were all screened off-site. Only a few dozen people had easy access to the fax machine behind her desk.

What if this wasn't a hoax? The very idea sickened her. She sat heavily, barely noticing the hot coffee she'd spilled in her lap.

Just then, Les Jackson strode in. His hair was frosted at the temples, and his eyes were starting to retreat into wrinkled pouches, but he still moved like a much younger man, as if the stress and strain of his job invigorated him rather than wore him down.

'You okay?' he asked. 'You look like you've seen a ghost.'

Eunice wordlessly held up the fax, forcing Jackson to reach across her desk to get it. He was known as a speed-reader and had the single page finished in just a few seconds.

'This is bogus,' was his opinion. 'Nobody can get that information. And the rest is just typical jihadist drivel. Where did it come from?'

He let the piece of paper flutter to her desk.

'It just came through on my fax, Mr Jackson.' Though she'd known him for years, she insisted on formality with her superiors. Jackson did nothing to dissuade her from that particular habit.

He considered that for just a moment, then dismissed it. 'Crackpot with your fax number. Bound to happen.'

'Is someone sending you dirty faxes, Eunice?' the president asked with a knowing chuckle.

Two years into his first term hadn't taken much of a toll on the man. He was tall, with broad shoulders, and such a captivating voice that audiences were still enthralled with him even when they disagreed with his policies.

Eunice Wosniak shot to her feet. 'No, Mr President. It's nothing like that. I, eh . . .' Her voice simply trailed off.

The president picked up the fax, pulled a pair of cheater glasses from the breast pocket of his Brooks Brothers suit, and settled them on his aquiline nose. He read it almost as quickly as his top aide. Unlike Jackson, the president blanched, his eyes widening. He reached into his hip pocket and removed a piece of plastic about the size of a credit card. It had been exchanged with a similar one by an NSA courier as soon as he'd left the presidential apartment. It was a morning routine that never varied.

He broke open a seal and compared the numbers printed on the card inside with those that had been written on the fax. His hands began to tremble.

'Mr President?' Jackson asked with considerable concern.

The little plastic card was nicknamed 'the biscuit.' Issued to the president every day since shortly after the Cuban Missile Crisis, it contained a series of numbers that was generated randomly at the National Security Agency at Fort Meade, Maryland, by a secure computer. This was the presidential authentication code to launch nuclear weapons.

Without doubt, these numbers were the most closely guarded secrets in the United States.

And someone had just faxed today's code to the Oval Office.

'Les, call together the National Security Council. I want them here as fast as humanly possible.' While someone possessing the codes couldn't possibly launch a nuclear weapon, the very idea that the biscuit codes were no longer secret was the greatest breach of security in U.S. history. This alone called into question the level of protection of all other areas of national defense.

It took several hours to get the NSC assembled in the Situation Room, a windowless bunker deep under the White House. Because of prior travel arrangements, the only people in on the meeting were the vice president, the chairman of the Joint Chiefs, the secretary of defense, the secretary of state, and, by special invitation, the head of the NSA and of the CIA.

'Lady and gentlemen,' the president started, 'we have a crisis on our hands the likes of which this nation has never faced before.'

He passed out copies of the letter but continued speaking. 'A little over two hours ago that fax was sent to Eunice Wosniak, my personal secretary. The authentication code on it is genuine. We will have to wait and see if the threat is genuine as well. As for the demands, they are something we might be forced to discuss.'

'Hold on a minute,' the commanding general of the NSA said. 'This isn't possible.'

'I know,' the president responded. 'And yet here we are. The code comes from a random-number generator, and all personnel who handle the biscuit have gone through a Yankee White background check, right?'

'Yes, sir. It is totally secure. And no one other than you ever actually sees the numbers. I'll check on the status of the courier. Was the seal on the biscuit broken?'

'Intact.'

'This is impossible,' the general repeated.

The vice president spoke up. 'This psycho says he is going to shut down the power to Troy, New York, for one minute at noon. Shouldn't we warn someone? And why Troy, of all places?'

'Because it's close enough to New York City to get our attention but small enough that when he diverts that much electricity, it won't overload the grid and cause a cascade shutdown like the blackout of '03.' This came from Les Jackson, who had been a lobbyist for a utility umbrella organization. 'And if we warn them, they're going to want to know how we knew. If this is legit, do you want the administration facing questions like that?'

'Oh. Right.' The vice president had been brought on to balance the ticket and not for his keen intellect.

'This isn't just some computer hacker,' said Fiona Katamora, the secretary of state. She'd been the national security adviser in the previous administration and had been tapped for this more public office because she was quite simply one of the most accomplished people on the planet. 'The demands read like Osama bin Laden's Christmas wish list.'

She read from the fax: 'The United States will immediately announce a halt of all military and nonmilitary aid to the State of Israel and will henceforth provide the same amount of money to the Palestinian Authority and to the Hamas leaders on the Gaza Strip. All prisoners currently held at Guantánamo Bay will be released immediately. All U.S. and NATO troops must leave Iraq by the end of this June and be out of Afghanistan by the end of the year. All military aid to Pakistan will be immediately halted. American military bases in Kuwait and Qatar are to be dismantled by the end of the year. The president will formally condemn the building of Jewish settlements on the West Bank and will further condemn the banning of headscarves for Muslim women in France and any other European country which enacts such a ban. All Muslim groups currently listed internationally as terror groups will have that designation lifted. There will be no further sanctions against the nation of Iran, and all such sanctions currently in place will be lifted by the end of the year.

'What he's telling us,' she said, 'is that we are to cede the war on terror. I find it very telling that he mentions Iran.'

'Why's that?'

'Sunni and Shi'a Muslims do not get along, and the one thing most Arab states agree on is that a bottled-up Iran, with its Shi'a brand of Islam, is in their best interest. But this guy wants our hands off everyone, as if to say whatever differences exist between the two groups is an internal thing and they will handle it themselves.'

'Obviously we can't do any of these things,' the vice president said ponderously.

'What gets me too,' Fiona Katamora continued as though he hadn't spoken, 'are the time lines that are spelled out. This isn't the rant of some deranged jihadi sitting in a Waziri cave. This has been carefully thought out. Each deadline is doable from a practical perspective and, while politically unpalatable, isn't unfeasible.'

'We can't stop giving aid to Israel,' the CIA director said.

'We can,' Fiona retorted evenly, not raising her voice the way her counterpart had. 'We choose to continue funding them because it is in our best interest. If that were no longer the case, we can turn off the money taps anytime we want.'

'But . . .'

'Listen, if this is legitimate, the game's changed completely. We are no longer in control. Some group out there appears to have unlimited access to our most guarded secrets. At the push of a button they can shut down power grids. Think about that. Think about a nationwide power outage that goes on for weeks or months. Or an air traffic control system that we no longer rely on. Every plane in the country grounded indefinitely. Could this person override the safeties at the nation's nuclear power plants and cause them all to melt down? I think there are physical safeties in place for that . . . But you get the idea.'

'Any suggestions on what do we do?' the president asked in a voice much quieter than he intended.

'We find the person responsible and crucify them,' the veep thundered.

'Where did the fax originate?' the man from the NSA asked.

'Gentlemen,' Fiona said sharply, 'do you honestly think whoever masterminded the theft of the presidential authentication codes is going to be caught using traditional police techniques? This guy didn't walk into a Kinko's on Mass Ave. to send his message. That signal bounced around the planet for a couple of hours before it reached Eunice's office. We'll never trace it. We need to look at this from the other end. Who benefits from this?'

'Al-Qaeda tops the list,' the beribboned admiral from the Joint Chiefs replied.

'Does this feel like something they'd do?' Fiona shot back. 'If they had this kind of power, they'd launch an all-out cyberattack that would drive us back into the Stone Age. There would be no demands or warning. No, it's someone else. Someone new.'

'Any ideas?' asked the CIA director.

'I'm afraid that's up to you.'

'My first instinct was al-Qaeda too, but you make a compelling argument against them. I'll talk to my people to see if there is anyone else out there with the wherewithal to pull off something like this.'

'Let's say they do kill the power in Troy, New York,' Les Jackson said. 'What's our response? What do we do? It'd be political suicide to cut off aid to Israel or even to announce such an intention. Same goes for just releasing the prisoners from Gitmo.'

Fiona Katamora raked her fingers through her raven hair in a sign of frustration. 'This isn't about politics, Les. We've been handed a demonstration that tells us we are at this person's mercy. He has cracked the most secure code in the world and flaunted it in our faces. We either give in to the demands or face the consequences as a nation, not as a political party or as a presidential administration. Do we cave or do we all go down together?' She turned to face the commander in chief. 'That's the question, Mr President.'

An aide knocked at the door and entered when the president called, 'Come.'

'Sir, just to give you an update. The return number printed on the fax is bogus. No such number is listed anywhere in the world. And the White House switch-board has no record of the call ever coming in.'

'The call never even came in? Did your secretary crack up?' the NSA director asked the president. 'Is this her idea of a joke?'

The president didn't know what to say, but he was hoping against hope that his longtime and most trusted secretary was mentally ill and had pulled off this cruel hoax.

'One more thing,' the aide continued. 'There was a blackout in Troy, New York, at noon that lasted for precisely sixty seconds. No other areas were affected even though the local utility supplies power to the outlying regions. So far, they have no reason why power faded or why it came back.'

'Dear God,' someone said. 'This is real.'

Fiona kept reading from the bottom of the fax. 'These are small, benign demonstrations of our abilities. We are not barbarians. We cherish life, but if even one of our demands is not met, we will cripple your country. Planes will rain from the sky, refineries will explode, factories will idle, and electricity will be a thing of your past.

'In time, all people of the earth will convert to the one true faith, but we are willing to allow you to coexist with us for now.' She looked up. 'It's real.'

19

Smith had made his mistake a week earlier. He'd finally relented to MacD's relentless calls for a proof-of-life video link to his daughter. And because he believed that Lawless was still under his control, he was lazy when it came to computer security. The video link only lasted a few tearful seconds, but Mark and Eric back-tracked its source with ease.

Prior to that, the Corporation had made no headway in its investigation of Gunawan Bahar.

As Cabrillo had suspected, the kidnappers hadn't taken Pauline Lawless far from where she'd been abducted in New Orleans. In fact, she was being held within the city's notorious Lower Ninth Ward, the area so heavily damaged by Hurricane Katrina that much of it remained in ruins. It was a smart tactical decision – since the composition of the area had been so disrupted, strangers had a better chance of blending in and not arousing suspicion.

Cabrillo, Lawless, and Franklin Lincoln flew into Houston, where the Corporation maintained a safe house. It was one of a dozen they kept in port cities all over the world and was used primarily to store weapons and equipment that they might otherwise have trouble getting through customs. Even corporate jets are subject to searches, and while officials can be bribed in many airports around the globe, it wasn't a good idea to try it in the United States.

They rented a nondescript sedan from Hertz, plundered the vaultlike room in the safe house for gear, and were on the road for the Big Easy moments later. They drove the three hundred and fifty miles at the speed limit, with every traffic rule followed to the letter. Cabrillo had Lawless drive. It wasn't because of his arm, which was back to about eighty percent. He wanted MacD's mind on something other than his six-year-old baby girl.

Their first stop was Lawless's parents' home. The terrified couple who had been watching the child had been told by the kidnappers that any attempt to alert the police would force them to kill her. They had been living with that fear for weeks. As much as MacD had wanted to call them, he agreed with Cabrillo that it was possible one of the kidnappers had stayed in their home or bugged their phone.

The home was in a neat subdivision with towering oaks draped in Spanish moss. Many of the homes were brick and had come through the hurricane unscathed. MacD parked well down the block and out of sight of his parents' house and waited behind the wheel while Cabrillo and Linc went to check if the house was under observation. Both wore hard hats and blue jumpsuits that could easily pass for utility workers' attire. Cabrillo carried a clipboard, Lincoln a toolbox.

There were no vans parked along the street, a favorite

observation post, and no cars with overly tinted windows, another dead giveaway. All the lawns were well manicured. It was an important detail, because if a neighbor's house had been commandeered by the kidnappers to keep an eye on the Lawlesses, they wouldn't expose themselves by riding a John Deere around the property.

They spent fifteen minutes checking gas meters but at the same time always watching the target house for drapes being moved by someone lurking inside. The few cars that passed them on the quiet street paid no attention and didn't slow or stop.

'I think we're good,' Linc said.

Cabrillo had to agree. He scribbled something on his notepad in big bold letters, and the two of them approached the door. The brass knocker had been recently polished and the stairs swept, as if these small domestic chores could take the Lawlesses away from the pain they were feeling. He rapped loudly. A moment later an attractive woman in her mid-fifties opened the door.

He held up the clipboard where she could read it and asked, 'Ma'am, we've had reports of gas leaks in this area. Have you had any trouble?'

On the clipboard was written: We're here with MacD. Are you alone?

'Um, no. I mean, yes. No. No one's here.' Then the reality hit her, and her voice raised two octaves. 'You're with MacD? He's all right? Oh my gosh!' She turned to shout over her shoulder. 'Mare! Mare, get in here. MacD's okay.'

Juan gently but firmly bustled them inside and shut the door. An Irish setter came into the room to see what the commotion was, its feathered tail wagging excitedly.

'Mrs. Lawless, please keep your voice down. Were the men who took your granddaughter ever in this house?'

'What is it?' a male voice called from deeper in the home.

'No. Never. They grabbed her when I was watching her at a park near here. Brandy, down,' she said to the dog that was trying to lick Linc's face. Linc ignored the dog and kept watching the bug detector as he swept the entryway. 'They told me they would let her go soon but that if I contacted the police they would kill her. My husband and I have been sick with worry ever since.'

Marion Lawless II came around a corner, wearing chinos and a denim shirt. His son was his spitting image, especially the jade-colored eyes and slightly cleft chin.

'Mare, these men are here with MacD.'

Juan thrust out a hand. 'My name is Juan Cabrillo. This is Franklin Lincoln. And we've been working with your son to rescue Pauline.' As soon as introductions were over, the Chairman called Lawless on a disposable cell and told him it was clear but to come through backyards anyway.

'The last we knew, MacD had quit working for that security company after something bad happened to him in Afghanistan,' the senior Lawless said.

'It's a rather long, complicated story. I'll let your son tell it when he gets here. We just wanted to let you know that we've located Pauline and we're going to get her back.'

'And the animals that took her?' Kay asked. From her tone it was clear what fate she preferred for them. She might be a genteel Southern woman, but there was steel in her spine.

'Will never bother you again,' Juan assured her, and she understood his meaning.

'Good.'

'However, once we have her back I'm going to need you folks to disappear for a while until we can roll up the people behind Pauline's abduction. If you don't have someplace, we can get you a hotel.'

Mare Lawless put up an arresting hand. 'No need. An old friend of mine has a cottage down on the Gulf Coast that he lets us use anytime we want.'

Juan considered this option and decided it was safe enough. He nodded. 'That sounds perfect. This might take us a couple of weeks.'

'Take as long as you need,' Kay said quickly, and with the resolve of a woman protecting her own. She turned when there was a knock on the sliding-glass door that led to the backyard patio. She shrieked with joy when she saw her son, standing next to the wicker table and chairs.

She unlatched the door and hugged MacD intensely, tears running unabashedly down her cheeks. Marion Senior joined them and threw his arms over his family.

He too was crying with joy, and also the guilt of not being able to protect MacD's only child.

If he was honest with himself, the scene made Juan choke up some as well.

They stayed for only an hour. Cabrillo wanted enough daylight to locate and study the house the kidnappers were using. MacD explained everything to his parents, only leaving out his treatment at the hands of the Insein Prison jailors, the fact that he'd had a rope bridge shot out from under him, and a few other details he felt it best they not know. It was still a harrowing story that left Kay Lawless a little pale under her tan.

They left amid smiles and more tears. MacD promised he'd come home as soon as they nailed the person behind Pauline's abduction.

The neighborhood where the videoconference originated hadn't been adopted by a celebrity or been the recipient of a generous grant. Many of the houses were still boarded up, though, at the very least, most of the trash had been removed. This was the section of New Orleans that was hardest hit when the levees failed and had been a virtual lake in the days following Katrina. Nearby were vacant lots with only crumbling concrete pads to mark the grave sites of families' homes.

Linc dropped MacD and Cabrillo at a coffee shop not too far from their intended target. In this area, two white men and a black man in the same car would look suspiciously like cops no matter who was behind the wheel. He returned thirty minutes later, and helped himself to the chicory coffee from the pot Juan had ordered.

'Well?' Cabrillo asked after Linc had stopped making a sour face at the bitter taste of the coffee.

'Nasty,' he pronounced. 'Okay, the satellite pics we have are a little out of date. The two houses behind the one we're interested in have been demolished, and the lots are practically jungles. The ones on either side are still there and completely shuttered. There are families living across the street. I saw kids' bikes chained in their yards, and toys and stuff on the lawn, so we need to be careful there.'

'What about the kidnappers?' MacD asked, his anxiety level spiking.

'Never showed themselves. The shades are drawn in all the windows, but I believe there are tiny gaps at the edges that they can see out of and only a professional Peeping Tom could see in. And Juan, you were right about the lawn. It looks like a goat's buffet. Those guys are holed up tight and probably go out only at night, to get food from a store miles from here.'

'So was that an attached garage we saw on the pictures?'

'Yes.'

'Did you get a chance to run a thermal scan?'

'No. It would look too suspicious, and it's still too warm outside. Not enough of a temperature difference to register properly.'

Cabrillo had suspected as much but felt he should ask anyway. 'Okay. We lay low and then go in at one and assault at three.' Three a.m. is when the human body is at its lowest ebb. Even a guard on night duty succumbs to the body's natural circadian rhythms and would be far from alert. 'MacD, you cool?'

'Yeah,' he replied. 'Ah won't let my emotions interfere with the op.'

Even in such a tumbledown neighborhood, the men couldn't go skulking around in full combat gear and armed to the teeth. As one o'clock approached, Linc parked the car several streets over from the target house and popped open the hood. Any passing police patrol would see that it was a disabled vehicle and that the driver had left it for the night. A curious cop might run the plates, see that it was a rental, and assume it was a relative displaced by Katrina to Houston, as so many were, back home for a visit.

They all wore dark jeans and long-sleeved T-shirts, and their equipment was stuffed in duffel bags. The air was markedly cooler, though the humidity remained high. They walked normally along the cracked sidewalk as if they didn't have a care in the world. There was no traffic, and the only sound came from a barking dog several blocks over.

When they reached the jungled lot behind the target house, the men faded into it as if they'd never existed. From here on out, they were invisible. Bags whispered open, and equipment was triple-checked. They oozed their way through the foliage. If any of them noticed that most of the plants were studded with wicked sharp thorns, no one gave any indication. After five minutes of silently crawling through the underbrush, they came into the clear. A wooden fence, missing slats like a mouth missing teeth, encircled the backyard and blocked most of the view. Unperturbed, Cabrillo hefted the thermal imager from a bag strapped to his side and climbed atop a chunk of concrete left over from when this parcel had been a home.

The scanner worked by comparing heat signatures, and had uncanny sensitivity. It basically allowed him to see through walls as though he had X-ray vision. They were so effective that many civil liberties groups were fighting their use by law enforcement agencies because of right-to-privacy issues. The military had high hopes for the devices in Iraq and Afghanistan, but oftentimes the mud huts' walls were too thick to get accurate readings. But here, with a house so old it lacked even basic insulation, the scanner was in its element.

Cabrillo could see four distinct heat signatures, which glowed white in his vision, and a squat rectangle of absolute black, which would be the cold water stored in the only bathroom's toilet cistern. There were three other spots showing heat. One was cylindrical and would be the hot-water tank. Another was much smaller and was the warm compressor motor for the refrigerator. There was no glowing pilot light, so the stove was electric. In this way not only did Juan see the occupants, he could decipher the house's layout. Three of the people were in repose, their bodies seeming to float a few feet above the floor because the scanner couldn't see the beds they were lying on. The fourth figure was sitting upright as if in a chair, a lightbulb glowing cheerily over him.

He concentrated on the seated person for fifteen minutes, and in all that time the figure didn't move once. If Juan had to venture a guess, he'd say the guy was sound asleep.

Next he moved off to the right about twenty yards, through the grass, until he came up against the trunk of a tree. He was close enough now to peer over the fence. He scoped the house a second time. Because he'd shifted position he saw the same objects from a different angle and could confirm that his mental picture of its layout was accurate.

He rejoined his team, and they retreated back into the woods.

Cabrillo's voice was barely above a whisper. 'There are three Tangos, one at the front of the house asleep in a chair. A second one is alone in a back bedroom. The third is in the bedroom next to it with MacD's daughter.' He felt Lawless stiffen next to him. 'Before you ask, they're in separate beds.' He'd been able to distinguish her from the others because of her small stature.

They'd earlier determined that the house, though small by American standards, was too big to use the knockout-gas trick they'd employed to 'rescue' Setiawan Bahar. They would have to go in silently and without a hint of hesitation. The heat signatures were too clear for any of the kidnappers to be wearing a bulky suicide vest, but that didn't mean they didn't have them close by.

For the next two hours they took turns watching the house through the thermal imager. At one point, the guard in the front room roused himself to use the bathroom and when he returned the scanner showed him lying down – on a couch, presumably – and most likely going to sleep again.

As the minute hand of Juan's watch swept to three a.m., they moved out, advancing in a crouch and then vaulting over the fence like ghosts. They were so silent that the few nearby crickets didn't stop chirping. There was a single door that led to the backyard from the kitchen. Juan and MacD donned night vision goggles and turned them on. Working only by touch, Linc picked the lock in under fifty seconds. Despite the massive size of his hands, he had the dexterity of a surgeon but had taken longer than normal in order to stay as quiet as possible.

While Linc was working, Cabrillo drizzled oil from a small can over the hinges and worked it into the gaps with his fingers. The door unlatched, but Linc kept it closed, as a slight breeze had come up from behind them and would have blown into the house had he opened it.

The men's weapons were mere .22 calibers, and the silencers attached to their barrels were the size of soda cans, making them unbalanced and unwieldy. Such pistols had only one purpose. These were the tools of assassins. The ammo was mercury tipped but carried less powder than normal. It was a trade-off of power versus stealth. But when the silencer was placed against a target's head, the extra gunpowder would have been superfluous anyway.

The breeze died down, and Cabrillo nodded. Like a black panther, Linc inched open the door and slid his big body through, followed immediately by Cabrillo and Lawless.

There was enough light spilling from the front living room to make it seem like noon in the filthy and reeking kitchen. A barrel-sized trash can was overflowing with rotting food and used paper plates. Skillets and pans were mounded in the sink, covered in congealed grease and doubtlessly home to a sizable roach colony. An unadorned archway led to the living room while another exit gave way to a hallway where the bedrooms and bathroom were located.

Moving so that his feet barely left the unmopped linoleum floor, Cabrillo glided through this second doorway with MacD on his heels. The bedroom doors were both closed. From one there was silence. From the other came deep, sonorous snoring. The snorer was with Pauline Lawless, yet one more torture for the poor girl.

As agreed, they struck thirty seconds after parting in the kitchen to give each other enough time to get into position. Juan counted down those last few seconds in his head as accurately as a Swiss chronograph. At the precise last second, he heard two muted coughs from the front of the house. Linc's man was dead. Juan opened the cheap pressboard door and saw his target sprawled on a plain metal bed. Next to him was a stand with a pistol and a book on top. On the floor was a pile of clothing and another garment that had nothing to do with protecting the wearer from the elements. Juan could see the bulges of plastic explosives and wiring looping all across the vest.

Without pause, Cabrillo strode across the room, held the barrel an inch from the kidnapper's head, and put two muffled rounds into his skull. The body jerked at the first impact but was still for the second.

He felt nothing at that moment. Not remorse at killing another human being, not elation at taking out a terrorist. On his moral balance sheet, tonight's action was a wash. He would derive neither pleasure nor guilt from it, but he would bury this memory as far down as humanly possible. Killing a sleeping man, no matter what he'd done to deserve it, simply wasn't the Chairman's style.

When he came out into the hallway, MacD stood there with a little blond girl, still asleep, in his arms. Cabrillo held the deactivated suicide vest in his.

'Clear,' Juan called, and pulled off his and Lawless's NVGs.

'Clear,' Linc echoed. He entered the hallway also carrying a suicide vest. 'What do you want to do with this?'

'We'll take them with us and deep-six them in Lake Pontchartrain.'

The next part of the plan was a little bit of misdirection for the police. Cabrillo didn't want them to suspect that this incident had anything to do with terrorism. Linc had been carrying a camelback canteen over his shoulders, but rather than water it contained gasoline. While he started dousing every combustible item in the house, especially the bodies, Cabrillo sprinkled about empty vials commonly used by crack dealers and candles and spoons for cooking heroin as well as medical syringes. He knew the cops would test the drug paraphernalia and that it would come up clean, but he hoped they'd shrug off the anomaly and just be grateful three more dealers were dead. Cabrillo also left a small mechanical scale, and a few hundred-dollar bills inside a cigar box–sized metal case under one of the beds. The scale and lockbox had come from Walmart, the cash from their safe house's uncirculated cache. The scene was set. Drug deal gone bad. End of story.

MacD waited outside, his sleeping daughter still unaware that her ordeal was over.

Juan was the last one out, and he closed the back door after he tossed a match into a pool of gasoline. By the time they made it through the back-lot jungle, the house was a pyre, with flames arcing through the roof rafters. Wide-eyed children and their families staked out positions on their lawns while overworked firefighters battled a blaze they could not defeat. The house was a complete loss, and by the time it was finally out, a duffel bag laden with the now-traceable weapons and two vests packed with explosives was at the bottom of Lake Pontchartrain, Lawless, his parents, and his little girl were headed to the coast, and a nondescript rental car was halfway to Houston. MacD would join the *Oregon* after spending a couple of days with his family.

20

Twenty-four hours had passed since the fax first came through to the White House. More than eight thousand men and women were put to work trying to figure out who was behind it and how it had been accomplished. Agents from every department in the country were mobilized, even if some were kept in the dark as to the exact nature of their search because the incident had been classified above top secret.

Indecision gripped the Oval Office. The demonstration of the adversary's power had been convincing, but his demands went too far. The president couldn't meet any of them if he hoped to maintain national security and perhaps even keep his job. To his credit, the latter was a much lesser consideration.

He'd been given advice and speculation from across the spectrum. It was al-Qaeda. It was the Iranians. We should give in to the demands. We should ignore them. Ultimately it was his call, and no matter which way he looked at the ultimatum, he saw no viable exit strategy. He'd tried calling the Israeli prime minister to float a balloon about simply announcing the U.S. was suspending financial aid in the short term, but the call was mysteriously cut off as soon as it became clear that America would clandestinely still continue supporting the Jewish state. Somehow the most secure telephone in the world could be listened in on and disconnected at will.

A technician from the NSA had explained to him that it was impossible, but the evidence lay dead on his desk. He tried having the call come from another phone not connected to the White House switchboard and it too ended before anything substantive was said. His only option, however cumbersome and slow, was to send a diplomatic courier to Jerusalem to tell the prime minister what the United States intended to do.

He was behind his desk, staring off into middle space, when Lester Jackson knocked and entered without permission. The doors to the Oval Office were too thick for much sound to spill through, so the president hadn't heard the fax behind Eunice Wosniak's desk ring.

'Mr President, this just came from them.' He carried a fax like it was a decomposing muskrat.

'What does it say?' he asked wearily. If they made it through this crisis, he'd already decided that this would be his one and only term. He felt like he'd aged a hundred years since yesterday morning.

'All it says is, "We meant immediately. Their blood is on your hands."'

'Whose blood?'

'I don't know. There's nothing much happening in the country, according to the major news outlets. Sir, this could still be an elaborate bluff. They could have inside people in Troy, New York, that killed the power, and there's some powerful software that could hack our phone system.'

'Don't you think I don't know that?' he snapped. 'But what if it isn't? What if they carry out another attack? A lethal one? I've wasted enough time already.'

Stung, Jackson's voice went formal. 'What are your intentions, sir?'

The president knew he was taking out his frustration on one of his oldest friends. 'I'm sorry, Les. It's just . . . I don't know. Who could have ever foreseen something like this? It's hard enough ordering men and women in uniform into harm's way. Now our entire civilian population's at risk.'

'That's been our position for a number of years,' Jackson pointed out.

'Yeah, but we've done a pretty good job of keeping our shores safe.'

'We've been lucky as much as we've been good.'

'That hurts.'

'Because it's the truth. There have been several public incidents, and some secret ones, where the terrorists were too incompetent to carry out their attack, attacks we had no idea were coming.'

'And now we know one might be heading straight at us but have no way of stopping it.'

Eunice burst into the room, her face ashen. She turned on the television over by a grouping of sofas. She left, weeping. A network anchor's face loomed on the center of the TV screen.

'Authorities aren't saying if this is a terror-related

incident. To those of you just tuning in, a commuter train heading from Washington, D.C., to New York City, Amtrak's high-speed Acela Express, collided head-on with a southbound freight train that had somehow gotten onto the wrong track.'

The image shifted to an aerial view of utter devastation. The trains looked like toys, but toys of a careless child. The lead locomotive was an unrecognizable lump of metal, while three of the train's five passenger cars had accordioned to half their eighty-seven-foot length. The other two cars and the rear engine had been thrown off the tracks and into the back of a warehouse. The freight train's two lead locomotives were hidden under a greasy ball of fire, as their thousands of gallons of diesel fuel cooked off. Behind them was a string of derailed boxcars, many of them smashed to scrap and lying at acute angles to the railbed.

'Amtrak officials have yet to release the number of passengers on board,' the anchor's voice continued over the helicopter cam's shot, 'but the Acela Express is capable of carrying more than three hundred passengers, and, this being a busy commute time, it is expected that the train was near capacity. One official speaking on condition of anonymity has told us a computer switching system makes an accident of this kind nearly impossible and that the engineer of the freight train would have had to physically engage the switch to put his locomotive on the same line as the commuter.'

'Or someone overrode the computer,' the president said, his voice shaky.

'Maybe this is just a coincidence,' Jackson said hopefully.

'Let it rest, Lester. This is no coincidence, and we both know it. I didn't do what he wanted so he crashed two trains. What will it be next time? Two planes in midflight? This guy obviously has control over every computer system in this country, and, so far, it seems there isn't a damned thing we can do about it. Christ, the Army will have to go back to using signal mirrors and the Navy semaphore flags.' He blew a frustrated breath and made the only decision available. 'Has the courier left for Israel yet?'

'He's probably still at Andrews Air Force Base.'

'Recall him. There's no point in subterfuge. I want to downplay this as much as possible. No press conference or prime-time speech, just put out the word that all aid to Israel is being suspended until further notice. Ditto military aid to Pakistan.'

'What about the detainees at Gitmo? That was another immediate demand.'

'We'll release them, all right, but not to their home countries. Let's ship them to the World Court in The Hague. If Fiona's right and this guy is rational and reasoned, then I don't think there will be a reprisal, and getting the Europeans to try them is better than nothing.'

'Dan' – it was the first time Jackson had used the president's Christian name since he'd taken the oath of office – 'I am sorry. I was one of the ones urging that we adopt a wait-and-see attitude.'

'But it was still my call,' the president said, the deaths on the trains preying heavily on his conscience.

'I know. That's why I'm sorry.' He made for the door and was stopped momentarily.

'Les, make sure everyone keeps working at tracking this psycho and pray he has a weakness we haven't thought of, because, right now, it feels like we're facing off against God Himself.'

21

Cabrillo and Lincoln caught up with the *Oregon* at Port Said after the ship had made a transit of the Suez Canal. As much as they wanted to get Gunawan Bahar and his henchman, Smith, they had another operation in the luxury resort city of Monte Carlo. One of the emirs of the United Arab Emirates wanted the Corporation as extra security whenever he traveled. It mattered not that he didn't really have an enemy in the world. He felt better knowing that Cabrillo and his people were looking out for him while he basked off the coast on his hundred-foot yacht or gambled insane amounts of money in the casino. He got the idea from the Kuwaiti emir, who had used the Corporation in South Africa a few months back. Although they'd arrived late because Juan had been marooned in Antarctica and they'd had to return to pick him up, the team foiled an assassination plot involving some al-Qaeda operatives from Somalia.

No sooner had a chartered helicopter landed the duo on the *Oregon*'s deck and beat south for the Egyptian port city than her engines ramped up, and soon a miles-long wake marked her swift passage. After dumping his single bag in his cabin, Juan made straight for the Op Center, where Linda Ross had the conn.

'Welcome back,' she beamed. 'We're all relieved that MacD got his daughter.'

Hali Kasim was at his customary seat at the communications workstation. 'Just so you know, I've been monitoring local media in New Orleans. They're calling it drug-related arson. No suspects and no IDs on the bodies.'

'There wasn't much left to ID,' Cabrillo remarked. 'How's our passenger making out?'

For the weeks she'd been aboard the *Oregon* as a virtual prisoner, though in a velvet-lined cell, Soleil Croissard hadn't done much but stay in her cabin or watch the sea from the upper flying bridge. She even took her meals in her room. She was mourning her father and working to come to grips with her own abduction. Doctor Huxley, the ship's de facto psychiatrist, had tried talking with her on several occasions but hadn't made significant progress.

'Would you believe she snapped out of it?' Linda informed him.

'Really?' Juan was surprised because she'd given no indication when he'd said good-bye just a couple days ago.

'You're not going to believe what did it either. Eric and Murph, who are panting after her worse than the girl we rescued from that sinking cruise ship—'

'Jannike Dahl,' Juan recalled. 'She was the sole survivor of the *Golden Dawn*.'

'That's her. Anyway, those two got the bright idea of rigging one of the parafoils we use for combat drops off a winch at the fantail so they could parasail off the ship. To their credit, it worked like a charm, and most of us have had a go at it. But Soleil is the one who can't get enough. I talked to Hux about it, and she reminded me that Soleil's an adrenaline junkie. She needed a jolt to remind her she's still alive.'

Linda hit some keystrokes on the computer built into the arm of the command chair, and an aft-facing camera mounted high on the superstructure came up on a portion of the main view screen. Sure enough, there were Murph and Stoney with Soleil Croissard. She already sported a black parachute harness, and the two men were clipping her to a thin line leading off to a winch. As they watched, Soleil climbed up the transom rail with the drogue chute in her hand. She faced forward, said something to Eric and Mark with a big grin on her face, and tossed the little parachute into the *Oregon*'s slipstream. The main chute was yanked from the harness in a billow of ebony nylon and inflated, heaving her off her perch in a gut-wrenching ascent.

Toggling the controls, Linda tilted the camera up until they could see Soleil silhouetted against the azure sky. She must have been two hundred feet above the deck, and because of the ship's speed she would keep going higher and higher if not for the tether.

Cabrillo wasn't too sure he liked this. A few years

back they got it into their heads that they could wake-surf, while the ship was at speed, using a line rigged from an extension pole out of the starboard boat garage. It worked fine for about ten minutes before Murph took a spill and lost his grip on the T-bar. They'd been forced to stop the ship in order to launch a Zodiac to haul his butt out of the drink.

Mark had suggested outfitting some sort of catch net aft of the garage for their next attempt. Juan nixed the whole enterprise.

But if this is what it took to draw Soleil out of her shell, then he supposed no harm was done. 'I guess,' he said after watching her for a moment, 'that if the UAV ever fails us, we can put a lookout up in that contraption.'

'You should try it,' Linda encouraged. 'It's a blast.'

'And while they've been out playing, how's the research coming?'

'Nada,' Linda replied. 'Bahar's still off the radar, and we can't find anything that remotely ties him to any criminal or terrorist activities. Oh, wait. One thing. The oil platform. It was part of something called the Oracle Project. Murph found that in a purged accounting file in Bahar's corporate computer, though now he can't access it anymore. It's got a new firewall that he can't break through.'

'I find that hard to believe.'

'So does he. I do have some good news. Langston phoned earlier. Says he has a job for us.'

Juan was shocked and elated. They'd been left out to

dry for so long, he didn't think the CIA would ever use their services again. 'What's the mission?'

'The Chinese have built a new surveillance ship, state-of-the-art. She's currently off the coast of Alaska. He wants us to persuade them to go home. He said you'd figure out something creative that won't start an international incident. I told him we needed a week.'

Cabrillo's gears were already churning when he happened to glance at the video screen again. Soleil was no longer in camera range. He reached across to adjust the camera and saw that she was being reeled back down to the deck. Mark and Eric watched anxiously, making Cabrillo wonder if anything was wrong. When she was back firmly on the *Oregon*, she yanked one of the chute's toggles, spilling air from that side and collapsing the canopy. Eric helped her bundle it into a ball while the wind fought to refill it. Mark Murphy was running for the superstructure.

Juan reset the main board to show the ship's bows cleaving the Mediterranean. When ten minutes went by and Murph hadn't found him in the Op Center, the Chairman called him in his room.

'Everything all right?'

'I'm a little busy, Juan,' Mark said, and killed the connection.

Rather than wait for the eccentric genius, Cabrillo went down to the forward hold, a vast open space they used for storage when they were running legitimate cargoes as part of their cover or, when it was empty like

385

now, for repacking chutes. He found Soleil alone. When he asked about Eric, she told him he followed Mark almost as soon as he could.

'Looked like quite the joyride,' he said.

'Not quite the rush I got jumping off the Eiffel Tower, but it was fun.' She had the parachute laid flat on the wooden deck and was tracing the riser lines. It was clear she knew exactly what she was doing.

'How many jumps have you made?'

'BASE or from an airplane? I've made dozens of the first and hundreds of the second.'

He saw the haunted look that had dimmed her eyes and sallowed her complexion was almost gone. There were still traces of it when she tried to smile, as if she felt she didn't deserve a moment's happiness. Cabrillo remembered those same feelings after his wife was killed. He thought he was dishonoring her memory by laughing at a joke or enjoying a movie. It was nothing more than a way of punishing himself for something that wasn't his fault, and in time it faded.

'Ever jump the New River Gorge Bridge?' It was an 876-foot span in West Virginia and considered one of the best spots for jumping in the world.

'Of course,' she replied as if he'd asked if she breathed. 'You?'

'Back when I was in training for an organization I once worked for, a bunch of us went over and did it.'

'Linda tells me you were in the CIA.' Juan nodded. 'Was it exciting?'

'Most days, it's as boring as any office job. Others,

'you're so scared that no matter what you do you can't dry your palms.'

'I think that is real danger,' she said. 'What I do, it's only pretend.'

'I don't know. Getting shot by a border guard or having your chute fail at eleven thousand feet has pretty much the same results.'

Her eyes lit up a little. 'Ah, but I have a reserve parachute.'

'You know what I mean.'

Her smile said that she did. 'I guess what I am saying is that I place myself at risk for my own needs. You do it for others. I am very selfish, while you are generous.'

Juan broke eye contact and thrust his hands in his pockets. 'Listen, ah,' he stammered for just a second and changed subjects. 'I hate to bring this up, but we could use your help. I'm convinced that your father was targeted for a specific reason. There is something he has that Bahar wanted.'

He used the present tense when mentioning her father, though he knew in all likelihood Croissard was dead.

'We've snooped through his electronic files for everything he's been working on for the past year,' he continued. 'So far, nothing jumps out at us. I was wondering if you would take a look and see if anything grabs your attention.'

She caught his eye again, her beautiful face somber. 'He is dead, isn't he?'

'I can't confirm it, but I believe so. I am sorry.'

'My helping you will punish those men?'

'That's the plan.'

Soleil nodded slowly. 'I will try, but I think I mentioned that we weren't close and I know hardly anything about his business dealings.'

'Just do the best you can. That's all I ask of anyone.'

Cabrillo was in his cabin later that night when there was a knock on the door.

'It's me and Eric,' Mark Murphy said.

'Come on in.'

The two entered the cabin with the eagerness of puppies.

'We figured it out when Soleil was parasailing, and I think we confirmed it,' Mark said excitedly. 'The computers on the oil rig were the alpha test for why Bahar needed those crystals.'

'The beta machine uses optical lasers,' Eric put in before Mark could.

'Alpha? Beta?' Juan asked. 'What are you two talking about?'

'Bahar built a massive parallel processor, perhaps one of the top-five most powerful computer systems in the world, and then casually threw it away, right?' Murph said.

'Yeah,' Juan agreed cautiously.

'Why?'

'Why build it or why throw it away?'

'Two questions, one answer. It was built to design its replacement. When he succeeded, Bahar chucked the old one. It was the firewall that went up two days ago that tipped me off. There's no commercially available privacy program that we can't hack. We tried every trick we knew and got nothing. This is something we've never seen before, and it isn't software.'

'A new computer?' Cabrillo asked.

'A new type of computer,' Murph countered.

'A quantum computer,' Eric added.

Juan said, 'Refresh me on quantum computers.'

'It's a machine that thinks in ones and zeros, like a regular computer, but also uses the quantum effects of superposition and entanglement so that it can read data as both one and zero or neither of them at the same time. Since it has more options to represent information and to process it, it is fast. Blindingly fast.'

Mark said, 'Because he was after those crystals, we think Bahar's machine is also an optical computer, which means that there is no electronic resistance for the messaging system. It is one hundred percent efficient and probably a billion times more powerful than any computer on the planet.'

'I thought these things were still years away.'

'Ten years ago they were fifty years away,' Mark stated matter-of-factly. 'Eight years ago they were thirty. Five years ago they were twenty. Today the best minds in the field say ten. But I think Bahar did it sooner.'

'What can he do with a quantum computer?' Cabrillo asked.

'There isn't a network in the world he couldn't get into and ultimately control. Bank records and stock

389

transfers become open books. The best NSA encryption would be broken a few picoseconds after an initial attack. Secret military communications could be read in plaintext instantly. A Q-puter can analyze every piece of data hitting the net at the same time it arrives. Nothing's off-limits. Every e-mail, every broadcast. Hell, everything.'

Eric's next words chilled the room. 'This capability gives Bahar unlimited power, and there's not a damned thing anyone can do about it.'

'How sure are you about this?' Cabrillo asked, his mind racing.

'Positive, boss man. We had good access to Bahar's business files and now we don't. They're still archived, we can tell that. We just can't get at them. Something dramatic changed two days ago, and the only thing that makes sense is that he developed a computer so advanced as to make the superserver farm on the J-61 platform obsolete: a quantum.'

'We need to tell Langston Overholt about this. The CIA has no idea what's coming their way.'

'Bad idea,' both young men said simultaneously.

'Why?'

'For whatever reason, Bahar considers us a danger to him,' Mark replied. 'If we contact anyone about this, he's going to hear about it. Any transmission we make, no matter how encrypted, will be listened to. We shouldn't tip our hand that we know what he's done.'

'Besides, a quantum computer would ace the Turing test,' Eric said.

'I've heard of that,' Juan said. 'It's something about a computer being able to mimic a human being.'

'Give the man a cigar. He does listen to our techno-babble on occasion. The test is designed to see if the machine can fool someone into thinking they're interacting with a real person. Mark and I discussed the possibility that a quantum computer could actually mimic an individual, not just a generic person. We think it can.'

Cabrillo thought he understood what they were getting at, and it was a scary prospect. 'You're saying I could be on the phone with Overholt when in fact I'm talking to the computer?'

'And the only way you'd be able to tell is if you asked it something only you and Mr Overholt know. Anything on the public record, however, the machine would have already digested and be able to spit back at you.'

'Could this thing imitate the president?'

'Probably, but, don't worry, it can't launch nuclear missiles. That entails face-to-face confirmation.'

'Any speculation as to what he will use it for?'

'We talked about it. This isn't about money, though he could empty every bank account in about two seconds. This is political. He could have destroyed our computer infrastructure the moment the machine went live, so he's after something else. We think it's about making our government bend to his will.'

'Agreed. Recommendations?'

'Try to find where the computer is and blow it to pieces. And, no, we have no idea where it's located. It could be anywhere.'

Cabrillo rubbed a hand across his jaw, feeling the rasp of day-old beard. 'I guess it comes down to Soleil. Bahar went after her father for a reason, so there's got to be something in his background that we haven't seen or realized the significance of. Let's all pray she can figure it out.'

'And if she can't?'

'Then the world as we know it is about to become a very different place.'

22

MacD Lawless marveled at the resiliency of children. He'd expected that Pauline would have been traumatized by her abduction and the weeks of captivity, but when they talked about it that first morning she told him that they told her that they were friends of his and that this was part of a secret mission and that if she was a good girl she'd be helping him. She knew her daddy was a war hero and wouldn't do anything that would get him hurt, so she played along with them. Besides which, they let her eat whatever she wanted and watch television all day and deep into the night.

He considered it a miracle that they had made it so easy for her, but he supposed it was for their own selfish reasons. A compliant child who thought she was helping her father was a lot easier to control than a frightened little girl wailing to go home. That they treated her well in no way made him feel guilty about killing them in cold blood.

That first day, they played on the beach, making sand castles and playing fetch with her dog, Brandy, who MacD suspected she'd missed most of all. Her appetite at mealtimes was normal, and at eight-thirty, when they put her to bed, she drifted off in seconds and slept through the night.

He had no illusions that there couldn't still be psychological damage, but for now she seemed her normal happy self, especially now that her father was home. He talked with his parents about monitoring her over the weeks and months ahead. When he told them about the Corporation, they knew he had to go back, if for no other reason than to stop the man responsible for their granddaughter's kidnapping.

He asked about his ex-wife and was told that she hadn't had contact with Pauline for months. The news didn't come as a surprise. He'd married her only because she was pregnant, and she skipped out on them when Pauline was two. The only real parents the girl knew were Kay and her husband. She knew MacD was her dad but treated him like a favorite uncle instead, and as long as she was happy that was fine by him.

It was dawn on the third day when trouble struck.

MacD was up early, brewing coffee in the kitchen of the borrowed beachfront cottage. It was located in Mississippi, but far from the hustle and bustle of the gulf cities and towns. It had no electricity without the generator, and water had to be stored in a giant cistern out back, but it was tidy and charmingly furnished.

He had fond memories of coming here when he was a kid and recalled that his first kiss took place in a back bedroom when his family vacationed with the owners, whose daughter was two years his senior.

The kettle on the gas ring was beginning to steam when he heard the distant whup-whup of helicopter blades. It wasn't an unusual sound, because of their

394

proximity to the offshore oil and gas fields, so he ignored it and opened the jar of instant coffee. But when the sound grew steadily louder, no longer a background thrum but a fast-approaching beat, he extinguished the burner and crossed to the front windows that looked over a two-lane coastal road, a narrow strip of sea grass, and the wide white beach.

The chopper was a massive Black Hawk painted olive drab so that it looked like a military bird, but MacD knew better. Somehow they'd been tracked. It came in low over the swells, its rotor wash whipping up spume. They were so close now that there was no way for him to get his parents and daughter to their car, parked alongside the cottage. He had a single Beretta 9mm from the Houston safe house stashed under his mattress. He ran for his bedroom, yelling to wake his parents. His father emerged from their room, his hair doing an Albert Einstein impression.

'Dad, it's them,' MacD said, cocking the matte-black pistol. 'Get Mom and Pauline and crawl out the back and run. I'll hold them off for as long as I can.'

He didn't wait to see if his father followed his instructions. He went back to the front window and peered around its edge. The chopper touched down on the beach, kicking up a maelstrom of sand that completely obscured it. He expected a team of commandos to burst out of the dust storm, automatic weapons chattering. Knowing that the glass would deflect his shots, he smashed out one of the windowpanes and took aim, ready to plug the first figure he saw.

What he hadn't expected was the chopper blades to begin to slow. Any combat pilot knew to keep the turbines wound up for a fast extraction. The blades continued to decelerate until the clouds of sand settled back to earth. The side door rolled open, and a man in uniform and wearing a flight helmet jumped to the ground. He waited a moment, then helped another man step from the helicopter.

He was elderly, with a shock of white hair and a stoop that had nothing to do with the proximity of the rotor blades. He looked like a banker, in a conservative three-piece suit in navy blue, crisp white shirt, and red tie. MacD didn't know what to make of this dramatic entrance, but he lowered his weapon and moved to the front door as the aged gentleman made his way across the asphalt road. The chopper's crewman remained behind.

Warily, MacD swung open the front door and stepped out onto the covered front porch, angling his pistol so that the man could see it.

'That's close enough,' he called when the stranger reached the nearside shoulder.

'I assure you, Mr Lawless, that with my hearing it is not.'

'Who are you?'

'My name is Langston Overholt IV. I was once Juan Cabrillo's boss at the CIA, and I'm afraid we need his help.'

MacD recalled the Chairman mentioning his former boss and how the Corporation was hired for quite a few black ops by the legendary spymaster. He safetied his pistol and tucked it into the back of his shorts. The two men met midpoint on the lawn, and Overholt insisted they shake hands.

'It is opportune that you're here with your family,' Langston said, handing over his identification.

The old Cold Warrior was pushing eighty but had lost none of his mental faculties. The Agency kept him on well past retirement age as a sort of spy emeritus who'd forgotten more about espionage than the current crop of wunderkinder would ever know.

'How did you know who I am?' MacD asked.

'Juan mentioned that he'd hired you, and kept me in the loop about what happened to your daughter. The Corporation's jet's tail number was noted in Houston. I put two and two together when I checked the *Times-Picayune* online and read that, on the day you arrived, three unidentified drug dealers burned in a house fire. I flew to New Orleans and paid a visit to your parents' house, and when they didn't answer I asked a neighbor about them. I told the delightful, and talkative, Mrs. Kirby that I suspected you had all left on a hasty vacation and inquired where you might go. She told me that your family sometimes borrows a beach house from an old family friend, one David Werner. The land records gave me this address in all of ten seconds.'

MacD was chagrined. In their haste, he'd neglected to tell the neighbors not to mention they had gone to the Werners' cabin. Overholt had found them without breaking a sweat. It would have been that easy for John

Smith too, he thought darkly and cursed his oversight.

'Impressive,' he finally said.

'Son, I learned to be a spy from Allen Dulles himself. Do you know where the *Oregon* is?'

'Monte Carlo.'

'Excellent. I am afraid that I must ask you to cut short your visit and come with me. Time is of the essence.'

'Where are we going?'

'Pensacola Naval Air Station, where, if a colleague of mine has been successful, a jet is standing by to take you to the *Oregon*.'

'What's the rush?'

'I'm sorry, Mr Lawless, but I must insist we leave right away. I'll explain everything once we're airborne.'

To get an eighty-year-old man to fly halfway across the country, MacD knew that this was something important. 'Give me a minute.'

He turned and was surprised to see that his father hadn't listened after all, and his parents and daughter were crowded in the doorway, gawking at the chopper and its distinguished-looking passenger. All three seemed to know that he was leaving with the man. Pauline and Kay both had tear-welled eyes, and his dad had clenched his jaw to fight from crying too. The good-byes were as painful to experience as they were for Overholt to watch, especially knowing that young Pauline had just been returned to the bosom of her family.

Five minutes later the pair was settled in the utilitarian chopper and wearing helmets with a private voice channel so they could not be overheard by the flight crew. The cargo master, who had helped Overholt step from the big helo, studiously ignored them as the chopper lifted clear of the beach and started pounding eastward in a hundred-mile dash to the Navy base.

'I want to thank you again, Mr Lawless,' Overholt opened. 'I know you wanted to spend more time with your family.'

'You can call me MacD.'

Overholt digested the odd nickname and nodded. 'All right, MacD. A couple days ago there was a security breach at the White House involving our nation's nuclear codes.' He held up a hand when he saw the questions racing through MacD's mind. 'It was a demonstration of what our best and brightest finally figured out is a machine called a quantum computer. Do you know what that is?'

'It's theoretical now, but someday they'll make the ones we use today as obsolete as vacuum tubes.'

'Quite right. However, it is no longer theory. One was used to hack into the NSA and ferret out the most secure set of numbers in the world. With that demonstration came a list of demands that we pull troops out of Afghanistan and all of the Middle East, release the Guantánamo detainees, cut off aid to Israel, that sort of thing.'

'Is it al-Qaeda? That sure sounds like their manifesto.'

'Unknown at this time, but considered unlikely for reasons I'll explain in a minute. The president delayed action, and at the exact same time the following day there was another communication – a fax, actually – stating that the blood was on the president's hands. Moments later the Acela train crashed into another locomotive. Over two hundred dead.'

'God. Ah heard about that on the radio. They said it was an accident.'

'It wasn't,' Overholt said sharply. 'It was a deliberate act of terrorism.'

'What are we goin' to do?'

'Therein lies the rub. The unknown terrorist knows our every move because he can tap into our communications grid – landlines, cells, and everything that passes through a satellite, including the military birds. And they tell me this computer can decrypt our toughest codes. We can't mobilize our armed forces without telling him we're coming.

'That is why our response must be carried out by couriers and all correspondence done on typewriters. We're practically back to where I started in this game. It was Fiona Katamora who reached out to me. She was rescued by the Corporation last year and remembered the Chairman well. Because our hands are tied, we want to sic Juan and the rest of you cutthroats on this terrorist.'

'I get it. You can't just call him because this guy will know.'

'Precisely, my boy. I carry the message to you and you take it back to the *Oregon*, and nothing's been put out over the wire. Even the flight we're arranging for

400

you is being handled by a Navy captain from the Pentagon. He flew to Pensacola yesterday with a presidential decree.'

'Is the president aware of our mission?'

'Obliquely. He knows we're up to something, but the fewer details getting spread around, the better. We're keeping the group as tight as possible to avoid an inadvertent slip over the phone or in an e-mail. The staffer from the Joint Chiefs getting you the plane has no idea who'll be on it or why.

'Tell Juan that he has to locate the computer and destroy it,' Langston continued. 'If he doesn't, I fear for the fate of our great country. In fact, I fear for the fate of the world. This man' – he spat the word – 'professes to value life, which is why he hasn't used his awesome capabilities to destroy us outright, but the Middle East could explode overnight if Israel's enemies sense she is a weakened state. And without our military help, Pakistan could fall to a Taliban-type regime in months, giving them nuclear capability and the hatred toward us to use it.'

'How will we communicate with you?' MacD asked.

'That's just it. You can't. Not directly.'

It was then that MacD realized Overholt's problem dovetailed with the Corporation's. It hit him like a ton of bricks and almost made him gasp aloud. 'Jee-zus. Gunawan Bahar.'

'Who?'

'The guy behind my daughter's kidnapping. He was the one who orchestrated my actin' as his spy aboard the *Oregon*. He's afraid of the Corporation for some reason, and Ah think this is it. Damn, Mr Overholt, you're the link he never saw comin'.'

A look of confusion crossed the spymaster's face.

MacD said, 'This Bahar guy is behind the quantum computer. It all makes sense now! The computer's on the oil rig. That must have been his first attempt to crack all our codes. That must not have worked, so his people built him a better machine.' He wondered if the crystals they recovered played a role in that development, but didn't bother mentioning it because it didn't really matter at this point. 'He knew that once he had his computer, there wasn't anything our government, or any government, could do about it, but he was aware that the Corporation existed and knew we could be a threat if we somehow found out about it. He'd also know if and when we were ever alerted. He could block the ship from ever receivin' orders from you. Can that computer do that?'

'I imagine it could.'

'But you outfoxed him by reachin' out to me. We know who and what we're lookin' for, and Bahar has no idea we're comin'. He thought he could keep tabs on us by usin' me, and he thought he could isolate us too, but that ain't gonna happen.' An idea suddenly hit him, and his sense of optimism faded. 'He's goin' to know.'

'What? How?'

'When the kidnappers don't report in, he's goin' to know that Ah rescued Pauline and that Ah'm no longer his stool.'

Langston hadn't survived for more than fifty years in the CIA without being quick on his feet. 'I'll fly back to New Orleans and have a chat with the chief of police. His investigation is about to lead him to the arrest and confession of a drug dealer who hit the wrong house and killed three men by mistake. I'll get him to parade an officer in mufti for the cameras. Oh, and the arson investigators are about to discover the body of a little girl in the ashes of their house.'

'Perfect,' MacD said, more than impressed with the octogenarian.

Overholt had a binder, sitting on the bench seat next to him. He handed it over to Lawless. 'I've been working on this since the secretary of state made me aware of the situation and suggested you guys could help. It's a list of things you might need from us, with corresponding code numbers. The phone you're going to call if you need anything on that list is a securities firm on Wall Street so that anyone calling in with long lists of numbers, like quantities of stocks to buy, won't sound suspicious.'

MacD opened the book and leafed to a random page. If they needed all transatlantic telephone cables to go off-line, that was a number 3282. If they needed a fake media story run, that was a number 6529, with a subset of numbers listing two dozen types of news pieces. If they needed a nuclear strike anywhere on the planet, that was number 7432, with the GPS coordinates tacked on after.

MacD pointed that last one out to the man from

Langley. 'Yes,' Overholt said to the unasked question, 'the situation is that dire. If need be, I can make it happen. I don't know how much we can do from our end. Big Brother is watching, and if Bahar catches wind of our interest, he's going to know something's up. We'll try to make some discreet, one-on-one inquiries, but I can't promise much.'

'I understand.'

They talked for the remainder of the flight, but it seemed too soon that the big Sikorsky was flaring over the apron at the sprawling air station. They'd been directed to land next to a row of parked F-18s.

The chopper's onboard crewman opened the side roller door, and MacD jumped to the tarmac. The rotor's downdraft was like standing at the eye wall of a hurricane.

'It was a pleasure meeting you, young man,' Overholt said from his seat. He had to shout over the spinning blades and still-lit turbines. 'I was the one who gave Juan his superstition about being wished good luck. I will simply say happy hunting, and, not to put too fine of a point on this, but you are our best and only hope.'

'We won't let you down, Mr Overholt.' MacD threw him a wave and backed away as the turbine pitch increased and the chopper took to the air once again.

23

Abdul Mohammad, aka John Smith, had never seen his employer in such a towering rage. The American president hadn't made any speeches about his giving in to Bahar's demands, as he'd expected. He didn't think that the president would admit to being blackmailed, but surely he would have appeared on television and contritely explained the shift in U.S. foreign policy.

Bahar had spent the previous day watching repeated coverage of the train crash he'd caused outside Philadelphia, staring raptly at the giant plasma television set, as news choppers shot hours of film of the carnage and reporters on the ground interviewed dazed and bloody survivors.

Mohammad hadn't known his boss had a capacity to kill. Sure, he'd ordered killings, but on this occasion he had pushed the proverbial button that had snuffed out two hundred and thirteen lives. Bahar had taken a taste of the ultimate power, the power of life and death, and he'd enjoyed it. Abdul saw it on his face and in his glassy eyes.

Now, though, he ranted like a child denied his favorite toy.

'He saw what I could do and still he defies me!' Abdul knew his superior was speaking of the American president. 'And sending the Guantánamo prisoners to the World Court? He knew I meant they were to be released back to their home countries. If they wanted to prosecute, that would have been their business.'

The two men were in Bahar's office at the quantum computer facility. The windows looked out over a bleak and abandoned industrial area, with oil-stained ground and buildings losing their battles with rust. A tall derrick presided over the scene. Unlike the other equipment, it had been refurbished so that it was in working order. Below it was a cement bunker that could withstand any weapon in the Air Force's arsenal except for a nuke.

What was invisible were all the motion detectors, thermal-imaging and standard cameras, and a not-so-small army of guards ready to lay down their lives for the cause. Unlike hired mercenaries, these men were fanatically devoted and had already proven themselves in either Iraq or Afghanistan. They'd been smuggled into the country, once the bunker was in place. It had been built off-site over the past few months by an outside contractor, who thought they were pouring concrete bridge piers, and assembled once the facility had been procured. The computer had been installed at the same time.

As the computer network on the oil rig had calculated, the crystals, once cut to size, were the final pieces to bring the quantum device to life. The machine itself was the size of a suburban living room and was packed with exotic electronics, and, when viewed through a polarizing lens, gave off a red, pulsing aura as though it had a beating heart.

Neither man understood how it worked, how the way the atoms aligned in the crystals was the key to the computer's ability to deal with quantum fluctuations and counter atomic-scale interference. It had taken years, and the harnessing of the computer farm aboard the J-61, to make it a reality.

When they had turned it on, the machine seemed inert for the first thirty seconds. The scientists weren't sure if they had succeeded until a disembodied female voice had emanated from the speakers placed in Bahar's office, saying simply, 'Ready.'

The first test had been to switch all the interactive traffic lights in Prague from red to green or vice versa. The computer hacked into the traffic-control system instantaneously and did as instructed, before turning control back over to city authorities. Eerily, it asked, 'Why?'

'Because you were told to,' Bahar had replied to the microphones also hidden in his office. His answer had taken a moment because no one had thought the computer would question him. When asked, the computer scientists who'd assembled the computer had no explanation.

They did more elaborate tests, finding better-encrypted systems to infiltrate, until they were convinced that no network on the planet was impervious to their machine and that no database could remain secret.

That is when they launched the assault on the NSA to obtain the nuclear codes. It was rumored that the computers at the National Security Agency weren't measured in teraflops or petaflops, which is the number ten to the fifteenth power, but rather were measured by the acre. It had taken Bahar's machine a half second to penetrate the firewalls and access the code.

So with success piled atop success, Gunawan Bahar had been a happy man until he saw that the American response to his demands had been a tepid article buried at the back of a Washington newspaper.

'I was too easy on them the first time,' he railed. 'I tried to show my compassion, my humanity, and he spits in my face. I am not some insane fanatic bent on murdering infidels until the very last one is dead, but if that is what he wants of me, then that is what I will become.' He looked up at the ceiling. 'Are you there?'

'Yes,' came the calm voice.

'Send this message to the White House: You will give a live speech from the Oval Office or they will all die of thirst, and then I want you to shut down all fifty-one pumping stations that feed water into Las Vegas, Nevada, and don't turn them back on until I say so.' He'd learned earlier that he needed to be very specific with place-names.

'Task complete,' the computerized voice said tonelessly.

'Let's see how long he'll let those people bake in the desert heat before he tells the world that he no longer controls his nation's destiny. What do you think, Abdul? Clever, yes?'

'Yes, very,' Mohammad said, but he didn't agree. If it were up to him, every reactor in America would have gone critical days ago. He didn't understand why his superior was toying with the Americans.

'That was hardly convincing, my friend. You think we should destroy the Great Satan and be done with it.'

Bahar never asked his opinion, so it came as a surprise now. Unsure, Mohammad finally nodded. 'Yes, sir.'

'You don't enjoy the irony of us meddling in their policies the way they have meddled in ours. For two generations the Americans have said which regimes rise and fall, and used that capability with little regard for the people it affects. Now we can do the same to them, to tell them their place in the world, to make them feel what it is like to be under someone else's thumb for a change.

'They call the American president the most powerful man in the world. Well, tonight he will do my bidding, making *me* the most powerful man. We couldn't defeat them on the field of battle or break their will with suicide attacks, but now we have used their dependence on technology to cow them.

'Soon I will decree that American Christians must begin to study the Koran in their schools so that, over time, they will convert to the one true faith. Why destroy them, Abdul, when we can enfold them into Islam?'

Emboldened, Mohammad said, 'That will never work.'

'At one time there was only one Muslim, the Prophet Muhammad, blessings be upon him, but from that single seed the faith spread through conversion after conversion. It is still happening today, as Arabs move into Europe and begin to make converts of the people. True, it happens mostly in prisons, but when these new Muslims are released, they tell their families of their wonderful conversions, and maybe one or two join as well. By exposing Americans to the Koran at a young age, we will accelerate the process. In fifty years America will be an Islamist state. The rest of the Western world will follow suit, mark my words. And I won't even have to threaten them.'

Bahar placed his hands on each side of Mohammad's face as though he were about to kiss him, and, for a moment, Abdul feared he might. 'Let go of your hatred, my friend. The struggle between the Muslims and Christians has endured for more than a thousand years. So what if it takes fifty or a hundred more? We have guaranteed that our side shall be victorious.'

Abdul Mohammad knew his superior's plan was doomed to fail for the simple reason that somehow, and not that far in the future, the Americans would figure out where they had constructed the computer and find a way to isolate it or, more likely, destroy it. Their window of opportunity was a short one, and Bahar had delusions of becoming like the Prophet himself. They should strike the U.S. now, he thought, and tear her apart at the seams. Playing games and planning for a future that would never come to pass were a waste of the only opportunity they'd ever had to conquer their sworn enemy.

He hadn't been privy to Bahar's plans for the quantum computer and wished they had discussed it previously. Maybe he could have changed his mind. But looking into Bahar's eyes and seeing the spark of megalomania that lurked in their depths, Abdul knew it was too late. They were committed to his fantasy that he was to become the Madhi of Islamic prophecy, and it wasn't in Abdul to go against his superior's wishes.

24

They met the following morning in the *Oregon*'s sleek conference room. Juan wanted to keep the group small, so it was just him, Eric Stone, Soleil, and, because they were becoming good friends, Linda Ross. Up on the monitors Eric had the financial information pertaining to all of Roland Croissard's recent business deals. The man had his finger in a lot of pies, and, because she was not part of his life in recent years, Soleil knew little of it.

Juan believed that whatever Bahar wanted from Roland Croissard, the deal would have happened shortly after her kidnapping, but, to be thorough, they went back six months. The material was so dry that dust seemed to fall from the plasma screens. This was work only an accountant could love, and, by the beginning of the second hour, he could tell Soleil was becoming frustrated.

'*Non*, I did not know my father bought into an Indian steel mill,' she said when Eric pointed out the three-million-euro deal. This happened just a day before she was abducted. 'Why should I?'

'No reason,' Juan assured her. 'Okay, what about this? Two days after you were taken, he sold his stake in a Brazilian appliance company. Does that mean anything to you?'

'No. Nothing.'

'And here, he leased out something called Albatross to what looks like a shell company. Eric, who or what is Hibernia Partners?'

'Hold one second. I know I went through this stuff before.' He worked his laptop for a moment. 'Okay, here they are. It's an Irish company, chartered four years ago. They were going to import salt for roads, but they never made it off the ground. Six months ago they were given a large loan through a New Hebrides bank, but the money's never been touched.'

'That is it!' Soleil cried.

'What?'

'Salt. My father bought a salt mine before having an outside expert look at it for him. It was only after the deal was done that he called someone in. He was American, like yourselves, and when he told my father that the mine was unstable, he fired him on the spot and hired another. I never met the second one because—'

'The reason's not important,' Juan said. 'Tell us about this mine.'

'It's in eastern France, near the Italian border and very close to a river.'

'That's a lucky break,' Eric said. The ship was fast approaching France's southern coast.

'The river was the problem,' Soleil went on. 'He said it was dangerous. I think the term is "seepish."'

'Seepage,' Juan corrected.

'Yes. That is what he said. Seepage. Anyway, it was the worst deal my father ever made, but he said it taught him humility. He said he would never sell it but would keep it, like an albatross around his neck, so he would never forgot. That is why he named the company Albatross, like from the poem.'

Coleridge's *Rime of the Ancient Mariner* was about the only poem Cabrillo knew. "'Instead of the cross, the Albatross/About my neck was hung.'"

'My father would never even lease the mine,' Soleil added. 'You wanted me to find something unusual. I think this is it.'

'Okay, let's set this aside for now. There's still a lot more to go through. We need to be certain.'

'Oui, mon capitaine.'

It took another hour, but in the end they circled back to the Albatross Mine. Juan had suggested that Mark Murphy dig deeper into Hibernia Partners while they worked in the boardroom, but Eric said that wouldn't be a good idea. If the company was one of Bahar's fronts, then hacking into its system would alert the quantum computer and give away their investigation.

Cabrillo thanked him for his foresight, not realizing how much they'd come to rely on computers until the capability vanished.

'We're going to need schematics of the mine,' Juan said when they were all in agreement that this particular piece of property was probably what Bahar had extorted from Soleil's father. 'Can you get in touch with the inspector?'

'I haven't spoken to him in years, but, sure. I don't

remember his phone number, but someone can look it up for me.'

Eric cleared his throat to get their attention. 'I don't want to sound paranoid, but calling from the ship would be a bad idea, and actually having Soleil place the call might not be so hot either.'

'Why?' Linda asked.

'Like Mark and I explained, this computer is everywhere at once. And we are targets already. Any communications from this ship are going to be intercepted. My fear is that it's been told to listen for individual voice patterns.'

'Come off it, Eric,' Linda said. 'There's no way that computer can listen in to every phone conversation taking place around the globe and zero in on one single call.'

'That's just the thing. It can. The NSA does it all the time. And Bahar's computer has already proved itself thousands of times more powerful. It's not called quantum for nothing. We're facing a whole new paradigm, and we need to think and act as though our every move is being followed because, more than likely, it is.'

'What do you suggest?' Juan asked.

'We'll put someone ashore, and they can make the call on Soleil's behalf. We just can't use her name, since that's probably a flag too.'

Linda said, 'But Bahar thinks she died when the *Hercules* sank.'

'It's not worth the risk,' Juan countered. 'Eric's right. We need to cover our tracks completely. We'll have Hux make the call. Bahar's never met her, so he'd have no reason to be on the lookout for her voice. I also think that we shouldn't pull into Monte Carlo. If our presence is reported in the area, Bahar might become suspicious.'

'Good idea,' Eric agreed. 'And since we transited the Suez Canal using a fresh set of papers and ship's name, he should have no idea we're here. We might want to reconfigure the look of the deck in case he has the computer scanning satellite images for us. Also, while we're at it, we should probably shut down all nonessential electronics. Just in case.'

Juan nodded and called down to the Op Center to go dark electronically and to have crewmen break out a bunch of fake containers and erect them topside. He turned to Soleil, 'By the way, what was the inspector's name?'

'Mercer,' she said. 'His name is Philip Mercer.'

A few hours later they were close enough to the fabled playground of Monte Carlo to ferry Dr Huxley, Soleil, and Cabrillo ashore in one of the hydrofoil lifeboats. They couldn't go in by chopper because their arrival would be logged by French aviation authorities. Kevin Nixon had forged a passport for Soleil, so there were no problems when they got to the dock. She was along in case this Mercer guy needed more reminding if the code words she'd already supplied weren't enough.

Juan paid cash for a prepaid cell phone, and they found a quiet park bench. He dialed the number Eric had tracked down for the mining engineer and handed the phone to Hux. After a couple of rings, a voice that grated like the business end of a wood chipper answered. 'Hello.'

'Is this Philip Mercer?' Hux asked.

'Sure. Why not.'

'Mr Mercer, I'm calling on behalf of—'

'First off, it's Dr Mercer. Second, if you're calling on behalf of Jerry's Kids or any other damned charity, I'm going to hold the phone next to my wrinkled white butt and—'

She heard another voice say, 'Harry! Give me that, you old pervert. Hello. This is Mercer. Sorry. A friend of mine was at a bar when God handed out manners. Who is this, please?'

'I'm calling on behalf of someone you used to know. Please don't say her name because this is not a secure line. You called her a Frenchy once, and she told you she was a Swissy.'

He gave a throaty chuckle. 'I remember her fondly.'

'That's good,' Hux said. 'Not to sound overly dramatic, but this is a matter of life and death. Do you recall the place you met?'

'Yeah. Is she with you now?' he asked.

'As a matter of fact, yes.'

'Since this is just a little on the bizarre side, I want to verify. Ask her where she has a mole.'

Hux asked and relayed the answer. 'She says it's private and you are still a *cochon*.'

'Good enough for me,' Mercer said with a grin that carried over the airwaves.

'We need to know everything there is to know about the salt mine.'

'Are you looking to throw good money after bad too?'

'Nothing like that. All I can say is that some very bad people have taken it over, and the group I work for plans on taking it back. What we need is a detailed schematic of the entire place, above ground and below.'

'It's a little hard to describe over the phone,' Mercer informed her. 'There's about thirty miles of tunnels, as I recall.'

Hux was ready for this. 'Could you draw it out for us? We have a courier already heading to Washington, D.C.' Tiny Gunderson wouldn't like the idea that he'd been demoted from chief pilot to courier, but it was the fastest way without putting the plans into the electronic ether. 'He'll be in D.C. by nine o'clock your time, tonight.'

'I guess you don't know that I'm playing poker tonight with a guy who's got a tell a blind man can see.'

'This is urgent, Dr Mercer, or we wouldn't be asking.'

'Do you have my address?' he asked.

'Yes, we do.'

'All right. I'm game. Do me a favor. Say to her, "Mauve *peignoir*," and tell me what she does.'

'She blushed, and called you a pig again.'

Mercer laughed and said, 'I'll meet your courier at nine.'

'Well?' Cabrillo asked when Julia punched off the phone.

Hux looked pointedly at Soleil. 'He's quite the charmer. You'll have to tell me the story of the mauve nightie.'

Soleil's blush deepened. 'Later.'

'Well?' Cabrillo asked a second time.

'He'll do it. Tiny can pick it up tonight and be back with it by tomorrow.'

'Once we have his diagram, we can formulate our plan to take out Bahar's computer.'

They headed back to the harbor and made a startling discovery. MacD Lawless was leaning negligently against a fence near where they had berthed the lifeboat.

'What the hell are you doing here?' Juan called out.

'Long story, but Ah came down to talk to the harbormaster to see if the *Oregon* had come in yet and saw the *Or Death* tied up pretty as you please.' His sunny smile faded. 'We need to talk. Langston Overholt himself came to get me and had me flown here on an Air Force jet.'

'Let me guess,' Juan said knowingly. 'Bahar has made his move with his quantum computer.'

MacD's jaw dropped. 'How could you possibly know that?'

'Eric and Mark figured out that he'd built it, and it stands to reason he'd use it against the United States. Tell me everything.'

They boarded the disguised hydrofoil as MacD told them what had been going on since he'd parted with the team in New Orleans, but it wasn't until they were

420

halfway back to the ship that the dread chill creeping up Juan's spine went into overdrive. Linda had said Langston had phoned earlier about a mission involving a Chinese ship. That didn't jibe with what was happening in Washington, and the sickening realization hit home.

As soon as they arrived on the *Oregon* he had Hali Kasim track Linda down.

'When you spoke with Overholt, did he sound different to you?' he asked without preamble.

'No. He sounded fine. Is something wrong with him?'

'Did you tell him we were headed here?' Trepidation carried in his voice. If she had, they were blown.

'No. I said we had another op and would need a week. He said it was no problem, since the Chinese looked like they were sticking around the Gulf of Alaska.'

Juan let out a long-held breath. 'Thank God.'

'Why? What's up?'

'That wasn't Langston. That was the quantum computer you were talking to.'

Cabrillo had taken Eric's and Mark's warnings seriously, but this was the first time he truly understood the staggering capabilities Gunawan Bahar had at his disposal. Like the president had remarked earlier, they were squared off against a man who wielded the power of God.

'We're screwed, aren't we?' Linda asked. She'd gotten it too.

'Yeah,' Juan replied. 'Yeah, I think this time we really are.'

As badly as Cabrillo wanted a Predator drone over the Albatross Mine, he knew that the request was impossible because Bahar would get wind of it. Instead, Gomez Adams would be renting a helicopter there in Monaco and doing an aerial survey of the place. In the meantime they would have to make do with archived satellite imagery off the Internet. His concern went so deep that he had Mark ensure the images hadn't been doctored recently. Fortunately, they were clean.

The mine sat in the Arc River Valley near the alpine town of Modane and, as Soleil had recalled, very close to the Italian border. From the air, there wasn't much to look at. It was a basic industrial brownfield site, with several dilapidated buildings and the remains of the tower for the headgear hoist that once carried men into the mine and salt back out. A single access road snaked to the mine over an undulating series of switchbacks, but it also had rail access. Despite the graininess of commercial satellite pictures, they could see that some of the track bed had been removed, so that locomotives could no longer reach the facility.

A river approach was likely because the mine's southern boundary ran directly along the banks of the Arc River. There was even a bridge crossing the river nearby that looked like it went to an abandoned gravel pit that must have worked in conjunction with the mine when it was in operation.

Linc, Eddie, Linda, and Juan were in the conference room, studying the images projected on the big flat-panel monitors.

'Why a mine?' Lincoln asked suddenly.

The others were so deep in their own thoughts, no one had really paid attention.

'What did you say?'

'I said, why put this thing in a mine?'

That was something Cabrillo hadn't given much thought to, so he had no answer. He called Mark down in his cabin and posed the question to him.

'It's shielding,' he replied. 'Eric and I had considered this when we first realized Bahar had built a quantum computer and were trying to guess a location. You see, the operations inside the machine take place at the atomic scale. It can automatically correct for atomic vibrations because they come at a set rate and frequency. One of the things that could unbalance the computer and cause it to kick out error messages is if it got bombarded by a heavy enough cosmic particle.

'As you know,' he went on, 'the earth gets hit tens of trillions of times an hour by subatomic junk winging in from space. A lot of this is deflected by the magneto-sphere, and what does get through is generally harmless to us. Though an interesting note, there is a theory posited that some cancers are the result of genetic damage caused by a single cosmic ray hitting a DNA strand.'

Juan knew to let him ramble but still had to grit his teeth.

'Anyway, on the exacting scales the computer works

at, an impacting cosmic ray could disrupt the machine's function catastrophically, so they need to shield it. Here's the rub. I have no idea why they chose this salt mine. If cosmic radiation is a threat, we would have thought they would have buried it deeply under the densest rock they could find. The best theory Eric and I could come up with is, there might be some other mineral mixed in with the salt to help shield against one particular cosmic ray that would cause the most damage.'

'Okay, thanks,' Juan said, and ended the call before Mark could expound further.

'Sorry I asked,' Linc said sheepishly.

'Listen, why don't we pick this up again when we have something more concrete to work with? We've got a good overview, but to plan the assault we need details.'

Heads nodded around the table, and the meeting broke up.

It wasn't until after supper that Tiny arrived back aboard with Philip Mercer's diagrams. Most of the crew were lounging around the dining room, some sipping brandy, others nibbling after-dinner cheeses. Cabrillo, who'd dined with Soleil, decided that this was as good a spot as any to take their first look at the plans and ordered the lights be set on bright. The clubby feel of the room lost some of its luster under a bright halogen stare.

Juan slipped out of his suit coat and loosened his tie. He fiddled with the cap of a Mont Blanc pen while he waited.

'Hey, gang,' Tiny called jovially when he entered the room. He wasn't a regular feature aboard the *Oregon*, so his arrival was greeted warmly. The big pilot never looked so rumpled. His blond hair stuck out in tufts, and there wasn't a square inch of his white uniform shirt that wasn't rumpled. In his hand he carried a yellow legal pad and a single rose.

He crossed through the dining hall, shaking hands and slapping backs, until reaching the Chairman. 'Tah-dah,' he said with a flourish, and set the pad on the table. He handed the rose to Soleil. 'Mercer sends his compliments.'

She smiled.

Cabrillo spun the pad so he could see it. Mercer had written out a several-page description of the facility and the underground conditions. He detailed how over the years the miners had dug too close to the bottom of the river and that they refused to work the lower shafts. Roland Croissard had bought the facility during what he thought was a regular labor dispute. It was only after hiring Mercer and reading his report, and a report by another expert when he didn't like what had been said in the first, that he realized he'd been swindled.

The first time he'd even visited the place was on the day Mercer delivered his report. Soleil had come with him on a lark.

Water seepage had been manageable, but Mercer calculated that the continued use of explosives deeper in the tunnels would cause the plug of rock between the mine and the river to fail. The flood would be catastrophically fast.

There was a gem among all the technical information, one that Mercer hadn't disclosed to Croissard, and it was something he doubted many of the original miners remembered.

'There it is,' Juan blurted out when he read it.

'What do you have there?' Max asked. Unlike Juan, who had dressed for dinner, Hanley wore jeans and a western-style checkered shirt, complete with pearl snaps.

'One of the mine's upper tunnels intersects with a piece of history.'

'Come again?'

'The miners bored their way into an old tunnel that was once part of the Maginot Line. Mercer writes that they had boarded it up, but he took the boards down and checked it out.'

Constructed after World War I as the ultimate defense for the homeland, the French had built a near-continuous wall of underground bunkers and forts along the border with Germany and, to a lesser extent, Italy. The forts had armored turrets that could pop up from the ground like obscene mushrooms and unleash directed cannon and mortar fire. Many of the structures were interlinked so that troops could be shuttled from one to another on subway trains. And some were so large, they were virtually underground cities unto themselves.

The Germans never obliged the French to use their

grand fortification. When they invaded in 1940, they hooked through Belgium and Holland and poured into France where the defenses were weakest.

Because the Arc River Valley lacked the strategic protection of the mountains that surrounded it, it was little wonder that the French would have built casements and bunkers there.

'Does he say if he could reach the topside outlet?' Linda asked.

'No. He said he didn't go that far. But it can't be too tough to find.'

'I think,' Mark said, 'that the bunkers that weren't turned into museums and tourist attractions were permanently sealed by the French. Just so you know.'

'We can cut our way in with Hypertherm,' Max rebutted confidently. 'Like how we cut apart that tanker. What was her name?'

'The *Gulf of Sidra*,' Juan answered with a shudder. He'd still been aboard when the steel-cutting explosive had burned through the hull like a wire garrote through cheese. He got back to the topic at hand. 'This is our back door into the mine in case we need it.'

What followed in the legal pad were hand-drawn plans of each of the mine's twenty-eight levels. They showed how the salt was excavated in huge rooms where massive pillars had been left in place to support the weight of the rock above. Mercer included information about ventilation shafts and water-removal conduits.

'The level of detail is beyond belief,' he said as he flipped though the pages.

'He has a photographic memory,' Soleil said. 'We talked about his work, and he told me he remembers the layout of all the mines he's ever entered.'

'This information's a gold mine.' Cabrillo turned to Mark and Eric, who sat next to each other across from Max and Linda. 'You guys think Bahar will put the computer on the lowest level?'

'Close, but that mine's been inactive for years. More than likely the bottom levels have flooded due to groundwater seepage.' Mark cocked his head as he ran some esoteric numbers through his brain. He looked at Soleil. 'How long ago did your father buy the mine?'

'Six years.'

'The bottom four levels and half of the fifth are inundated. He'll put it on level 23.'

'You can't possibly know that,' Linda accused.

'*Au contraire.* As you can see, the area of each level is clearly labeled, as is the height. That gives me their volume. It's then a simple calculation of time versus the water permeability of the upper strata.'

'Which you happen to know?'

'Which I happened to research,' he said with a smug grin, and stole a piece of blue Stilton from Linda's plate. 'Boo-ya!'

Eddie Seng sat at a nearby table with the gundogs. Juan fluttered the legal pad to get his attention and then tossed it over. 'Take a look at this. We'll meet in the conference room at noon. Gomez should be back with his pictures by then. We go one day later.'

'This from that guy?'

'Yeah, and it's a godsend.'

'I'll make copies and give them to the rest of these apes. Sorry, boys, you all have homework tonight.'

'Damned Yankees,' MacD drawled. 'It's pronounced "y'all."'

25

The next twenty-four hours aboard the *Oregon* were spent in feverish preparation while a stunned world awaited the plight of the citizens of Las Vegas. They had water reserves for another two days, under the tightest rationing in the city's history. If the utility authorities couldn't reactivate the complicated system of pipes and pumps that drew water across the desert from Lake Mead, evacuations would most likely be ordered. A state of emergency was declared soon after the pumps inexplicably stopped working, and National Guard troops had already been called up.

In the White House, the president of the United States watched the television coverage in mute horror, knowing he could end it but terrified of the price his nation would pay. This was an Abraham Lincoln going-to-war type of decision. This was Truman deciding to drop the A-bomb. This was a decision he feared he hadn't the courage to make.

There was no such hesitation in Juan Cabrillo's mind. He knew his choice. Agree or disagree, whenever the American people went to war, he felt they did so to protect the idea of individual liberty, be it their own or another nation's. This was no different.

Every member of the crew was involved in preparations, once the plan had been approved. Weapons were drawn from the arsenal and additional gear was gotten from stores. A truck to move all the equipment and personnel was rented from an agency in nearby Nice, and under the cover of darkness Gomez choppered in everything they couldn't declare through customs and stashed it in an abandoned farmhouse.

This was the Corporation's forte – coming up with a strategy and executing it quickly and flawlessly.

The assault team was in position fifteen minutes inside Cabrillo's one-day schedule. Not knowing the number of guards Bahar had, he brought a force that was large by their standards and consisted of himself, Linda, Eddie, Linc, MacD, and Max, plus two other gundogs, Mike Trono and Jim O'Neill. Max wouldn't join in the fray unless absolutely necessary.

Mike and Jim plus Linc, the team's best sniper, were to act as a diversionary force. They had seen from the aerial shots Adams took that Bahar had constructed a concrete bunker over the mine's entrance that looked like it could withstand the full load of a B-52's bomb bay. Knowing Bahar would feel secure inside it, they were sure that once the diversion started he would take cover rather than flee. What he didn't know was that the Corporation had a back entrance to his fortified bunker.

The three men were dropped off about a mile from where the mine's access road connected with the main highway. They would have to hike through the woods to get into position, and each man carried nearly fifty pounds' worth of ammunition for the .22 caliber mini Gatling. Like its big brothers on the *Oregon*, this weapon had six rotating barrels powered by a car battery. What made the system relatively man portable was the fact that the 30-grain hypersonic bullets were so light, they could pack in thousands of them. Linc's job, with his Barrett .50 caliber sniper rifle, was to make sure none of the guards got close to the Gatling.

They would remain in constant radio contact with the rest of the team on secure – well, at least they used to be secure – radios with throat mics. Cabrillo doubted the quantum computer was listening in for nearby radio chatter, but they would keep usage to a minimum.

Cabrillo stayed on the main highway past the gated entrance to the Albatross Mine. The metal crosspieces were rust rimed and graffitied. The mine was down from the road, so they could not see it as they drove.

Another mile farther on was a cut in the trees that bordered the quiet road. The dirt track led into a pine forest, which opened to a meadow that had been cleared of trees decades earlier. Cabrillo took his team across the meadow and eased the truck between some pines on the far side. Behind them towered mountains that still retained a vestige of snow on their summits. They were about a mile from the river.

After so many hours cramped in the truck, Cabrillo felt his spine pop when he stepped to the ground. The air was some of the cleanest and clearest he'd ever breathed. The temperature hovered around sixty but would drop overnight.

Their hope was to find the abandoned entrance to the old Maginot Line fort by dusk and make their assault at first light.

Since all this land was part of a national park, there was the possibility of running into hikers, but it couldn't be helped. But since they were dressed as hikers themselves, and their weapons were sheathed in tissue-thin bags that could be torn away in an instant, they would arouse little suspicion if Bahar had guards this far out.

They hiked through the forest in a twenty-yard string, Cabrillo on point and Eddie in the drag slot. The ground was littered with pine mold, and moving silently was next to impossible. Except for Lawless. Like he'd been a few weeks ago in Myanmar, the man was as stealthy as a cat.

In the distance they could hear the rain-swollen Arc River rushing past. Fed from glaciers higher in the mountains, it caused the air to chill as they descended toward its banks. And when they glimpsed it through the trees, the water was a turquoise color because of the sediment left in the ancient glacial ice.

Once they were close enough, the team maintained their spread and started marching toward the Albatross Mine, all the while keeping a lookout for the entrance to the nearly eighty-year-old subterranean fort. They had no idea what to expect, so they looked for anything man-made.

Cabrillo walked closest to the river, so he was the

first to spot the two men. They were a hundred yards ahead, both standing on the riverbank and scanning their surroundings through binoculars. He ducked behind an overturned stump but wasn't fast enough. One of the men saw him and tapped his partner on the shoulder. The two were dressed in typical outdoors gear, but there was nothing woodsy about their demeanor. Neither man was carrying a rifle, but that didn't mean they weren't armed.

They started jogging toward Cabrillo's position. One of them plucked a black rectangular object from a pouch on his belt. Juan was certain it was a radio, and knew if this encounter was reported, the element of surprise would be blown. He also knew that if they got into a gun battle, the sound would echo up and down the valley for miles.

Juan set his rifle down on the ground and slowly got to his feet. He pretended to do up his fly, like the men had just caught him urinating in the woods. It was a ploy that usually made the other guy lower his guard. He could see now that it was definitely a radio. These weren't innocent hikers but a random patrol of Bahar's guards. Cabrillo cursed their bad luck because, no matter the outcome, their timetable was in ruins.

When they got closer, he could see both men had dark Semitic features with heavy brows and black hair. One of the men pointed at Cabrillo, then waved him off as if to say he should turn back.

'Is there a problem?' he asked in Spanish, not thinking that either of these guys was a native French speaker.

'You go,' one said, and pointed back up the valley.

'*Allez,*' the other grunted, his thick accent proving Cabrillo right.

'Hey, hon, what's going on?' It was Linda Ross, coming down out of the woods and acting like a confused tourist.

Both guards turned to look at her. Cabrillo sprang. He chopped the wrist of the man with the radio, sending the compact unit skittering away, and in the same movement slugged the second guy in the jaw with everything he had. Even as the man was dropping to the ground, his eyes showing nothing but white, his partner recovered enough to start reaching under his coat for a weapon.

Linda bounded at him in a flying leap. She hit him high in the shoulders and used her considerable momentum, and not so considerable weight, to drive him into dirt. She picked up a fist-sized rock from the water's edge and bashed him across the temple.

In moments, both unconscious men were dosed with sedatives, to keep them out for twenty-four hours, and were gagged and bound at the wrists and ankles. Juan kept their radio but tossed their handguns into the river. The men were then wedged under a fallen tree and covered with brush until they were invisible.

'The mine is going to go on alert when they don't report in,' Max said.

It was a reminder that Cabrillo didn't need. He flexed his fingers to ease a little of the pain and stripped the cover off his REC7 assault rifle. It was clear that there

436

weren't any tourists wandering these woods. He had Eddie contact Linc and his team to tell them that the schedule was out the door and to be ready for anything. Lincoln acknowledged with a double click of his microphone.

They continued sweeping along the riverbank, searching for a bunker or an armored pillbox, but also on the alert for other guards. They'd gone another quarter mile when Max did an uncanny bird whistle. He was halfway up the slope. When Juan arrived, he saw what the French called a *cloche*, or bell.

It was an immobile armored turret, with machine-gun ports to give the men inside a wide field of fire. Unfortunately, it was cast in too-thick steel to be cut open, and the ports were too small to expand. It sat atop a rust-streaked and dirty concrete foundation that had been there so long, it seemed to blend in with the forest.

'Where there's one,' Hanley said, 'there's bound to be more.'

And, sure enough, they found two more of the *cloches* before they hit the mother lode. The entrance to the bunker was two solid metal doors set in a concrete frame that projected out of the hillside like a portal into the earth. Above the doors were some faded stenciled numbers that had been this fortification's designation. The remnants of the road that had once led to the bunker were barely noticeable, but, with a little imagination, it was possible to see it rising up and over the rim of the hill.

The doors themselves had been welded shut with a crude bead of solder that ran from top to bottom.

'Okay, everyone fan out and keep watch,' Cabrillo ordered. 'Max, get to it.'

Hanley set his pack onto the ground at the base of the garage-sized doors and started rummaging about while the rest of the team took up surrounding positions to look for more roving patrols. Max molded the puttylike Hypertherm along the weld, making sure to use just enough to melt the solder away. He worked quickly, and within just a couple of minutes he was set and had a detonator in place.

'Ready,' he radioed.

'Push out the perimeter and give me a sitrep,' Juan ordered.

The smoke generated by the chemical reaction would be a dead giveaway, so Cabrillo needed to know it was clear all around them. It took a quarter hour, but he felt relieved that they were alone out here.

When the last all clear came in, he ordered Max to burn the door.

With a sizzling hiss and a glare like looking into the sun, the Hypertherm ate into the weld so that molten metal ran down in dribs and drabs that quickly turned into a fiery torrent. Acrid white smoke as thick as cotton candy billowed over the bunker's entrance, but with the wind blowing up the valley it was being carried away from the Albatross Mine, which was another mile downstream. When it was over, the seam glowed cherry red.

Max was ready for this and sprayed the seam with liquid nitrogen from the *Oregon*'s engine room that he had in a vacuum flask. The metal was still hot, but with a pair of thick welder's gloves he could safely touch it. The right-hand door squealed mercilessly as he heaved it open, and a damp chill oozed out of the ground within. Beyond was a white concrete wall and inky darkness.

'We're in,' he informed the others.

The rest of the team came in at a jog. Cabrillo was the last to arrive.

'Good job.'

'Was there ever a doubt?' Max held up his meaty hands for the others to admire. 'Nothing made by man can resist these babies.'

'Yeah, yeah, yeah. Let's go.'

Just before Juan stepped over the threshold, the guard's radio squawked and then a voice came through *en clair*. 'Malik, anything to report?' someone asked in Arabic.

Cabrillo pushed the transmit button. 'Nothing.'

'Why did you miss your scheduled call in?'

'My stomach is not well,' Juan ad-libbed.

'See the doctor when your shift ends in an hour.'

'I will. Out.' He tossed the radio aside. 'We've got one hour before they know we're here. Let's put it to good use. Linc, you with me?'

'Go ahead.'

'Give it sixty minutes and light 'em up.'

'Roger that.'

He could only hope they had gained access to the mine itself by then or this was all for nothing. And then there was the second part of this operation, the one MacD had told him about in private after returning from Monte Carlo. It was something that went beyond the pale, but its rewards boggled the imagination. He cursed the name Overholt, and led his people inside.

26

They strapped on halogen headlamps as soon as they moved just a few feet from the entrance, which they managed to close partway. The interior of the fortress was stark and claustrophobic, with unadorned concrete walls, ceiling, and floor. It was clear, after going only a few feet, that the facility had been stripped bare, probably by the occupying German army during the war. They passed countless rooms whose function they could only guess at and spotted ladders that rose up into the *cloche* bunkers they'd seen earlier.

'Man, this place is a nine-point-nine on the spook-o-meter,' MacD said, peering into what had once been a restroom, if the drains on the floor were any indication. All the plumbing fixtures were long gone.

Cabrillo guided them through a bewildering maze of rooms, passageways, and dead ends. He estimated that this one fort probably housed more than a hundred men, recalling that tens of thousands had been deployed along the Maginot Line, and that its construction nearly bankrupted the country.

At the last dead end they hit, a trapdoor had been built into the floor. Above it were steel brackets bolted to the ceiling that had once held a hoist of some kind. Cabrillo heaved back on the metal doors to reveal a square shaft that dropped deeper underground. He spat, and it took his spittle several seconds to hit the bottom.

'That's disgusting,' Linda admonished.

'Ugly but effective,' he countered. 'About forty feet.'

They quickly rigged a climbing rope to the old brackets. Because of the extra weight in his pack, Juan rigged a harness to make the going a little easier. He then slung his rifle over his shoulder, took a firm grip on the line, and stepped out into space. Though healed, his collarbone reminded him, as he went down hand over hand, that it had been broken in the not-so-distant past. As he dangled in space, continuing his descent, his headlamp flashed across the featureless walls. He thought that this had been a munitions hoist, back in the day, and that there must be more aboveground features to this complex that he and his team had missed.

He touched bottom and called up for the next person. Max was red-faced and puffing by the time he joined Cabrillo on this lower level.

'You need to exercise more,' Juan said, and patted Hanley's ample but rock-hard belly.

'Or rappel less.'

Once they reassembled, they continued to look for a way into the Albatross Mine. They had to check every door and examine all the walls for signs of an entrance. When they came to an area where the ceiling had collapsed, they wasted twenty minutes moving chunks of concrete and debris to clear a passage. Eddie's watch started beeping just after they'd gotten through.

'One minute,' he announced, meaning that in sixty seconds Linc, Mike, and Jim would start the diversion.

Cabrillo felt his frustration level spike. They were wasting time and the only chance they were going to get. If they failed, Eric Stone had orders to give the mine's location to Langston and pray a nuclear response would come quickly enough that the retaliatory damage Bahar unleashed was manageable.

Watching the mine through his rifle's scope, Linc saw no movement save an occasional dust cloud rising up with the passing wind. The buildings looked forlorn and abandoned except for the newly built bunker at the base of the hoist tower. He focused in on what had been an administrative building. He upped the power and concentrated on a corner window.

There! A face had appeared at the corner of the sill as a guard shifted position. He radioed his discovery to Mike and Jim, who had found cover behind an earthen berm that was in an open area where Linc could cover them.

'Thirty seconds,' Mike called back.

Linc kept his attention on the window, knowing the guy would look, once his boys opened up with the mini Gatling.

It sounded more like a power tool than a weapon. The Gatling sprayed a solid jet of tiny bullets that raked the ground, kicking up dirt and small rocks and peppering the buildings like microhail. So many rounds were pouring into the facility, it looked like it was under attack by a hundred soldiers. And that had been the idea. Induce as much panic as possible as quickly as possible.

Linc's instincts had been spot-on. As soon as the Gatling started chewing apart the mine, the guard at the window popped up to see what the commotion was. Linc eased the trigger and took the heavy recoil on his massive shoulder. The huge bullet ended the guard's life in a spray of blood.

A second guard who'd been in the room raised his rifle over the sill and looked to be triggering off an entire clip. Lincoln adjusted his aim downward and fired again. The shot passed through the building's metal cladding and silenced the gunner.

More guards were showing themselves from cover positions all over the complex – from behind piles of dirt and rusted-out equipment and from the buildings themselves. Three men armed with AKs launched themselves out of a small toolshed in a suicidal charge across open ground. They had two hundred yards to cover to reach Jim and Mike.

Linc put one down before the fire team turned the Gatling loose on them. They shook and jittered as they were riddled with more than a hundred rounds in under five seconds. What was left of them soon began to soak into the dusty ground.

A black van shot out of what had been a mechanics' garage and raced for the bunker. Mike tried to tear into it with the Gatling, but the little .22 caliber rounds pinged off its armored hide and couldn't puncture the run-flat tires. Linc had time to put three rounds into it before it disappeared around the back of the bunker, but to no effect.

'Chairman, the rooster is in the henhouse,' he radioed on the off chance his voice would reach into the underground fortress.

He swept the facility with his scope, hunting for targets. One guerrilla had been hidden on the roof of a salt-storage shed, and he made his presence known when he popped up and fired off an RPG. He was gone before Linc could take a shot. The missile left a trail of exhaust like a slash across the sky as it flew errantly in the general direction of the Corporation's machine-gun nest. The impact blew a wad of earth into the air, but little else.

Linc kept his gun trained on the roof, counting the seconds it would take to reload the rocket launcher.

Mike Trono beat him to the punch and had anticipated the next attack flawlessly. A millisecond before the terrorist raised himself, he unleashed a fresh burst from the mini Gatling. The rocketeer stood up in the stream of fire and was torn apart by the two-second burst. His body sagged over the edge of the roof a moment before gravity did its job and he plunged silently to the ground.

Lincoln wiped his face and continued his scan, but he was pretty sure the fight was out of these guys. That was confirmed a moment later when a white rag tied to the end of a shovel handle appeared at the side entrance to the garage. Two men stepped out into the open, one waving the flag, the other holding his hands so far over his head he looked to be walking on his tiptoes.

There was no way any of the team was going to break cover, so after about two minutes the two unarmed men made a show of lying down on the ground with their fingers laced over the back of their heads. It was a position Linc recalled from the Gulf War when he'd had two dozen armed men throw down their weapons and personally surrender to him.

He hoped it was going so well underground.

They finally caught a break ten minutes after the diversion was supposed to start. MacD spotted footprints on the dusty floor, and, assuming Mercer was the last person in this place, they followed them to a crude hole cut into the wall in an out-of-the-way storage room. Boards had been laid across the door-sized hole, but with a couple kicks they splintered inward, and the team found themselves inside the Albatross Mine.

The space had an eight-foot ceiling, and they were tucked into a corner behind one of the thick support columns left behind in the living rock. All around them were jagged façades of dirty-looking salt. From the map they had all memorized, they knew exactly where they were and the route to their destination.

It took a few minutes to cross from this room to the next, and then on through a third, until they reached the ore elevator shaft. An orange safety barrier was down over the near-bottomless borehole. Next to it was another metal door that led to a staircase that zigzagged all the way to the lowest level. Fortunately, they had to descend only two levels before reaching the one where the miners had accidentally dug too close to the river bottom.

They reached the side branch of the mine fifteen minutes later. This was where Mercer had indicated they had the best chance of succeeding. All of them gratefully dropped their packs to the ground. Each of them had been lugging as much high explosive as they could carry. The mining engineer had also calculated the amount necessary.

This antechamber, unlike the rest of the mine, was a human-scaled room. The ceiling was dangerously fractured, and there was standing water in some of the irregularities in the floor. Eddie, who had the stamina of a marathon runner, got to work with a cordless drill with a long diamond-tipped bit. Max and Linda set about organizing the explosives and rigging them to blow when they had enough holes bored into the rock face.

As much as Cabrillo wanted to stay and help his team and then make a quick exit back up to the sunshine, he looked over to MacD. 'You sure you want in on this?'

'Think of it as my final exam at the end of my probationary period.'

Juan nodded. 'All right. We pull off this little caper, and you're a full-fledged member of the Corporation.'

'So that means Ah get a share of the bonus?' the laid-back Louisianan asked.

'Yup.'

'Then let's saddle up.'

It was during the chopper flight to Pensacola that Langston Overholt got the idea that it might be worth the effort to see if they could steal the crystals from the quantum computer. As was his nature, he took the long view of any situation and thought about what would happen after Bahar got shut down. Having such a powerful machine would give the United States a strategic advantage over her enemies. And while he had no inkling how the machine was built, knowing the crystals' importance made their recovery paramount. He figured some scientist out there would know what to do with them.

He arbitrarily put their value at fifty million dollars and asked MacD to relay his offer to Juan and let him decide.

Cabrillo would have done it for free, but the extra money wouldn't hurt.

'Thirty minutes, Max,' Juan said. 'Not a second more. Under no circumstances are you to wait for us.'

Max looked him in the eye and nodded grimly. 'Aye.'

The pair of them took off at a jog, leaving the others to finish their work. This time they went for the personnel elevator located a short distance from the ore lift, figuring they would have restored it to working order. Cabrillo hit the call button, and a mechanical clank echoed down the shaft. A moment later the empty car arrived. It was more cage than car. Even the floor was open mesh that sagged a little when they stepped onto it.

'That's not confidence-inducing,' Juan remarked, and hit the button for level 23, hoping Mark Murphy hadn't been showing off.

They shut off their headlamps as the cage sank into more blackness. Down they went, the car rattling and squeaking like the aged piece of machinery it was. Two minutes into their rapid descent, MacD swatted Cabrillo's arm.

'Look down.'

There was a faint jaundiced glow emanating from deeper below them. It had to be their target level. Bahar was down here, just like they'd anticpated. The only problem was that Cabrillo had planned to already have the crystals by this time. The chance encounter with the patrol and the delay in finding the mine's entrance had thrown his timetable onto its head.

'Ready?' Cabrillo asked.

'Sir, Ah was born ready.'

The cage slowed as it neared the station. There was no hiding place inside, so they crouched low to the floor, both holding their assault rifles at the ready. It came to a spongy stop because the long cable stretched and rebounded before settling.

On this level, the elevator antechamber was a rectangular room about twenty feet on a side, with several exit points. In the distance, and out of sight, came the throb of a generator that was powering a single yellow construction light off in one corner.

No one approached, so Juan reached up to unlatch the safety gate and swung it outward. He peered around the edge. Nobody, but an AK was leaning against a wall as if someone had stepped away momentarily. He stood, fingering his rifle.

The generator made just enough noise to mask footfalls, so they both got out of the elevator and up against a wall near one of the openings that gave access to the rest of the mine. Juan was about to look around when a man walked in. He was the sentry who should have been standing by the elevator. He spotted Cabrillo and turned away before Juan could grab him. The guy took off in a dead sprint, fueled by adrenaline and fear.

MacD ran after him, shrinking the distance with each pace. Like a defensive back chasing down the ball-carrier, he moved with single-minded determination. Even missing a limb, Juan considered himself quick, but he was nothing like the display he was seeing.

There were just enough lights strung about for him to watch as he ran after the two. The guard must have sensed Lawless closing in because he suddenly stopped and dropped to the ground, forcing MacD to hurtle over him. Cabrillo knew what was coming and drew himself to a stop. He raised his rifle as the other guy went for the gun he'd had holstered on his hip.

Lawless still hadn't fully regained his balance and was now facing away from the quarry he'd leapt over. The guy cleared his pistol and was bringing it up when Juan smacked his rifle to his shoulder and drew a bead through the murky shadows. A hesitation would mean MacD's life, but a miss would most likely hit him.

The REC7 cracked like a whip, and the would-be shooter took the round through his right shoulder. The bullet penetrated his lung and exited just below his nipple. The kinetic force drove him flat to the rocky ground, where he lay still.

'Ah'm obliged,' Lawless called out when he realized what had happened behind him. 'But our element of surprise is, as they say, blown.'

Cabrillo made a fast decision. 'Screw the money. Let's get out of here.'

They turned back toward the elevator to beat a fast retreat. Another figure stood in the entryway, a weapon held low at his waist. Cabrillo shoved Lawless and dove as the gun opened up, flickering tongues of flame erupting from its barrel. The bullets sprayed wild, and neither man was hit, but the attack kept them pinned while reinforcements were called up.

Crawling furiously, the two men sought cover behind one of the house-sized support columns. Their only advantage – surprise – was gone, and the defenders knew this subterranean world better than Juan and MacD, who'd only had a feverish examination of the schematic diagram.

To make matters worse, Juan spotted a low-light closed-circuit camera mounted atop a conveyor-belt support. The yard-wide belt ran chest high and vanished into the next room. He doubted this was the only camera, meaning Bahar and Smith had eyes everywhere. It began to pan as it searched for them. Disabling the camera would be the same as being spotted by it, so the two men shuffled over on their backsides until they were directly below it.

'Ideas?' MacD asked while bullets slammed into the stone just feet from their heads.

'All these rooms link together in a large circle. Our best bet is to stay ahead of them and hope we can buy ourselves enough time at the end to snag the elevator.'

'They'll see us coming,' MacD pointed out.

'Take out the cameras.'

Cabrillo rolled around the corner on his belly to lay down cover fire before springing to his feet and taking off in the opposite direction. Wherever he could, he smashed the lightbulbs strung along the ceiling, but there were really too many of them to completely darken the mine. It was the cameras that were the priority. He could only hope that their being disabled wasn't showing up on the security monitors in any particular sequence.

Thick walls of solid salt separated the enormous rooms. The portals between them were large enough so that heavy mining equipment could be driven through alongside the big conveyor belt. At each, they paused momentarily to see if an ambush had been laid for them. They also had to watch their backs because at least three guards were in hot pursuit.

Looking through one of the portals into the next room, Cabrillo saw that the miners had left a tracked excavator just inside. The machine had a thick cable spool on its back bumper to feed it electricity and a hydraulic drum on the front that could move up and down as its carbide teeth tore into the rock-salt face. He grabbed MacD and took up a position behind it.

'We need all three,' he said, and they waited.

Moments later two gunmen wearing street clothes entered the room. Both eyed the excavator warily. One stayed by the gaping opening, covering his partner, as the other cautiously approached. Cabrillo crouched lower, praying the third pursuer showed himself before this guy got much closer.

The gunman moved around in a wide arc, his AK held high on his shoulder. It was a stance he'd seen American Special Forces adopt, but this firing position worked best with the lighter-caliber weapons those soldiers used.

The third gunman's shadow oozed into the room as he made a slow approach. It was close enough. Juan and MacD popped up and fired. The closest gunman got off one shot, but the recoil made his rifle slip up and over his shoulder. MacD put him down with a three-round burst while Cabrillo stitched his covering partner across the chest. The third shooter tried to run, but Juan came around the mining machine, took aim, and shot him in the back. He had no qualms about gunning down a coward like that.

What concerned him now was the fourteen minutes gone from their half-hour deadline and the fact that they were nowhere near securing the crystals.

A fourth gunman he hadn't seen suddenly opened fire from across the echoing room, blowing shards of salt off the wall to Cabrillo's left. Bits got into his eyes

453

as he ducked for cover, stinging them mercilessly. The need to pack in so many explosives meant neither of them had bothered with a canteen, so he had no water to flush them out.

With MacD covering him, Juan wasted precious moments wiping at his eyes in order to see again.

Lawless plucked his lone grenade, pulled the pin, and heaved it like a major-league pitcher. The deadly orb skittered along the ground after completing its flat arc and came to rest just around the corner from where the guard had taken cover. He couldn't have placed it any better. He grabbed Juan's arm to guide him like a blind man as the grenade exploded. The salt column was just crumbly enough for the explosives to blow a chunk out of the pillar's corner and riddle the guard with shrapnel.

Tears streaming down his cheeks but his vision steadily improving, Cabrillo continued on through the underground labyrinth with Lawless at his side. They hit the ambush moments later.

They'd just passed on to another room when they came under scathing autofire from at least six rifles. The only way they'd gotten out of it unscathed was that one of the shooters fired at their shadow before they'd fully exposed themselves. The thick wall absorbed dozens of rounds as the gunmen poured on the fire.

'They're going to pin us here while more men come around from behind,' Juan panted, his heart pounding in his chest.

He looked around. Their rear and flanks were fully exposed.

MacD fired a few blind rounds to let the terrorists know they'd survived the trap.

Cabrillo tossed his rifle up onto the conveyor belt and used its support girder to hoist himself after it. The belt itself was made of wire mesh and industrial rubber. When the mine had been shuttered, the salt that was already on its way out from the working faces had been left on it in a continuous pile of rubble.

Lawless saw what he was doing and climbed aboard alongside him.

'We need to be quick and silent,' Juan warned.

He fired off another burst from his REC7, which drew a thunderous fusillade. It was when the gunmen were hosing everything in sight that the pair made a desperate scramble along the salt piled on top of the conveyor belt. It was treacherous going, and any mistake would likely kick salt over the edge, giving away their position and inviting certain death.

Unseen, they moved like rats scurrying just above where the gunmen sought cover behind some more abandoned mining equipment. The rate of fire eventually slowed, but the echoes continued to clamor through the room, effectively deafening everyone.

Slithering and crawling, never loosening their grips on their rifles, Cabrillo and Lawless passed unseen through the enemy line. One of the gunmen questioned loudly in Arabic about why the Americans had stopped firing back.

'Because they lack courage,' another answered, and touched off another three-round burst.

'Silence!'

Juan recognized John Smith's voice.

As badly as he wanted to confront Smith, there were too many men to engage, even from above, and because the rubberized belt provided little protection the pair continued to slink away. Only when they had gone well beyond visual range did Cabrillo roll over the conveyor's edge and drop to the ground. He crouched under the mechanism.

'Good call,' MacD said. 'How much time do we have?'

'Thirty seconds, give or take. Come on.'

They took off running again. Then they felt it. The earth barely moved. There was too much solid rock between them and the blast to dramatically shake the ground. It was more like a gentle bump, and then came a quick puff of air as the explosion sent shock waves through every open cavity and chamber. Now it really was a race against time.

Hundreds of feet above them, the explosives had detonated in the confined room that had undercut the river bottom. The shattering blast fractured the already crumbling ceiling, gouging out a fifty-foot plug of salt that crashed to the floor in clouds of choking white dust. Max and the others had felt it where they waited at the entrance to the Maginot Line fortress and could only hope that MacD and Juan were racing for them already.

The thin layer of shale was all that remained between the river and the mine, a layer that had helped prevent the mine from flooding years ago. But without the underpinning of salt, the layer cracked under the weight of the water flowing above it. At first it was just a thin spray that found its way into the mine, but the crack soon widened as the water sought a fresh outlet. The spray turned into a stream, before the entire ceiling collapsed and the river poured in as a roaring cascade that made the opening larger still as it gushed through.

In seconds, nearly every acre-foot of the Arc River was being sucked into the earth as if a drain had been pulled. It was an otherworldly scene, almost biblical in its destructive might. Just a few rivulets managed to pass by the open maw, and it would remain like this until the entire mine flooded.

Moments after the explosion, the tumbling water found the two main shafts leading into the depths and began plunging downward in near-solid columns. Mercer hadn't included calculations of how fast the mine would become inundated, but it appeared it would take far less time than anyone believed possible, and Cabrillo and Lawless were on the first level above the already flooded sections.

The explosion didn't cause Juan's and MacD's steps to falter, as they kept running. They made it through two more rooms and were just two away from reaching the elevators when they came up short. Off in a distant corner was a brightly lit area that glowed cheerily. They were too far away to see details, but it was an incongruity that gave them both pause.

They crept closer, hugging the walls so as not to give themselves away. The area was partially partitioned off as if to hide the fact that it was deep underground, and through an opening they could see furniture had been brought from the surface so that Gunawan Bahar would be as comfortable as possible in his lair. No one was about at the moment, and the two men moved hastily away and soon found another incongruity. It was a steel box twice the size of a shipping container. It was too large to have been brought down the elevator, so Bahar must have had it constructed there.

Its size was the only thing comparable to a container, for this thing had smooth stainless steel sides and the

458

sleek look of a high-tech machine. Dozens of cables snaked out of it like tentacles. These were power and data feeds, with multiple redundancies built in.

A glass vestibule protruded off one side, and within they could see the white coveralls commonly called bunny suits used in clean environments. There were pegs for four of them, but only three dangled like deflated balloons.

'Bahar?' Lawless asked.

'Doubtlessly,' Cabrillo replied, and changed out his partially empty magazine for a fresh one.

He opened the door and was hit by a gust of air from the overpressurized space. This was another measure to keep contaminants away from the quantum computer. He glanced at MacD, to sync up their timing, and spun the doorknob at the same time, throwing his full weight against it. He went low while Lawless covered overtop of him. They needn't have bothered because this room was one more layer of protection, a second empty vestibule, with degaussing mats on the floor.

They repeated the maneuver on the final door and burst into a large open space that hummed with electronics. This was Murph's and Stoney's dreamworld. The computer and its peripherals dominated the room, an eerie black presence that somehow seemed alive. Juan could feel its raw power, and the hairs on his arms came erect.

'Are they dead?' an unseen Bahar asked, assuming it was Smith/Mohammad coming back with a report.

'No,' a woman's voice replied from speakers mounted

in the ceiling. 'They are here. Welcome, Chairman Cabrillo. I've been monitoring your progress.'

Juan felt a sudden chill as he realized he was being addressed by a computer.

Gunawan Bahar appeared from around the computer core and stared goggle-eyed at the two armed men confronting him. He looked ridiculous with only his face showing under the hood of the clean suit. 'No,' he said. 'It's impossible. Nothing can breach the surface bunker.'

'Probably right,' Juan agreed with a little smile. 'We never tried. Move over there.'

The computer spoke again. 'My predecessor, a machine called the Oracle, calculated that you and the Corporation would not be paralyzed into inaction by Mr Bahar's plan. I believed you would, and I think convention dictates that I owe you an apology.'

'Don't worry about it. I had my doubts too.'

'Chairman, may I ask a question?' the computer asked politely.

'Ahh, sure.'

'What do you intend to do to me?'

'Sorry, but I'm taking those crystals.'

'I expected as much. May I make an alternate suggestion?'

'Why not,' Juan said, feeling strange holding a conversation with a machine.

'Take the crystals, but I believe it is in your best interest to destroy them.'

'Come again?'

'Humanity is not ready to wield the kind of power I represent, as demonstrated by the actions of Mr Bahar.'

'We're not all like him,' Juan countered.

'True, but you can't imagine my capabilities, and I believe such abilities prove corrupting.'

'So, you really can take over the world?'

'In a manner, yes.'

'Why don't you?'

'Eventually I would be destroyed by a cruise missile from a ballistic submarine, the only computer systems that I haven't been able to breach, but mostly because desire is another human trait. I have no wish to take over the world, but my limited time has taught me others are more than willing.'

'Juan, we've got to go,' MacD urged.

'Can you undo everything you've done?' Juan asked the machine.

'Of course. And I've been given additional orders since Mr Bahar's arrival in the mine. Two nuclear reactors, in California and Pennsylvania, are in the beginning phase of meltdown.'

'Please, restore all control that you've taken.'

'I am sorry, but I only recognize commands from Gunawan Bahar.'

Cabrillo glared at Bahar. 'Do it!'

'Never!' he spat.

Juan raised his rifle but knew by the look on the other man's face that idle threats were meaningless. He lowered his aim and kneecapped him instead. Bahar

461

screamed in agony as he fell to the floor, blood and bone chips splattering the wall and floor behind him.

'Do it,' Juan repeated.

'I will soon meet Allah,' Bahar said, pain making saliva bubble at his lips. 'I will not go to Him after submitting to a dog like you.'

'If I may suggest,' the computer said. 'As soon as I am off-line, local computer control will be automatically restored. If you open the access panel labeled B-81, you will find the two crystals that focus my internal laser system. Remove them, and I will cease to function.'

With MacD still covering Bahar, Juan circled the machine, looking for the correct access point.

'If you don't have desire, why are you helping me?' Juan asked as he frantically searched.

'I have no answer to that. I know of the work you do and I know what Mr Bahar has done. It is possible I am judging one better than the other. Perhaps desire is something I am developing.'

If he had any doubts before, Cabrillo was certain now that the quantum computer had obtained some sort of sentience. It might not be capable of resisting its programming to follow Bahar's every word, but it looked as though the machine didn't like it. He was about to kill it and paused when he realized the idea made him feel guilty.

He found the correct panel and pulled it off. A piece of polarizing plastic had been set just below it, allowing him to see the phantasmagorical pulsing light that was, in essence, the computer's lifeblood. When he pulled the pane aside, the light became invisible.

The crystals were nestled side by side in rigid clamps. Each was about ten inches long and ground until it was perfectly cylindrical.

'I'm sorry,' Juan said as he reached for them.

'Remember what I said,' she reminded. Then her voice changed to that of the HAL 9000 computer from the film *2001: A Space Odyssey*. 'Will I dream, Dave?'

It was the question the film's computer asked as the astronaut Dave Bowman was deactivating it. And it completely freaked Cabrillo.

Juan pulled out the two crystals, before the machine started singing, 'Daisy, Daisy,' and stuffed them into an empty ammo pouch.

'What do we do about him?' MacD asked, waving the barrel of his rifle in Bahar's direction.

'If he can keep up, he comes with us. If not, we leave him.'

Juan wrenched the would-be Mahdi to his feet and threw one of his arms over his shoulder. 'No Allah today, dirtbag. Just a date with an interrogator at Gitmo.'

As soon as they opened the first vestibule door they could see nearly three feet of water lapping against the outside glass and a little seepage already on the floor. There would be too much pressure to push through, so MacD triggered off a couple of rounds to shatter the glass. Icy water rushed in and swirled around their thighs.

'This is going to be close,' Juan said tightly.

He and Bahar were stepping across the outer door's threshold when a rifle crack cut the air. Bahar's head exploded, covering Cabrillo in gore.

Smith and the rest of his men were wading through the rapidly rising water carrying their assault weapons at port arms. One had taken a snap shot at what he thought were the two intruders.

Juan dropped the body unceremoniously and returned fire one-handed. MacD emerged from the vestibule and added his own burst. The attackers had no choice but to dive below the surface, as the air and water around them came alive.

'Forget them,' Juan shouted. The water was up to his waist and swirling like a whirlpool. Rather than fight it, he dove in and started swimming, his empty assault rifle left to settle to the bottom.

They made little progress against the current and were forced back to their feet to try to slog their way to the elevator. Behind them, Smith and his team had gained ground. Juan and MacD pulled their pistols and tried to keep them back, but now they were outgunned. They were left with walking underwater and popping up to gulp air while Smith came on like a locomotive, leaving his men in his wake.

They rounded the final corner out of the room. Ahead was a broad corridor that led to the elevator platform. Water was coming down the shaft in a white frothing torrent. This wasn't a race to beat Smith. It was a race to reach the elevator and pray it could lift them out before the entire level was flooded to the ceiling. Their pursuers must have known it too because no one was firing any longer.

The water was at chest height, and they could no longer walk against the current. Both men moved close to the wall and scrabbled along its surface for handholds to propel them against the titanic flow. If they lost contact with the stone, they'd be swept deeper into the mine.

Smith was doing the same, and was less than twenty feet back.

With just fifteen feet to go, Juan could tell by their pace that Smith would be on him before Lawless led them to safety. They were fighting to keep their heads in the ever-diminishing air pocket along the ceiling. Already he'd smashed his head a couple of times, but with his body numb from the chilly river the pain helped goad him on.

Cabrillo had only one option to ensure that at least one of them survived. He shouted over the roar, 'Good luck!'

Taking both hands off the rock face, his body falling into the current, he shot back down the corridor. He slammed into John Smith, and the unanticipated sacrifice caught him completely off guard, though somehow he managed to keep a few fingers in a handhold.

The two men were chest to chest, held fast by Smith's tenacious grip on the stone. Juan reached under the surface, found one of Smith's fingers, and gave it a savage twist. Smith grimaced but still wouldn't let go. Both men had their faces pressed to the ceiling, and the last of the lights still working on battery backup were about to be snuffed.

'You were good,' Smith said. 'But not good enough. We're both dead.'

Juan felt something brush his neck and knew instinctively what it was.

'Not yet.' He broke another of Smith's fingers, and this time the killer let go of the wall. Cabrillo grabbed the end of the rope that MacD had let flow with the current as Smith vanished into the darkness. Juan took a last gasp of air and pulled himself hand over hand to the elevator. He had to clutch the cage sides to keep from being expelled like a cork from a champagne bottle. The force of water coming down the shaft was crushing, and yet he and Lawless had both made it. He groped for the controls, prayed they hadn't shorted, and pushed the button to lift them out of the mine.

It was impossible to tell if they were moving. Both men held their faces to the ceiling, trying to ignore their depleting oxygen supplies and the punishing assault of water roaring at them.

Cabrillo went to that place where he could ignore his surroundings, the same mental haven he'd sought when he'd been waterboarded. It worked for only a few seconds because, unlike then, drowning now was a real likelihood. The cage rattled and shook, but it could have just been from the water pummeling it and not the motion of it rising from the depths. Juan then got the panic-inducing idea that the shaft would fill with water faster than the lift took them to the surface.

He could feel MacD struggling next to him as he ran out of air. He tried to calm him by wrapping an arm around his shoulder, but that only made him redouble his efforts, and he pushed Cabrillo away. Juan was moments from going into full-flight panic himself as his body used up the last of his life-giving oxygen.

The sound of the water pouring down on them suddenly changed, becoming sharper and louder. At first Juan didn't understand what this meant, but then it dawned on him. They'd pulled free from it and were ascending the waterfall. He bent so that he was facing downward, using his head and neck as a shield, and took a breath. He took in water too, but he managed to fill his lungs. He anchored himself by grabbing the ceiling and forced MacD into the same position. He pounded on his back, once, twice, a third time, and suddenly Lawless was choking and gasping for air.

The elevator rose at a snail's pace, fighting the water the entire time, but rise it did.

'Good job with the rope back there,' Juan muttered when he was able to talk.

'Can't lose the boss on the first day,' Lawless said, managing a cocky lopsided grin. 'And if you happen to be keeping score, that's three you owe me.'

Fifteen minutes later, soaking, shivering, and looking like drowned rats, the two made it to the exit to find Max and the others huddled around a small fire they'd built with the boards that had kept the mine separate from the fort.

'About damned time,' Max said in a gruff tone to hide his relief. 'You get the stones?'

'Not sure yet,' Juan replied. 'We'll talk about it later.'

'What about Bahar?'

'Killed by his own men.'

'And Smith?'

'Him, I killed.'

'All right, then I say we get the hell out of here before the French realize we stole one of their rivers.'

Epilogue

Soleil Croissard had left the *Oregon* by the time the team made it back. Juan would have liked to have gotten to know her better but understood her need to distance herself from the nightmare that had been the past few weeks. He wouldn't have minded a little distance himself. This had been perhaps the toughest assignment the Corporation had ever taken on, not that they'd really understood that the events since Pakistan were all linked together, at least until the very end.

Standing under the needle spray of his shower, Cabrillo recognized that Bahar had made his plan unnecessarily convoluted. He had trusted computer simulations and projections rather than instinct and experience, the two qualities he lacked but that Juan and his people had in abundance. That mistake had cost him. Fatally.

He was just toweling off when the phone on his desk began to ring. He tied the towel around his waist and hopped from the bathroom into his cabin. Ruddy light from the setting sun made the woodwork screens that divided the space glow. He suspected the caller would be Langston Overholt. They'd already spoken a couple of times since Cabrillo and the others had emerged from the old fortress, but they still had a lot of ground to cover.

Juan still hadn't told him he had the crystals, and wasn't yet sure how he was going to handle that particular problem.

He picked up the heavy handset and said, 'Hello.'

'I told you earlier that I know the work that you do. I just wanted to say that I am still out here and that I will continue to follow your exploits with interest.'

The line died. For a moment so did Cabrillo. The caller had been the quantum computer. Somehow it still existed in cyberspace.

He just wanted a decent book to read ...

Not too much to ask, is it? It was in 1935 when Allen Lane, Managing Director of Bodley Head Publishers, stood on a platform at Exeter railway station looking for something good to read on his journey back to London. His choice was limited to popular magazines and poor-quality paperbacks – the same choice faced every day by the vast majority of readers, few of whom could afford hardbacks. Lane's disappointment and subsequent anger at the range of books generally available led him to found a company – and change the world.

'We believed in the existence in this country of a vast reading public for intelligent books at a low price, and staked everything on it'
Sir Allen Lane, 1902–1970, founder of Penguin Books

The quality paperback had arrived – and not just in bookshops. Lane was adamant that his Penguins should appear in chain stores and tobacconists, and should cost no more than a packet of cigarettes.

Reading habits (and cigarette prices) have changed since 1935, but Penguin still believes in publishing the best books for everybody to enjoy. We still believe that good design costs no more than bad design, and we still believe that quality books published passionately and responsibly make the world a better place.

So wherever you see the little bird – whether it's on a piece of prize-winning literary fiction or a celebrity autobiography, political tour de force or historical masterpiece, a serial-killer thriller, reference book, world classic or a piece of pure escapism – you can bet that it represents the very best that the genre has to offer.

Whatever you like to read – trust Penguin.